PRAISE FOR ELIZABETH BEVARLY

"Elizabeth Bevarly knows how to show readers a good time."

—*The Oakland Press*

"If you like your romantic fantasies delivered with all the wit, fireworks, and tenderness of a Tracy/Hepburn movie, Elizabeth Bevarly can't be beat." —Lisa Kleypas, *New York Times* bestselling author

"Lots of fun, lots of style, lots of heart."

—Christina Dodd, *New York Times* bestselling author

AND HER NOVELS

Neck & Neck

"Brisk and breezy." —*Midwest Book Review*

"Laugh-out-loud funny." —*Night Owl Reviews*

"An exhilarating tale which should not be missed."

—*Fallen Angel Reviews*

"Smart, witty . . . [A] very sweet romance you will remember."

—*TwoLips Reviews*

"Bevarly's fun-filled, saucy story has spot-on timing and laugh-out-loud humor. Likable characters make it easy to cheer for everyone in this feel-good book. Just don't read it in a public place—unless you're comfortable laughing alone!" —*Romantic Times*

continued . . .

Ready & Willing

"[A] great paranormal contemporary romance . . . Well-written."

—*Night Owl Reviews*

"[A] wonderful story . . . Heartwarming and inspired."

—*Romantic Times*

"Engaging." —*Midwest Book Review*

Fast & Loose

"[A] fabulous romance . . . Captures the spirit of the Kentucky Derby . . . With well-developed, entertaining characters and humorous dialogue . . . Will keep you reading until the end of the race."

—*Fresh Fiction*

"Fans will enjoy this lighthearted romp." —*The Best Reviews*

"This warm, easygoing story, set in the world of horse racing, has very likable characters, especially a hero who's basically a nice guy and some great secondary characters. The way the hero pursues the heroine is lovely."

—*Romantic Times*

"A fast-paced romance with a light touch of humor [and] engaging characters."

—*The Road to Romance*

MORE PRAISE FOR ELIZABETH BEVARLY AND HER BESTSELLING NOVELS

"Elizabeth Bevarly writes with irresistible style and wit."

—Teresa Medeiros

"[Bevarly's] writing is quirky and funny, and her heroes are hot."

—*The Oakland Press*

"Full of hijinks and belly laughs." —*Detroit Free Press*

"A supersteamy beach novel." —*Cosmopolitan*

"This is a book that's like a drink of fresh water to all of us who are tired of reading about perfect women. There's a bit of a mystery, a sexy hero, and a lot of terrific one-liners."

—Eloisa James, *New York Times* bestselling author

"A delightful, humorous, and smoothly written book—a must-read." —*Rocky Mountain News*

"This practically perfect romance has . . . writing that is pure joy."

—*Library Journal*

"Wyatt and Julian are quirkily appealing romantic heroes, and Bevarly's voice is fresh and funny." —*Publishers Weekly*

"Full of the author's trademark humor, this witty romance is a jaunty romp through the world of the rich and mischievous."

—*Romantic Times*

"Enjoyable and funny." —*Booklist*

Titles by Elizabeth Bevarly

FAST & LOOSE

READY & WILLING

NECK & NECK

* * *

THE HOUSE ON BUTTERFLY WAY

The House on Butterfly Way

ELIZABETH BEVARLY

BERKLEY SENSATION, NEW YORK

THE BERKLEY PUBLISHING GROUP
Published by the Penguin Group
Penguin Group (USA) Inc.
375 Hudson Street, New York, New York 10014, USA
Penguin Group (Canada), 90 Eglinton Avenue East, Suite 700, Toronto, Ontario M4P 2Y3, Canada
(a division of Pearson Penguin Canada Inc.)
Penguin Books Ltd., 80 Strand, London WC2R 0RL, England
Penguin Group Ireland, 25 St. Stephen's Green, Dublin 2, Ireland (a division of Penguin Books Ltd.)
Penguin Group (Australia), 250 Camberwell Road, Camberwell, Victoria 3124, Australia
(a division of Pearson Australia Group Pty. Ltd.)
Penguin Books India Pvt. Ltd., 11 Community Centre, Panchsheel Park, New Delhi—110 017, India
Penguin Group (NZ), 67 Apollo Drive, Rosedale, Auckland 0632, New Zealand
(a division of Pearson New Zealand Ltd.)
Penguin Books (South Africa) (Pty.) Ltd., 24 Sturdee Avenue, Rosebank, Johannesburg 2196,
South Africa

Penguin Books Ltd., Registered Offices: 80 Strand, London WC2R 0RL, England

This book is an original publication of The Berkley Publishing Group.

ISBN 978-1-61793-588-6

PRINTED IN THE UNITED STATES OF AMERICA

For David and Eli, my family, my home, with much gratitude and even more love

Acknowledgments

I have so many people I need to thank for being so (a) supportive, (b) insightful, (c) helpful, (d) tolerant, and (e) patient. First, thanks to my agent, Karen Solem, for being so enthusiastic about the book and making such excellent suggestions. Thanks to Cindy Hwang for those things, too, and for encouraging me to try my hand at writing something new and different. It's a brave new world, this trade paperback stuff, but I'm liking it *a lot*.

Thanks to good writing friends Christie Ridgway and Barbara O'Neal for always responding to my panicky and needy e-mails with good cheer and wise counsel. I have treasured both. (But seriously, we all need to take a vacation together where there's a lot of water and drinks with umbrellas.)

Thank you, too, to writer, filmmaker, and friend Keith Snyder for answering all my pesky questions about bicycles and cycling. If I screwed anything up with that, it's totally my fault, because I don't think there's a person on this planet who loves or is more knowledgeable about cycling than you. (But truly, Keith, you haven't cycled until you've taken U.S. Highway 42 from Louisville to Cincinnati. I promise to wave to you from my chaise longue as you pedal past me.)

Thank you to my readers, both those who have followed me from the romance genre and those who have picked me up for the first time. I adore each and every one of you and would be lost without you. Writing is great fun (usually), and enormously satisfying (ditto). But being able to share it with others and knowing they enjoy it, too? I don't know that there are words to describe that feeling. Other than awesome.

But the biggest thanks go to my husband, David, and son, Eli, for their intrepidness when it comes to living with a writer. And not just any writer. A writer on a new and scary venture. A writer filled with doubts and fears. A writer who would, most days, just as soon crawl under the bed and try to channel winning lottery numbers than open her laptop and get to work. You two are my reason for getting up in the morning. You're the reason my days are filled with light, even when it's raining (or there's a tornado on the horizon). And you're why I don't have scary dreams at night. You guys are the *best*.

Prologue

Eugenie Dashner had always loved the house on Butterfly Way. When she was a little girl, her friend Marianne Weatherly lived one street over from it, and whenever they rode their bikes around the neighborhood of Manitou Hills, they inevitably pedaled past. As a child, she thought the house looked like a wedding cake. A giant three-tiered wedding cake dappled with buttercream frills and meringue lace, its pale pink front door a frosting rose at its base. The child Eugenie had been certain that gypsies lived in the house, because bright fringed curtains framed the front windows, and she once heard accordion music coming from inside. She was sure that fairies frolicked in the baskets of fuchsia dripping along the front porch, that sprites splashed in the sparkling side yard fountain, and that pixies pranced in the purple clematis twining through the gazebo nearby.

She even convinced Marianne once during a slumber party to sneak out and visit the house under cover of darkness, to see if they could catch a glimpse of the magic. But the pixies, sprites, and fairies must have heard them coming and quelled their wild rumpus before the girls arrived—though Eugenie did spy of one of the gypsies watching them when a curtain on the second floor twitched enough to allow a slice of pale lamplight to sneak through. When she pointed out to her friend the faint profile of a woman in that window, Marianne squealed and dropped her flashlight, then scampered off into the night. But Eugenie waited until the curtain fell back into place before following. She'd never seen a real gypsy before.

As a college student, she had rented an apartment not far from the house, and she had deliberately routed her morning runs to include Butterfly Way. By then, though, the wedding cake had begun to spoil. Its once-white frosting was smudged, its frills and lace were frayed, its rosy front door was blistered. The fuchsia grew feral, the fountain went dry, and the gazebo listed to one side. Some mornings, the mailbox overflowed with uncollected correspondence, and others, the fading curtains were drawn tight. The magic that had made the house resplendent when she was a child had begun to fail, and something inside Eugenie grieved to see it.

Eventually, she graduated from college, then married and moved away. But often, when she came home to visit, she would find an excuse to drive through Manitou Hills to see how the house was faring. Each passing year brought greater failure to the enchantment. The house grew more weary, more unhappy, more hopeless. The frosting decayed. The fuchsia withered. The gazebo fell. And all she could do was watch helplessly as the palace of her childish dreams collapsed.

But then, a lot of things collapsed for Eugenie during those years. A lot decayed and withered and fell. Not just her dreams but her career and her marriage, too. For a long time, she didn't come home. For a long time, no place felt like home. Until one day, when she realized she had nowhere to go except back to the place where she grew up. On that day, with her son riding in the passenger's seat and everything they owned in a trailer chasing behind, Eugenie returned to Louisville. But before driving to her brother's house, where she would be staying for now, she turned into Manitou Hills, down Butterfly Way, to see her old friend. Her old friend who looked much like Eugenie now—exhausted, broken, and old. Except, she noted, for one small difference.

A sign in the front yard that read FOR SALE . . .

One

The day Eugenie Dashner toured the house for the first time, there was a *Damnation Alley*–sized cockroach in the master bath. Dead, fortunately, though thoughts about what might still be prowling the house that ended the life of a creature she'd heard could survive the next apocalypse did give her pause. There were also mousetraps in the attic that contained only pieces of mice. (She didn't want to think about what had happened to the parts that weren't there.) Mold sullied walls in the basement, the study, and a downstairs bath. Cracks crimped all three chimneys and bisected the terra-cotta patio. Wallpaper peeled and plaster was scattered in virtually every room. The carpeting throughout was filthy. And the smell festering over all of it was . . .

Well. A charitable person might say the house smelled piquant. But Eugenie wasn't charitable when it came to the safety and well-being of her family. She thought the house smelled like a bloated, fetid wildebeest.

On the upside, the place had been updated and redecorated relatively recently. On the downside, since it had been built in the eighteen eighties, *relatively recently* translated to *the nineteen seventies*. So unless one had a fondness for harvest gold shag carpeting and avocado appliances (which Eugenie did not), and unless one was enchanted by that phony antiquing crap people of that era brushed on their cabinetry (which Eugenie was not), no one in her right mind would want the place.

"You're right, Eugenie. It's perfect."

But then, her brother, Julien, had never exactly been in his right mind.

"We have to buy it."

They were exactly the words she had been hoping to hear him say when she convinced him to look at the house with her. But her sanity—the bulk of it, anyway—was one thing Lawrence hadn't received in the divorce settlement, and she knew it would be nuts to take on a project like this. It was one thing to do some home improvement. A little paint here, a little spackle there. A jug of Murphy's Oil Soap and a bottle of Febreze. But this . . .

This went beyond extreme makeover. This went beyond *Damnation Alley*. There wasn't a cubic centimeter of the house that wasn't damaged in some way.

She shook her head reluctantly. "I was wrong, Jules. From the outside, it looked like the place might have a chance. But after seeing its insides, it's obvious there's no way to salvage it. This place needs way more than just repair and renovation. What happened here . . ." She swallowed against the disappointment tightening her throat. "This is heartbreaking."

"It's a disaster, no question," Julien agreed. "But c'mon, Eugene. You've never been one to back down from a challenge."

Uh-oh. When he called her Eugene, it was an endearment—to

him, anyway, never mind that their mother had always insisted she be called by the French version of the name, giving the second syllable a long *a* sound instead of a long *e*. That *Eugene* meant Jules was totally on board with using their pooled finances to buy this place together. And he was determined to bring Eugenie back to that way of thinking, too.

"This isn't a challenge," she said. "This is irreparable damage."

Julien threw her one of his *C'mon, Eugene* smiles. "There's no such thing as irreparable damage. Things that are broken can always be fixed."

Spoken like a man who made his living fixing things. But even Julien knew that wasn't true. In a lot of ways, he knew that better than anyone.

She sighed heavily, driving her gaze around the ugly kitchen again. It wasn't a good idea, she told herself. It didn't matter that she was half as solvent as she'd been before her divorce or that she had a teenage son who was fast becoming a stranger. She didn't care if Julien's investment in the place would be twice what hers would be because he'd made a boatload of money flipping houses before the real estate market collapsed. It made no difference that he had two motherless daughters who needed an adult female role model as much as her son needed someone like Julien to fill the empty space left by his dumbass father. And it was irrelevant that her and Julien's mother had reached a point in her life where she wasn't able to live by herself—or with anyone else who wasn't obligated by blood ties to take care of her.

Okay, okay. All those things did matter, and Eugenie did care about them. She still wasn't convinced this house could ever be restored to the bloom and buoyancy of its former self.

"It's twice the size of all the other houses we've looked at in this price range," Julien cajoled.

That, she had to admit, did indeed make it perfect for blending the bunch of mismatched personalities that was her family. Which was an inescapable merger now thanks to (a) Julien's financial worth being a fraction of what it had been before his portfolio evaporated in the Wall Street debacle, (b) Eugenie's employment prospects looking equally evaporative in the current economy (provided *evaporative* was actually a word), and (c) their mother having become even more of a handful than their children were, not to mention more childish.

"Mom will have a bedroom and bath to herself on the first floor," Julien added, knowing it would count for a lot, keeping at least a floor between them and Lorraine. "The girls and I can take the second floor, and you can have the third."

Oh, well done, Jules. Put two *floors between me and Mom.* How could Eugenie resist that?

"And we can convert a good chunk of the attic for Seth," he concluded, "so he'll have his own space. That's important when you're sixteen, you know. A kid's gotta have someplace to stash his stolen *Playboy*s and Colt 45 tallboys."

Eugenie managed a thin smile. "My, what a convincing argument that is. There's nothing that will sway my decision faster than envisioning my emotionally fragile, grossly underage son passed out in a drunken stupor on top of Miss February. Just show me where to sign."

Julien expelled one of those sighs that told her he was worried about her. The same sort of sigh she'd heard from him the night she'd brought home Lawrence for the first time. "Seth isn't emotionally fragile, Eugene. He just has an asshole for a father."

"Oh, is that all?"

"Hey, we had an asshole for a father, too."

"And look where we are. Buying a house together so we can

live with our mom. Is it just me, or does this feel like junior high school all over again?"

"Mom paid for the house that time," he pointed out. "And it was about the size of an electron compared to this one, not to mention a rental. And it was junior high for you, kid. I was embarking on my senior year when Dad took off, remember?"

Oh, did she ever. She'd just been starting seventh grade, completely unprepared for the turbulent social life that awaited her, ill equipped as she'd been with braces, pimples, a bracken of unwieldy dishwater curls, and absolutely no breasts to speak of.

Wow. This really was just like seventh grade again. Except for the braces. And the bracken of curls was more of a shrub now. A well-tended shrub. But still a shrub.

"There's nothing wrong with this house that a little Clorox and paint won't fix," Julien said.

"Or a little nitro and acetylene," she muttered.

"The kitchen is gigantic," he pointed out, throwing his arms wide to encompass the room in which they stood. "Plenty of space for you to cook. The whole family could have breakfast and dinner together at the same table. I know that means a lot to you. You love to cook."

No, she used to love to cook. Back when she cooked for her roommates in college. And early in her marriage when she and Lawrence could use up as many hours, bottles of wine, and sticks of butter as they wanted to prepare dinner together. Then be together. But then had come two careers. Then Seth. Then suburbia and the whole fantasy-mom thing she'd bought into before having to return it unused. Eugenie hadn't actually enjoyed cooking since . . . Well, for a very long time. But then, she hadn't enjoyed a lot of things for a very long time.

"Who was responsible for the seventies, anyway?" she grumbled at the green appliances. "They should be taken out and flogged with a macramé belt."

Julien moved to a countertop where the Realtor had set out an incomplete place setting of stoneware and picked up a plate to inspect it. "Look," he said, turning it so she could see. "This house even has its own dishes. Dishes with its name painted on them. Hell, the house has a name, period." He pointed to the single word executed by hand in arcing, filigreed lettering around the rim. "Fleurissant," he murmured with affected reverence. "That's French. It means 'blooming.' Like when a flower blooms, not like how the English use it as a cuss word."

Which would have been infinitely more appropriate, Eugenie thought. "And you know that how?" she asked.

In spite of their mother's insistence that their surname had originally been D'Ashner and that she had endowed both of her children with Gallic names, and in spite of her insistence all her life that she would someday return to her "native France," a place she had never even visited, Julien didn't speak a word of French other than *garage*. He hadn't even gone to college. Before flipping houses—and meeting Cassie—he'd made his living being kept by women who had a lot more money than he did.

"The name was in the listing," he said. "So I Googled it."

Eugenie made her way over to have a closer look. The dinner, salad, and bread plates bore a whimsical rendition of the house, but they and the soup bowl, cup, and saucer were all either chipped or cracked or broken. She started to point out the significance of that, then decided it would be lost on Julien. Having educated himself in the arts of carpentry, masonry, plumbing, and hanging drywall, he was gifted at repairing things and making them whole again. Little faults like chips and cracks didn't bother him. He'd experienced brokenness a lot worse than that.

He'd watched his wife succumb to lymphoma, helpless to do anything that might fix her. If he could have Cassie back again, alive and healthy, he certainly wouldn't have minded a few chips and cracks in her.

"Think how great it would be," he said, "if the next time you talk to Lawrence, you can tell him you're doing so well without him that you just bought a mansion with a French name."

"Well, considering the fact that he knows exactly how much I received in the divorce settlement, he's going to think it must not be a mansion—which it isn't—and that it's filled with mold, nasty carpeting, and dismembered mice—which it is."

Julien frowned. "So you saw Mickey up there in the attic, huh?"

She nodded. "Minus his little gloves, jacket, bow tie . . . and, oh yeah, his head."

Her brother laughed lightly, his pale green eyes—the only feature they shared in common—crinkling adorably. Damn him. He was a half decade older than she, but the lines on his face and threads of silver in his dark hair had only improved his rugged good looks. The same traits on Eugenie made her look haggard. Or maybe it was Lawrence who had made her look—and feel—that way. But Lawrence was gone now, and she still felt like that. What did a woman have to do to feel blooming and buoyant again?

"Will you stop worrying?" Julien said. "There's nothing wrong with this house except that it's been neglected for too long. All it needs is a little hard work." At her expression, he hastily amended, "A *lot* of hard work and a couple bottles of environmentally friendly cleaner—"

She hardened her expression.

"Several vats of industrial strength cleaner, hundreds of thousands of nails, and a warehouse full of building materials." He smiled again. His charming-women smile, she noted. "And with your extremely gifted eye for color and fabrics, not to mention your exquisite taste in antiques, this place will look like the Beaux-Arts beauty she was back before the rest of the neighborhood sprang up around her. Just close your eyes for a minute and imagine how this place could look."

Eugenie didn't have to imagine. She remembered too well the frothy, fairy-tale facade and the enchanted gardens she'd loved as a child. That was why she'd wanted to look at the house in the first place. But that facade was decrepit now, and the gardens were blighted. Who would want a house like this? How could it ever be made whole again?

"It costs more than we allotted in our budget," she said halfheartedly, the foundation of her misgivings beginning to crumble. Maybe aiming for Julien's wallet would yield a deeper nick than talking about mold and mortar.

"It's been on the market for almost three years," he replied, "and it's way overpriced. Hell, the owners couldn't have gotten their current asking price for the place even *before* the housing collapse. They haven't had an offer in over a year. They'll come down. A lot, I bet."

Eugenie didn't doubt he knew what he was talking about. In addition to flipping houses, Julien had been a card-carrying Realtor for more than a decade.

"Who are the owners, anyway?" she asked, deliberately stalling when she felt the crack in her convictions widen. "How could they have let a house like this, in a *very* upscale neighborhood like Manitou Hills, deteriorate so much?"

"The owner's agent told me the house has been empty for five years. That's when the previous owner went into a nursing home.

When she died, it went to a second or third cousin, I think, up in Indiana somewhere. When he saw the comps for the rest of the neighborhood, he thought he could make a bundle off of it, not realizing—or wanting to accept—just how bad a shape it's in. But he's gotta be starting to sweat. Taxes for this neighborhood aren't exactly easy on the wallet."

"Every other house on this street would sell for high six figures, maybe seven, even in this market," she said. In Louisville, houses didn't get much more expensive than that. Not unless they *were* mansions. "And this house is way bigger than the others in this neighborhood, with double the lot. The owner may not be as amenable as you think."

Julien sighed sadly. "This house isn't like the other houses in the neighborhood. He has to realize that by now, too. The others have all been pampered like heiresses. They've been topped with tiaras, spoon-fed champagne and danced around ballrooms, then kissed by a worthy suitor beneath a plump, pink sunrise while Daddy smiled indulgently from an upstairs window." He gazed through the door that led to the dining room, with its cloudy chandelier and ragged wallpaper. "This beauty deserved no less. I can't understand how someone could have mistreated her so badly. She deserved better."

Now Eugenie was the one to smile. Her brother could be a raging poet when it came to old houses. And this one had been magnificent once upon a time. But it looked out of place now amid the other homes on Butterfly Way, all of them proud Tudors and Queen Annes or elegant Colonials and Neo-Classicals. It went beyond neglect, what had happened here. For some reason, she just couldn't quite let it go.

What's your story? she asked the house. *Why didn't they take better care of you?*

But the house didn't answer. Maybe the house didn't understand, either.

Eugenie told herself she was crazy. The place was going to take more time, work, and inclination than she had in her to invest. But when she turned to look at her brother again with the word *no* firmly on her lips, she instead heard herself say, "No one moves in until the last vestige of mold and pestilence is gone."

Julien grinned. "Not a problem, Eugene."

She could only laugh at that. No, the house wasn't *a* problem. It was scores of problems. So many, she didn't even know where to begin.

But Julien did. Obviously fearing she would change her mind, he whipped out his phone, scrolled through his contacts, and pushed a button. "Joanie?" he said when someone picked up at the other end. "Yeah, Julien Dashner. My sister and I would like to make an offer on the house on Butterfly Way."

Two

The Garden Atrium assisted living facility had neither a garden nor an atrium as far as Eugenie had been able to tell during her twice-weekly visits to see her mother. Even so, it was a nice enough place to live, with everything a person could need under one roof, and its monthly fee covered all of it. Lorraine Dashner had not only her own studio apartment (even if it wasn't much bigger than a college dorm room) and restaurant-style meals three times a day (even if they weren't served in a place that began with the word *Chez*) but also access to a hair salon, exercise room, indoor pool, computer lab, library, music room, and game room. Not that she ever took advantage of any of those things, in spite of Eugenie's and Julien's efforts to get her more involved with the activities she was able to enjoy. Since moving into the facility six months earlier, Lorraine had—as she had done at the half-dozen other facilities the Dashner siblings had tried before it—spent most of her time complaining and becoming more bitter and making sure everyone who came within shouting distance knew it.

Now Eugenie sat in the parking lot of the Garden Atrium, steeling herself to go inside. She and Julien had closed on the house three days earlier and were now the official owners of the home where they would be settling themselves, their families, and their mother.

Home, she repeated to herself. The word felt awkward in her brain. Maybe because *home* was, at the moment, a house that was barely fit for occupation, let alone habitation, let alone being a home. Maybe because *home* was a nebulous condition she had never quite been able to make substantial. Or maybe it was just because Lorraine Dashner would be spending the rest of her life in that home with the children she had booted from her own nest as soon as they turned eighteen, making clear they should never return.

Julien hadn't minded. He'd gone straight to work after high school and found a dump of an apartment to share with his best friend, both of whom were content to live in a dump. But Eugenie had wanted to go to college, and she hadn't wanted to live in a dump, and UofL had been less than five miles from her not-quite-a-dump home. Lorraine, however, had been adamant that living on her own would be character building for Eugenie. After all, Lorraine left home at eighteen, and look how well she turned out.

Amazingly, Eugenie had been able to refrain from commenting on that. Even more amazingly, she found an affordable apartment marginally less dumpy than Julien's. She also found a job on campus, then a second job off campus, to pay for rent, food, tuition, and anything else that came up. Her character had grown *a lot* during that time. Certainly more than her bank account had.

With both children gone, Lorraine had taken off, too, to spend the rest of her life traveling to exotic places and meeting exotic people. Especially exotic male people. Especially rich exotic male people. Unfortunately, the income of an insurance company receptionist only went so far in achieving that exotic travel thing—even after the receptionist in question cut her children loose—so what Lorraine had really ended up doing was working as a receptionist in places other than Louisville, and she had called it travel. *Immersion* travel at that.

More than anyplace else, she had wanted to visit France, the country she always called her homeland. This in spite of the fact that her parents immigrated to her native Mississippi from the Florida panhandle and in spite of the fact that her maiden name was Higgenbotham. Lorraine had always insisted her surname was merely a corruption of the word *Huguenot*. Which meant that in addition to being French, her family had a long history of being persecuted, so just lay off the Higgenbotham thing already.

After marrying Douglas Dashner, Lorraine had immediately begun signing her last name D'Ashner and pronouncing it Dash-NAY, insisting its true origin referred to a person—a *French* person—who lived in a forest of ash trees. Never mind that Ancestry.com said the name's origin was actually German, a variation of Taschner, an occupational name for a maker of purses.

Eugenie wondered how her mother's character—or perhaps she should say *caractère*—was these days. Lorraine had been on her own for three decades. But the closest she'd come to living in France had been a three-year stint in Vincennes, Indiana, where she'd lived with a guy named Chris whom she'd called Christophe. The entire time she was with him, Lorraine had introduced Christophe as her fiancé, even though Eugenie was fairly certain he'd never had any intention of making Lorraine his madame. Not the way Lorraine translated the word, anyway.

Inhaling a fortifying breath, Eugenie squared her shoulders, pushed open the car door, and unfolded herself from inside. When she'd told her mother the day before about closing on the house, Lorraine had insisted on seeing it immediately. Eugenie had tried to stall her for a few weeks . . . months . . . millennia . . . telling her there was a lot of work to do before they could move in, and she wouldn't be able to get a good feel for the house until some of it had been completed in a few weeks . . . months . . . millennia. But Lorraine had been adamant. She told Eugenie she would meet her in the lobby of the Garden Atrium at ten o'clock this morning on the dot. Glancing at her watch, Eugenie saw that ten o'clock was only three dots away. So she forced her feet to move forward.

The lobby of the facility strove to look like a luxury hotel, right down to its marble floor, potted palms, skylights, and posh tapestry sofas and chairs. It might have succeeded with the illusion had it not been for the extrawide spacing of the furnishings to accommodate wheelchairs and walkers and the oxygen tanks tucked into discreet places. Even the staff members in this part of the facility were dressed to look like hotel concierges and receptionists, with dark blue suits and crisp white shirts. Farther in, there were RNs, nurse's aides, orderlies, social workers, and geriatric psychiatrists, but even they wore khakis and polo shirts to give them the look of hospitality people on a cruise ship. None of them was referred to by what they actually were. At the Garden Atrium, everyone was a "staff member," so that the inmates—ah, Eugenie meant residents—could better convince themselves that their living wasn't assisted at all. They just had lots of housekeepers, gardeners, and drivers.

Soon, Lorraine would have only Eugenie and Julien to be her staff. They would be not just her housekeepers, gardeners, and drivers but her nurses, orderlies, social workers, and psychiatrists, too. Jobs neither of them had ever performed before. Jobs neither of them was trained to do. Jobs neither of them wanted, quite frankly. Jobs that would be theirs for the rest of Lorraine's life.

Something akin to terror knotted Eugenie's belly. Buying a house and combining their families had seemed like such a good idea six months ago when she and Julien made the decision. Now, suddenly, she felt as if she were condemned to prison—a moldy, crumbling, pestilent prison—for the rest of her natural life.

Home, she repeated to herself, striving for more optimism. The house *would* be a home. Not a prison. Not an assisted living facility. Not a degenerated, neglected, decomposing building that was beyond repair. It would be a home. Dammit. It would.

Out of nowhere, she was assailed by the voice of Bette Davis spouting her famous "What a dump" line. Over and over and over again. Lorraine loved Bette Davis. Eugenie, not so much.

She approached the faux concierge desk on the other side of the lobby and smiled at the faux concierge. "Hello, Diane," she said. "I've come to fetch my mother for the day."

Diane, a woman in her mid-thirties with cropped brown hair and dark eyes, smiled back. The same kind of smile all the staff members at the Garden Atrium smiled, one that offered not a clue as to whether it was borne of enthusiasm or erudition, mordancy or lunacy. Eugenie wondered if they learned it in employee training or if she and Julien would be smiling that way in a few months, too.

"Madame Dash-NAY is on her way down now," Diane chirped. "Evelyn's gotten her bathed and dressed, and she's ready to go."

Funny, but the way she said *ready to go* made it sound as if Diane were hoping Lorraine's going would be a terminal condition.

"Please thank Evelyn for being there for Mrs. Dashner," Eugenie said. "I'm sure my mother appreciated the help."

She could tell by the way the Diane's eye twitched that Mrs. Dashner didn't appreciate much of anything they did for her at the Garden Atrium. If there was one thing Lorraine hated, it was being dependent on others. Which was ironic in light of the fact that she'd spent her entire adult life looking for a man who would take care of her. The kind of caregiver Lorraine wanted was the kind whose care came in the form of cash, cars, and carats. The kind she'd actually found had been more likely to offer hardship, hopelessness, and heartbreak.

Diane said, "I'm sure Madame Dash-NAY will be much happier once she's moved out of the Garden Atrium and has her children to take care of her at home."

It was a nice thought. But Eugenie knew the only thing that would make her mother happy would be draping herself across a chaise longue on the balcony of a small pension on the Boulevard Saint-Germain while a guy named Étienne mixed up a batch of champagne cocktails. For now, however—forever—Eugenie and Julien would have to do.

"I'm sure you're right," she told Diane. "It's been a while since Mrs. Dashner has been able to spend much time with her family."

She didn't add that that was because every time Eugenie or Julien came to see her, Lorraine began the visit with an invasive interrogation, segued into a harangue, and ended with throwing something. Occasionally at them. Not that she'd ever hit either of them, since she could barely hold an item, let alone manage enough strength or grace to fling it any distance. Whether they hit their target or not, however, airborne projectiles had a way of curbing conversation. Fortunately, there was nothing at the house at this point that could be hurled. Other than the contents of one's stomach. Which, all things considered, still wasn't outside the realm of possibility later in the day.

The two women stood in awkward silence for a few moments, until Eugenie heard the elevator at the end of the hall ding its arrival. It was followed by the sound she had come to associate with her mother—the metallic *chink-creak-chink-creak-chink-creak* of the walker Lorraine needed in order to get around. Involuntarily, Eugenie stiffened, and her stomach knotted tighter.

Chink-creak. Chink-creak. Chink-creak.

Lorraine was getting closer. Eugenie strode slowly to a place where she could gaze down the corridor beyond the lobby and tamped down the ribbon of unease that unwound inside her.

Chink-creak. Chink-creak. Chink-creak.

The sound grew louder as Lorraine drew nearer.

Chink-creak. Chink-creak. Chink-creak.

Then she was there, rounding a corner, defiantly walking in front of the aide who was pushing a wheelchair behind her, even though her progress, not to mention her pain level, would have been better had she taken advantage of the alternate mode of transportation. The fingers hooked over the handles of her walker were buckled and gnarled, but the nails were manicured, painted a fabulous forties film red. The color actually made Lorraine's fingers look more monstrous than the rheumatoid arthritis did. Then again, that was probably the reason she had chosen the color. Her left foot turned inward and was bent at the ankle, and she dragged her right one behind her.

Chink-creak. Chink-creak. Chink-creak.

There was a time when Lorraine had tried to hide her twisted limbs with long sleeves and pants or skirts. Today, in spite of the fact that March was still chilly, she wore turquoise capri pants and a short-sleeved scarlet top that battled her fingernails for brilliance. Instead of the sneakers she was supposed to wear to help her keep her balance, she had on red-beaded, open-toed pumps—three sizes larger than the tiny size fives she used to wear, in order to accommodate her sprawling joints and digits. Her toenails, too, were painted hematic red. As was her mouth. Red, too, were the sunglasses studded with rhinestones that hid the green eyes she shared with her children. On a lesser woman, all that red would have clashed with the flaming orange hair, but on Lorraine, it didn't dare.

In her own khaki cargo pants, olive drab sweater, and Birkenstocks, Eugenie felt like a carrier pigeon standing in the path of a peacock. Not that that was a new feeling, however. Before her mother became Madame Lorraine Dash-NAY, before she was even Lorraine Dashner, she was Lorie Higgenbotham who, in her native Natchez, had been Someone. Not only a cheerleader and homecoming queen for four years straight at Calhoun High School but also a Miss May Fest, a Tomato Days Princess, and the Safe Boating Queen. Then she was Miss Natchez. Then Miss Mississippi. And when she went to the Miss America pageant that year, she was fourth runner-up for the crown. Lorraine claimed dozens of tiaras and sashes in her collection, starting with the tiny ones she was awarded in a beautiful baby contest at the Mississippi State Fair and ending with the ones she earned as Mrs. Kentucky the year after Eugenie was born.

Rhinestones, satin, and sequins. That was what Lorraine Dashner was made of. Or had been. Until the year the vessel she'd spent her life honing and currying began to wither. It started when she was living in Chicago—that time with a fiancé named Bob/Robert-with-a-silent-*t*-at-the-end. Eugenie would call her mother to check up on her, and Lorraine would complain of "hurting all over" and being too tired to talk. At the time, Eugenie had feared Robert-with-a-silent-*t*-at-the-end was abusing her. She'd asked Julien to drive up to Indianapolis to get her so the two of them could go to Chicago together to investigate.

What they discovered when they got there was Lorraine living alone and looking like hell. Watery eyes, pale skin with patches of red, swollen joints. Had she been to the doctor? they asked. Of course not, Lorraine told them. She was simply suffering from a broken heart in the wake of Robert-with-a-silent-*t*-at-the-end's desertion. A trip to the ER, however, indicated something slightly more problematic. Anemia, pleurisy, and swollen glands for starters. Rheumatoid arthritis for finishers.

In addition to twisting her hands and feet in the ensuing years, the disease had now begun to gnarl other joints, bow her back, and warp her shoulders. Eugenie wasn't sure, but her mother's head might even be listing a bit to the left now where it hadn't been before. Or that could simply be because Lorraine was giving her the evil eye even harder than usual.

Chink-creak. Chink-creak. Chink-creak.

Eugenie waited silently, willing the tension in her own body to lessen. Which, she supposed, was more than her mother would ever be able to do.

"Mom," she said by way of a greeting when Lorraine drew within earshot. As always, she had to halt herself before asking the question she would have asked of anyone else: *How are you?* Not only was her mother's condition obvious, but she didn't want to get hit by a flying walker or wheelchair or staff member.

"What are you dressed for? Camp?" her mother asked. "Honestly, Eugenie, if you'd take even five minutes in the morning, you could at least look halfway decent. It's no wonder Lawrence had a wandering eye."

The knot in Eugenie's belly cinched tighter. "No, Mom, I'm

dressed for the weather and for looking at a house that's in need of renovation." Somehow, she managed to keep her voice level. After all, her mother's comment was nothing out of the ordinary, and Eugenie's mode of dress hadn't changed any more over the years than her mother's had.

She allowed a moment for each of them to get a handle on their acrimony, then continued, "Well. Looks like you're good to go. You ready to see our new home?"

Lorraine smirked at that. "I could ask if you're the one who's ready."

Eugenie waited to see if her mother would and was relieved when she didn't. She reached for Lorraine's coat, slung over one side of the walker. "Maybe Diane can help you with your coat while I bring the car around," she said to no one in particular. "Then we can go . . ." For the first time since looking at the house, Eugenie stumbled over the word. "Home," she finally made herself say. "Then we can go home."

Three

"What a dump."

Eugenie couldn't quite halt her grin when she heard her mother's commentary. The words coincided perfectly with the Bette Davis refrain still cycling through her head, right down to the sighs that bookended it. It was the first time she could remember her and her mother ever being in sync.

"It'll get better, Mom. Just you wait."

It was Julien, not Eugenie, who replied, since he was the only person in the room who could say that with a straight face. Eugenie was barely able to stifle the strangled sound clawing for escape at the back of her throat.

"Well, it couldn't get any worse," Lorraine said with even more conviction than Julien.

No one contradicted her, even though everyone who would be living in the house had come to see it this afternoon. Eugenie and Julien had tried to put them all off until they could at least delouse . . . ah, demouse . . . ah, demouse-part the place. But Julien's daughters, Sophie and Chloe, had been dancing with anticipation about seeing their new rooms *now* (and Julien had guiltily indulged them with whatever they wanted since their mother's death), Lorraine had made clear in her own roundabout way that she wanted to be sure Julien and Eugenie hadn't bought a death trap to hasten her death (which hadn't been so roundabout, since what she'd said was, "I want to make sure you haven't bought a death trap to hasten my death"), and Eugenie's son, Seth, had wanted . . .

Well, actually, Seth hadn't wanted to come and genuinely couldn't care less about the new house. Where Chloe and Sophie had been zipping from room to room squealing with every new discovery they made ("Look! A little elevator in the kitchen!" "Hey! The floor here is lower than over there!" "Yuck! A dead cricket!" "Gross! Something smells like poop!"), Seth had retreated to the kitchen, hoisted himself onto a countertop, and, eyes closed and earbuds firmly in place, proceeded to ignore them all.

But then, that had been his pattern since his father moved out of their old house. His iPod was the last thing Lawrence had bought for him, and even though Eugenie had offered to upgrade Seth to an iPod touch in an effort to cheer him up, he'd declined. More accurately, he'd ignored her.

She knew ignoring was a big part of the average teenager's life, but with Seth, it seemed to be the only part. The solid B average he'd maintained all through grade and middle school had plummeted to a D during his sophomore year, and so much anger simmered just below his surface (and, too often, spilled over the top) that he'd driven away most of his friends. Eugenie had hoped moving to a new city might give him as much of a fresh start as returning to her hometown would give her. But Seth just seemed to be withdrawing even more.

She started toward the kitchen to see if she could coax him out to join the rest of the family, but towheaded five-year-old Chloe careened into her from behind, grabbing her around the legs and halting her.

"Aunt Eugenie!" she cried. "When can I see *my* room?"

"Very soon," Eugenie told her. "We'll look at the whole house before we leave. But your daddy needs to go up first to make sure, um . . ."

To make sure there were no carcasses in any of the rooms up there that would keep the girls awake at night and scar them for life. Even without carcasses, Eugenie was going to have nightmares enough for all of them. Julien was supposed to have come yesterday to get rid of all the dead stuff, but had he? She threw her brother a searching look.

He understood immediately and nodded. "We can head up anytime and decide which room will be whose," he said.

Dark-haired seven-year-old Sophie, who looked as much like her father as her sister looked like their mother, joined them, leaning into her father's side and curling an arm around his waist. "I think I should decide that," she said. "I'm the oldest."

"Maybe you could draw straws," Eugenie said.

Julien shook his head. "We'll decide together," he told both girls. "The same way you two and me and Mommy have always decided things like that together."

"But Mommy's not here anymore," Sophie said with the matter-of-factness of a child who never really had the chance to know her mother and probably didn't remember her very well. Evidently, no decisions had been made in the family since Cassie's death.

Julien sobered at the mention of his late wife, but he sounded almost normal when he told his daughter, "Mommy will *always* be here." He dropped to his haunches in front of his youngest and tapped his finger against her chest, over her heart. "She'll always be there," he said. Then he pointed his finger at Sophie's heart. "And she'll always be there." Then he moved his hand to his own chest, splaying his fingers wide over his heart. "And she'll always, *always*, be here."

Chloe's eyebrows arrowed downward. "Daddy, what did Mommy look like?"

Julien's expression would have been the same had someone just driven a stake through his heart. "You, uh . . . you don't remember what Mommy looked like, sweetie?"

Chloe's loose curls danced as she shook her head. "No."

"But there's a picture of her in your room," he reminded her.

Other than an identical photo of Cassie in Sophie's room, it was the only picture of Cassie in the house, Eugenie knew. A lot of people were comforted by photos of their dead loved ones, but Julien wasn't one of them. After Cassie's memorial service, he'd boxed up every image of her that had been displayed in their house except for two he'd placed in the girls' rooms. Although he'd ventured halfheartedly back into dating about a year ago, the handful of women he'd gone out with were all physical opposites of Cassie. Eugenie didn't think he'd seen any of them more than a few times before deciding the relationship would never work out.

"I know, but that's just a picture," Chloe said. "I don't really remember Mommy. What did she look like?"

When Eugenie looked at Julien, his expression was so bleak, and so devastated, it was all she could do not to reach out to him. Instead, she cupped Chloe's chin in her hand and turned her niece's earnest little face toward her own. She truly was a miniature version of Cassie, right down to the pale freckles scattered across her cheeks. It must be hell for Julien to look into that face every day and see his dead wife.

"Your mommy looked just you, Chloe," Eugenie told her. Then she smiled. "Except she was a little bit taller."

"When we get home," Julien said, "we'll talk about your mom, okay?"

Chloe turned to her dad and nodded.

"And I'll, um, I'll get out some more pictures to show you," he added. "And the videos of . . ." He swallowed hard again. "Of our wedding, and of when we brought you two home from the hospital." He straightened and, still looking a little dazed, turned to Lorraine. "You're going to have the entire first floor to yourself," he said as if nothing had interrupted the house talk in the first place. "The master suite is huge. It even has a fireplace. Also an attached bath. And look at this." He strode to a sunken library area in a far corner of the living room, danced down the three steps, and spun around at its middle. "Your own library."

It took Lorraine a few minutes to hobble over the distance Julien had covered so quickly—*chink-creak-chink-creak-chink-creak*—and when she finally arrived at the top of the steps, she frowned. "I can't go up and down stairs. You know that."

Julien's smile dimmed not at all. "Nash and I are going to raise the floor for you."

Nash Ridley was Julien's boyhood friend with whom he had run his house-flipping business once upon a time, and who still freelanced on renovations where he could—like he would on their house. Nash was as gifted as Eugenie's brother when it came to repairing old, worn-out things, but he wasn't as good with the responsibility part, so Julien had always been the one in charge when they were professional partners.

Nash had also been the sole occupant of Eugenie's romantic fantasies while she was growing up, since he was the first boy she ever had a crush on. Okay, the only boy she ever had a crush on. And the only teenager she ever had a crush on. And the only young man she ever had a crush on. Thankfully, she met Lawrence in college and that had been the end of all her crushes. On Nash, she meant. Of course she'd had a crush on Lawrence. At some point. She must have. She just couldn't remember the details now that she was a bitter divorcée.

At the mention of Nash's name, Lorraine brightened. But then, she'd always brightened whenever Nash was around. So did Sophie and Chloe, for that matter. Nash was an equal-opportunity crush.

"How is Nash?" Lorraine asked.

"Same as always," Julien told her. "You'll be seeing him before long, since he's going to be doing a lot of work around here."

"And just how long," Lorraine said, "is it going to take you to get this death trap whipped into shape?"

"It's not a death trap, Mom," Julien said. Still smiling, Eugenie noted. Amazing. "It just needs a little TLC."

Lorraine shook her head. "More like a little TNT."

"It's gonna be fine, I promise." As Julien segued into a list of all the reasons why buying the house was a good idea, Sophie and Chloe scrambled up the stairs, and Eugenie headed for the kitchen. Seth hadn't moved a muscle since assuming the position and still had his eyes closed. Eugenie turned around and gripped the countertop beside him and, with considerably less grace than a sixteen-year-old boy was able to manage, maneuvered herself up beside him. Although there was no way he couldn't have noticed her presence—she had elbowed him in the ribs more than once—he still didn't open his eyes. So she poked him on the shoulder. Three times. Then she reached up and tugged on the cord of the earbud that dangled from beneath his razor-straight brown hair until it popped free.

That, finally, got his attention. He even—gasp—reacted. He actually opened his eyes! Or at least the eye she could see that wasn't covered by the sweep of his overly long bangs. It was the same bottle-glass green that the elder Dashners claimed. Then—Eugenie tried to contain her excitement at so much reacting—he even *turned his head*. And then—*Be still my heart!*—he glared at her.

"So what do you think?" she asked.

He said nothing for a moment, but the gaze of that one eye remained fixed on her face. Finally, he said, "I think the world is going to hell in a handbasket."

She nodded. "It was on its way when I was your age, too. It's going to take a while to get there, I promise. What I meant was, what do you think of the house?"

There was another moment of silence, then Seth said, "I think the house is evidence that the world's trip is picking up speed."

Ignoring, for now, that the same thought had crossed her own mind more than once today, she asked, "Do you want to see your room?" Hastily, she amended, "Well, what will eventually be your room. There's a lot of work to do up there before it will actually *be* a room. Right now it's just . . ." She stopped herself before saying "a mouse morgue" and instead concluded, "The attic. It's going to be really cool when Uncle Jules finishes with it."

For an infinitesimal moment, something flickered to life in Seth's expression that made Eugenie remember the sunny little kid he used to be. But he doused it as quickly as it had ignited, then snatched the earbud from her hand and tucked it back under his hair.

"Whatev," he said as he completed the gesture. Then he closed his eyes and leaned his head back against the cabinet again. Just like that, her son was gone.

"Whatev*er*," Eugenie corrected him, even though she knew he couldn't hear her. She had given up trying to squelch his profanity, but she'd be damned if she would let him butcher the English language.

Still, she conceded, he had a point. Words did sort of fail when it came to a place like Fleurissant. Closing her own eyes and doing her best to tune out her mother's complaints from the other room, she leaned her head back against the cabinet, too. She'd see Seth's *whatev* and raise him a *terribad*. The whole situation was FUBAR, anyway.

Four

Springtime came to Louisville symbolically more than anything else, since the weather that time of year swung from blizzard to blistering with the occasional tornado thrown in for good measure. Bags of cypress mulch sprouted at gas stations where rickets of firewood had begun to lay dormant. Derby hats bloomed in boutiques in dizzying colors. Brilliant patches of bicyclists sprang up along River Road. Eugenie drove past one of those last on her way downtown, but their bright splashes of green and yellow did little to lift her mood. And not just because, as always, they rode in bunches instead of single file, then flipped her off as she swerved around them, because they evidently needed more than an entire lane while they flouted the rules of the road.

Where Julien had spent the month since closing on the house seeing to its detox and trying to sell his own, she had been looking for a job. Any job. Something inside her balked at the idea of having to rely solely on Lawrence for income. She wasn't sure if that was due to some primal instinct that she could take care of herself and her cub on her own, or if it was because of some deep-buried feminist conviction that she didn't need a man. Maybe it was just because Lawrence hadn't taken care of her for a long time, anyway. Not in more than a financial sense.

Unfortunately, the world wasn't exactly friendly to employment seekers these days, and more than a decade had passed since Eugenie last held a job. That one had been in advertising, a business that had changed significantly since she'd been a part of it—a fact that was hammered home when she was almost immediately dismissed from the three interviews she managed to win at local agencies.

At this point, she was beginning to feel ill equipped to do anything, in spite of having whittled down what had already been a slim list of requisites for prospective employment. In fact, she currently had only two requirements of a job. Number one: that she would earn at least minimum wage. And number two: that she wouldn't have to make balloon animals.

Which was how she came to be exiting the elevator on the eighth floor of the Starks Building in downtown Louisville. She looked left, then right, down the deserted hall, the blunt silence seeming to echo off the marble walls and mahogany doors. The setting was like something from a film noir, from the arching porcelain water fountains to the gold paint on opaque glass that identified the businesses behind those doors. She heard what must have been the sound of fingers search-and-pecking on a computer keyboard, but if she closed her eyes—and she did for a moment—she could convince herself it was the staccato report of an old manual typewriter.

This was the last place on her list of tolerable employment possibilities. If this interview didn't work out, she was going to have to delve into the kind of work that necessitated dealing with—she swallowed her terror—the general public. Like retail or telemarketing. Next on the list came the really chilling prospects. Like food service. Then food preparation. Then food delivery. Then food stamps.

She paused in front of suite 842 to straighten her charcoal pencil skirt, and while she was at it, she unbuttoned her dove gray jacket. Then she buttoned it again. Then unbuttoned it. Casual or serious? Which would make her look less desperate?

Open, she finally decided. Instinctively, she also unpinned the brooch holding closed the collar of her white shirt. Too eighties. Though maybe it could be construed as fashionably retro? Nah. Nothing about the eighties had been fashionable. She stuffed the brooch into her pocket with one hand while loosing the top two buttons of her shirt with the other. She scrubbed both hands through her hair, gave her head a shake, and took a couple of fortifying breaths. Casual, she told herself. Casual was better for something like this. Definitely.

Probably.

Maybe?

Oh, dammit . . .

The gold letters on the frosted glass of this door were blocked and formal, but their sentiment was not. HEARTMENDERS, the letters spelled in an arch at the top. Below that: SPECIALISTS IN FINDING THAT PERFECT SOMEONE. A third line announced, SPALDING CHASAN, PROPRIETOR. Below that, on a final line: MAISY CHASAN, FOUNDER.

The ad in the online classifieds had said HeartMenders was looking to hire a "relationship facilitator." Eugenie had been about to ignore it and move to the next listing when she realized the company wasn't, in fact, a massage parlor but a dating service, and "relationship facilitator" appeared to be a perfectly legal and in no way contagious secretarial position.

She gripped the knob and pushed the door open, stepping into a small, crowded waiting room—though the crowd consisted not of people, but of empty chairs. Except for one that was behind a desk much too large for such a tiny space, overflowing with a woman whose orange helix of hair was topped by two pencils resembling Martian antennae. She looked up when she heard Eugenie enter, smiling in a way that was neither warm nor cool, both distant and familiar. There was no way to gauge the woman's age—she might have been fifty-five or twenty-five—but her name, according to the plastic sign perched on the desk's edge, was Iris Philpot.

"Can I help you?" she asked.

Eugenie smiled. "Yes. Thank you. I'm Eugenie Dashner. I have an appointment with Mr. Chasan? I'm here about the position of, ah . . ." She reminded herself that if she wanted to land this job, she was going to have to get used to calling herself a, ah . . . "Relationship facilitator."

Damn. She'd still managed to say it in a way that made her sound like she was applying for a job at a massage parlor.

Iris seemed to think so, too. "Just a minute," she said coolly.

The woman's knees snapped as she stood, then clickety-clacked like a night train when she made her way across the room. As she disappeared behind one door, Eugenie noticed there were two others, both closed, neither identifying what might be behind them. Once Iris was gone, the room was thrown again into numb silence. Either this building had amazing soundproofing or HeartMenders' business wasn't exactly booming.

To distract herself from having to think about that, Eugenie absorbed the surroundings of her prospective workplace. The walls were kind of a noncolor between beige and eggshell, the hardwood floor was scarred in places, and patches of the broad

Persian rug spanning it were worn nearly to the backing. The furniture was vintage Danish Modern, the artwork WPA-style prints. She half expected the reading materials on the tables beside them to be decades-old issues of *Life* and *Look* blaring headlines about Normandy and Ernest Hemingway. But it was the usual supermarket fodder of couples so indistinguishable they had been endowed by the media with fused names.

Had she and Lawrence been a celebrity couple, they would have been known as Eugrence. No wonder their marriage had been doomed.

Iris Philpot thankfully emerged then and announced, "Mr. Chasan will see you now."

Eugenie nodded her thanks and crossed to the door. She expected Iris to move out of the way to let her pass, but instead the other woman held the door open, mostly by standing in front of it. It was all Eugenie could do to squeeze between her and the doorjamb—in addition to being big-boned, the woman must have stood more than six feet tall—something that caused Eugenie to pop out on the other side like a scary jack-in-the-box clown.

Thank goodness she was making such a good first impression.

Spalding Chasan looked like the kind of guy who might have chatted up Ward Cleaver at a cocktail party, right down to the slender lapels of his jacket and the skinny necktie. Not that Ward Cleaver had ever gone to cocktail parties. Well, not that they'd shown on TV, anyway. But Eugenie would bet good money her prospective employer could have comfortably traded bons mots with Ward at the bar of the American Legion Post on a Saturday night. His hair was nearly fifty-fifty salt and pepper—obviously prematurely—his eyes were kind, and his smile was real. Best of all, he pretended not to notice she'd just breached the hull of his office like an atomic warhead.

"Hello," she said a little breathlessly, forcing her feet forward. "I'm Eugenie Dashner. Thank you for seeing me."

He stood and extended his right hand. "Spalding Chasan. Please, have a seat."

He gestured toward the—also Danish Modern—chair on the opposite side of his—also Danish Modern—desk. His office was an extension of the reception area, right down to the worn Persian carpet. Except that this room was even more crowded than the other, and instead of being crowded with furniture—the desk and two chairs were the only bit of that—the office was crammed with . . . stuff. Lots and lots of stuff.

His desk was obscured by untidy stacks of paper, scattered among which were things that didn't seem in any way pertinent to running a dating service. A coffee cup commemorating the royal wedding—not of William and Kate or even Charles and Diana but of Elizabeth II and Prince Philip—housed a spray of pens and pencils, a kazoo, a C-3PO action figure, and a Cuban flag. Near that, a Matchbox-sized El Camino was parked beside a bobblehead Marilyn Monroe. Peeking out from beneath what looked like a handwritten thank-you note was an iPod. First generation. Roughly the size of Rhode Island.

On the wall behind him was an array of framed photographs featuring beaming couples of all ages and ethnicities, presumably some of HeartMenders' success stories. There was also a large grouping of Best of Louisville plaques—though the most recent, she observed, was dated two years earlier—and two framed degrees: a bachelor's in social work and an MBA, both from the University of Louisville.

Homegrown boy, she realized. Not many people came from elsewhere to go to UofL, unless it was to attend the engineering or medical schools.

"So, Ms. Dashner," he said, bringing her attention back to the matter at hand. "Just out of curiosity, how did you hear about the opening at HeartMenders?"

He really did have a nice smile, the kind that made her feel like he was completely focused on her and nothing else. Then she decided it wasn't just his smile that did that. It was his eyes, too. The irises were the rich, warm amber of good whiskey, and his gaze never wavered from hers. She couldn't remember the last time a man had looked at her for any length of time without glancing away, even for a second. She'd begun to think they weren't wired for eye contact.

"I saw it in the *Courier-Journal* classifieds," she told him.

His smile broadened at that. "So you're a newspaper reader, then."

"Actually, I found it in the online classifieds."

His smile fell some. "Ah."

"But I do like to read the paper, too," she hastened to add when he seemed disappointed in her answer. On Sunday morning. When she had time to enjoy it. "I assume you've had time to look over my résumé?" she hurried on, changing the subject.

"I have."

She expected him to whip out a laptop and pull up the document she'd uploaded with her query on the website, but he instead began to rifle through the stacks of papers on his desk. It took him only a few seconds to find the single sheet of ivory vellum that was much nicer than the discount printer paper Eugenie always bought.

"I have to be honest with you, Ms. Dashner," he said as he gave her résumé another quick scan. "You're a little overqualified for the position."

"Yes, well, it's kind of you to say that," she told him, fighting back her fear of being dismissed again before even being given a chance. "But the position sounds so interesting, and I think I'd enjoy it and be very good at it. I've always loved learning new things, and I'm *such* a people person." The only way she managed to say that last without tripping over the words was because she'd had so much practice over the past few weeks. Although not quite as adept at saying, "And I'm such a romantic at heart," she managed to get those words out, too. "Plus," she hurried on, "I'm a Louisville native, so I know the city well. I'm familiar with all the restaurants and clubs and venues. And I know what it's like to be single here."

The amber eyes twinkled a little. Honestly. Twinkled. Suddenly it wasn't Ward Cleaver that Eugenie was thinking about. It was George Clooney.

"So you're not married?" he asked.

Eugenie bit back a strangled sound. "No. I'm not."

"Never married?"

"Divorced."

He nodded, a gesture that told her nothing of what he might be thinking. "So, tell me a little bit about yourself and what brought you to HeartMenders today."

She relaxed a little. His request was one she had heard at every interview in some form, so she was ready for it now. In fact, so familiar with her reply had she become that she could recite it without even thinking about it. Just toss out the vital statistics of her educational and professional background in a way that made her sound confident and capable and provide a few snippets of her personal life without giving away too much.

Piece of cake.

She looked at Spalding Chasan, at his twinkling George Clooney eyes and his comforting Ward Cleaver jacket and tie, leaning back in his chair and seeming sincerely interested in her reply.

So she replied, "Two years ago—two years ago today, as a matter of fact—I woke up an hour before everyone else like I always do, then I had my coffee and made a nutritious, wholesome breakfast and two nutritious, wholesome lunches for my husband and son, whom I then sent off to work and school, then I ate breakfast myself and went to the spin class I used to go to every day with my friend Susan Stoddard, whose son, Ethan, is the same age as my son, Seth—honestly, the two of them are almost like brothers, or, at least, they used to be until Seth starting turning into this reclusive stranger I hardly recognize anymore—then I volunteered at the teacher appreciation lunch at school, then I went to Kroger because I didn't realize we were out of turmeric when I went to the grocery the day before, then I went back to school to pick up Seth and dropped him off at track practice, then I went to pick up Lawrence's dry cleaning and Lawrence's psoriasis prescription and renew Lawrence's gym membership and blah blah blah, it was always something for Lawrence, wasn't it, then I went back for Seth after track practice, then home to fix dinner—chicken tikka masala because Lawrence asked for Indian that night—then I cleaned up the kitchen and paid some bills and balanced the checkbook, then I said good night to Seth and poured myself a glass of wine, and then—*then*—just as I was sitting down to watch *CSI: New York*, which was the *only* show I *ever* took the time to watch without DVRing it, it was the *one hour* every week that was *just for me, dammit,* Lawrence comes in and tells me he's having an affair with Dolores Hastings, so I ask, 'Who the hell is Dolores Hastings?' and he tells me she's the woman who came to work for his firm six months before, five of which he's spent sleeping with her, by the way, and then I remember meeting Dolores Hastings, and not only is she *not* young and beautiful with perky, non-child-bearing breasts, she's in fact pushing sixty and looks *a lot* like Ethel Merman."

It was only then, when Eugenie finally paused to take a breath, that she realized how long she'd been talking. Then she realized what she had said. To a complete stranger. Who she had hoped would hire her for a job. And who was now looking at her like . . .

Hmm. That was odd. Spalding Chasan was looking at her exactly the same way he had been when she started talking. Hastily, Eugenie lifted a hand to cover her eyes, before she could see the look of abject horror darken his features.

For a moment, she said nothing. Mostly because she had no idea what to say. Except, of course, for *I'm sorry I wasted your time, Mr. Chasan. I can find my own way out.* Finally, though, she said softly, "And you know what the hell of it is?"

Spalding Chasan said nothing for a few seconds, but then, even more quietly than she had spoken, he asked, "What's the hell of it?"

She dropped her hand and discovered he was now looking at her with mild amusement, which she wasn't sure was any better than the look of abject horror would have been. "The hell of it is I can't even watch *CSI: New York* anymore. The *one* thing I had *just for me* in that marriage, and Lawrence took it, too."

Spalding Chasan arched one dark brow but said nothing.

"I apologize," she said with great understatement. "I have no idea where all of that came from. Well, I do, but I don't know why it chose now to chew off the restraints and make its escape."

"Not a problem," Chasan replied. "This kind of thing happens to me with some regularity. I think it's the Ward Cleaver thing."

Eugenie managed a small, resigned smile for that. Then she

pried her fingers free from the chair and stood. "Well. I'm sorry I wasted your time, Mr. Chasan. I can find my own way out."

"Call me Spalding," he said as he rose, too. "Everyone who works here goes by his or her first name. Makes things a little friendlier. I'll expect you tomorrow morning at nine, when the office opens. We can take care of all the formalities then. But if you have a few minutes right now, I can show you around a bit."

At his words, something inside Eugenie that had been wound too tight for too long slowly began to unknot. Strangely, something told her it wasn't just because she'd finally landed a job.

"Welcome to HeartMenders, Eugenie," he said, pronouncing her name perfectly. "I think you're going to fit right in."

Five

Somewhere in the dark, dusty corners of Nash Ridley's attic, there had to be a portrait of him in which he appeared heinously disfigured.

That was all Eugenie could think when she stopped by Fleurissant after her interview at HeartMenders to find her brother's best friend slash business partner standing dirty and half naked in her newish house. Some kind of Dorian Gray, Oscar Wildean thing had to be taking place for him to still look, after all this time, so very . . . ah, good.

He was patching a section of plaster on a wall of what would be one of her nieces' bedrooms and had doubtless been performing similarly dirty, sweaty tasks all day—hence his current state. Not that Nash had ever needed a reason for being half naked. She'd known the guy since she was a kid, and any time the thermostat had registered higher than seventy, his shirt had always sort of automatically come off. Interestingly, he'd also always managed to find some way to become sweaty and dirty once it was off.

Well, Eugenie had always thought that was interesting.

She was only eight when Julien brought his thirteen-year-old friend home for the first time, but puberty and adolescence had cemented her affections for Nash nicely. Everything she knew about being a woman, she'd learned from reading her mother's Harlequin romances and casting herself and Nash in the lead roles. She had been Eugenie Dashner, RN, and he had been Dr. Ridley. She had been Housekeeper Eugenie Dashner, and he had been Rancher Ridley. She had been American Student Visiting the Greek Isles Eugenie Dashner, and he had been Shipping Magnate Ridley.

Ah, good times. Good times.

Now she was Bitter Divorcée Eugenie Dashner, and he was Handyman Ridley. Which admittedly still had the potential to be a good read, had Eugenie still believed in romance, Harlequin or otherwise. Which she did not. She didn't care if she had just been hired for a job that required she believe in exactly that.

Nash wasn't the kind of man who inspired thoughts of romance in a woman, anyway. More than three decades had passed since the guy graduated from high school, but he still looked as if he'd been sculpted by the hands of the gods. Blasting "Don't You Want Me?" from a boom box on the floor, he stood on the far side of the room, ignorant of her presence, his bare back a landscape of muscle and sinew. His white painter's pants—she'd swear they were the same ones he'd worn in high school—hung low enough on his hips to reveal two tantalizing dimples above his bum, and he'd tied a red bandanna around his head to contain his perspiration. That, too, was a throwback to high school. Eugenie had always thought him exceedingly cool for wearing it. His hair may have gone from golden blond to silver blond, and perhaps there were lines around his eyes and mouth that hadn't been there thirty years ago. But little else about the guy had changed.

She must have made some kind of sound, because he abruptly spun around, a broad smile splitting his features when he saw her. Immediately, he tossed aside his spackling knife, then hooked his hands on his hips.

"Eugene!" he cried with heartfelt delight. Damn Julien for ever endowing her with that nickname. "Long time, no see!"

It had indeed been years since she'd seen Nash. But looking at him now, Eugenie wouldn't have thought any time at all had passed since he and Julien were cobbling together their first business venture, right around the time she was starting her freshman year in college. He leaned over and turned off the boom box, throwing the room into silence, something for which she was thankful. She hadn't liked New Wave even when it actually was new.

"You know, there's some great stuff on the radio these days," she told him. "Cocktail Slippers. Ting Tings. White Rabbits. Hey, I know. You seem like a Metric kind of guy to me. Give me one night with your iPod, Nash. I'll make you a new man."

"I don't have an iPod. Besides, today's music sucks. Now come on over here," he told her, swinging an arm in a wide semicircle. "Come give Uncle Nash a big ol' hug."

She dipped her head toward his sweaty, dirty chest. "Gosh, thanks, Uncle Nash, but I think I'll pass."

He grinned again. And *zing* went the strings of her heart. "Yeah, you look like you're headed off someplace important. Look at you, all grown up, wearing a suit. Hell, wearing shoes. I hardly would've recognized you."

"It hasn't been that long since we saw each other," she reminded him. "I know I've run into you when I had Seth with me."

"Ah, yes. The boy. How is the little tyke?"

"He's not a tyke anymore. He's a fully mellowed teenager. Except that he's not mellow. On account of he's a teenager. So I guess he's more of a fully churlished teenager."

Nash shook his head. "That's impossible. If he's a teenager, I'm gonna start feeling old."

"Well, you know, Nash, you and Julien *have* both passed that half-centu—"

"Bite your tongue," he interrupted, lifting a hand palm out as if he could physically halt both the word and the condition. "You're as young as you feel."

Oh, she sincerely hoped not.

"And you," he said, "don't look a day older than you were when you graduated from college, Janey."

Nash was the only person who had ever phonetically shortened her name to Janey. In spite of her assurances to him every time he used it that her name wasn't Janey, and that he should please stop calling her Janey, she'd always kind of liked the way he called her Janey.

"My name isn't Janey," she said. "Please stop calling me that."

He kept grinning. She kept *zing*ing.

"It's good to see you, Janey. And not just because you look incredible. Got a job interview?" he asked before she had a chance to contradict him about that *incredible* business.

"Had," she corrected him. "I had a job interview."

He made a sympathetic face. "Got shot down, huh?"

She shook her head. "No, actually, I got the job."

"Oh. You don't sound too happy about it."

She lifted one shoulder and let it drop. "I'm happy to have it. It's just not exactly what I thought I'd be doing."

"What's it—"

"Is this going to be Sophie's room or Chloe's?" she asked. She took a few restless steps to her left, pretending to inspect a part of one wall where the plaster was still in bad shape.

Nash hesitated a moment, then said, "Chloe's. Julien said Sophie could have the bigger room since she's oldest. Which didn't go over too well with Chloe. I'm thinkin' a five-year-old probably doesn't buy into seven being that much more mature."

"Au contraire," Eugenie said. "Chloe's not even in kindergarten yet. Sophie's had almost a whole year of real school. And don't think Sophie doesn't remind her of that all the time. That's probably why the bigger room didn't go over well with Chloe."

"She'll get over it. She has a better view."

Eugenie went to one of two broad windows harboring rotting upholstered tragedies that would eventually go back to being the window seats they once were. The yard beyond was still a tangle of brambles and mud, so there wasn't much to see, save an intrepid cardinal who was busily building a nest in a skeletal lilac bush. Her brown body was plain and sturdy compared to her flamboyant red partner, who attended her from a low-lying maple branch above. It doubtless would be a gorgeous view from this window eventually. Probably right around the time Chloe was heading off to college herself.

"There's an awful lot to do."

Surprisingly, the comment came not from Eugenie but from Nash.

"Yep," she agreed, feeling a little lightheaded at the prospect.

He strode over to stand beside her, smelling of plaster and

perspiration and the past. Instead of gazing out the window, however, he looked at Eugenie. But he said nothing.

"What?" she asked, making it a point to keep staring out the window and not at him.

Another weighty moment passed before he told her, "You cost me a hundred bucks, you know that?"

Now Eugenie did turn to look at him. "What are you talking about?"

"I bet Jules a hundred bucks you'd back out of the deal before closing. I told him you were too smart and too careful to try something like this. Not to mention too fastidious."

This time Eugenie was the one to smile at him. "Look at you. All grown up, using the big words." When he only made a face at her in response, she looked out the window again. "Yeah, well, I guess life has a way of making people stupid, reckless, and messy sometimes, doesn't it?"

"Life does that?" he echoed. "Or Lawrence does?"

Instead of answering, Eugenie changed the subject. "Do you guys have an ETA yet for when we can move into the house? Julien thinks he might have a solid offer on his, and Mom's got a deadline at the home. They told us if we don't have her out of there by the end of May, they're going to perform an exorcism. That's only a couple of months away."

"I think the timeline will work out okay," Nash said after a moment, not even remarking on the exorcism thing since, hey, he knew Lorraine. He thought for a moment more, then added, "The mold and pestilence problems aren't problems anymore, and the roofers are coming day after tomorrow. You need to get on the stick and find appliances you like so they can be ordered and installed by then. Ditto the hot-water heater, and we'll have to get the HVAC guy in. The plumbing and wiring are in better shape than we thought, though, so that won't take as much time as we first planned on them taking. The fireplaces won't be an issue till fall, so those can wait for now. The bedrooms will be . . ." He hesitated. "Habitable," he decided. "Though Lorraine's and the girls' might be finished because Jules said we should get those as close to done as possible before moving day. He said you and he won't mind waiting till after moving in to start on your own. Attic will have to wait a bit, though, so if Seth doesn't mind taking that second bedroom on the third floor and sharing a bathroom with you for a little while—"

"Oh, he'll mind," Eugenie said. "But don't let that throw off the timeline."

"Then if y'all don't mind some inconvenience for the first few months, it shouldn't be a problem to have everyone moved in when you need. We can finish as we go, troubleshooting whatever problems come up as they come up."

Which had really been the plan all along. Now that it was coming to fruition, however, Eugenie felt that tight mass clotting in her stomach again.

"The kitchen and bathrooms will be functional?" she asked.

Nash nodded. "Jules wants to have Lorraine's bathroom finished before any of the others—by moving day, if possible, which it should be—but for the rest of them, it'll just be cosmetic stuff by then. I just hope you don't mind a whole lot of ugly for a while."

Miraculously, she refrained from making any comments about having lived with Lawrence for twenty years.

"Like I said, there just might need to be some room juggling," Nash continued. "I think Jules wants to knock out a wall or two in a couple places but not anywhere that it will create a problem with sleeping or eating or privacy."

All good, Eugenie thought. She and Julien had laid out a plan for resuscitating the house that started with safety and function and ended with comfort and beauty. He and Nash would be doing the bulk of the work, and she and Seth would do what they could to help out, but their skills didn't extend much beyond painting, cleaning, and hauling. Even in the yard, she was fairly useless unless it involved raking or yanking. There really was an awful lot to do. And it really was going to take an awful lot of work to do it.

Funny, but why did it suddenly feel as if she were thinking about more than the house as that last thought unfolded?

"Okay," she said, swallowing what she told herself was a revisit of the drive-thru burrito she'd consumed on the way to the house, not stark-raving terror. "So first of June, we can start moving in."

"I'll double check with Jules, but yeah, I think that's doable."

"Great." She forced a smile. "Thanks, Nash."

"No problem, Janey."

No problem, she echoed to herself. Yeah, right. She was the owner of a house that would be better served by bricks of C4 than bricks and mortar, she'd just been pity-hired for a job to which she wasn't even suited, her mother was about to be evicted from the last assisted living facility in town, and her husband—her *ex*-husband, she hastily corrected herself—would rather be boinking Ethel Merman than her. *No problem*. That was a good one. Eugenie would pencil in *laugh* on her to-do list just as soon as she found the time.

Six

Eugenie was seven months pregnant with Seth the last time she saw Marianne Weatherly—now Marianne Weatherly-Blankenbaker. She and Lawrence had come to Louisville to spend a rare Thanksgiving with Julien *and* Lorraine (who had been between fiancés at the time), and she'd had to make a last-minute dash to Kroger for fresh sage on the eve of the holiday. In the produce section, she'd seen a woman's top half so deeply immersed in the massive but nearly depleted sweet potato bin that her feet had actually lifted from the floor. Eugenie had been marveling at her fellow shopper's pilgrimlike tenacity when said shopper came up for air, clutching a few straggling yams, and Eugenie recognized her as her childhood friend from Manitou Hills. She also noted that Marianne was almost as pregnant as she was at the time.

They ended up talking until the produce manager chased them out of the store at closing; then they embraced in the deserted parking lot with promises to meet over the weekend before Eugenie went back to Indianapolis. But, as happened over holidays, their plans never quite came together. Even though they exchanged phone numbers and addresses, neither ever found the time to call the other, and the Christmas cards gradually tapered off.

So, although Eugenie had thought about Marianne a time or two since she and Julien closed on the house on Butterfly Way she and her friend used to pedal past all the time, it was with some surprise that she opened her back door two weeks after moving in to find Marianne standing on the other side. She bore a veritable cornucopia of comestibles in two oversized willow baskets, and the little girl by her side, who was about ten years too young to be the product of that Thanksgiving pregnancy (unless, of course, Marianne had suffered one of those elephantine pregnancies, which, admittedly, some did seem to be), carried a third basket filled with wine and cheeses.

"Oh my God, Eugenie!" Marianne cried when she saw her. "I didn't know it was you and Lawrence who bought this place! I didn't even know you were back in town!"

Before Eugenie had a chance to correct her about Lawrence or even say hello, Marianne was setting the baskets on the patio and pulling her into a fierce hug. Eugenie laughed as she hugged her friend back, unable to fathom how sixteen years could have passed since that afternoon by the yam box.

"It is so good to see you," she told Marianne, hugging her back just as fiercely.

Only as she spoke the words did Eugenie really appreciate what a huge span of time sixteen years was. The last time she saw Marianne, neither had become mothers yet. Neither had had an inkling of the colossal changes the arrival of a baby would bring to their marriages and to themselves. They had both been so happy. So full of plans and dreams. So very, very young.

"Jesus, how long has it been?" Marianne asked as she drew back to look at Eugenie again. "No, wait, I remember," she answered her own question. "D.J. turned sixteen in January, so it's been more than sixteen years. You look incredible," she continued, again before giving Eugenie a chance to reply. She eyed her up and down, then settled her hands on her hips. "You must have stopped at one, otherwise your ass would be as fat as mine. I have four kids now."

Although it was true that there was a bit more of Marianne than there had been the last time Eugenie saw her, at no time would she have considered her friend in any way—

"Four?" she asked incredulously when the import of Marianne's remark finally registered. "How did that happen?"

"The same way it always does. Obviously, I should have listened to the older girls in Brownies when they warned us about the dangers of using public bathrooms."

Eugenie nodded sagely. "I always suspected there was some truth to that. Fortunately, I only used a public bathroom that one time at the state fair, where Seth was obviously conceived."

Marianne sighed melodramatically. "Would that I had had your smarts, I might have fulfilled my dream to become a professional dog walker. Instead, fifteen months after D.J. was born—oops, so much for not being able to get pregnant while you're still breastfeeding—Dale and I had another boy, Eddie. After Eddie, we were a lot more careful . . . until that anniversary trip to the Virgin Islands where Claire was conceived after an evening of killer rum punches. She's ten now." Marianne draped an arm around the shoulders of the little girl beside her. "And this is Abby, my youngest, who was determined to be born no matter how religiously I took my birth control pills every day." She pulled her daughter closer and bent to press a kiss on the crown of her head. "My last," she stated emphatically after completing the gesture. "I had them lock up the baby factory and turn out the lights after they pulled this one out."

Unfazed by her mother's comments or language, Abby, who, with her short dark hair and wide-spaced brown eyes, bore a striking resemblance to her mother at that age, raised a hand, wiggled her fingers, and said, "Hi."

"Abby, honey, this is Mrs. MacPherson," Marianne told her daughter. "She and I have been friends since we were even younger than you."

"Call me Eugenie," she told Abby. Then, looking back at Marianne, she added, "It's not MacPherson anymore. It's back to Dashner."

Marianne's mouth dropped open at that. "Holy shit. You finally left the sonofabitch?"

Eugenie spared a glance for Abby's sake, but again, she seemed in no way surprised or bothered by her mother's vocabulary.

"Actually, Lawrence left me," she said.

She could tell Marianne wanted to ask more, but she managed to restrain herself in front of Abby—well, as restrained as Marianne was ever able to be—and instead said, "Okay, now that makes sense. Because Sarah Munson, who lives behind me on Sparrow, told me she met the new owner when she was out walking Bruno the other day, and it was some buff, hunky guy. And since I don't remember anyone ever using the words 'buff,' 'hunky,' and 'Lawrence' in the same sentence, you must have done much better in his wake."

"The divorce was just final last fall," she told Marianne.

Now her friend's eyes went wide. "Well, yay, you, moving on so quickly with the Abercrombie and Fitch stallion."

"Sarah Munson met Julien," Eugenie said before Marianne could draw any more erroneous conclusions. "He and I bought the house together so we could move Mom in with us and take care of her. She's had rheumatoid arthritis for a while now, and it's really started to take its toll. We figured we could maybe help each other out in the parenting department, too. He lost his wife to lymphoma a couple of years ago, and now with Lawrence out of the picture . . ." She let her voice trail off since, really, there wasn't much need to say anything else.

It took a minute for Marianne to process all the news. Probably, it was the part about *move Mom in with us and take care of her* that she got hung up on. Eugenie's struggles with her mother had been the topic of more than one slumber party when they were kids, and Marianne had constantly marveled at how different Lorraine was from her own mother, who had been the president of the local NOW chapter and subscribed to *Ms.* and *Mother Jones.* It hadn't been unusual for Marianne to miss school when they were kids because she and her mother and older sister were marching on the Capitol in Washington, D.C., with signs that read ERA NOW or WOMEN AGAINST NUKES or HANDS OFF ANGELA DAVIS. The only time Eugenie could remember Lorraine protesting anything, it had been when she wrote a letter to Avon after they discontinued her favorite lipstick shade, Magenta to the Max.

"Lorraine is living with you?" Marianne asked.

Eugenie nodded.

"So . . . how's that going?"

"We just moved in two weeks ago."

"Right. I'll wait a week and ask you again. Provided one of you hasn't been locked up for something like, oh, I don't know. Murder."

"It'll be fine," Eugenie said. "She and I have two whole floors separating us."

Marianne laughed at that. "There have been times when you had two whole states separating you, and she was—"

"Abby," Eugenie interrupted, turning her attention to Marianne's daughter. "Do you like Moxie Girlz?"

The little girl nodded shyly.

"Well, I happen to know for a fact that my nieces, Sophie and Chloe, are upstairs right now unpacking what must have been ten boxes full of Moxie stuff. I bet they could use a hand with that. Why don't you go up and introduce yourself, and your mom and I will bring up some cookies and lemonade after we've had a chance to catch up. You can see the stairs from the kitchen doorway. Just go on up, and they're in the last room on the right at the top."

Abby looked at her mother for permission. Marianne said, "Go ahead, peanut. Eugenie and I will be up in a little while."

Abby handed her basket to Eugenie, who thanked her and took a step back from the door to allow both her and her mother inside. She was about to close the door behind them when a movement near the garage caught her eye, and she saw Seth wheeling his bicycle onto the driveway. She called out to him and asked where he was going, but he either didn't hear her or—more likely—pretended not to. Nevertheless, she decided to give him the benefit of the doubt. He might have his earbuds in under his helmet—maybe, possibly, perhaps—so there was some small chance he really hadn't heard her. Maybe. Possibly. Perhaps. Eugenie watched as he pedaled down the driveway and, after a quick glance to his left, turned right onto Butterfly Way and disappeared.

But then, disappearing down Butterfly Way on his bicycle had been Seth's daily habit since they moved in two weeks before. Every evening, Eugenie asked him over dinner where he went, only to have him shrug, mumble something about exploring the neighborhood, then go back to glowering at his plate. Although she always wanted to press him, she invariably told herself she should just be grateful he was even at the dinner table, and she let him get away with ducking the question. For now. Soon, though, the two of them were going to have a talk about . . . Well, all the stuff they should have talked about long before now.

She sighed as she closed the back door, then turned to Marianne. The two women were silent until Abby was out of earshot, then Eugenie said, "Maybe you should just kill me now."

"What and take the rap for Lorraine? No way." Marianne picked up her two discarded baskets and moved ahead of Eugenie, into the kitchen proper. "Still, hearing this news, I wonder if—" She stopped abruptly, turning in a full circle to inspect the kitchen. "Holy shit, Eugenie, this house is a wreck."

Eugenie stopped behind her. "Yeah. It is."

"I mean, it's been obvious for a long time from the outside that this place isn't what it used to be. But, wow, the inside is way, *way* worse. It needs like . . . *massive* renovation."

"Yep."

"One might even go so far as to call it a disaster."

"One might."

Marianne studied her curiously for a moment. "You hate disasters, Eugenie. You hate messes. Whenever you came to my house when we were kids, the first thing you did was clean up my room."

"I remember."

Marianne narrowed her gaze. "And then you organized my closet so all my shirts were together, followed by my skirts, then my dresses, then my pants. And you lined up all my shoes in order from dressy to casual."

"Mm-hm."

"Are you sure you know what you're getting into here?"

"Probably not."

Eugenie strode a little farther into the kitchen and let her gaze follow the same trail Marianne's had taken. She'd been in the middle of stripping the wallpaper when her friend knocked, but big patches of the ugly yellow and brown stuff still adhered to the walls. Even where she'd yanked away the offending pattern, the plaster left behind was chipped and scarred, some of it clinging to her T-shirt, shorts, and arms. The revolting linoleum was still in place, but it had been torn ragged in places by the movement of old appliances out and new ones in. Bare wires hung like a dead spider from the ceiling where the unsightly plastic light fixture used to be. The cabinet doors had been removed, but she hadn't had a chance to clean the insides yet, so the cupboards were not only bare but filthy. She hadn't thought it would be possible for the room to be any nastier than it was before they bought Fleurissant, but, wow, was it ever.

"I know it seems like an impossible task right now, but as lost and dilapidated as the house looks . . ." Eugenie turned to her friend again. "I don't know. Something about it spoke to me when we looked at it that first time. Something about it still speaks to me. Like maybe we're kindred spirits or something. Does that make sense?"

"Not really," Marianne told her. "But then you always were the weird one."

"Oh, so says the woman who went to the senior Halloween party dressed as a giant spoon."

"It was an homage."

"To what? Pudding?"

"But then, we were talking about you and Lorraine murdering each other," Marianne backtracked. "Maybe you could suffocate her in her sleep and get off on an insanity defense. I'm already wondering about your state of mind to have done something like this in the first place. What the hell were you thinking moving Lorraine in with you? There was a time when you wanted to run away and live with me."

"I still want to run away and live with you."

They wove through scattered cardboard boxes and black plastic garbage bags in varying stages of unpackedness, until they arrived at a tiny trapezoid of countertop that wasn't crowded with more clutter. After shoving aside two gallons of paint, Eugenie settled the basket of cheeses next to a Brownsboro Hardware bag full of drawer pulls and cabinet hinges, then helped Marianne wrestle the other two baskets up beside it.

"It was nice of you to bring all this stuff," Eugenie said. "You must have cleaned out Lotsa Pasta."

"If I were really a good neighbor, I would have baked you something myself. But that way lay madness. Besides, like I said, I thought you were some buff, hunky guy. I thought maybe bringing all this stuff would score me a few points, give me something to do when Dale is out of town. Had I known it was you and Julien and Joan Crawford, I would have just packed a jar of peanut butter and a box of Ritz crackers."

"You always did say the nicest things."

Marianne plucked a bottle of pinot noir out of the cheese basket, along with a professional-looking corkscrew. "Lemonade schmemonade," she said as she went to work on the bottle's foil cap. "It's Mama's day off."

"It's not even noon," Eugenie pointed out.

Marianne halted the corkscrew midturn. "So you'd rather have Bloody Marys? 'Cause there's a bottle of Grey Goose and some tomato juice in one of the big baskets."

Eugenie laughed, mostly because she knew Marianne was serious. It really was good to see her again. Marianne had always been the yang to Eugenie's yin, impulsive and outgoing when Eugenie had been content to play it safe, saying the first thing that came into her head when Eugenie had always had to think two or three times before saying anything at all. In return, Eugenie had been the one to keep Marianne from going too far, reining her in before she would have been (a) suspended from school, (b) arrested for public indecency, (c) prescribed an antibiotic for chlamydia, or (d) all of the above.

"Wine is fine," she told her friend. As she surveyed the box city around them, she added, "Though I have no idea where the glasses are."

"That's okay," Marianne said as she went to the nearest open box and began rummaging through it. "It'll be a quest. Whoever finds them gets first crack at Lorraine."

Chink-creak. Chink-creak. Chink-creak.

As if the comment had conjured the dragon, Lorraine appeared in the doorway just as Marianne finished the incantation. Eugenie had been so caught up in the conversation that she hadn't heard the metallic rumblings of the beast that normally heralded Lorraine's approach. Now she went rigid and spun stiffly around to greet her mother, every muscle in her body flexed tight. Marianne looked up from the box she had begun to search and smiled.

"Why, Madame Dash-NAY," she said without missing a beat, looking in no way guilty for having just suggested they plot *la mort de Lorraine*. "It's been ages. How are you?"

Although it was the customary question to ask someone you hadn't seen for a long time, it was also the question everyone who was acquainted with Lorraine knew better than to ask. Because Lorraine always answered it the same way:

"How the hell do you think I am? Are you blind? Can't you see for yourself? I'm a G.D. cripple."

Lorraine always said "G.D." instead of "goddamn," because you could take the girl out of the pageant circuit, but you could never take the pageant circuit out of the girl. No self-respecting beauty queen would ever take the Lord's name in vain.

Marianne ignored Lorraine's rancor and said, "Gee, Madame Dash-NAY, I don't think you look like a goddamn cripple at all. Me, I would never think of mixing chartreuse shorts with a turquoise halter that way, but on you, it looks fabulous."

Eugenie would have thought Marianne was being sarcastic about that last, but the truth was her mother did look great in chartreuse and turquoise, and Marianne would have looked ridiculous. Still, the cut of the halter did display the ruddy, twisted knots of her shoulders and elbows in a way that was anything but fabulous. Even Marianne, though, was decent enough not to comment on that.

Lorraine opened her mouth to say something else but finally registered the fact that she was acquainted with Eugenie's companion. "Marianne?" she asked. "Marianne Weatherly, is that you?"

"It's Marianne Weatherly-Blankenbaker now, Madame D."

Lorraine shook her head. "I do not get this hyphenated last name silliness," she said by way of a greeting. "Either you're married or you're not. Either you belong to your father or you belong to your husband. You can't have it both ways. You feminists"—she said the word *feminists* the way most people said the words *child molester*—"must get writer's cramp every time you sign your name."

"Every goddamn time," Marianne agreed.

"Look, Mom, Marianne brought us a welcome gift," Eugenie said. She swept a hand in front of the three baskets with all the elegance of Vanna White presenting a shiny new Subaru. "Look at all this gorgeous stuff."

Chink-creak. Chink-creak. Chink-creak.

Lorraine made it as far as the first two boxes she encountered, then realized there wouldn't be enough room to get her walker through the narrow passage between them.

"I can't look at it," she said. "I can't see it from here, and I can't get through."

Eugenie froze her smile in place as she crossed the length of the kitchen, shoving boxes out of her way as she went, until she'd cleared an ample path for her mother. Instead of making her way to the counter where the baskets were easily visible now, Lorraine only leaned on her walker and said, "I'll take your word for it."

She turned to Marianne again. "How's your mother? Did they finally put her in jail with the other Communists?"

"My mother wasn't a Communist, Madame D," Marianne said with surprising restraint. "She just wanted her daughters to grow up in a better America than she did. She wanted us to receive equal pay for equal work and have the same educational opportunities all the Y chromosomes had. She wanted it to be a criminal offense if our husbands beat or raped us, and she wanted us to be legally entitled to take our children with us should we divorce them. She wanted *us*, not a male-dominated government, to be the ones who made decisions about our sexual activities and our bodies. I know it sounds a bit nutty, but that's just the kind of woman she is."

Lorraine leaned forward on her walker, narrowed her eyes at

Marianne, and opened her mouth to say something else. But Marianne continued blithely, "Oh, right, I didn't answer the jail question. No, my folks are living in Key West now where they publish a small weekly manifesto filled with subversive rants about charter boat excursions and where to find the best crab bisque. Dale and I bought the house from them after they retired, and now I'm raising my kids in the house on Hummingbird Way where I grew up."

"Wow, Mare, how incredibly midwestern of you," Eugenie said, more to keep her mother from bringing up the Communist thing again by showing how normal Marianne turned out, in spite of her Marxist upbringing.

"Yeah, well, that's what happens when you hit middle age," Marianne said. "You will be assimilated, resistance is futile, and all that. But I have enough of my mother in me to protest for a while longer."

Eugenie said nothing in response to that. Mostly because she didn't want to think about how much of her own mother she might have in her. Not a drop, Lorraine would assure her. But there was something in Eugenie that wasn't so sure. Maybe she hadn't gotten the tiara or Phyllis Schlafly parts of her mother, but there were lots of other parts up for grabs. Her mother was a complicated machine. Maybe her external drives were failing, but her circuits, processors, and memory were chugging along quite nicely, thanks. And her motherboard? Fuhgeddabuddit. Totally intact. Lorraine was a prime example of mid-twentieth-century female technology. Yes, there were a few bugs in her at this point, but some of her components could conceivably be atomic. Best not to probe too deeply or push too many buttons.

"So," Marianne said, looking from Eugenie back to Lorraine, "you want a glass of wine, Madame D?"

Lorraine frowned. "It's not even noon," she pointed out.

"Bloody Mary, then?" Marianne asked.

"Or I could make lemonade," Eugenie tried helpfully.

"Your lemonade is always too sour and too weak, Eugenie. You never were much good in the kitchen. It's no wonder Lawrence had a wandering eye."

Marianne looked at Eugenie, waiting for the comeback, the quip, the rejoinder. Eugenie wished she had one. When none was forthcoming, Marianne took it upon herself to provide one.

"Lawrence had a wandering eye? You know, there's a surgery they can do for that now. They don't even have to take the eye out of the socket." Then, feigning a sudden understanding of Lorraine's meaning, she added melodramatically, "Ooooh, you mean *that* kind of wandering eye. There's a surgery for that, too, but Eugenie would have to perform it herself."

Since it was clear Lorraine wanted neither wine nor Bloody Mary nor lemonade, and since Eugenie suddenly wanted something quite a lot, she crossed to where Marianne held the open bottle of wine, took it from her friend's hand, and, eschewing both glass and decorum, lifted the bottle to her lips and drank. When she lowered it, she wiped her mouth with the back of her hand and said, "I'll get right to work on the lemonade. And I'll be more careful with the lemon-to-sugar ratio this time."

Wine bottle still in hand, she made her way through the warren of boxes back to the counter where she and Marianne had placed the baskets and began to rummage through the larger of the two. Maybe a splash of Grey Goose would keep the lemonade—or something—from being too sour.

Seven

By June, after working at HeartMenders for three months, Eugenie was fairly comfortable there. Spalding had been right about her being overqualified for the position, but there was a lot to be said for undemanding work when one's nonworking life demanded too much. Also nice was how traditional and steadfast a business it was when Eugenie's life seemed to be hurtling so turbulently in so many directions.

The matches completed by HeartMenders were decided by Spalding alone. He started by evaluating each application that came into the agency and arranging likely compatibles in different groups. From those groups, he further narrowed down each applicant's qualifications according to their likes and dislikes, lifestyle habits, personal philosophies, and so forth. Eugenie was responsible for making the reservations he requested for each date and was the one who stayed in touch with the clients before and after any outing. It was she who contacted them to give them the details of their upcoming rendezvous, and it was she who followed up with them afterward to see how things went. She then wrote up reports and handed those over to Spalding, who either planned the next outing for the two clients or attempted another match if they didn't hit it off.

What struck Eugenie most about the matches he made was not only how often Spalding was successful in pairing people—in the three months she had worked there, she'd written only one report of an unsuccessful date, and the second matches for each of those clients had gone swimmingly—but also how old-fashioned the operation of HeartMenders was. Although they had a computer—they even had a tech guy named Marco who managed the website and took care of any techie challenges that arose (including, on one occasion, changing the battery in Eugenie's cell phone and, on another, downloading a casserole recipe app for Iris's iPhone)—Spalding eschewed the use of technology himself. Another of Eugenie's duties was printing up paper copies of any applications or correspondence that came via the Internet and leaving them on his desk for his perusal. She also typed up his handwritten letters and left them for his signature. Even though he couldn't be more than a few years older than she, he simply did not abide the hurry-hurry-hurry of the World Wide Web. Or even the IBM Selectric.

His archaic iPod had been a gift from a girlfriend who was determined to drag him into the twenty-first century, he said, and had eventually grown on him (the iPod, not the girlfriend). He'd liked the convenience of taking all his Motown and surf music with him wherever he went. Other than that, however, Eugenie never saw him use any gadgetry other than the office phone. He didn't even own a cell.

But it wasn't just the operation of HeartMenders and its proprietor that were old-fashioned. The dates Spalding arranged were, too. Although Fourth Street Live!, with its plethora of flashy nightclubs and trendy restaurants was right next door, and although such a destination seemed the most obvious to send a couple on a first date, Spalding never even considered it. Instead, he sent his clients back in time, to picnic at Shawnee Park or to take long walks along the river or to visit the arboretum at Bernheim Forest. Eugenie wrote up one report following an outing to a revival of *The Sound of Music* at the Baxter Avenue Theatres followed by scoops of spumoni at the Homemade Ice Cream and Pie Kitchen. She wrote another for a couple who attended a Bats game followed by sidecars at Jack Fry's, a Louisville landmark whose original owner was known for his bootlegging and bookmaking in the back room.

It was all in keeping with the otherworldly, old-world feel of the business. In many ways, HeartMenders seemed trapped in a time warp it maybe didn't want to escape, because there were still things to like about the period it was trapped in. As much social injustice and cultural tumult as mid-twentieth-century America had seen, there was a lot to be said for white gloves and fedoras. Or at least what white gloves and fedoras had signified. Maybe that was why people still liked vintage stuff so much. They were looking for a happy medium between now and then, trying to blend the more courteous and simple past with the more just and comfortable present. Maybe it was because they wanted today to be as easily managed and maneuvered as yesterday had been. Only with fairer laws and grande lattes.

Eugenie had just returned from her Monday afternoon lunch break with one of those last, in fact, when Spalding summoned her into his office. He was, as always, wearing a suit and tie, the former dark and skinny-lapelled, the latter narrow and pin-striped, as if he'd jumped into his time-traveling DeLorean to buy both during the Eisenhower era at a place called Buddy's Man about Town on Main Street, USA. He was seated behind his desk (Eugenie had come to realize the state of chaos she'd seen that first day was a terminal condition) and still working on his own lunch, which (she had also come to realize) he brought from home every day. As was the case each time she had seen him eating his lunch at his desk, it was peanut butter and jelly on white bread, a plastic cup of diced peaches, four Oreos wrapped in cellophane, and a thermos of what appeared to be Big Red.

She took her seat opposite his desk, sweeping her khaki skirt beneath her fanny before tucking her legs under the chair. Inescapably, her gaze fell to the mode of transportation in which he carried his midday repast, an old metal lunch box featuring characters from a TV show she remembered watching with Julien when they were kids: *The Rat Patrol.* There was Christopher George looking rakish with his Australian bush hat snapped on only one side, and there was Eric Braeden as Captain Hans Dietrich, on whom Eugenie had always had a crush, even though he was the enemy.

Probably, she thought, that should have tipped her off early that she had bad judgment in men.

"You're doing it again," Spalding said as she set her latte down on the corner of his desk.

She looked at him, puzzled. "I'm doing what?"

He dipped his head toward the lunch box. "Giving Hans Dietrich that come-hither look."

Halfheartedly, she denied, "No, I was just wondering how much that lunch box would bring if you listed it on eBay. There's not a bit of rust. You've taken very good care of it."

And really, what did that say about a man, that he took better care of his childhood lunch box than he did his current-day work environment?

"Actually, I owe that to Aunt Maisy," he said. "I don't know how she ended up having it, but she's the one who took good care of it. I always thought Marty Derkin up the street swiped it one day when he was playing at my house." Parenthetically, he added, "Looking back, I think Marty lusted after ol' Hans even more than you. But Maisy literally made a deathbed confession to me that she was the one who had it, that she kept it after she found it lying outside in the rain to teach me a lesson about taking better care of my things. The day before she died, she made me promise I would carry my lunch to work in it every day for the rest of my life."

It seemed an odd deathbed request. Unless, perhaps, her death had been due to something for which dementia was a symptom. "Why would she do that?"

"No idea. She was still in full possession of her faculties when she went," he said, answering that question. "But she must have had her reasons."

Eugenie hesitated, then leaned forward and said conspiratorially, "You know, Spalding, she probably wouldn't know if you decided to start brown-bagging it."

He shook his head. "Nah. Number one, somehow, Maisy probably would know. And number two"—he lifted one shoulder and let it drop—"she could have made a way worse deathbed request. She could have made me promise to get married and have kids. Or to start each day with a smile. Or, worst of all, to dance like there's no one watching, love like I'll never be hurt, and sing like there's nobody listening. As promises to dying aunts go, carrying my boyhood lunch box to work every day isn't such a bad one."

Meaning Eugenie could strike through *deathbed promise to*

aunt on her "Reasons Why Spalding Chasan Has Never Married" list. Not that that one had been particularly high on the list or that she had suspected an aunt who made matches for a living would have required her nephew to remain single, but it brought the number down from around a hundred to around ninety-nine. Nevertheless, she did wonder why Spalding had never married. He was attractive, smart, gentle, kind, all the things women looked for in a man, and she was reasonably certain he wasn't gay. Then she remembered how marriage had turned out for her, and she decided the reason for his state of singlehood was as clear as the Hans Dietrich thing should have been. Marriage = Heartbreak. Ergo, do not go there.

But then, that was Eugenie—always flirting with the obvious.

It wasn't the first time she had heard him talk about his aunt Maisy, the original proprietor of HeartMenders, but she hadn't heard a lot about the woman. So she asked, "How long ago did you take over the business from her?"

Spalding sipped his Big Red from the plastic thermos cup and thought for a moment. Then he said, "Wow. It'll be twenty years this October since she died. But I worked with her here before her death for about fifteen years."

"You must have been in high school when you started."

He smiled and touched his nose with his index finger, telling her she was right. "My sophomore year of high school. Maisy hired me to sort the mail and run errands for her."

"Same last name, so she must have been your father's sister. Or else married to your father's brother."

"She was his sister."

"Then she was either light-years ahead of her time in keeping her maiden name or else she never married."

"The latter."

"Interesting."

"Why?"

"Here she was making matches for a living, finding that perfect someone for everyone else, but she never found one for herself."

"Actually, she met her perfect Mr. Right when she was a teenager," Spalding said. "But he was killed in the Battle of Normandy. I think opening the business was her way of dealing with the grief. If she couldn't spend her life with her perfect someone, maybe she could help others find their perfect someone to spend their lives with."

Eugenie nodded. "That was how she mended her own heart."

"As best as she could, anyway. She specialized in clients who had been heartbroken themselves. That was how she chose her employees, too."

From what Eugenie could tell, Spalding had upheld both traditions. Although she wasn't privy to anything a client divulged in a personal meeting with Spalding, she had noticed that an inordinate number of people ticked off the box on the application that indicated they were divorced or widowed. And she had been there long enough to have learned about her co-workers, all of whom shared stories of love either lost or stolen. Iris's significant other had left the house for an appointment one morning and never returned. Marco the tech guy had lost his partner to complications from AIDS. Natalie, their part-timer who worked on promotion and advertising, had left her high school sweetheart at the altar just last summer after learning that what happened in Vegas actually didn't always stay in Vegas, and that sometimes it found a guy in Louisville after tracking him down on the Internet and then showed up at his wedding with a two-month-old in one hand and a court order for a DNA sample and child support in the other, thereby having a legitimate reason to not hold its peace after the minister said that part about how if anyone knew any reason why these two people should not be joined in matrimony, they should speak now.

Obviously, Spalding had been right when he told Eugenie she would fit right in at HeartMenders.

Of course, that didn't answer the question of Spalding. Did he suffer from a broken heart, too? If he'd come to work for Maisy when he was a teenager, he probably hadn't had time to experience one of those by the time he was hired, so maybe he was the exception to the rule. Of course, a lot of time had passed since he was hired, so, then again, maybe he wasn't. And why did Eugenie wish so much that she knew which it was?

She felt sadness for all of them, but mostly for Maisy. As bad as things had become between Eugenie and Lawrence toward the end, at least they'd had a lot of years' worth of good times—and good memories—that she could try and focus on instead of the bad. They'd made Seth together, who would always be proof that at least some of her time with Lawrence had been precious. But someone like Maisy, whose young love had gone off to war before the two of them even had a chance to get started on a life together . . . To have so few memories to sustain her after he was gone . . .

"That really is heartbreaking," she said. "That Maisy saw all these happy unions come about without ever having one of her own."

Spalding said nothing for a moment, only took another sip of his Big Red and watched Eugenie over the rim of the cup. For some reason, she suddenly felt as if she were being given her first employee evaluation since being hired.

As if he'd read her mind—or maybe she read his—he said,

"You noticed that first day during your interview, I think, the Best of Louisville awards up there behind me."

He'd noticed her noticing? And remembered? Interesting. Or at least it would be interesting if she had any idea how it was significant.

"Yes, I did," she concurred, glancing up at them again. There were one, two, three, four . . . twelve of them in all, consecutively numbered for twelve straight years. But there was none for last year or the year before it.

"You probably also noticed," he continued, "or else you're noticing as we speak, that after receiving them consistently for a long time, HeartMenders missed out two years in a row."

"I did notice that my first time here, actually," Eugenie admitted. Diplomatically—and because she was, after all, still kind of new to the job—she added, "I just figured *Louisville* magazine stopped giving them out for dating services."

Spalding shook his head. "They did not. Another service won both years, and I have it on good authority that they'll be winning again this year. Strangely, they opened barely six months before the magazine tallied their ballots two years ago. I would have thought something fishy was going on if they hadn't taken the next two years, too. So what that first year tells me is that they took the lead in town immediately after opening, even though we'd been here for generations."

Not sure what else to say—and not really sure where the conversation was going or what it could have to do with her—Eugenie said simply, "Ah."

"That other service is called DreamMakers."

Eugenie nodded, still not sure what she was supposed to be taking from the conversation. So she repeated, "Ah."

"They're kind of the anti-HeartMenders," Spalding told her.

This time, Eugenie only thought *Ah*. Because she was afraid if she said it again, she would sound as if she were still not following. Which, actually, she wasn't.

"In fact, they're so opposite us that it's kind of obvious they took HeartMenders' model and deliberately turned it on its head in an effort to outdo us. Or maybe, more accurately, to *un*do us."

Okay, now Eugenie could sort of see where the conversation was going. Sort of.

At her lack of response, he continued, "It's beginning to really piss me off."

"Ooohhh," Eugenie replied, grateful to have a different syllable to utter. "You think they're *deliberately* trying to sabotage HeartMenders."

"No, I know they're deliberately trying to sabotage us. I also know they're starting to succeed. Our client list right now is down almost thirty percent from what it was this time last year. Prior to DreamMakers' arrival, it had been growing consistently every year. This should be our busy time. Wedding season is upon us, and that's when people begin to feel acutely their state of singlehood and start wanting to do something about it. So the shrinkage of the client list is doubly alarming."

"I gather they're not a local business?" Eugenie asked.

He shook his head. "A chain. This one is a franchise, meaning the proprietors can do some of their own stuff—or, as is the case here, some of *my* stuff that they twist around to fit their style—and still have a lot of corporate money behind them for promotion and advertising and razzmatazz."

Razzmatazz? Had he actually just used the word *razzmatazz*? Was there anyone still alive who would understand that word? Would spell check even recognize it?

"Maisy built this business—and I've kept it growing until now—by getting people together the old-fashioned way," he said. "By sending them into safe, sober environments that sowed the seeds of emotional intimacy, not sexual intimacy. She knew people needed to get to know each other slowly and gradually over a long period of time and reveal their secrets in installments if they wanted to have a successful lifelong relationship. Not regurgitate all their baggage up front over too many martinis with some stranger in a bar where it's too dark to see who you're talking to and too loud to talk in the first place."

Although it felt as if he was finally cueing Eugenie to comment, she had no idea what he expected—or wanted—her to say. Once again, she must have missed the obvious. Whatever the obvious was.

"That's why Maisy was so successful," he said in response to her silence. "Because she knew love—true, permanent, monogamous love—takes a long time to create. And in that long time, it has to become a lot more than just love. It has to be tolerance. It has to be patience. It has to be forgiveness. Love molds and is molded by every other emotion human beings bring into the mix. Passion, fear, happiness, sadness, anger, humor, resentment, mercy—"

He halted abruptly and smiled a little guiltily. "Sorry. I'm probably preaching to the choir with that, aren't I?"

Only if the choir is singing "How Fake Thou Art," Eugenie thought. "Actually, I assumed you'd switched gears and were talking about the stages of grief now," she quipped.

He did the arched eyebrow thing again. But all he said was, "Grief is a part of love, too."

Now she sobered. "Yeah, I know."

"All of us here do."

Aha. So he *had* suffered from a broken heart himself. Maybe possibly perhaps. It made sense that he would have and that his own heartbreak had, as it had done for Maisy, given him a perception into the human psyche—and the human heart—that a lot of other people didn't have. When people had known love and lost it, they tended to have a better understanding of and appreciation for the emotion than those who were still looking for it. Something like that would give Spalding a recognition of what people were missing from their lives that they may not recognize themselves.

Eugenie wanted very much for him to elaborate on his own interrupted relationship, but she knew better than to ask. She also knew better than to expect him to elaborate.

Instead, he continued, "HeartMenders strives to make matches based on things like the shared values and mutual likes and dislikes of our clients, and our goal is to place them in a respectful and committed relationship for life. *But.* We also try to pair people based on the empty places they may have in their lives or in themselves that could be made full by the addition of the right person in their lives. Does that make sense?"

Actually, it not only made sense, but it answered a lot of questions. Eugenie had never thought about that when she was setting up dates beforehand and filling out reports afterward—that Spalding took into account not just the obvious, and perhaps even superficial, commonalities of their clients, but the intangibles, too, that the clients themselves might not even be aware of. That went a long way toward explaining how two people she wouldn't have thought would hit it off because, say, one was a Republican and one was a Democrat, or one was a dog person and one was a cat person, or even that one was a Cards fan and the other loved the Cats, actually ended up enjoying their time together very much. There were more important things in life—and in love—than personal preferences and values, deeper holes that needed to be filled. One could overlook much of the former if it meant the latter overflowed with joy.

"DreamMakers, on the other hand," Spalding continued, "focuses on fat wallets and great cheekbones and little else, and their ultimate goal isn't a relationship—it's a good time."

"But for a lot of people, that's enough," she said, feeling compelled, for some reason, to rise to those people's defense. "And sometimes a good time can lead to a good relationship."

"Not without hard times interrupting them at some point," Spalding said. "At HeartMenders, it's a priority for us to make matches that are strong enough from the beginning to withstand those hard times, and we do it in a way that means the couple has a long time to bond before those hard times come. DreamMakers throws two people together willy-nilly—"

Willy-nilly? Eugenie thought. Had he just used willy-nilly *and* razzmatazz in the same conversation? Had anyone done that since 1929?

"—and when the good time for that poorly matched couple doesn't last, the clients just put it down to, 'Oh, well, that didn't work. Let's try another person instead. Here's more money.' Which DreamMakers is happy to pocket before matching them up just as badly a second time. Then a third. Then a fourth." He leaned back in his chair, his expression nothing short of glacial. "After enough of that," he said flatly, "a person begins to think they'll never be matched up with their perfect someone. Enough of that, and they begin to think there *is* no perfect someone. Then, after losing a ton of money to a corporation that doesn't give a damn about their happiness, they give up on ever finding someone. And that," he added, "is a tragedy. Because there's always someone.

There's always a perfect someone. For everyone. But they'll never find that someone if they don't do it right."

He spoke so eloquently, and so passionately, that Eugenie almost forgot she was sitting in the office of her employer while said employer described the way his business worked. Business and emotion weren't traditionally things that went hand in hand. But this was what Spalding did every workday. He came to the office and changed lives. For the better. Beyond the walls that surrounded them, people were walking around with smiles on their faces and joy in their hearts because of his work. They were planning their weddings, their vacations, their house hunts, their lives because of his work. They were pushing baby strollers, teaching their kids how to ride bikes, and helping their teenagers find the right college because of his work. Their entire lives were unfolding because of Spalding's work. Hundreds of them. Perhaps thousands. All leading lives that were happy and satisfying. Because of him.

And if she continued to work here, she realized, she would be partly responsible for that, too.

Wow. Just . . . wow. Talk about an awesome responsibility . . . That she really wasn't prepared to think about assuming right now . . . So she backpedaled to what he had been saying before everything went all Zen.

"You're saying DreamMakers sees a better profit if their matches *don't* work out than they would if the matches did."

Spalding nodded. "Yep. So would we, if that was the way we did business. But we have scruples."

"Damn. There goes my big holiday bonus."

He grinned. "Don't worry. You'll get a nice gift certificate to my favorite deli."

"Oh, thank goodness."

Spalding began to pick apart his Oreos, unscrewing each to stack the sides with cream still clinging to them in one pillar and the clean sides in another. As he did, his righteous indignation about DreamMakers took on epic proportions. He talked about how reality TV bombarded people with the message that love could happen anytime, anywhere, with anybody, so people started thinking the most important aspect of a relationship wasn't how well it might work out between two people—or how hard two people needed to *work* to make it work out—but how easily it was supposed to happen. He was also troubled by how pop culture had turned dating into a competition whose prize wasn't a loving, committed relationship, but a guy with great abs and a fat wallet or a girl with a great rack and the potential to drink too much in a hot tub. And then there was all that potential to take one's fifteen minutes of fame and parlay it into fifteen days by working the YouTube angle.

"Ah, romance," Eugenie said wistfully after Spalding wound up his diatribe. "Who says it's dead? Besides DreamMakers, I mean."

"What bugs me the most," he said, "is how many people actually buy into it."

"What, that having a good time for as long as it lasts is better than having a loving, committed relationship that lasts a lifetime but takes a lot of work?"

"That people can't see how having a loving, committed relationship *is* having a good time," he corrected her. "A good time that lasts forever."

Eugenie straightened a little in her chair. "Not that I want to play devil's advocate, but how do you know a temporary good time *isn't* what people want these days? Maybe long-term, monogamous relationships are an outmoded thing of the past.

Maybe contemporary American society is more suited to serial dating, or even dating a lot of people at the same time, than it is to a lifelong monogamous marriage."

The eyebrow went up again. "Is that what you think?"

She had no idea why the question made her feel defensive. "I don't know. I haven't really thought about it. I'm just playing devil's advocate."

"I thought you said you didn't want to play devil's advocate."

"I don't. I just—"

"What?" he asked before she had a chance to form her explanation.

Which was just as well, since Eugenie really didn't actually have an explanation. She'd hoped it would come to her in a lightning strike of brilliance just before the words tumbled eloquently out of her mouth. The way it always happened when . . . Never.

Still watching her, he unscrewed the last of his Oreos and stacked each side on its appropriate base, so that the naked sides formed a little tower and the creamy sides made a little pagoda.

"I've loved Oreos all my life," he said, suddenly changing the subject. "My mother packed them in my lunch every day all through elementary school. Some days, I barely noticed them. Just took them for granted, knowing they'd be in there. Other days, days when there was a pop quiz I wasn't prepared for, or when Brian Dooley threatened me with a swirly or when I found out Debbie McKinley had a crush on that jerk Leonard Moriarty instead of me, seeing those Oreos in my lunch box waiting for me was just so . . . comforting. Like in the great sea of elementary school, so full of disappointment and peril and treachery, I could count on my Oreos to make me feel better, you know?"

Um, okay, sure, Eugenie thought, wondering what hand had changed gears from true love to Nabisco products. Wondering, too, just which gear did that. It could really come in handy. "Yeah. I guess so," she said. "I mean . . . Okay, not really," she finally confessed. "I mean, I understand the whole emotional eating thing, but I don't relate to the consistency thing. Julien and I always bought our lunch at school. There was no consistency. Except that it always tasted like crap."

Which was kind of odd, now that she thought about it. Not the part about school lunches tasting like crap—no mystery there—but the part about how she and Julien had always bought their lunch. Their mother ultimately had become Mrs. Kentucky, after all, a big part of which back then was the recognition of superior housekeeping and cooking skills. And Lorraine had been a good cook. As long as their father was home. But on those occasions when he was traveling for his job—"traveling for his job" actually being a euphemism for activities that ranged from, in Lorraine's words, "porking that little Lolita at Woolworth's" to "steaming up the sheets with that bottle blonde at Lucky Strikes Lanes"—she pretty much left Eugenie and Julien to their own devices. Which meant dinners of Swanson's Salisbury steak, Sara Lee brownies, and Jiffy Pop. They figured that last was, technically, a vegetable, and the brownies had contained pretty much the same ingredients as bread, so together the three foodstuffs provided a balanced meal.

The Dashner *house*, however, *had* been a domestic wonder and absolutely spotless all the time. In fact, Eugenie and Julien had grown up in that house every nineteen sixties Wonder Bread suburban neighborhood claimed, where all the furniture was encased in plastic slipcovers, and Lucite runners in varying shades crisscrossed the house from one room to another. Eugenie and Marianne had always liked to pretend each color was enchanted in a different way and led to a different magical kingdom. The blue one led to Candyland (the kitchen), the lavender one led to Fairyland (Lorraine's pageant trophy room), the pink to Barbieland (Eugenie's bedroom), and the yellow to Oz (for obvious reasons, even though it really led to the bathroom—and don't think the crassness of the color symbolism there wasn't a constant source of amusement). If anyone ever stepped off of one of the enchanted paths, they risked being attacked by an ogre or eaten by a troll. Or, even worse, being yelled at by Mrs. Kentucky.

This time, Spalding was the one to say, "Ah." But he obviously did know where the conversation was headed and what he was expected to say next, because he immediately followed it with, "When I started junior high school, my mom thought I'd want a dessert in my lunch that was more suited to a teenager. So she tried packing other things instead. Banana pudding. Ding Dongs. Chunky candy bars. I really still wanted Oreos, but to make my mother happy—she was one of those moms who did, in fact, tell my sisters and me to clean our plates because children were starving in Africa—I always ate whatever she put in there, and I didn't complain." He sighed heavily as he lifted the stack of four clean-sided Oreo halves. "But I sure missed my Oreos," he said. "That's why I still carry them in my lunch, even after all these years. Because they make me feel good." He popped the entire tower into his mouth.

As he chewed—and because she was more confused now than ever about what the hell they were talking about—Eugenie said, "I've never seen anyone eat Oreos like that."

Spalding swallowed his cookies and washed them down with a slug of Big Red. Eugenie did her best not to gag. "I've eaten them this way since I was a kid," he said once his mouth was no longer full. "Oh sure, there were times when I tried eating them right out of the bag without separating them. Or I separated them quickly to lick the cream off both sides before going after the wafer. But in the long run, I always came back to this way because I like it best. It's slow, methodical, and predictable, but I find comfort in performing the ritual the same way time after time. It makes me feel secure. It makes me happy."

Oooh, Eugenie thought. *Oookaaay. Now* she got it. They weren't talking about Oreos. They were talking about marriage. Weren't they? But wait . . . Spalding wasn't married.

"So what you're saying," she ventured, "is that people get married not just because they fall in love, but because they want to have someone around to comfort them and make them happy and provide solace when pop quiz day doesn't quite go as planned."

He tilted his head left, then right, then left again. "That, but even more than providing comfort and happiness and solace, a lifelong mate provides an anchor. A place you can return to when the journey you undertake doesn't turn out quite as well as you thought or hoped it would."

"What if the journey involves going in search of another anchor?" Eugenie asked. "Will the old anchor be as forgiving when the journeyer returns?"

He met her gaze unflinchingly when he said, "It will if it's really, truly, genuinely in love."

Eugenie thought about that for a minute. If Lawrence showed up at the house tonight and told her that he and Ethel Merman had split up, that he'd made a terrible mistake, that he loved her and her alone and begged her to take him back, would she?

She was surprised to discover how quickly the answer came to her. No. She wouldn't. No question. Then she reminded herself of Seth and how his life had been turned upside down by his parents' divorce. What if reuniting with Lawrence would make things easier for Seth and bring him back from whatever dark place he had retreated to following the divorce? Would she take Lawrence back for Seth's sake?

She made herself take longer to consider that, but even so, the decision she made was the same. No. She wouldn't take Lawrence back, not even for the sake of her child.

So what did that say about her as a mother? What did it say about her as a woman? What did it say about the love she'd felt for a man with whom she had, at one time, promised to spend the rest of her life, for better or for worse, which the situation with Ethel Merman certainly was?

Instead of looking for answers to those questions, Eugenie posed one to Spalding instead. "Why did you ask me to come in here?"

The pointedness of the demand and complete change of topic didn't faze him, and he answered without hesitation. "I want to add another paragraph to your job description."

As she had in response to so many other things he'd said today, she murmured a mental *Huh?* Then she wondered if an additional paragraph would result in additional pay.

"What will this additional paragraph involve?"

"Additional duties."

"With additional pay?"

"Overtime."

"Which is?"

He grinned. "Don't you want to know what the additional duties will be?"

Only because she didn't want to sound as mercenary as she felt, Eugenie said, "Okay."

He met her gaze levelly and said, "I want you to become a client of DreamMakers'."

Before she realized what she was doing, Eugenie felt her eyebrow arch in exactly the way Spalding's did whenever she said something unexpected to him. He was clearly as surprised to see it as she was to have done it, because his lips parted fractionally . . . before curving into a grin.

"So that's what that looks like," he said.

She lowered the brow and leaned forward a little, as if her ears were telling her brain they needed to be sure they were hearing correctly. "You want to pay me for dating?" she asked. "Isn't that illegal?"

"No, what would be illegal is if I paid you for mating," he told her. "But that's okay. Sometimes the letters of the alphabet confuse me, too."

Now it was Eugenie's turn to grin. All she said, though, was, "So I'd be going undercover with our rivals and reporting back to you."

He nodded. "Everything you see, hear, and do."

"Like a spy?" she asked, lowering her voice without knowing why.

"Exactly like that. You can even have a code name if you want."

She brightened. She'd never had a code name before. "Really? Like what?"

She could tell he was doing his best to look Very Serious about the situation, but the somberness didn't quite reach his eyes. "I don't know. What kind of code name do you want?"

She thought for a minute, then said the first thing that popped into her head. Although why that name would be "Vixen," she had no idea.

It didn't help that, upon hearing it, Spalding lost his battle to remain Very Serious and began to chuckle.

"What's so funny?" she demanded.

He shook his head. "Nothing. I just thought you'd come up with a different kind of code name, that's all."

"Oh?" she asked indignantly. "You don't think Vixen suits me?"

"It's not that," he denied. "I just thought you'd be more suited to something else. Something like . . . uh . . . Pixie or something."

"Pixie?" she cried. "*Pixie*? You think I'm more pixie than vixen?"

He held up both hands, palms out, as if that might ward off any further outrage. "Sorry. Wrong word. Just mixing up letters again. I mean, the two words do have a lot of letters in common. But obviously, vixen was what I meant to say."

Hmpf, Eugenie thought. "Obviously."

"And, Agent Vixen, I'd be willing to pay you time and a half for any, ah, dating you do with DreamMakers. Not to mention foot the bill for the membership fee and any other ensuing expenses."

Eugenie was about to accept—Hey, more money? Sign her up!—but had one last question before committing. "Why me?"

As was so often the case, Spalding hesitated a moment before answering. But for some reason, his hesitation in this instance made something in her belly do a little flip-flop. "Because," he finally said, "you're new enough to HeartMenders that no one at DreamMakers is acquainted with you. And because you wouldn't have to lie to become a client. You can go in there as a recently divorced woman who's testing the waters of the single life."

For some reason, Eugenie felt it necessary to take exception to that. "Although it's true that I am a divorced woman, I am *not* testing the waters of the single life. That's the last thing I need."

Ignoring the last part of her statement, he said, "So what do you say, Eugenie? Will you be my agent provocateur?"

"Well, gee, when you speak French like that, how can I resist?"

It was only after the comment was out of her mouth that Eugenie realized how flirtatious she sounded. Then she thought about how flirtatious Spalding had sounded for the last few minutes, too. Then she wondered if they were, in fact, flirting. And, if so, did that mean—

Well, anything?

Maybe the real question she should be looking for an answer to, though, was, why was she kind of hoping it meant—

Well, something?

Eight

By the time Eugenie arrived home that night, the last thing she wanted to do was dive into dinner preparations. No, wait. That was actually the second-, no, third-last thing she wanted to dive into. The first last thing she wanted to do was strip more wallpaper, since every square inch of it so far had been demonically possessed and in need of something more powerful than vinegar and holy water to exorcise it. The second-last thing she wanted to do was yank up linoleum, since not even Julien had been able to identify yet what lay beneath it. Whatever it was, it, too, had been hell-spawned if the smell was any indication.

Okay, then. Dinner it would be. Then linoleum yanking. Then wallpaper exorcising.

But first, wine.

She went to the kitchen—the still-ugly, still-demoralizing kitchen—to pour herself a glass, drinking half of it in a couple of greedy gulps before refilling it. Then she turned to make her way upstairs to change out of her work clothes and into something more comfortable. This in spite of the fact that, considering both the state of Fleurissant and Spalding's recent assignment, comfort was looking to be a long way off.

She halted when she entered the dining room, however, which, like the kitchen, remained in a state of unfulfilled potential that was in no way ready for furniture. (The Dashners were currently taking their meals at a couple of card tables shoved together in a mud room that was, for now, referred to as "the breakfast nook"—though not with anything resembling a straight face.) Sitting in the center of the floor, atop a pink-flowered sheet and surrounded by straggling crumbs of plaster, was the massive chandelier that had been hanging from the dining room ceiling that morning.

Julien had told Eugenie a few days ago that its care and cleaning were up to her, since he sure as hell didn't want to be responsible for something so fragile. Not that she minded. She was certain it was original to the house and must have been a magnificent piece once upon a time, its crystal prisms devouring light and coruscating radiance in return. She didn't want to trust its restoration to a stranger. But she had thought Julien would move the chandelier to another room for its resurrection, not leave it out in the middle of everything where anything could mess it up. Men.

Right on cue, Julien entered the dining room from the door on the other side, his paint-spattered jeans and perspiration-slathered T-shirt a testament to how he had spent his day. The punctuation mark was the orange-striped Porter Paint can he carried in one hand, its paper streaked with the robin's egg blue Lorraine had demanded for her bedroom, even though both of her children had assured her that that particular shade had fallen out of fashion right around the same time Nixon had. Lorraine didn't care. She'd liked Nixon, too.

"Oh, hey," Julien said when he saw Eugenie. "I didn't hear you come in." He turned the wrist of his free hand to look at his watch. "Wow. I didn't realize how late it is."

Eugenie nodded her understanding. "Days with Mom do tend to have a time-altering effect."

"Yeah, but they usually make time go slower."

She grinned at that. "How's her room coming?"

"Pretty well. I stripped a corner of the flooring to see how big a job that was going to be and was pleasantly surprised to only find three layers of varnish, as opposed to the eighty billion I was expecting."

They had by now pulled up the rancid carpeting throughout the first level of Fleurissant to uncover random-width cherry flooring in every room outside the kitchen and baths. Eventually, it would be rich and lustrous. For now, the floorboards were caked and cracked with varnish in some places and dull and grimy in others, gasping for someone to bathe them with gentle strokes and massage them with oil to restore their youthful splendor. Eugenie sympathized completely.

"How was work?" Julien asked.

"Interesting," she replied.

"I guess it would be, hooking people up right after you've unhooked yourself from Lawrence."

She was surprised to discover she didn't have a sarcastic quip about her ex at the ready. Not because she was normally quick to have a quip for anything—on the contrary—but because she honestly didn't feel sarcastic about Lawrence today. Instead, she just felt . . . weary. Weary and unwilling to take even a moment out of this overfull day to think about him. Maybe because she was exhausted from trying to do too much these past few months. Or maybe because she was just fatigued from the day's work. Perhaps she was just finally growing tired of all the Lawrence shrapnel. Or perhaps the shrapnel that had embedded itself in her was finally beginning to work its way out.

"You know," she ventured cautiously, "if you want, I could bring home an application for HeartMenders for you to fill out. Spalding is amazingly good when it comes to fitting people together. I've seen a lot of—"

"Not interested, Eugene," Julien interrupted her, holding up his free hand, palm out, as if he wanted to physically ward off her words, too. "It doesn't happen a second time. The real thing only comes along once."

Neither of them needed to mention how his real thing had come and gone. Julien had indeed had something special with Cassie, something Eugenie hadn't seen with any other couple she knew. It had been obvious to anyone who saw the two of them together. Even when Eugenie was happy in her marriage, she had been envious, in a way, that her brother had something with his wife she knew she would never have with her husband. Julien and Cassie had been friends in addition to lovers. They'd communicated verbally, physically, emotionally, and every other way two people could communicate. They'd taken care of each other. They'd watched each other's backs. When Sophie and Chloe came along, they'd shared equally in all the parental demands and devoted one hundred percent of their weekends to being a foursome. They had been a family in a way that was almost never seen.

Even before the girls' births, Julien and Cassie had been a family. A family of two. That, she supposed, was where she and Lawrence had differed from them the most. It hadn't been until Seth came along that either of them had spoken in terms of their being a family. Strangely, though, even with Lawrence gone, she and Seth still felt like a family. She wondered if Julien felt the same way about himself and the girls without Cassie being there. Probably, the three of them were still a family. But, probably, it was a family that had as many cracks and missing pieces as Fleurissant did.

"Fair enough," she said, knowing it was pointless to try and change his mind about Cassie being the real thing and the real thing only happening once when what he said was undeniably true. "But that doesn't mean there's not someone else out there you could find happiness with. A different kind of happiness," she hastened to add when she saw his expression darkening. "But happiness nonetheless. You'll never know if you don't give it a chance."

"Right," he said crisply. "The same way you're all ready to jump in and start dating again, right?"

Touché, she thought. Of course, she *was* about to jump in and start dating again, but that was only for time and a half, not because she thought there was actually a perfect someone for her out there in the wake of her divorce. Not that Lawrence had been her perfect someone to begin with, so maybe there was actually someone else out there who was perfect for her. With Eugenie's luck, however, that person probably lived in Abu Dhabi.

"It's too early for me," she said, knowing that wasn't the reason she didn't want to date again, but thinking it sounded plausible enough. "It's been two and a half years since Cassie—" Eugenie stopped herself before finishing the sentence, then hurried on, "I know Spalding could find someone you'd like, Jules. He's so perceptive about people's wants and needs."

Julien was shaking his head and striding past her toward the kitchen before Eugenie even finished talking. She let him go. She didn't know what she was thinking to have even suggested such a thing, knowing how hard he had resisted getting involved with anyone since Cassie's death. She just hated seeing her brother alone with two little girls when he had so much to bring to a relationship. Yes, he'd been a major player as a young man, but when he finally did fall in love, he fell *hard*. Julien's emotional well went deep. Maybe it had grown shallow since Cassie's death, but there was no way it would ever run dry. All it would take was one good rain to refill it. Then he could grow a relationship crop out the wazoo. So to speak.

"I'll grill tonight," he said over his shoulder as he went into the kitchen. "Don't worry about cooking."

It was his apology for cutting her off, so Eugenie thanked him, told him she couldn't wait, and began her journey to her bedroom once again. As she topped the stairs on the third floor, she saw that the door to Seth's temporary room was closed, meaning that he was, for a change, home before dinner was on the table, even if he obviously wanted to make himself unavailable. But then, he hadn't been available since moving day. Come to think of it, he hadn't been available since March 2010. Eugenie started to walk past that closed door the same way she did every evening when it was open, then hesitated. Carefully, she pressed her ear against the seam where it joined with the jamb, to see if she could hear anything from the other side. But Seth must have had his earbuds in to tune out the rest of the world, because she didn't detect the slightest vibration of sound. She started to move away, then halted again, and lifted her hand to rap hard on the door three times.

No response.

"Seth?" she called.

Nothing.

"Seth? It's Mom."

Like it would be anyone else. Like he wouldn't recognize her voice in the first place and know who was at the door. Like that wasn't precisely the reason he stuffed those damned earbuds into his ears. Half the time she wondered if he even had anything playing on his iPod, or if he simply used the earbuds as an excuse to not engage. What she ought to do was identify herself as, well, whoever the latest Internet hottie was—did kids still use the word *hottie*?—or else as . . . as whoever young cyclists were looking up to now. Had someone come along to replace Lance Armstrong? Lance Armstrong was finally retired now, wasn't he? Then again, was it Lance whom Seth had admired in the first place, or was it someone else?

"Seth," she said again, more forcefully this time and without a question mark to punctuate it. "Open the door. I need to ask you something."

Silence greeted her again for a few seconds, then she heard the shuffle—the very slow shuffle—of someone moving—very slowly—around. She shifted her weight from one foot to the other a half-dozen times before he finally opened the door, and when he did, it was only to glare at her with that one eye visible beneath the sweep of dark hair that had now grown to nearly his shoulders. There was a game headset arced over the crown of his head, but the mike part was turned upward, meaning he was playing some game online, but he wasn't speaking to anyone there, either.

When he said nothing to greet her, she asked, "How are you?"

His expression changed not at all. "Is that the something you needed to ask me?"

"That was the first thing."

"What else?"

"How are you?" she repeated.

"Fine. What else?"

Now that was an open-ended question if ever there was one.

There were a hundred questions bouncing around inside her head that she wanted to ask her son. Did he like their new neighborhood? Were he and Marianne's son D.J. getting along? Had he made any other friends besides D.J., a friendship he'd only forged in the first place because she and Marianne had forced it? Was there a girl he liked? Had he read any good books lately? Seen any good movies? Where did he go when he left the house in the morning and didn't return until dusk? Why wouldn't he talk to her? Why did he dislike her? Why couldn't he see that it was his father who had screwed up everything, not her?

Then again, she probably already knew the answers to most of those questions: No. Probably not. Doubtful. Yes, but no way would he admit it. Possibly, not that he would ever talk about it with her. Ditto. Not telling. Because. Because. Whatever.

Wow, look at that. She already knew the answers to all of them. Who said she didn't recognize her son anymore? So she skipped over those for now and went for the ones that would be easier. "Do kids still use the word 'hottie' when they talk about good-looking members of the opposite sex?" she asked.

To his credit, Seth didn't bat an eye. Unless it was the one hidden by his hair, but Eugenie doubted he would bat one without the other. Which made her wonder why the phrase only mentioned one eye in the first place.

But she digressed.

"Do they?" she asked when Seth remained silent.

"Uh, I guesso."

"Do you ever use it?"

"No."

"Well, what would you call a pretty girl?"

"I'd call her whatever her name was."

Okay, so maybe not the best opening volley, Eugenie realized.

Perhaps she should move along. "So who's the biggest hottie on the Internet today? Female," she clarified. Although maybe she shouldn't have. If Seth named a guy instead of a girl, it would be a very telling statement and might explain why he'd become so withdrawn. He was at an age where a lot of kids were becoming confused about their sexual identity, and if that was the case with Seth, then—

Then she was jumping to a lot of conclusions and, again, digressing and, again, avoiding the task at hand.

The one eye she could see narrowed a bit. Nevertheless, he replied, "Kesha."

Not a name she recognized.

Seth obviously realized that. "She's a singer."

"Oh. So you think Kesha is a hottie?"

He said nothing for a moment, then, "Mom?"

"Yes?"

"How much wine have you had to drink tonight?"

She looked down at the glass she'd brought upstairs with her. "This is my first glass," she said. No reason she had to mention she'd already refilled it once. Alcohol had nothing to do with her questions. Motherly love did.

"Why are you asking me this stuff?" he said.

"Because I hardly ever see you anymore," she said. "I miss talking to you. You've barely spoken ten words since we moved into this house. And even before that, you . . ."

Before she could stop herself, she lifted a hand with the intention of brushing his hair back from his face so that she could see him better. There was a time when touching Seth's hair would have been a simple gesture he barely noticed. When he was little and first became proficient at walking, he'd been too independent to hold her hand, so Eugenie had always cupped hers over the crown of his head in substitution, weaving her fingers gently through his hair to prevent his straying from her side. When he started elementary school, his hair was always so matted when he woke up in the morning that she had to use a spray bottle full of water they kept in his bathroom to comb him out before he left. As more years passed and he grew uncomfortable with hugs and kisses from his mother, he would still allow Eugenie to brush his hair from his forehead as an acceptable way of showing affection—provided she didn't do it in front of his friends.

But today, the moment he saw her hand approaching his face, he jerked his head back before she could make contact. Something pinched hard in her chest when he did, but she dropped her hand back to her side and pretended she didn't notice.

"So . . . um . . . How's Lance Armstrong doing these days?" she asked.

"He's retired. Finally."

The reply was tinted with no small contempt, and she wondered when he had stopped liking Lance. He had liked Lance once upon a time—she was sure of it. But it had clearly been some time since she'd last checked. Then again, she had at least been right about the retirement thing. So why didn't she feel a little better about that?

"Then who do you—"

"Dave Wiens."

"Oh?" she asked, not recognizing the name.

This was the perfect thing for Seth to talk about. Maybe as she listened to him talking about his latest hero, she would hear things from her son that she hadn't heard before and learn things about him she didn't already know. Which was everything except for knowing how he would answer every question in the negative.

"I don't recognize Dave Wiens's name," she said. "Maybe you could tell me a little bit more about—"

"Mom."

"What?"

"I'm kinda busy right now."

She looked past him, into his room, which, like her own, was sparsely furnished and barely habitable. His old twin bed—she'd promised him they would buy a queen size once his attic room was finished—was shoved into one corner, covered with only a set of red sheets. The walls still bore water marks and open fissures, and bare wires beetled from a hole in the ceiling where that light fixture had been removed. Eugenie had found a very nice dresser and desk for him at Goss Avenue Antiques, but both were barely visible behind and beneath half-empty boxes, scattered teenage boy paraphernalia, and abandoned bits of clothing. The only things that were clearly visible were the checkmark-shaped gaming chair he'd clearly just vacated and the TV set sitting on the floor in front of it where a video game had been freeze-framed on what appeared to be the detonation of an atomic bomb.

"So you're playing a game?" she asked.

Oh, nicely done, Eugenie. Yet another question with an obvious answer. No wonder Seth enjoys talking to you so much.

He nodded quickly. "Yeah. And I need to get back to it."

She was about to say something else, but Seth closed the door, thereby hindering further conversation. Just in case she didn't get the message, however, he punctuated the action with the click of a lock on the other side. That was followed by the thump of footsteps across the floor, then what sounded like a very heavy weight being thrown against the wall. Probably, though, it was only Seth falling back into his chair. Probably.

Eugenie pressed her forehead against the door and sighed, replaying the conversation in her head. The only new thing she'd learned about her son was the name of a cyclist he now admired. That was if he hadn't just pulled that name out of thin air to appease her and hasten the end of their exchange. She didn't even know how he felt about Kesha. Or what term boys his age used for girls like Kesha or if he liked Kesha more than Dave Wiens or vice versa.

She pushed herself away from his door and turned toward her own room at the end of the hall. And she tried not to think about how the names Kesha and Dave Wiens were as alien to her as her own son had become.

Nine

As she approached her room, Eugenie simultaneously lifted the glass of wine to her mouth for another sip and tugged free the tail of her sleeveless white shirt from the waistband of her skirt. Then she went to work on the buttons, starting at the collar and working her way down. Her door was pushed closed but wasn't latched, so she nudged it open with her foot just as she finished unfastening the last button. She was immediately assailed by the odor of fresh paint mingling with the scent of linseed oil. Neither was an uncommon aroma in the house these days, but this was the first time she'd smelled them above the first floor, where Julien and Nash had been focusing their work. Granted, Lorraine's bedroom was situated almost directly beneath Eugenie's on the first floor, so maybe the smell was just wafting up from there through the air vents or fireplace, since the women's rooms shared a chimney.

Eugenie halted just over the threshold, however, when she

realized that the color of the wall on the far side of her room, behind her bed, was a different color than it had been when she readied herself for work that morning. Twelve hours ago, it had been the grayish white of dried plaster from Julien's efforts of the week before. Now it was a voluptuous scarlet she had chosen from a paint chip only the day before, but which she hadn't thought would actually appear on her walls for another month. The only reason Julien had plastered that one wall was because he'd mixed more than he needed for Lorraine's room and didn't want to waste it. The other walls were still pocked and scarred from the stripping of wallpaper. Hence the need for replastering.

Even more surprising, the floorboards throughout the room were completely refinished. She had completed the sanding and cleaning of them a few days ago, since the floors on this level hadn't been shellacked within an inch of their lives the way they had downstairs, and the task had been one Eugenie could complete in one day—so she did. Now, however, the narrow pine planking shone like ebbing satin, having been oiled and massaged with gentle strokes to restore its youthful splendor. A pair of multihued paint-spattered tarpaulins trailed from the doorway to the adjoining bathroom on the right side of the room, whose door was also mostly closed but not latched. A slice of fluorescent light spilled through the crack between it and the jamb, suggesting either that she had neglected to turn it off when she left that morning or, more likely, that Julien had neglected to do that after working in here earlier today. Though why he would be painting in here when Lorraine's room still needed it, not to mention skip the entire second floor between, she had no idea.

Eugenie strode across the tarp toward the bathroom and nudged the door open with the hand still holding her wine. Unfortunately, since the movement of the door surprised the hell out of Nash, who was lying on the floor beneath the sink, and who jackknifed up to bang his head on its bowl. His appearance was equally startling to Eugenie, who jumped backward, sloshing wine onto her shirt.

"Oh, dammit!" they chorused as one, if for different reasons. Nash lifted a hand to the place where his forehead had made contact with the sink while Eugenie began to brush at the wine stain with her free hand.

He was shirtless, as always, the elegant lines of his chest interrupted only by the earbuds' white cord that bisected it from his neck to the iPod affixed at his waist. He'd bought it a couple of weeks before and asked Eugenie to fill it with whatever music she saw fit, provided there was plenty of seventies and eighties rock and pop to comfort him when all that new alternative crap crept into the mix. She'd been gentle with him, however, downloading lots of Paramore and Plain White T's to temper the Green Day and Linkin Park.

Although it was only mid-June, his skin was already burnished to a honeyed bronze, thanks to all the work he'd performed on the exterior of the house. She didn't think he'd gotten a haircut since that first day she'd seen him, and it now hung nearly to his shoulders. His painter's pants, as spattered and ragged as the tarp in the other room, claimed a new color, the one that had suddenly appeared on the wall behind her bed. Fevered Passion, the hue was called. Not that any kind of wishful thinking on her part had had anything to do with why Eugenie chose it, of course. She'd just liked it better than the runner-up on another chip called New Cherry.

When Nash saw who had been responsible for the door's opening, he smiled and stopped rubbing his forehead to pluck the earbud out of one ear. "Janey!" he cried in the same tone a high school basketball star might show for Selection Sunday of March Madness. "When did you get home? I was just—" He halted abruptly as his gaze fell from her face to some point below it, where . . .

Oh, dammit. Where her blouse was hanging open over her bra. But even as she seized both sides of her shirt with her free hand to close it, what embarrassed her most wasn't so much that she had flashed her brother's best friend, but that the only thing she had to flash him with was a pair of no-nonsense, no-frills white cotton B cups that had no decoration whatsoever, not even one of those asinine little satin bows they stuck on no-nonsense, no-frills white cotton bras to embellish them, because the designers obviously didn't think women could really want something no-nonsense and no-frills and which Eugenie always removed because she really wanted her bras to be no-nonsense and no-frills, the way she was herself. And okay, so maybe at the moment, she was rethinking that particular philosophy and might have actually liked a little something extra on—and okay, *in*—her bra, but that didn't mean she didn't like no-nonsense, no-frills white cotton on other occasions or that she had—

Or that she had even the merest grip on the runaway voice in her head that was trying to make her think of anything other than the fact that Nash Ridley had just seen her no-nonsense, no-frills B cups.

Button it, she told the voice. Hopefully not confusing her brain in the process, since the voice might think she was talking about her shirt instead of its mouth, when, really, she was talking about both. Fortunately, her brain got the gist of it, because the voice quieted at the same time she began to look for a place to set down her wine to free both hands for the task of buttoning her shirt. Unfortunately, Nash stood between her and the only visible surfaces that would support a glass of wine.

He seemed to notice her predicament, though, because he lifted one hand to cover his eyes while extending the other toward her. "Here, let me hold that while you . . . you know."

She extended the glass toward him, and after a bit of fumbling, he managed to get a good grip on it. Hastily, Eugenie buttoned herself, but it wasn't until she reached the last two buttons near her collar that she realized she only had one hole left and had skipped one somewhere along the way.

Oh, bugger it, she thought, reaching for her wine. Everything was covered that needed to be. Not that she had exactly been on display to begin with. That would require having something *to* display, after all.

"You can look now," she said as she retrieved her glass. "I'm decent."

He grinned as he removed his hand from in front of his eyes, tugged free the other earbud, and dropped both hands to his hips. "I already knew that. You've always been eminently decent, Janey."

And, oh, wasn't that the kind of thing a woman wanted to hear from the man who had been her childhood, adolescent, and young adult crush. And, okay, maybe her middle adult crush, too. And, *oh, all right,* maybe her later adult crush as well.

"So what are you doing up here?" she asked. "I thought the goal was to finish the first floor before moving upstairs. And even then, the girls' rooms are supposed to be next. Then Seth's. We parents are making the huge sacrifices of going last. Well, not all of us parents," she quickly amended. "But Jules and I are."

Although Eugenie had wanted to start the renovation with the completion of the kitchen, Julien had suggested they finish Lorraine's rooms first, to make their mother more comfortable and keep her complaints to a minimum. Even at that, however, the progress had been slower than any of them had hoped, and Lorraine had complained plenty, most recently about the pedestal sink for her bathroom. She said it was "too froufrou" for her tastes, something Eugenie wouldn't have thought possible for a woman who had been known to cook dinner while wearing her Mrs. Kentucky tiara.

Nash shrugged. "I wanted to see how the color you picked out would look. It's pretty damn red. I wasn't sure if you realized just how red. I mean . . ." His eyes widened comically. "It's really, really red."

"I like red," she told him crisply.

He held up his hands before himself, palms out, as if in surrender. "Hey, I think it looks great now that it's on the wall. I was surprised. You have a good eye."

"You're surprised that the red looks good, or you're surprised I have a good eye?"

He gave her an indulgent look. "Not gonna go there, Janey. I'm just thinking maybe I'll plaster the other walls tomorrow and then get the rest of the paint on next week."

His offer surprised her. They really did have far more pressing matters in the house than her bedroom. "What about the girls' rooms? They're supposed to come after my mother's. Jules promised."

"And Jules is getting started on the plastering of both rooms tomorrow. It'll be a couple days before they're dry enough to paint, and he doesn't want to work on the floors until the walls are painted." Parenthetically, he added, "He doesn't have as steady a hand as I do. It's never been a problem for me starting at the bottom and working my way up. At least I've never had any complaints."

Eugenie wasn't positive, but she was pretty sure he was talking about something besides home renovation now. In a word, *Hmm*.

"But Mom's floor still needs stripping and refinishing," she said. "My room can wait. Besides, I can do it myself when the time comes."

He grinned in a way she'd never quite seen from him before—at least when he was grinning at her. "You shouldn't have to do it by yourself, Janey. Not when I can help you. Please. Let me take care of your room."

There was something in his voice when he said that last part that went way beyond *Hmm*. Oh, yeah. There was definitely something else going on here besides home improvement. Now if she could just figure out what exactly it was, maybe she would have some idea how to react.

"Were you the one who finished up the floor today?" she asked, backtracking to his earlier comment because something made her hesitate about going forward with anything else he'd said.

He nodded, then took a step forward, bringing his body to within a couple of inches of her own. Involuntarily, Eugenie took a step backward until she was framed by the doorjamb. So Nash followed, stepping even closer this time. Heat bloomed in her belly at his nearness, but she ignored it. It was nothing but a little leftover fevered passion from her adolescent fixation on him. He had always been a safe object of her affections, because there had never been a chance he would ever see his best friend's sister as anything but New Cherry. Just because she was an adult, albeit divorced and sexually deprived, woman, that didn't change anything. To Nash, Eugenie would always be Julien's kid sister. And to Eugenie, Nash would always be a safe but silly crush.

Right? Right.

No sooner had the thought formed, however, than did her safe, silly crush lift an arm and prop it against the jamb near her head. Then he bent forward to move his head closer to hers. She told herself she only imagined the way the air around her suddenly turned electric. But the scent of him, a brew of linseed, dirt, and sweat, was all too real. It was also kind of intoxicating, she had to admit.

"I want to do something nice for you, Janey," he said softly. "I mean, you come home from work every night and cook dinner for all of us, and then you clean up everything and work on the house for hours. It's like you're doing two jobs, only one of which you get paid for. It's nice of you to do that for us."

Nice. Another one of those words women loved to hear a man use in reference to her. Next, Nash would be telling her she had a great personality.

Instead, he told her, "I just want to do something nice for you, too. You deserve it."

What would be nice of him would be to stop standing there with her, straddling the two most intimate rooms of her house. "Um, thanks, Nash. That's nice of you, too."

Take that, *adolescent crush*, she thought. See how he liked being called *nice*.

Very slowly, he started to draw nearer, and for one insane moment, Eugenie actually thought he was going to kiss her. But just as his face swooped in on hers, he swayed to the right and went back to the sink to collect a wrench he'd left behind.

"Be careful with the floor in the bedroom for now," he said as he straightened and tucked the wrench into his back pocket. "It could still be a little tacky, so you might want to wear a pair of old socks to bed tonight."

Really, he had to stop murmuring such sweet romantic nothings to her. If he didn't cut it out, she was going to get the vapors.

"So what have you been working on in here?" she asked, lifting her chin to indicate the bathroom, which didn't look any different than it had that morning.

"I installed a new showerhead for you," he told her. "I heard you mention to Julien that you wanted one of those big ones that make you feel like you're standing in a rain forest downpour, so I went ahead and picked one up. And you know me—anytime I get something in my hand I have to find the right place to put it. So . . ." He jerked back the shower curtain with a flourish, making Eugenie jump a little. Her rusty, worn-out conical showerhead had been replaced with one that was dewy, round, and . . . dare she say . . . tumescent?

"Turn this baby on," Nash said, "and she'll be a real gusher."

No doubt, Eugenie thought. Oh, but wait. He meant the showerhead, didn't he?

"Ah, thanks, Nash. I can't wait to, um . . . shower with it."

"Anytime."

As Nash moved toward the door again, Eugenie made sure she took enough steps backward this time to land on the tarp, but he followed right along until they were both standing inside the bedroom. Except for the floor and one wall, nothing in here had improved since moving day. Eugenie hadn't even finished unpacking yet and still had a half-dozen boxes stacked in a corner. They held all the things that were inessential to life but important for living: photographs and mementos, accessories to make the room pretty, and the sort of clothing she only wore on special occasions. Even the furniture was at a bare minimum—a mattress and box springs on a metal frame (the feet of which were all resting on rags at the moment) and an old maple chest she'd found at a flea market and planned to eventually move into a stairway landing for storing linens. She hadn't even chosen curtains for the windows and was relying on a pair of cheap white shades she'd bought for the sake of privacy and nothing more.

She knew exactly how she wanted the room to look when it was finished, though. As a counterpoint to the ripe red walls, she wanted lush mahogany furniture—a highboy, an armoire, and a sleigh bed, all overblown and baroque, because the size of the room and the decorative molding warranted bold, brash contents. She wanted a chandelier at the ceiling's center dripping with crystals, and she wanted luscious bronze curtains that puddled beneath the windows. She wanted original artwork on the walls executed in vigorous colors by an exuberant hand. She wanted the room to percolate with energy and radiate beauty. No matter how long it took her to achieve both.

When she turned to look at Nash, she saw him surveying the room, too, as if he were also trying to picture what it needed to finish it. Though his idea of finished doubtless consisted of simply completing the plastering and painting and wiring. His gaze halted, however, on the wall opposite them. Turning to see what he was looking at, Eugenie found herself staring at the fireplace.

"Please tell me it works," she said, glancing back at Nash. "I'm so looking forward to having fires in it this winter."

"It'll work," Nash said. "I think."

He toed off his sneakers and then in his old socks padded over to give the fireplace a closer inspection. Eugenie followed as far as the end of the tarp and kicked off her own shoes, but because her feet were bare, she took little shuffling steps that dragged the tarp along under her feet until she was standing next to Nash.

She'd only given the mantelpiece a perfunctory inspection

after moving in, to see if it was salvageable. Thankfully, it was. A few inches taller than Eugenie, it had Doric-inspired triglyphs dented with a half-dozen guttae that resembled tassels. Because that was typical styling of the Beaux-Arts period, she was reasonably certain the mantel, too, was original to the house. Although someone somewhere along the line had painted it white, it was, like so much else in Fleurissant, flaking and chipped in places, hinting at what might possibly be a gorgeous mahogany beneath. (Another inspiration for her furniture plans.) Fortunately, whoever had wielded the paintbrush had left the chestnut-colored tiles surrounding the fireplace alone so that all they needed was a good cleaning.

Nash dropped to his haunches near where the floor and tiles connected, twisting his body so that he could look up into the flue. Then he lay down on his back, sucking in a quick breath at what must have been cold tiling against his bare skin before settling himself inside, looking up.

"Oh yeah, it'll work. Eventually," he said. "It's just really jammed up tight right now."

Not sure why she did it, Eugenie shuffled a little closer, then knelt on the floor and lay down beside him so she could look up into the chimney, too. But all she saw were walls streaked with soot and creosote, smelling of desiccation and disuse.

Nash reached up and rubbed a hand along one of those walls, slowly, deliberately, once, twice, three times, before bringing it back down just as carefully. Eugenie's breath caught somewhere in her chest as she watched the slow motion of those fingers caressing the brick insides, up and down, up and down, up and down, until she began to feel a little lightheaded. When he finally pulled his hand back out, his palm and fingertips were stained and sooty with the chimney's release.

"It's dryer than I thought it would be in there," he said.

No kidding, Eugenie thought. That was what happened when a woman went too long without—

Oh, right. He was talking about the chimney. Wasn't he? Or was he? Somehow they still seemed to be talking about something other than home renovation. Although if they *weren't* talking about home renovation, it probably wasn't in good taste to tell a woman her chimney was dry.

"That sounds bad," she said. "That sounds like it could disintegrate any minute and blow away like a pile of dust."

"No, dryness is good," he assured her. Which meant that they must be talking about home renovation, on account of no man would ever want a woman's chimney to be dry under other circumstances. "It means there's no fungus or mold or anything."

Well, no, there wouldn't be. In order for there to be that, a woman's chimney would have had to see some action from time to time.

"It shouldn't be too hard to bring it back to life," he said. "I'll just have to go slow and be gentle."

Okay, so then they *were* talking about something other than home renovation. Right? They must be. Weren't they?

She turned her head to look at Nash, but he didn't say anything, only turned his head to look back at her. She wanted to say something to him but wasn't sure what. It wasn't like she could talk about her chimney with just anyone. Especially her brother's best friend who had been the subject of so many of her youthful fantasies. She needed some kind of clarification about what he was saying. She needed even more clarification about what he *wasn't* saying. Was he talking about her chimney? Or was he talking about, you know, her *chimney*?

Before she could say anything at all, he asked, "Hey, Janey, you wanna go out and have a beer with me sometime?"

The heat she had felt before blossomed in her belly again. Again, she tried to ignore it, but this time, she couldn't quite manage it. She was surprised when she heard herself reply, "Sure," because she honestly hadn't made a conscious decision to do so. Once out, however, she didn't know how to retract the reply without sounding like an adolescent girl who didn't know the first thing about boys and couldn't figure out what this particular one had on his mind.

Still, she wondered what this particular one had on his mind. Nash's expression was no different from any other time she had seen him. He didn't look or sound like he was asking her out on a date, even if the question itself had kind of sounded that way. Maybe he really did just want to have a beer. Not that they couldn't have a beer here anytime they wanted. So it must be a date, right? Unless he just wanted to talk to her about her plans for the house. Or for her bedroom. Or her bathroom. Or her, you know, chimney.

"How about Saturday?" he asked. "You doing anything?"

"Nada," she replied, proud that she sounded as nonchalant as he did. She made a mental note to remind herself that when she contacted DreamMakers tomorrow, she needed to tell them she couldn't go out on Saturday because she had a date. Except that she'd have to make up something, since she would ostensibly be signing on with them because she was dateless. So she'd just tell them she couldn't go out Saturday on account of she was having chimney issues. Or something like that.

"Great," Nash said. "A friend of mine has a band playing at Stevie Ray's Blues Bar that night. Maybe we can grab a bite to eat, too. What do you think?"

Probably, it was best not to answer truthfully, because she was still wondering if this had something to do with unjamming her dry chimney. So she only said, "Sounds like fun."

Which was true, since both of those things did sound like fun. One just sounded more fun than the other. Provided, of course, she was remembering correctly how one went about unjamming one's chimney. It had been a while since she'd even had hers inspected.

And just when had she started thinking it was a good idea to let Nash anywhere near her chimney? Any woman who had even a vague acquaintance with him knew he was only after one thing when it came to women. Even if he was probably the best chimney sweep in metro Louisville—including Oldham and Bullitt counties and much of southern Indiana—Eugenie had a lot more renovating to complete before she could even think about having a fire in her bedroom.

On the other hand . . .

On the other hand, if Eugenie *did* want to start thinking about working on her chimney, who better to call on than a man who did *excellent* work when it came to rehabilitating them? Maybe she was being too hasty in putting off further renovation to her bedroom. Maybe the timing of Nash's proposition . . . ah, proposal . . . ah, suggestion . . . was spot-on. Then again, maybe he really did just want to go out for a beer.

So the big question, Eugenie supposed, was whether or not she just wanted to go out for a beer, too?

She looked up at the dry chimney again and, unable to help herself, called out, "Hellooo in there . . ."

Her voice ricocheted off the walls and curled up into the darkness, echoing back in a way that sounded empty and hollow and lost. Did she really want a dry, empty chimney and plain white bedroom walls indefinitely? Did she really want to put off that kind of restoration for what could be months when she had someone who could restore it right now? Especially after everything had already been neglected for so long? It seemed unfair—unnatural even—that her mother's bedroom was finished and full when Eugenie's was so barren.

No, not quite barren, she reminded herself. One wall, after all, was aflame with Fevered Passion. And the floorboards had been oiled and massaged with gentle strokes.

She looked at Nash again. He was still gazing at her the same way he had been all afternoon, giving her absolutely no clue behind his own intentions. But that was okay. Hers were becoming a little clearer.

"So, what time Saturday?" she asked him.

Ten

Spalding was right about DreamMakers, Eugenie discovered the next day as she pulled to a halt in their parking lot. Even before entering the building, she could tell they were the antithesis of HeartMenders. Whereas HeartMenders was a single suite of rooms in one of Louisville's oldest and most charming buildings located in the heart of downtown, DreamMakers was encased within a glass-and-steel cube structure situated on the periphery of the far east end in a patch of newly spawned businesses. And whereas HeartMenders advertised itself as "specialists in finding that perfect someone," DreamMakers' slogan, flashing in the front window beneath its neon logo, promised they were "experts in locating that ideal someone."

Clever use of the thesaurus, that. Especially since "ideal" could be interpreted two different ways. Yes, an ideal someone could be a perfect match for the client. But an ideal someone could also simply be a compilation of traits that the client found most desirable in a mate. The problem with that second interpretation was that what seemed most desirable didn't always end up being a perfect match. Lawrence had seemed perfect for her once upon a time. They had shared the same values, interests, and loves; the same hopes, plans, and dreams. Before marrying, they had made sure they were on the same page about *every*thing, right down to planning the perfect family—when to start, when to stop, where to live once their twosome became a threesome, where to send that third person to school and what to involve him in after school was out for the day.

They'd planned their ideal family and ideal life together ideally. And all of it had gone to the innermost circle of hell.

As if to illustrate that realization, when Eugenie tugged open the glass-and-steel door to DreamMakers, a blast of air swept over her that was cold enough to raise goosebumps. Amping up the chill was the synthesizer-infused *thumpa-thumpa-thumpa* of club music and a woman's auto-tuned voice welcoming Eugenie to the after par-tay. Coolest of all—if you were the kind of person who liked synthesizers and auto-tuning, at least—was the decor.

Just as HeartMenders' furnishings were in keeping with the old-fashioned feel of its practices, DreamMakers' were as newfangled as its exterior. Everything was either blue or white or both, from the sapphire carpet to the blanched walls and chairs to the two cobalt-uniformed blondes behind the counter. Eugenie found herself surrounded by oversized and equally colorless photographs of aberrantly beautiful people, though whether they were actual clients or part of the dream, she couldn't have said.

She had been prepared for the aberrant beauty part, since any dream made here would, it went without saying, include perfect looks. Understandably worried about being turned down for membership owing to her own not-particularly aberrant beauty, she had snuck into her mother's bathroom and borrowed as many cosmetics as she could identify, then had pulled into a church parking lot two miles from Fleurissant before applying them. To further her tarty image, she had donned a snug red T-shirt, made snugger by a push-up bra she had purchased specifically for the occasion (but which she probably wouldn't include on the itemized expense list she would eventually hand over to Spalding).

Although Spalding had told her there was no reason for her to lie about anything on her application except for the name of her employer (for obvious reasons), Eugenie had decided to enhance more than just her cheekbones and bustline to maximize her potential to become someone's ideal herself. In fact, she had spent the entire drive across town rehearsing her DreamMaker persona. She would be the proprietor of a pastry business she ran out of her home, which supplied high-end confections to local restaurants and caterers. She would also be world-traveled and enjoy a variety of adventures, from photography safaris in Kenya to bungee jumping over Angel Falls in Venezuela. She had decided to be child-free, too, so now Seth was her nephew, not her son. Also, she was only thirty-seven. And she had never been married.

Wow, look at that. She hadn't even signed on with DreamMakers yet, and they were already responsible for a damned nice dream.

She strode to the counter, taking care not to twist her ankle in the only pair of high heels she owned—"high" being a relative term, since she normally always wore flats, but, hey, two extra inches was two extra inches, and they complimented the skinny jeans that were admittedly less skinny than they would have been when Eugenie really was thirty-seven. Then she pushed her sunglasses to the top of her head and struck a pose she was reasonably certain she had seen one of the Victoria's Secret models strike in a recent catalog.

"May I help you?" asked Blonde Number One, whose name tag read BARBI. No, really. It actually said "Barbi." With an *i*. It *did*. Too bad name tag makers didn't have a printing option that would allow its *i* to be dotted with a heart, otherwise the picture would have been perfect.

"Yes, you may," Eugenie told her. "I called yesterday. I have a ten o'clock appointment? I'd like for DreamMakers to locate that ideal someone for me."

Barbi-who-would-definitely-dot-her-*i*-with-a-heart smiled, revealing a dimple that may or may not have been put there surgically. After consulting a clipboard behind the counter, she said, "You must be . . . Is it Eu-jean-ie Dashner?"

"Eu-jane-ie," said Blonde Number Two, whose name tag identified her as Helen.

It was a name with which Eugenie couldn't find a single fault, because it sounded straightforward, efficient, and in no way blond. Not that Eugenie was in any position to put down blondes, seeing as she was one herself. She'd just never much felt like a blonde. And no one had ever mistaken her for being a blonde. Which, now that she thought about it, might go a long way toward explaining why she was trying to put down Barbi and Helen now when, probably, both of them were perfectly nice women, even if they did work for the enemy.

"Yes, Eu-jane-ie," Eugenie said. "Dashner. But call me Janey."

The name popped out of her mouth without her even intending to say it. She had no idea why. Although she had thought about giving herself a fictional name to go with her fictional persona, she'd figured she would, at some point, have to produce ID. But she could be Jáney here. Janey fit well the woman she wanted to be for DreamMakers.

"Pretty name," Helen said. "That's French, isn't it?"

"Yes. It is. Though I'm not French myself. Wishful thinking on my mother's part, I'm afraid."

She didn't add that had the rest of Lorraine's wishes come true, she wouldn't be standing here right now, because she would be a former Miss America who was now married to a professional baseball player and hosted a popular morning talk show with guests who were movie stars, celebrity doctors, pet psychics, and mob accountants. But that was neither here nor there.

"If you want to come with me," Helen said, "there's some paperwork and a brief questionnaire for you to fill out, and we'll need to snap a photo. Once that's done, we'll be able to cross-check your vitals with our other clients and find you a whole list of ideal someones to get you started."

Eugenie decided not to point out the incongruity of there being a whole list of ideal someones, when, technically, there could only be one *ideal* someone for her. There could be lots of *potential* someones or *promising* someones or *possible* someones. But if someone was *ideal* for her, then, really, there was no reason for there to be a list of others. Spalding never gave his clients lists of someones. He found one someone. And if that someone wasn't the perfect someone, then he went back to the drawing board and tried again.

Nevertheless, "That would be wonderful," Eugenie said.

She followed Helen to a row of glass-enclosed cubicles that offered absolutely no privacy for the people who were in them filling out paperwork and brief questionnaires with other DreamMakers' employees who were dressed like Barbi and Helen. Eugenie did her best not to stare, but her inner voyeur got the best of her. There were only three other people besides herself applying with DreamMakers today, all of them younger than she, all physically attractive, all looking quite successful in both work and life.

She wondered about that for a second. Why would young, physically attractive, successful people need to use a dating service to meet other eligible singles? Not that all of HeartMenders' clients were ugly. They just looked more . . . real. More normal. Some were attractive but not like this. The people signing on with DreamMakers looked like dreams themselves. They were definitely the kind of people who would get noticed in any social setting. Yet here they were, paying a membership fee to find an ideal someone.

"Right through here," Helen said, leading Eugenie into a glass cubicle at the end of the row.

As had been the case elsewhere in the building, there were few decorations in here other than more photographs of impossibly beautiful people. Though here, the color scheme was reversed—a white tile floor bled into blue walls. Helen positioned her against one of those where there were no pictures hanging and snapped a few photos with a digital camera. Then she seated herself behind a spare white desk and opened the MacBook sitting atop it to upload them. After letting Eugenie choose the one she liked best—not that Eugenie liked any of them at all, because none looked like what she normally looked like—Helen tapped a few keys to bring up a new screen.

She turned to Eugenie. "Now then, Janey, I need for you to place your right hand on the desk, palm down, fingers together."

Certain she must have misheard—not that there were a lot of ways to mishear something like that—Eugenie said, "I beg your pardon?"

Helen smiled. "I need to do a digit ratio analysis."

Okay, Eugenie may have been out of the dating world for a while, but she was reasonably certain it hadn't evolved to a point where it had a whole new language.

She eyed Helen curiously. "I don't understand."

Helen's smile didn't alter so much as a millimeter. "I'll show you. Put your right hand on the desk like this."

She placed her own in the position she had first described, and Eugenie mimicked it. Then she pulled a small white tape measure out of her pocket and measured the length first of Eugenie's index finger, then of her ring finger.

"Identical," she said as she wound up the tape and returned it to her pocket. Then she typed the information into the computer.

"What does finger length have to do with anything?" Eugenie asked.

Helen opened a drawer behind the desk and began to pull forms out of it as she spoke. "There have been studies to show that the length of a person's fingers and their ratio to each other—ring and index, anyway—are good indicators of exposure to hormones in the womb. Men tend to have ring fingers longer than their index fingers and women tend to have those fingers the same length, or the index finger slightly longer than the ring. Testosterone versus estrogen. That kind of thing."

Which was sort of interesting, but Eugenie still didn't see how it might lend itself to adventures in dating.

Her expression must have reflected her confusion, because Helen elucidated some. "It's been suggested that digit ratio is a good indicator of masculine and feminine traits in an individual. So if a man came in whose ring and index fingers were the same length, he would have had less testosterone exposure in the womb and therefore exhibit more feminine qualities than a typical male.

And a woman whose ring finger was longer than her index finger would exhibit more masculine qualities than a typical female."

"So you end up with a guy who likes musicals and a woman who likes tractor pulls."

Helen's smile faltered not at all. "In a way. And we wouldn't want to match those two up, would we?"

Well, not unless the guy who liked musicals was looking for a woman who liked tractor pulls or vice versa. Which—call Eugenie crazy—seems like something that would be made clear on the questionnaire: *Would you object to dating a man who likes musicals or a woman who likes tractor pulls?* But maybe they just wanted to keep the questionnaire to a single page.

"Anyway, you appear to be a typical female, so I'm guessing you're not a big fan of tractor pulls, are you?"

"I've never been to one, actually. I don't know if I'm a fan or not."

Helen continued to smile her unwavering smile. "According to your fingers, you're not."

Well, she wouldn't want to call her fingers liars, would she?

"Here's the application," Helen said, turning a sheet of paper toward Eugenie. "We'll just need all the usual stuff—name, address, birth date, marital status, et cetera." She laid another sheet atop it. "And this is a brief questionnaire about you."

Before Eugenie had a chance to look at either, Helen ran through all the payment plans DreamMakers offered, then asked which credit card Eugenie would be using today and if she'd like to go ahead and give it to Helen, then Helen would give her a few moments to fill out all the paperwork, and then they could move ahead with that ideal someone thing.

After surrendering her Visa, Eugenie picked up the questionnaire first, thinking it would be the more challenging and therefore time-consuming of the two documents to fill out. At HeartMenders, the client questionnaire was like a sacred text that held all the answers to the mysteries of the universe. Spalding spent days poring over each one, using great care to filter and match each client's personality, morality, and propensity. But he also looked at places where differences of opinion between two people might actually make for conversation that was more lively than it was divisive. Yes, he looked for similarities when considering who to match with whom. But he also looked for complementary differences.

DreamMakers' questions started off being almost identical to HeartMenders, taking into account lifestyle habits like smoking, drinking, and socializing. But where HeartMenders left blanks after each one so that the client could describe his or her habits with whatever words they chose—*Lips that touch liquor will never touch mine,* say, or *A day without nicotine is like a day without sunshine*—DreamMakers' questions were all multiple choice. *I drink (a) never, (b) occasionally, (c) socially, (d) on weekends, (e) like a fish.* Except that *like a fish* was actually *daily,* giving it none of the whimsy a daily drinker probably would have preferred to give it so it wouldn't make him or her sound like a daily drinker.

Down the list she went, ticking off the proper letter for each of her replies even though, for many of them, none of the answers was exactly right. The smoking one was easy—lips that touched cigarettes would never touch hers, so that would be *(a) never*—but the religious affiliation one didn't offer *Emersonian Transcendentalist* as a choice so Eugenie had to go with *(e) unaffiliated.* Toward the middle, where HeartMenders generally started getting into things like hobbies and interests, DreamMakers asked about birth order and energy levels. Then there was a series of visual tests. Could Eugenie tell which of these four people were smiling real smiles and which were smiling fake smiles? Which of the lines in the plus sign was longer, the horizontal one or the vertical one? Which of these doodles looked the most like her own doodles?

But how was she supposed to know whose smile was real and whose was fake when she'd never met any of the people before and had no idea how they operated? What difference did it make which side of the plus sign was longer? How could any of those doodles look like hers when she never doodled anything? This questionnaire sucked.

At the bottom of the page, there were a handful of questions about spontaneity, adventurousness, and risk taking, none of which went any deeper than *(a) never* to *(e) all the time,* even though Eugenie would have liked some kind of clarification as to just how spontaneous, adventurous, and risky they were talking. She could be all those things if they were talking about skydiving. Not so much if they were talking about dog collars and riding crops.

She turned the page over, expecting to find more questions on the other side, but it was blank. When DreamMakers said brief questionnaire, they really meant brief questionnaire. Where was the part about her expectations in a relationship? About whether she was looking for marriage or just a fun weekend? About whether she intended to stay child-free, was willing to adopt, or wanted to eventually star in a reality show called *Janey Plus Eighty*? Where were the questions about sex, for God's sake?

HeartMenders asked about all those things and more. They asked about how a client envisioned decision making and the division of household chores in a relationship. They asked about a client's friends and how they liked to spend both a Saturday night and a Sunday afternoon. They asked about the sharing of personal matters, personal wealth, and personal space. Hell, they even asked if the glass was half empty or half full. Evidently DreamMakers was confident they could find Eugenie an ideal someone without knowing any of those things about her *or* a potential match. As long as they had her Visa number, everything was A-okay.

As if conjured by the thought, Helen returned and placed the credit card on the desk in front of Eugenie, then returned to her seat. "Did you have enough time to fill everything out, Janey?"

"Only the questionnaire," Eugenie said. "I haven't gotten to the application yet."

Helen looked surprised. "Were there questions you didn't understand?"

"No. I just needed to think about some of them before answering, because I wasn't entirely comfortable with any of the choices."

"Well, as long as you chose the one closest to your true feelings, it should be fine."

Which, actually, was the problem. Virtually none of the questions had involved her feelings.

Obviously not bothered a bit by the fact that Eugenie was a bit bothered, Helen said, "If you're done with the questionnaire, Janey, I can input the information while you fill out the application."

Translation: *Move along, Janey.*

Helen finished her task only a moment after Eugenie finished the application, and literally with the push of a button, her vital statistics were intermingled with all the others in DreamMakers' database.

She asked, "How long will it take before I hear something on—"

A chime pinged from the computer that sounded like an eruption from Tinkerbell's wand, and Helen said, "Here's the first batch now."

So then Buddy Holly was wrong. True love doesn't wait at all. Not at DreamMakers, anyway.

"Lucky you," Helen said further as she pivoted the laptop so Eugenie could see the screen. "The computer's capabilities don't allow for more than ten matches at a time, but we seldom have that many for a client the first time out. Yet here are ten right off the bat who should be ideal for you."

Ten? Eugenie wanted to ask. She'd spent twenty years of her life with Lawrence when there were at least ten men in this city alone who were ideal for her?

Then she reminded herself of how vague the questionnaire had been and how the computer knew almost nothing important about her. She probably could have found ten ideal matches inputting the same information into the database of eligible adoptions from the Louisville Humane Society.

"What kind of criteria does the computer use to make the matches?" she asked.

Helen's never-say-die smile persevered yet again. "We use your responses to the questionnaire."

"No, I meant how does the computer rate the responses? Were they asked in order of importance? Like does the computer put more importance on my nonsmoking, social-drinking habits than it does my birth order or my doodles?"

"I'm not sure I understand."

Eugenie wasn't sure she understood why Helen didn't understand. "Then do all the responses carry equal weight? Did my matches reply on their questionnaires the same way I replied on mine?"

"I—"

Eugenie could tell by the look in Helen's eyes that her thoughts were currently in a place not yet occupied by her smile, and that place was the land of confusion.

"I don't know," she finally said. "We input your responses and the computer does the rest."

"So my romantic future is in the hands of a computer?" Eugenie asked. "Which, when you get right down to it, doesn't actually have hands?"

"It's state-of-the-art and cutting-edge," Helen assured her. "DreamMakers has matchmaking down to a science. Our success rate speaks for itself. We're not the number one dating service in Louisville for nothing."

No, Eugenie supposed not. Still, it would be nice if the number one dating service in Louisville could say why they *were* number one.

"Now, let's have a look at your matches," Helen said, quickly shifting gears. "This one's cute. His name is Thomas. He's self-employed, like you, and is a youngest child, like you."

Both of which were at the very bottom of Eugenie's "What I Look for in a Potential Mate" list. Why on earth was this place so popular?

"He's forty-four and lives in the east end."

Which told her nothing of significance.

"Judging by your responses, a good dating scenario for the two of you would be dinner at J. Gumbo's, followed by a show at the Improv, then drinks at Red Star Tavern."

All located at Fourth Street Live!, the entertainment complex next to HeartMenders where Spalding never sent dates because it was such an obvious and generic choice. Imagine that. How had the computer arrived at that destination? Eugenie had said nothing about liking stand-up comedy or Cajun food or enjoying a drink after hours. In a word, *Hmm.*

"When would you like for us to set something up? Is this week too soon?"

Definitely, Eugenie thought. "Of course not," she told Helen. "I have an engagement Saturday night, but any other time this week would be fine."

Inescapably, she then thought, *Let the dating games begin.*

Eleven

It was with more than a little relief that Eugenie opened her back door to Marianne and Abby on Tuesday, shortly after arriving home from work. It was with even more relief that she saw the pitcher of martinis in Marianne's hand. Eugenie sent Abby up to collect the girls so the three friends could grab some time in the inflatable ring pool Julien had set up near the patio, in hopes of both stimulating their appetite for dinner and hastening their desire to go to bed not long thereafter. Then she went back into the kitchen long enough to grab a couple of coffee mugs out of the dish drainer for the martinis, since she still hadn't located the box containing the barware.

She tried to reassure herself that she and Marianne didn't *always* meet over something alcoholic. In fact, several times, they had met over coffee. It was just that, somehow, Marianne always seemed to know when coffee wasn't enough. Or maybe, at their age, life just consisted of two kinds of moments: coffee moments and cocktail moments. If it wasn't one, it must be the other, and something about gentle summer evenings like this one simply demanded the latter instead of the former. June was the kindest of the summer months in the Ohio Valley, its skies infinite blue smeared with gauzy clouds, its breezes amiable and unhurried. July would sully the city with brown hazes and stifling heat, and August would smother with soggy humidity. By the end of summer, everyone in Louisville would be weary and cross. But in lighthearted June, with school just finished and months of potential ahead, children were joyful and parents unruffled, and everyone found it much easier to breathe. That had to be a cause for celebration.

"Still haven't found the box with the cocktail glasses?" Marianne asked when she saw the mugs.

"I'm still not sure I even got the cocktail glasses in the divorce," Eugenie told her. "I'm beginning to think Lawrence got all the best stuff. Including an especially lovely beaded black tank top that I was planning to wear Saturday night for my . . . On my . . . When I . . ." She finally halted when she realized she still didn't know what to call her thing with Nash.

"When you go out with Nash pretending you're only doing it because it sounds like it might be fun when, in fact, you're doing it because there's an *ex*cellent chance you'll get laid?" Marianne supplied oh so helpfully.

"Um, yeah, for that," Eugenie said.

"I'd loan you something of mine, but I gave up tank tops thirty pounds ago."

Since she and Marianne had begun their regular visits, Eugenie had put some meager effort into making the patio outside a more comfortable place to gather. The tiles were still chipped and fractured, but she'd yanked out the weeds that had flourished between the cracks and swept and power-washed away as much of the grime as she could. She'd found some old cast-iron furniture abandoned in the garage from which she'd sanded away the rust and applied a new coat of black enamel, and she'd situated them close enough to one of the less crumbled walls to make a small sitting area with a surface for drinks—be they coffee or cocktails. She'd planted pots of peonies, pansies, and petunias and scattered them about for color, and she'd trimmed off the lowest-lying branches from the nearest trees. The patio still had a long way to go before it would be back at its best, but at least it seemed hopeful and happy now, instead of discarded and dreary.

As the trio of girls screeched past them toward the pool, Eugenie and Marianne made their way to the chairs as they had on previous evenings. Eugenie placed the mugs on the wall and, after stirring the pitcher a few times, Marianne filled both to the brim with the martinis, reaching back into the pitcher with her fingers to fish out a couple of olives to drop into each.

"I washed my hands," she stated almost credibly as she completed the gesture. "But even if I hadn't, the alcohol will take care of any germs."

"That's not all it will take care of," Eugenie told her.

"Good point," Marianne agreed. "But then, we were talking about you having sex with Nash."

Eugenie flinched at her friend's candor. Certainly it was no secret between the two women how Eugenie had felt about Nash since they were kids. It was likewise no secret that Nash's sexual appetite was notorious and that he had set the gold standard for man 'ho before the concept had even been invented.

Marianne sipped her drink, savored it for a moment, then swallowed and said, "I'm still marveling at the fact that when he asked you out, you didn't scream and crawl under the bed."

"I'm still marveling at the fact that he asked me out," Eugenie replied.

"Oh, stop," Marianne said. "Why wouldn't he ask you out? You have a vagina."

"Don't flatter me."

"Just sayin'."

"Yeah, but I've had a vagina all my life, and he never asked me out before."

Marianne stirred her drink with her finger. "That's because when he met you, your vagina was way too young to date. Then it was because your vagina had braces and pimples. Then it was because your vagina was attached to someone else—often literally. But now your vagina is open for business, and since Nash is such a conspicuous consumer, it makes sense that he would want to shop in yours."

Eugenie couldn't help laughing at that. "How have I made it all these years without you around to put everything into perspective for me?"

Marianne enjoyed another taste of her drink, then stretched her legs out comfortably in front of herself, crossing her ankles and wiggling her bare toes. Her extra pounds suited her. When they were kids, she'd been a stick-thin collection of planes and angles and jutting-out body parts. Now she was all curves and hills and orbits, something that made the blunt words she spoke come out less pointed.

"I just wonder about your motives," she said, the words tinted with concern. "If you just want to get laid, I'm all for that. But even having been separated from you for a few decades, Eugenie, I know you. Getting laid has never been for you what it is for someone like, oh . . . I don't know. Nash, for instance."

"Maybe a few decades ago, that was true," Eugenie agreed. "But the passage of that much time changes things. Changes people. A lot."

"It does change a lot," Marianne concurred. "But it doesn't change what has been there at the core all along. Just look at this house," she added, sweeping a hand upward at the towering edifice beside them. "Look how crappy it looks on the outside, how much it's changed since it was first built. Hell, even just since we were kids. It was gorgeous then."

"It looks crappy on the inside, too," Eugenie reminded her unnecessarily.

"Yeah, but it's starting to get its old mojo back in there, thanks to you guys. Julien said its foundation is sound and its bones are good, the way they've always been. Plus, the place has a lot of its original character and charm. Not even ten decades could strip that away. Essentially, it's still the house it always was. It's just succumbed to exterior forces that have left it *looking* like it's changed. But it hasn't changed. Not really."

"Thirteen decades," Eugenie corrected. Mostly because she didn't want to consider any of the other stuff Marianne had said. "The place was built in the eighteen eighties."

"Which makes it even more awesome that in all the places where you can't see it—but where it counts—it's still the place it always was. And which makes my point even more applicable. What happens after Saturday night? You and Nash have sex, and then you have to see him every day around here. Can you be okay with that? 'Cause he sure as hell will be. In fact, he'll be assuming you're available anytime he wants it."

Eugenie's back literally went up at that. "Who says I won't want it anytime, too?"

Marianne smiled. "Of course you'll want it anytime. But what you'll want and what Nash wants won't necessarily be the same thing."

"Sex is sex," Eugenie said.

"Nuh-uh," Marianne corrected. "Sex is sex for men. Sex is something different for women."

Eugenie couldn't exactly disagree. She just wished she could define what sex was for her. What it had ever been for her. When she was an adolescent and the time had come to have the Talk with her mother, Lorraine had been in no way informative. Most of what Eugenie learned about sex in those early years came from Marianne. And although she was sure Mrs. Weatherly had been extremely forthcoming with information where her two daughters were concerned, that information had been filtered through the brain of twelve-year-old Marianne by the time it reached Eugenie. ("When you get your period," Marianne once told a room full of prepubescent friends at a slumber party, "it's like peeing, only blood comes out instead." Leaving Eugenie and the others to wonder just how long they would have to sit on the toilet before their period was over and how it could potentially affect their grades if they had to miss classes because they were in the bathroom for their monthly bloodletting.) And although when Eugenie was a teenager, she had dates for all the major school events, they'd always been with boys who were more friends than objects of desire. She hadn't had a serious boyfriend until Lawrence.

Which was another reason Saturday night's whatever-the-hell-it-was-with-Nash weighed so heavily in her brain—not to mention other body parts. Eugenie hadn't had a sexual partner other than Lawrence. The closest she'd come was during a game of Seven Minutes in Heaven at Leslie Burke's sweet sixteen party, and that had mostly been groping for things neither participant had ever held before, so they hadn't even looked in the right places to begin with.

Therefore it was understandable why Eugenie would have some misgivings about Saturday night. She was pretty sure that anything that happened with Nash would last more than seven minutes. And she was extremely sure he knew exactly where to find what he was looking for. She just hoped she could remember where to look for things, too.

This was all provided, of course, that she and Nash both had more than beer on their minds. Even if Nash didn't, once Eugenie gave off any signal to indicate she *was* thinking about something other than dinner, Nash would be all over it. All over her. All over her . . . whatever.

Marianne suddenly snapped forward in her chair, staring hard at Eugenie. "I just thought of something. Please tell me you've dated since the divorce was final."

Since Eugenie couldn't do that, she said nothing.

"Before the divorce was final?"

Now Eugenie glared.

Marianne's expression grew more panicked. "Then please tell me that, in an effort to stick it to Lawrence, you had a quickie fling with one of his friends or co-workers."

Eugenie remained silent.

Marianne's agitation doubled. "Then please tell me there was one night when you were so horny you went to the nearest bar and deliberately had too much to drink, then went home with a stranger and did something outrageously, if later regrettably, sexual in nature."

Eugenie maintained her silence.

Since Eugenie was so unwilling to comment, Marianne took it upon herself to state the obvious. "Oh. Shit."

A commentary with which Eugenie could do nothing but agree. So she looked away from her friend, pretending it was to check the girls to make sure none of them was floating facedown in the pool in spite of them all being able to swim like fish. None of them was. On the contrary, the scene that greeted her was the definition of serenity. The girls bobbed in the water like dragonflies, their voices melding into an easy purr against the susurrant breeze. A redbud tree beyond the patio wall had exploded some weeks earlier in rampant fuchsia and coral. Closer to Eugenie and Marianne, a determined dogwood still clutched a few of its snowy blooms, surrendering an occasional petal when the breeze became too playful.

On its lowest branch sat a scarlet cardinal, the male half of the couple that was nesting in the lilac bush. Eugenie had watched them often from the kitchen window while she prepared dinner, the plain brown female growing plumper as spring wore on until finally laying the eggs upon which she now sat. The male spent the better part of his day flying back and forth, bringing her food or filling in the nest or singing her a song to help pass the time.

"Did you know cardinals are monogamous and that they mate for life?" she asked Marianne.

The change of subject didn't seem to faze Marianne. In fact, her gaze went straight to the cardinal sitting in the dogwood tree, so she must have seen him, too. "No," she said.

"I read that somewhere," Eugenie told her. "Only after one of them dies will the other look for a new mate."

"Interesting," Marianne said. Though she didn't sound as interested as Eugenie was.

"I've been watching that little guy and his missus since we moved in. They have a nest in the lilac bush. They're really sweet together. He takes such good care of her."

"Mm."

"She built the nest, but he kept watch for predators while she did it. She's sitting on the eggs, but he brings her food. After the eggs hatch, they'll both feed the babies—I read that, too. It's a pretty equitable relationship, you know? People could learn a lot from cardinals."

She looked at Marianne to find her friend eyeing her with something akin to worry. "Need a refill?" she asked, holding up the pitcher.

Eugenie shook her head and leaned back in her chair. As she stretched out her bare legs before her on the cool terra-cotta tiles, she cataloged every impression to recollect and replay later. It was one of those odd, extraordinary moments where every sensation—every sight, every smell, every sound—seemed interwoven into the perfect pattern of a life well spent. She both loved and hated such moments, because as soon as she recognized them for what they were, they were always snatched away, and she was left feeling as if she'd stolen a glimpse of something she was never meant to see—a glimmer of how life could be if everything worked the way it was supposed to.

Then she noticed how the fabric of her T-shirt snagged on the back of the chair behind her. She felt a crack in the tile beneath her bare foot, heard the screech of an angry blue jay, possibly the meanest bird in Mother Nature's oeuvre. She remembered how Seth had left on his bike that morning without telling her where he was going or when he would return, without even saying good-bye, and how he hadn't yet returned. She sipped her martini, relishing the cool liquid as it warmed her throat and belly. Then she tipped her head back to enjoy what was left of the tepid sunlight and closed her eyes.

When had her son become such a stranger? When had she stopped knowing all the important things a mother knew instinctively about her child? When he was a baby, she had known Seth would go to sleep fastest if she sang "It Had to Be You." On his first day of preschool, she had known to tuck the book *Here Comes Tommy Tow Truck* into his backpack, to provide some measure of familiarity and comfort. As a kindergartner, she had known he wouldn't eat the grapes in his lunch unless they were purple and there were exactly ten. In middle school, she had known his favorite band was Rise Against, that he'd secretly loved the movie *Titanic,* and that he would never, ever, wear clothes from any of the trendy stores most teenagers frequented. Now . . .

Now his ever-present earbuds silenced from her everything that went into his brain. Even before she and Lawrence split, he had begun to pull away. She'd told herself it was his age. His gender. His prerogative. It was healthy for adolescent boys to separate from their mothers. Seth was supposed to change when he became a teenager. He was supposed to have a life separate from his parents. He was supposed to have secrets.

She just hadn't thought he would be so secretive about it.

She looked at the little girls in the pool again, laughing and squealing and dousing each other. She wondered if girls were easier to raise than boys. Did daughters share things with their mothers that sons didn't? Did they talk more? Understand better? Were they friends?

"So, how is it with four kids?" she asked Marianne, deliberately steering the conversation—and her thoughts—away from the men in her life.

"Busy," Marianne replied, evidently not minding the change of topic. At least for now. Eugenie knew her friend would return to it before the night was through. "They attend three different schools, and none of them has the same after-school interests. Dale and I limit them to two extracurriculars each, so D.J. has football and guitar, Eddie runs track and is involved in this fantasy card game league, Claire has basketball and art classes, and Abby plays piano and takes riding lessons."

"Wow. You must be running all the time."

Marianne turned to watch the little girls, too, sounding mellow when she replied. "It's not as bad as it sounds. None of the sports overlap much from one season to the next, and the guitar and piano classes run simultaneously at Mom's Music, which is a stone's throw from the Water Tower, where the art class meets. The store where Eddie plays his games is close enough to the gym where Claire plays basketball, so I can drop them off and then run errands before going back to get them. The riding lessons are the biggest pain in the ass because they're way out in Crestwood, but I can usually fill the time with grocery shopping." She smiled at Eugenie. "Besides, I really love driving around Republican white-bread Oldham County with the sunroof open while I blast my hard-core hip-hop tunes. It's just so wonderfully"—she sighed with relish—"satisfying."

Eugenie chuckled at that. "You've come a long way. I remember when you bought your first album. It was Barry Manilow. And your first forty-five was the Archies' 'Sugar Sugar.'"

Marianne feigned affront. "Whatsamatta, sucka? You can't see me rollin' with my mothafuckin' homies?"

Eugenie laughed. "No."

Marianne grinned. "Well, I never actually said I *like* hard-core hip-hop. I said I like to play it when I'm driving around Republican white-bread Oldham County with the sunroof open." She suddenly jackknifed forward and pinned Eugenie with her gaze. "But I don't like Barry Manilow or the Archies anymore," she stated emphatically. "I'm still as cool as I was when I was a teenager. I *am*. I even have a Green Day sticker on my car."

"You drive a minivan."

"I even have a Green Day sticker on my minivan."

Eugenie eyed her with interest. "Why am I suddenly reminded of a certain Don Henley lyric?"

"No clue," Marianne assured her. "A Green Day sticker on a Caravan is way different from a Dead Head sticker on a Cadillac."

"But is a little voice inside your head saying, 'Don't look back, you can never look back?' "

"Hell no. I look back all the time. There's some great stuff back there."

"So, then, you disagree with Don that those days are gone forever and we should just let them go?"

Marianne sat forward, tucking her legs under her chair, enjoying another sip of her coffee-mugged martini. "No. I know those days are gone forever. But what happened in those days shaped what happens today. Those days made me what I am now. Why would I want to forget them?"

"Spoken like a woman who has no regrets."

"Nah. Spoken like a woman who knows regrets are a part of life."

Eugenie dipped her head reverently toward her friend. "O, mother of four, you are very wise in the ways of the world."

Marianne shook her head. "Only in my little corner of it. Just call me the Queen of Sparrow Way."

"Okay, Your Majesty. Then tell me this. Where's my kid at this very moment?"

Marianne turned to look at her, her expression puzzled. "You don't know where Seth is?"

Eugenie shook her head. "He takes off in the morning and doesn't come home sometimes until dark."

Marianne's expression cleared. "He's sixteen. He could be anywhere. Does he have his driver's license yet?"

"No. He's a cycling nut. He hasn't shown the slightest interest in learning how to drive."

"Could he be waiting for his father to take an interest in teaching him?"

Eugenie hadn't thought of that. "I suppose he could. But he'll have a long wait. Lawrence and Ethel Merman are still enthralled by the early stages of their November–December romance."

"Meaning," Marianne said, "it could be hours, maybe even a whole day, before he's no longer able to get it up and keep Ethel satisfied."

"Exactly."

"Does he take any interest in Seth at all?"

Eugenie shook her head. "He hasn't called once since we moved down here. It's always Seth who calls him. And Lawrence always finds some reason to hang up after ten minutes."

"They could be e-mailing," Marianne said. "Or texting."

"Not texting. Lawrence hates it. And the e-mail is doubtful. Lawrence has never used it for anything but business."

"It's got to be tough on a boy that age, losing his father. Especially when his father is still around and has voluntarily removed himself from the boy's life. Seth has to be pissed off about that."

"He won't admit it," Eugenie said. "Whenever I've tried to explain to him about his father and me and remind him that the divorce had nothing to do with him, he just blows me off."

"That's because trying to explain something like that to a kid is pointless," Marianne told her.

"But that's what all the books say to do," Eugenie said. "Talk to your kids about the divorce. Reassure them that it wasn't their fault."

"The books always tell us to talk," Marianne said. "Talk to your kids about sex. Talk to your kids about drugs. Talk to your kids about drinking. Talk to your kids about STDs and HIV. We should always talk talk talk talk talk talk talk. That's like the stupidest parenting advice in the world."

"And what do you suggest, oh great and powerful Oz?"

Marianne stubbed the toe of her sandal against a cracked tile, fracturing the terra-cotta clay even more. "I know it's a radical idea, but what's worked for Dale and me is listening to our kids instead of talking to them."

"I'd listen, but Seth never talks," Eugenie said. "That's why I have to talk to him."

"They talk a lot if they're in the right surroundings and have the right medium to do it. And if they're given the time. They say even more when they're not talking. You just have to listen."

"I don't understand."

Marianne enjoyed a thoughtful sip of her martini, then said, "Seth must be into gaming, right?"

"Oh, yeah. Next to his bike, it's his greatest passion."

"Do you ever play with him?"

"What? Me? No. I hate those things. I'm terrible at them."

"Yeah, I was, too, when I first started playing," Marianne told her. "But now I'm made of awesome at Call of Duty: Black Ops. And I'm merciless when it comes to pwning n00bs on Xbox Live."

Eugenie stared at her friend as if she were speaking a foreign language. Which, of course, she was.

Marianne smiled again. "All your base are belong to us, babe."

Eugenie frowned. "I have no idea what you're talking about."

"Yeah, I know. But Seth would. And so would you, if you spent a little time taking an interest in what he does. The best communicating D.J. and I have ever achieved has been when we're gaming. Or afterward. It's amazing what kind of conversations can come out of a recap of an especially brutal battle campaign."

"But Seth always acts like I'm an idiot when I ask him about the music he's listening to or what movies he likes or what games he's playing. He acts like I'm not supposed to be a part of any of that stuff."

"Of course he does," Marianne said. "But if you educate yourself about the things he loves and then ask him questions that prove you know what you're talking about, it will first leave him flummoxed but then, eventually, willing to open up a little. And once that facade cracks, it doesn't take long to get to what's inside and start working on it."

"But—"

"Look, Eugenie," Marianne interrupted before she had a chance to object again, "just try to take some interest in the things that are important to Seth, even if you find them mind-numbingly boring or brain-scrambling confusing. When I'm playing Xbox with D.J. and Eddie, when I talk WNBA stats with Claire or horse breeds with Abby, they know I'm listening to them. They know I'm interested in the same things they are, even if I'm really not all that interested in the same things they are. And they start to talk to me. I'm not Ozzie Nelson, pipe in hand, standing in their doorway spewing TV pith. I'm letting them tell me what's going on."

"But that's like a having a second full-time job," Eugenie said.

"News flash, Eugenie. Parenting should be your *first* full-time job."

"But what about, you know, me time?"

Marianne laughed outright at that. "Oh, *me* time. Right. That's another one of those things some consumer-driven think tank came up with, probably during the Reagan era, to make us spend even more money on frivolity than we already do. They're all laughing their asses off at how easily manipulated we are."

"But our parents' generation never took me time," Eugenie

pointed out. "And look how messed up our generation is. Maybe if they'd—"

"Oh, please," Marianne interrupted her again. "Eugenie, our parents were the most selfish fucking generation ever put on this planet. They did as little for their kids as they could. As long as we were fed, clothed, and enrolled in school, they figured they were doing their job, and then they could hit the club or the salon or the golf course or whatever. They opened the door in the morning to boot us out of the house and let us run wild through the neighborhood all day, never knowing, or giving a shit, where we were unless we didn't come home when they told us to. They had nothing *but* me time. *That's* why our generation is a mess."

"Yeah, my parents, for sure, were like that," Eugenie agreed. "But not yours. Your mom was always there for you. She took you and Sharon to all those cool marches on Washington, and you did all that political volunteering with her. You all were always doing stuff together."

"Yeah, stuff Mom wanted us to do. I didn't care if Bella Abzug got elected to Congress. I wanted to go to Camp Piomingo that summer, and Natalie wanted to volunteer at the Humane Society. Instead, we both spent eight weeks up in New York campaigning with my mom and my aunt Marian."

"And my folks sent me and Julien to Camp Piomingo to get us out of their hair so they could go to Florida."

"If people want me time, then they shouldn't get married and have kids."

Eugenie thought about that. Why, really, had she gotten married? Because she loved Lawrence? She had genuinely loved him when they decided to get married, but by the time they married, it wasn't necessary for two people to make it legal just because they were in love. There was no stigma to living together by then.

And legal documents could be drawn up for joint ownership of houses and bank accounts and such. They'd each had health-care benefits from their respective employers, and at the time they were years away from starting a family. So, really, why *had* they married?

Probably, she answered herself, it was because, on some level, they hadn't wanted to be alone. They had each wanted a promise that there would always be someone there for them, someone to give them meaning, someone to validate their importance in the world. They had both wanted some kind of guarantee that neither would end up lonely and living in solitary confinement. Yet marriage hadn't offered any such guarantee. It hadn't offered any kind of validation. In the end, they had been as separated and alone as two strangers.

Eugenie hesitated before admitting, "My mother thinks that my taking too much me time was part of why Lawrence had a wandering eye."

Marianne leaned back in her chair again and stretched her legs, crossing them at the ankles. "This would be the same mother who assigns a woman's worth according to the kind of man she's able to rope into marriage, right?"

"That would be the one."

Marianne nodded. "The same mother who, coincidentally, roped herself a man who, whattaya know, ended up having a wandering eye, despite the fact that she made it her life's work to keep him happy, even to the exclusion of her own children, and who then was never able to rope another man again. Not sure that's the kind of expert I'd want to take advice from myself."

"I know," Eugenie said dispiritedly. "But sometimes I wonder if I had just been a little better at—"

"It wouldn't have changed the outcome," Marianne interrupted again, way more adamantly than before.

"You don't even know what I was about to say."

"It doesn't matter what you were about to say. Nothing you did, and nothing you might have done differently, would have made Lawrence act any other way than he did. His affair with Ethel Merman had *nothing* to do with *you*. Deep down, you do know that, right? It happened because he's a dick who cares more about himself than anyone else in the world, including the woman he promised to put before all others. That's the only reason the affair happened."

Eugenie glanced away, her gaze falling on a rope of dead morning glory that spilled out of a jagged crack in the chimney nearby. "I guess."

With a jarring *scrape-clank, scrape-clank, scrape-clank,* Marianne scooted her chair over until she had moved herself between Eugenie and the chimney, forcing Eugenie to look at her. "No, I don't think you do. I think you believe Lorraine. You blame yourself, at least in part. You think if you'd had sex more often or done more things together or kept the house cleaner, or if the three of you had sat down to more family dinners together every night, then Lawrence wouldn't have had an affair. But the affair had nothing to do with any of that. It had nothing to do with you."

"How do you know?"

Marianne hesitated a moment, then said quietly, "Because Dale and I went through the same thing a few years ago."

Eugenie looked up at that. "Dale cheated?"

Marianne met her gaze levelly, then shook her head. "No. I did."

Before either of the women could say anything more, Abby came running up to her mother, laughing and dripping wet, shaking her hair and loosing a spray of water over both women. She launched herself at Marianne, who caught her soggy daughter in her lap, then buried her face in the girl's neck to make slurpy animal sounds, as if she would devour her right there on the patio.

"Don't!" Abby squealed, laughing. "I have to pee!"

Marianne backed off on the devouring but didn't release her daughter. "We should probably get going, anyway," she said. "It's way past suppertime, and I still have no idea what to fix."

"Pancakes!" Abby immediately suggested.

"You want pancakes?" Marianne asked, only mildly surprised.

Abby nodded.

"Okay. Pancakes it is."

"And applesauce. The blue kind."

Marianne turned to Eugenie. "I love it when dinner takes care of itself this way."

Eugenie tried to grin, but was still a little stunned by Marianne's revelation. "And here I go to all the trouble every night to coordinate a meal that has one lean protein, one green, leafy vegetable, another vegetable in the red-yellow family, and one whole grain starch."

Marianne turned back to Abby. "We can count the applesauce as something red, even if it is blue, but Eugenie says you have to have a protein and something green. So we need to put green food coloring in at least some of the pancakes, and you have to drink milk."

"Chocolate milk," Abby said.

"Okay, chocolate milk," Marianne conceded. "But you have to drink every drop, young lady. I mean it now."

Abby grinned. "'Kay."

She looked at Eugenie again. "See how easy that was? Seriously, stop sweating the small stuff. You've got a cataclysmic disaster of a house to renovate."

Eugenie ignored that last and said, "I bet they're not even going to be whole wheat pancakes."

"Nope," Marianne said. "They'll be straight from a box. And it'll be a store brand, too. On account of that's how we rebel moms roll."

"All my base are belong to you, is that it?"

Marianne set down Abby long enough to stand, then scooped her daughter up again. When Eugenie was standing, too, Marianne shifted her daughter to one hip, then leaned forward to lay a loud, smacking kiss on Eugenie's cheek. "Now you're learning," she said. "But you've still got a long way to go, n00b. Just 'cause it's summer doesn't mean school is out."

"So I should use my plethora of spare time to learn to play Xbox? Is that what you're saying?"

"Among other things. It's never too late to get to know your son. And you know what?" she added. "It's not too late to get to know your mom, either. Maybe Lorraine would like Xbox, too."

"The only things Mom likes are in French."

"I'm sure eBay *français* has Xboxes for sale. I know I've seen characters in some of D.J.'s games who wear berets. I bet she'd be fine with that. And she'd be an even bigger n00b than you. Work it right, Eugenie, and all Lorraine's base could belong to you." With that, she shifted Abby to her other hip, pulled the little girl's towel around them both, and headed home to make what passed for dinner in the Weatherly–Blankenbaker home.

Which, for some reason, made Eugenie start craving green pancakes and blue applesauce really bad.

Twelve

Wednesday morning found Eugenie wrapped in her bathrobe and standing in front of her open closet, contemplating her wardrobe more critically than she normally would for work. Because Wednesday morning, she wasn't dressing for work. She was dressing for a lunch date. With cute, self-employed, forty-four-year-old, youngest child, east-end-dwelling Thomas, whom Helen at DreamMakers had designated as the most ideal of Eugenie's first ten—she still gave her head a mental shake when she considered the number—ideal someones. She had asked Helen to ease her into the dating thing by arranging a lunch date instead of dinner, telling the matchmaker—though it was odd to think of her performing the same service Spalding did when she relied on a computer she hadn't even programmed herself—it would be less stressful. As much as her rational mind recognized that this date was actually a professional responsibility, not a social engagement, there was another part of her—an irrational part, obviously—that had kicked into social engagement mode. If she thought too much about it, her stomach even knotted with nerves. And she truly didn't think it was all because she would be acting as Spalding's Mata Hari. Still, it might help to reduce the stress level if she arrived for the appointment early enough to swill a glass of wine before Thomas's arrival. But she was probably getting ahead of herself there.

In an effort to move the date to someplace other than HeartMenders' backyard, she'd also asked Helen to send them someplace other than Fourth Street Live!, allegedly because neither of them worked downtown—another indication DreamMakers didn't do their homework where the whole dating thing was concerned, if that was where they planned to send two people who didn't work downtown—and instead find a place, preferably locally owned, midway between her and Thomas's home offices in two separate suburban neighborhoods. Surprisingly, Helen had been stumped to think of a place, even though Eugenie could have ticked off a quick half dozen, thanks to her work for HeartMenders. So she had helped the matchmaker out by suggesting Mojito.

Unfortunately, her wardrobe wasn't cooperating with her search for proper date wear, because all Eugenie saw in her closet was the usual assortment of work-related clothing—straight skirts and tailored shirts and dresses, all in a color palette more suited to a charcoal or sienna sketch artist than to a woman who was hoping to attract an ideal someone.

"Oh, screw it," she finally muttered, reaching for a taupe sheath that buttoned down the front. She wasn't dressing for a date. She was dressing for work. Spalding would be paying her overtime for going out to lunch today.

In spite of that, Eugenie donned her push-up bra before slipping on the dress, and she dabbed on a little more makeup than usual after. Thomas would, after all, have seen the photo Helen placed in her file—or, as Eugenie preferred to think of it, her *fauxto*—and would be expecting her to bear some vague resemblance to it.

That made her wonder what Helen had told Thomas about her. Had she told him Eugenie was cute, self-employed, thirty-seven—hah!—and a youngest child who lived in Manitou Hills? If so, what image had Thomas formed of her? It must be as nebulous as the one she had formed of him. Then again, unless he was spying on DreamMakers for his employer, his expectations of her were probably a lot higher than her expectations of him.

Not that that was saying much.

Wouldn't it be funny, she thought as she made her way downstairs to the kitchen, if he turned out to be a very nice guy with whom she had a lot in common? Hey, it could happen. Maybe the two of them would actually have a good time over lunch today. Maybe she would end up really liking him. Maybe he truly was her ideal someone.

And maybe an asteroid the size of Lithuania would hurtle into the earth tonight while they were all asleep, crumbling it like a gingersnap. Hey, that could happen, too.

Eugenie was still pondering that possibility—of Thomas's being a nice guy, not the earth's annihilation—as she brewed a pot of coffee in their shiny new coffeemaker and nuked a frozen breakfast sandwich in their ultramodern microwave. She wished the rest of the kitchen was as state-of-the-art. Although both the nauseating wallpaper and heinous linoleum were finally gone, both had left behind residues that defied every attempt to remove them. Clearly, the decimation of chemical adhesives from the seventies commanded a weapon of mass destruction unlike anything now available outside the military's secret stash. Or possibly even inside the military's secret stash. Damn those Carter-era EPA regulations, anyway.

Ah, well. At least the kitchen was clean and no longer smelled of fetid wildebeest. Thanks to the industrial strength cleaners Julien had promised, the kitchen these days smelled as fresh as a forest full of chemically fabricated pine trees.

Chink-creak. Chink-creak. Chink-creak.

Something that hadn't changed, however, was the lump of anxiety that settled in Eugenie's stomach every time she heard Lorraine's metallic approach. Doing her best to ignore both the sound and the knot, she forced a bright smile onto her face before turning around to tell her mother good morning.

Chink-creak. Chink-creak. Chink-creak.

Chink-creak. Chink-creak. Chink-creak.

Chink-creak. Chink-creak. Chink-creak.

Only it took a lot longer for Lorraine to arrive than Eugenie thought it would, so her face was beginning to ache from the phony cheerfulness by the time her mother actually appeared in the doorway. Even in sleep, Lorraine was a riot of color, her lime green pajamas and robe spattered with swirls of yellow and orange, the fuzzy slippers on her feet hot pink.

Inescapably, Eugenie glanced down at her beige attire. The additional X chromosome on her double helix must have detached at some point during her gestation and been sucked back into the umbilical cord, thereby giving her mother an additional jolt of estrogen. That could be the only explanation for how Lorraine had ended up with the femininity of Sophia Loren while Eugenie had been left with the femininity of Charles Bronson. How had she ever sprung from the loins of a woman like her mother?

"Good morning, Mom," she said as cheerfully as she could. "I hope you slept well."

"I barely slept at all," her mother said by way of a greeting. "Not that last night was any different from any other. I lie awake most nights wondering what you and Julien were thinking to buy this place. I've never seen anything so ugly in my life."

Although Eugenie reminded herself that her mother's complaining was simply a habit she would never be able to break, the barb stung. The house might still be ugly, but there were plenty of places where improvements were evident. Renovations like the one they were undertaking took a long time to complete. In some ways, they would never be done making improvements. But Fleurissant *was* in a better place than it had been four months ago. Even four weeks ago. It was unfair of Lorraine to expect beauty to happen just because she insisted on it.

But then, she had expected beauty under those terms for as long as Eugenie could remember. Her mother was, after all, an expert on beauty, having been defined by hers her entire life. Why wouldn't she use the same dictionary to define everyone else?

"The house won't be ugly forever," Eugenie said. "You need to look beneath the surface it has now to see its future potential." *You know—the way you never did with me.*

"Its surface is the whole problem," Lorraine fired back. "It doesn't matter how sound the foundation is or how reliable the wiring and plumbing are. That's not what people care about."

"It is if they value their lives," Eugenie countered. "If the foundation or wiring or plumbing go bad, then you're left with nothing but a beautiful shell, which won't do anyone any good."

"No one notices any of those underlying things," Lorraine said in what might or might not have been an amendment to her charge. "And some things can't be made beautiful no matter how much work you put into them. You can spend years trying to make a silk purse out of a sow's ear, but it will still be a sow's ear."

What was so terrible about a sow's ear? Eugenie wanted to ask. Other pigs must not have a problem with sow's ears, because they all wallowed together happily and never even paid attention to each other's ears. And if you gave a silk purse to a pig, that pig would look at you like you were an idiot. What did a pig need with a silk purse? It would just get dirty, and then nobody would want it.

"The house will be lovely when it's finished," Eugenie said again, ignoring the jab as well as she could. "Look how beautifully your rooms have turned out. Just give the rest of the place a little time. The whole house can be beautiful, if given a chance."

"How long before it's finished?" Lorraine demanded. "Because it's no picnic having to put up with it the way it is right now."

"I know, Mom, I don't like it much right now, either. But it's a work in progress and I'm doing the best that I—"

"It's deplorable," Lorraine interrupted.

She released the walker long enough to sweep a gnarled hand in front of her. Eugenie tried to reassure herself that her mother wasn't talking about anything other than the ugly kitchen. Unfortunately, she wasn't quite reassured.

"I don't know why you're even trying to fix this place. It's been neglected for too long. It's too damaged."

"There's no such thing as irreparable damage," Eugenie said, echoing Julien's words from their first visit to the house, even though she wasn't sure she believed them, either.

Her mother nodded vehemently. "Oh yes there is."

"Then I guess we'll just have to patch it up as best we can and overlook what little minor flaws are left. Can I fix you some breakfast?" Eugenie hurried on in an effort to change the subject. "I have some extra time this morning. I could make you a Spanish omelet with a couple of tomato slices on the side. In fact, I've been thinking maybe you and I could put out some tomato plants in a part of the backyard that Jules has cleared. I don't think it's too late in the season to do that."

Actually, Eugenie hadn't been thinking any of that until this minute, and only because she really did want to change the subject. Now that she thought about it, though, why not? Tomatoes were something of a religion in Louisville. Perhaps even a cult. Everyone had a personal philosophy for growing them, too—different ways to treat the plants, different places to plant them, different nutrients to feed them.

When Eugenie was a little girl, Lorraine had put out plants every year, just like everyone else in the neighborhood. They always had to be placed on the same side of the garage—not too close, but not too distant, either—in a narrow patch of earth where the shade from the maple and oak trees didn't fall at any point during the day to stunt them. She went outside every evening and massaged the leaves with garlic water to keep away the aphids and beetles. She lavished the tiny yellow blossoms with praise when they flourished and coaxed them with encouraging words if they started to fail. Every summer, she was rewarded with gorgeous, plump, fiery fruits the size of softballs that bled juice at the first prick of a knife blade. Lorraine's tomatoes never let her down. Not the way her daughter did.

"It's too late," her mother said now. "To get good tomatoes, you have to start early. You have to put them out right after Derby. There's a tiny window of opportunity, and if you miss it, it's pointless. You might as well not even try."

"Derby was a full week into May this year," Eugenie reminded her. "Not even two months ago. That's not much time to make up."

Lorraine shook her head and repeated, "It's too late. It's pointless to even try."

Lorraine turned to make her way to the table—*chink-creak-chink-creak-chink-creak*—so Eugenie opened the refrigerator to extract an egg, a pepper, and a tomato. As she set them on the counter, she noticed the tomato had a brown spot near its stem and a bruise at its base. She always bought the less-than-perfect fruits and vegetables at the market, knowing everyone else rejected them. It was easy enough to trim off the imperfections and cut around the dark spots. What lay beneath was always as good as the more perfect-looking produce in the bins.

"Well, Paul's still had some tomato plants that looked promising when I was in there the other day," she called over her shoulder to her mother. "Maybe I'll go back and pick up a few to put out this weekend. You never know unless you try."

Her mother's only response was a derisive sound as she continued toward the table in the mud room/breakfast nook. *Chink-creak. Chink-creak. Chink-creak.*

Eugenie relaxed a little when her mother seated herself and silence descended. She relaxed even more as she opened a drawer and withdrew a sharp knife, then began to whittle away the flaws on the tomato. *Nope,* she thought as she worked, *you never know anything unless you try.*

Unfortunately, thanks to an overly full morning, Eugenie wasn't able to arrive for her lunch date with Thomas early enough to swill a glass of wine before he got there. In fact, by the time she arrived, he was already halfway through one of his own. Irrationally, she was a little put off by the fact that he hadn't waited for her before having the hostess seat him and ordering a drink—not to mention pursue said drink's consumption. She wasn't sure if that constituted strike one against the guy—since it wasn't like she hadn't had the same plan herself—but it wasn't exactly a good omen, either.

He was kind of cute, though, she had to admit as she approached, with sandy hair and trendy glasses and a sturdy jawline, but she was reasonably certain he had lied as much about his age as she had her own. He was clearly well on the other side of fifty. Since he was sitting down, she couldn't tell much about his build, though he didn't seem to be overly anything in any direction. He wore a pale yellow polo embroidered with some kind of logo beneath the left shoulder and khakis, a good indication that he had at least been telling the truth about the self-employed part since most men meeting this time of day would be wearing business attire.

He glanced up as Eugenie drew near the table, but the moment his gaze lit on her, it ricocheted off again, over her shoulder, toward the entrance, as if he were expecting someone. Which, of course, he was, but he clearly didn't recognize the woman he was supposedly waiting for. Even when she stopped on the other side of the table, bringing his attention back to herself, he looked at her for a long moment before recognition—or something—finally dawned. Dawned like a good, solid blow to the back of the head, if his expression was any indication.

Oh, come on. Maybe she'd gone a little lighter on the makeup this morning than she had the day she went to DreamMakers, but she didn't look *that* different. Unless, of course, DreamMakers had altered her fauxto to make it even more faux, which wasn't outside the realm of possibility, all things considered. Which would mean they'd probably altered Thomas's picture, too, hence the post-fifty thing passing for forty-four. God knew what they'd done to her own likeness to keep her up to DreamMakers' standards.

"Are you Thomas?" she asked, even though she knew he was.

For a moment, she thought he might try to deny it, but he finally nodded and said, "Yes. Yes, I am. You must be Janey."

She waited for him to stand and/or offer his hand, since she was pretty sure dating hadn't changed so much in the time that she was away from it that people had dropped basic introductory courtesy, but he did neither. Which—just a shot in the dark—probably meant he wasn't going to pull out her chair for her to sit on, either. Not that Eugenie expected such chivalry in this day and age, from a blind date or anyone else, but—yo, Einstein—maybe it would have been a nice gesture from a blind date, or anyone else, who should have been trying to make a good impression or just be a thoughtful person.

Fine. She'd just pull out her own damned chair. Which she did.

After setting her purse on the floor, she turned to see Thomas tipping his glass back to empty it. She told herself not to take it personally, since, had the tables been turned, she probably would have been doing the same thing. When he lowered it again, instead of looking at her, he scanned the restaurant desperately, lifting a hand at someone and pointing to his glass, then nodding. Eugenie waited to see if he would ask her what she wanted, but he only glanced back at her and folded his arms on the table.

"Why, yes, I'd love a glass of sangria," she told him. "Thank you so much for asking."

Thomas looked a little confused for a minute—maybe that hadn't been his first glass—then glanced around the restaurant again, considerably less desperately this time.

"I don't see our server," he said, finally looking at Eugenie—for all of two seconds before his gaze skittered off again. "I'll let him know when he gets back with mine."

She lifted the menu that had been placed at her spot on the table—at least Thomas had been thoughtful enough to tell the hostess there would be someone joining him—and scanned the choices. She'd never eaten here before—another reason she'd suggested it to Helen—but liked the place immediately upon entering, thanks to its dazzling, Caribbean-inspired colors and artwork and the bubbly bits of majolica scattered about. At the moment, the decor and menu selections were the only reasons she was staying. So far, Thomas was anything but dazzling or bubbly. In fact, she was starting to reassess the whole "cute" thing, too. So there.

"So," she said as she continued to scan the menu selections, "I understand you're self-employed. What is it you do?"

"I own Magic Lube."

That gave Eugenie pause. Mostly because she wasn't sure whether he was telling her he was the owner of a car repair place or letting her know of his sexual proclivities right off the bat.

"The place that fixes cars?" she asked hopefully.

"That's the one."

Whew.

"Where's the one you own located?" she asked. She was pretty sure there was one not far from where she lived. She remembered the logo depicting a top-hat-wearing rabbit crawling out of some car orifice.

Definitely glad he had been talking about his occupation, not his sexual appetites. Even so, she kind of hoped that wasn't the Magic Lube Thomas owned. Because if it was, there really did go the neighborhood.

"I own all of them," he said with great pride.

Damn.

He pointed to the logo on his polo with great flourish, and she noted then that it was the purple-embroidered image of the orifice-ejected rabbit. "See?"

"Wow," she said, striving to infuse just the right amount of awe into the word. Since, of course, all it took to convince her of his veracity was the fact that he was wearing a logo-spattered polo.

"'Wow' is right," he agreed, thumping his fist on the table to punctuate his righteousness. "Even in these tough times, I'm raking in a bundle. No matter how much other businesses tank, people still need their cars, even if it's just to get them to the unemployment office. Hell, even welfare skanks have cars. It's only those namby-pamby *bicyclists*"—Eugenie's back went up, literally, at the unmitigated disgust with which he uttered the word by which her son identified himself—"those tree-hugging, hummus-eating, go-green enviro-wimpalists who would get rid of their cars just because of a little burp in the economy. People will always need to maintain their vehicles. And I'll always be there to take their money for it."

"Enviro-wimpalists?" Eugenie echoed. Mostly because she couldn't think of a single other response to his outburst. At least, not one that didn't contain profanity.

He grinned. "Coined that word myself. I use it online whenever I can. I'm hoping it will go viral."

Eugenie nodded. She hoped something went viral in Thomas's pants. Soon.

"So," he said, snapping up his menu to give it a quick peruse. "What looks good to you?"

Probably, it would be best if she didn't answer that truthfully. She still hadn't moved beyond the something viral in his pants.

So she told him, "I'm having the hummus to start. Then I'll probably go green for my main course."

She looked up to find him still gazing at his menu, her less-than-subtle innuendo obviously not registering at all. Amazing.

"I'm having the steak."

Now there was a shocker.

"That's about the only American-looking thing I see on this menu."

Oh, now he was just trying to be charming.

Their server arrived with Thomas's wine, then greeted Eugenie warmly with an expectant smile. "And what can I get for you?" he asked.

Eugenie considered her choices. On one hand, the restaurant was enchanting, the menu looked mouthwatering, and it had been a long time since she'd gone out for lunch. In that same hand was the knowledge that not only would she not be paying for the meal, since Spalding would cover her portion, but she was also being paid to sit in said enchanting restaurant enjoying its mouthwatering fare. On the other hand . . .

On the other hand, there was Thomas.

"You know what?" she said brightly to both men. "I just remembered I'm supposed to take my mother for a doctor's appointment today." She made a big show of looking at her watch. "Gosh, I really don't think I have time for lunch." She grabbed her purse from the floor and stood, then hurried on before either Thomas or their server could say anything. "It was so interesting meeting you, Thomas," she told him. "I'll be in touch." *Someday. In another life. One where you're reincarnated as a cockroach, and I come back as a Doc Marten.*

Before he had a chance to say anything—not that she thought he was going to say anything she wanted to hear, anyway—she wiggled her fingers in farewell and turned to make her way to the exit. Her stomach rumbled in protest as she passed the hostess stand, and Eugenie made it a silent promise that she would come back some other time. Sometime when they had two-for-one sangria, for instance. That would be enormously helpful should a situation like this arise again. For lunch today . . .

Well. Maybe Spalding hadn't eaten all his Oreos yet.

Thirteen

When Eugenie opened the front door upon returning home from work that night, she was greeted by the frantic whir of an electric sander, the chalky taste of plaster dust, and the bitter redolence of something about to catch fire. She followed all three through the foyer and living room, toward the far right side of the house where lay a broad, brightly lit room they had deemed the family room immediately after moving in. Ironically, on the order list of rooms to be renovated, it had been placed dead last, because neither Eugenie nor Julien had been able to think of a single reason why they would use such a room.

Evidently, Julien had conjured one at some point, because it was in that room where she found him, spattered with both plaster flakes and sawdust, a white particle respirator covering the lower half of his face. It wasn't he wielding the sander, however—that task belonged to Seth, who was as bespeckled and masked as his uncle was. The late afternoon sun angled through the long row of windows behind them, transforming the fragmented jots of Fleurissant dancing around them into golden bits of fairy dust. Beyond the windows, perched atop the lilac bush, sat the ruby red cardinal, his head cocked to one side as he looked into Eugenie's home from his own, obviously wondering the same thing she was: What the hell is going on?

Seth was crouched in the far corner sanding what appeared to be the last section of flooring that needed it, and Julien was on the opposite side of the room, sponging down the wall on that side. Neither had noted her arrival, and with the buzzing of the sander, they weren't likely to unless she announced it. So she strode to the middle of the room and shouted, "Hey!"

The sander shut off immediately. Julien spun around and Seth stood, the former pulling his particle respirator down over his throat, the latter pushing his atop his head.

"Oh, hey," Julien greeted her. "You're home early."

"Not really. It's almost five thirty." She smiled at her son. "Hi, Seth. It's good to see you home. Helping your uncle Jules." *Without your earbuds in to ward off your family or your surly attitude on to ward off everything else.*

Seth wiped his grimy forehead with the sleeve of his grimy T-shirt. "He didn't give me any choice."

Well, okay. Without the earbuds at least.

"It's still good to see you home."

Julien glanced down at his watch. "It's five thirty? When did that happen?"

"A little after five twenty-five," she told him. "What are you doing? I thought we were renovating this room last."

Julien dropped his sponge into a bucket of opaque gray water near his feet. "We were. Until Mom decided she needs it done now."

"Why?"

"She wants a place where she can read and relax," Julien said.

"I thought that was what her bedroom was for."

He shook his head. "No, that's where she lives. She wants another room for an escape."

Eugenie wanted another life for an escape. But you can't always get what you want. Still, she tried to be sympathetic. It couldn't be much fun being, for all intents and purposes, housebound. Especially when the house to which one was bound was in such disarray. In the long term, Lorraine would have lots of places to call her own in Fleurissant—the entire substantial first floor would be hers to roam. For now, however, her horizons were pretty limited.

"You've done a lot in one day," Eugenie said.

Granted, the room was a narrow one, but it spanned the entirety of the side of the house, from front to back. Still, one entire wall was nothing but windows, and the opposite one sported a wide entrance at each end, so there wasn't a huge amount of plaster to tend to. This was also one of a handful of rooms that hadn't been wallpapered, so there was none of that to strip. When they'd pulled up the carpeting throughout the first floor, the wood in here hadn't been shellacked within an inch of its life as it had elsewhere in the house, either. This actually might have been a good room to start in, since it needed less work than many of the others. But, hey, it was a family room. Why bother?

"Seth has been a huge help," Julien said. "He sanded the entire floor himself. The plaster wasn't buckled in here the way it was in other rooms, so a good scrub with the sandpaper did the trick. All the sunlight streaming in kept this room in relatively good shape. Sophie and Chloe were in here until the sander started again, washing the walls as I finished sanding them." He grinned.

"Well, as high as they could reach. They're in the kitchen with Mom making sandwiches for all of us now."

In other words, Eugenie thought, the entire family was chipping in for the family room.

"Let me change," she said, "and I'll help."

By the time she returned in her painting shorts and T-shirt, her mother and nieces had joined the menfolk, and all of them were munching contentedly on their dinner. Someone had dragged in a chair for Lorraine, who sat in the entryway farthest from where Seth had been sanding, describing what she wanted the room to look like when it was done.

"And lace curtains on the windows," she said as Eugenie accepted a sandwich from Sophie, whose lopsided ponytails were threaded with plaster dust. "And cabbage rose wallpaper on the walls."

"Oh no," Eugenie said adamantly. "No wallpaper. We'll paint in here."

"I want wallpaper," Lorraine told her.

Eugenie sent her a pleading look. "Mom. We've stripped enough wallpaper and paste from this place to build a wasp nest the size of New Zealand. Why would you want to put up more?"

"Wallpaper," Lorraine decreed. "With cabbage roses."

Eugenie sighed. She should have seen this coming. When she and Julien were kids, Lorraine had changed the wallpaper in their dining room on a regular basis, and none of it had been attractive. Eugenie could remember some that had fishing trawlers and lobster traps. At another point, the images had been of peacock feathers. For the Bicentennial, her mother had pasted on some that was red, white, and blue, with sketches of fifes and drums and thirteen-starred flags. Now she wanted big, nasty cabbage roses.

Knowing it would be pointless to argue—for now—Eugenie let the matter drop. For now.

Julien seemed to think it was a good idea to change the subject, too, because he asked, "How was work today, Eugene?"

"It was good. Now that I know what I'm doing there, I really enjoy it," she said, sounding a little surprised. Feeling a little surprised.

"You sound surprised by that," Lorraine said.

Eugenie looked at her mother, who was picking apart her BLT to get to the tomatoes first. "I guess I kind of am," she told her mother. "It's not exactly what I ever saw myself doing."

"You could look for work somewhere else to find something that suits you better," Lorraine said.

Well, Eugenie could, but . . . She didn't want to. That kind of surprised her, too. "No, I couldn't."

"Why not?"

Actually, she kind of wondered that herself. Hadn't she, from the day she got the job at HeartMenders, approached it for what it was—simply a means to make money she needed? Hadn't she considered herself as overqualified as Spalding had? So why hadn't she kept looking for something that might bring her greater professional satisfaction, not to mention better pay?

When she didn't reply right away, Lorraine prompted, "What do you like so much about working there that keeps you from looking for something else you're more suited to? Something that would pay better? I would think you'd want to make as much money as you can, being a single woman with no man to support her."

Of course Lorraine would think that. But there was a time when Eugenie would have thought that, too. Not so much the part about needing a man to support her. But certainly the part about making as much money as possible. The person who took home the largest paycheck was the winner of the game, after all. That was how her generation had been taught to look at the American Dream. It didn't matter if one liked what one did for a living. It only mattered that one be well paid for whatever one did.

Eugenie scrunched up her shoulders and relaxed them. "I like the people I work with," she told her mother. Knowing the reply would sound lame to Lorraine but knowing it was true nonetheless. "And I like seeing the dates Spalding puts together for our clients. I like discovering how well two people can fit together, especially when I don't see at first how they're going to fit together at all. It's fun being part of what makes all that happen." She smiled. "It's very romantic."

Julien uttered a derisive sound at that. "I can't believe you still think romance exists after what Lawrence put you through."

He didn't add that what made the notion of romance even more incredible was how bitterly it had treated him, robbing him of Cassie so soon—and so heinously—after bestowing such a wonderful gift upon him. It was impossible to talk to Julien without seeing a reminder of that. His grief was a shroud that settled more resolutely around him with every passing year.

"Just because a person thinks something is romantic doesn't mean they believe in romance," Eugenie said.

"That doesn't make sense, Eugene."

"Sure it does," she told him. "Just because I like watching a movie or reading a book where two people find romance and fall in love and live happily ever after, that doesn't mean I expect it to happen in real life. I like the movie *The Haunting* and the book *Watership Down*, too, but that doesn't mean ghosts and talking rabbits exist. I just suspend my disbelief for a little while for the sake of being entertained. True love makes for great entertainment, but it's kind of unrealistic to expect to find it in real life."

Julien feigned shock. "First you don't believe in romance, and now you're saying you don't believe in true love or happy endings, either?"

Even though she knew he was being sarcastic, Eugenie answered the question. "Let's just say I think anyone who believes in fairy tales like love conquers all, or that there's a perfect someone out there for everyone, or that happy endings really happen where everything is tied up neatly with a big red bow . . . Anyone who buys into all that is going to be disappointed."

Julien sobered immediately. And he said nothing. Eugenie was stunned by the way his expression changed. Her brother *did* believe in those things, she realized. Or at least he had. Until Cassie's death.

"So you don't know any couples," he said, "who have clung to each other through times of adversity or difficulty knowing that if they just loved each other enough, everything would work out? You don't know any couples who were determined to do that work together—whatever it took—to make sure they found the happily-ever-after they knew was waiting for them? Everyone you know who commits to a relationship just ditches on it the minute things get tough or go sour?"

He was talking about himself and Cassie, Eugenie knew. The two of them had indeed clung to each other during her illness, and they had done everything they knew to do to battle it. Even with the lousy prognosis her doctors gave her immediately following her diagnosis, they had both been certain that if they just worked hard enough and had enough faith in her recovery and loved each other enough, they could beat it. When Cassie died, Julien's grief was rivaled only by his disbelief. He truly had thought the love he and his wife shared would conquer anything. Even cancer. But fate had had an entirely different plan for them both.

But his question made Eugenie think about Marianne, too, and her confession that she had cheated on Dale. Something had obviously gone wrong at some point in that marriage if her friend had been unfaithful. But whatever it was had obviously been corrected. From everything Eugenie had seen and heard from Marianne since the two became reacquainted, she was perfectly happy with the way things were in her life and in her family. Everything Eugenie had observed on the occasions when she was at Marianne's house supported that. Her kids were friendly, bright, and cheerful, and Dale was gregarious and loving toward his wife.

Admittedly, Eugenie had only a couple of weeks' worth of observations to go by, but it had been her experience that when a family was fractured, it became clear to even the most casual observer almost immediately. How many people had she seen since her split from Lawrence who had been in no way surprised to hear she had split from Lawrence? How obvious had it been to everyone but her that things were wrong in her marriage a long time before she realized it herself? A lot of her friends had told her they were surprised she ever married him in the first place.

Looking back in hindsight—which, hey, what do you know, really was twenty-twenty—even Seth had shown signs of withdrawal long before the problems between his parents had become evident to her. Eugenie had always put his behavior down to puberty and adolescence. Kids always became withdrawn and surly when their hormones started getting the better of them, right? The thing was, she had known plenty of kids Seth's age who weren't surly or withdrawn at all, plenty who had perfectly good relationships with their parents. Because their parents had a perfectly good relationship with each other.

"That's not what I meant," she told Julien. "I just think there can be romance without love and love without romance. The two don't necessarily go hand in hand all the time."

"So, then, you do think romance exists," he told her.

She started to object again, then realized she had just pretty much said that she did think romance existed—it just wasn't always tied to love. Nevertheless, she told him, "Okay. Maybe romance exists. Hell, maybe even true love exists—I don't know. But neither of them work unless you're a believer. And I'm not." She hesitated only a moment before adding, "But you are, aren't you, Jules?"

He dropped his gaze to the thin crust of sandwich he held in one hand. Instead of finishing it, he tossed it onto the napkin unfolded near his thigh. "We're burning daylight," he said. "I'd like to at least finish sanding the floor and cleaning the walls before we call it a night. Sophie and Chloe," he called to his daughters as he pushed himself to standing, "do you remember where I left the Windex? You two could get started cleaning the windows down at this end."

Eugenie stood, too, grabbing her nieces before they could escape to give each of them a quick squeeze because . . . well, maybe because she just thought they needed it. And because she needed it, too. They squealed and fidgeted, but eventually hugged her back, Chloe even going so far as to land a smacking kiss on her aunt's chin. Then they were gone, in a flurry of girlish giggles, and Eugenie was straightening again, looking at her son.

Seth had watched her as she hugged her nieces, but when her gaze met his, he began busying himself with the sander, steadfastly ignoring her. The little hum of well-being that had blossomed in her belly as she enveloped the girls withered.

His disappearances from the house were becoming more frequent, and he had been coming home even later after dark than before, during a season when darkness didn't happen until after nine o'clock. There had been a few days when he'd come home abraded and bruised, as if he'd been fighting. Eugenie tried to talk to him about it the first time it happened, but he told her it was nothing, a mishap on his bike, and no, he didn't want dinner, he ate while he was out, and if anyone needed him, he'd be in his room.

Eugenie might have laughed at that last part about anyone needing him, since everyone in the family needed him—if for nothing else, then to at least join the family—and every knock to his bedroom door met with silence. Either silence or an increase in the volume of whatever game he was playing that drowned out any further knocking.

As her nieces' happy chattering grew more distant behind her, Eugenie looked at her silent son and instinctively began to turn away. She made it two full steps before telling her instincts to take a hike. Then she spun back around and crossed the room to her son. Seth remained focused on the mechanism in his hand, his gaze cast heartily downward, even when she stood right beside him.

"Seth," she said.

"What?" he replied without looking up.

"Look at me."

He hesitated, but finally did as she asked. He even jerked his head to one side so his hair wasn't covering that one eye. "What?" he repeated, more sullenly this time.

Eugenie hesitated not at all. She extended her arms, wrapping them around Seth's shoulders, and pulled him close. He didn't squeal or giggle as the girls did, but he fidgeted. A lot. Eugenie didn't care. She just held him tighter.

"Mom!" he finally objected, trying to thread his arms up through hers to break the embrace.

But Eugenie held him tighter still. "I love you," she said. Because, honestly, she didn't know what else to say. "More than anything in the world, Seth. I. Love. You."

He stopped fidgeting then, long enough to say, "I know that, Mom."

"And you know what happened between me and your dad—"

"Had nothing to do with me. I know that, too."

"And you know that if I could have, I would have—"

What? she asked herself now. *Stayed with Lawrence? Tried to make the break less acrimonious? Never married him to begin with?*

"If I could have, I would have never put you through all that," she finally finished. "It was my and your father's crap. But it got all over you, too. And I'm sorry for that."

"I know that, too, Mom."

"Do you?"

"Yeah."

She still wasn't quite convinced of that, but she loosened her hold on Seth a little. "Hey, if I ask Spalding for a day off next week, will you stay home that day and not take off on your bike?"

He narrowed his eyes at her. "Why?"

"So you and I can—" She started to say *talk*, then remembered Marianne's admonition. "So you can teach me how to play . . ." She tried to remember the game Marianne said she played with D.J. "Call of Duty?"

Seth opened his mouth, but no words came out.

"Is that what it's called?"

"Um, yeah, but I don't play that one. It's rated M. You don't let me play M-rated games."

"I know that." What she didn't know was that Seth had respected her wishes. What she also didn't know was why that surprised her. Probably because she'd spent most of her teens blowing off her mother's wishes. If Lorraine had told her she couldn't play an M-rated game, the first thing Eugenie would have done would be enlist Julien's help in procuring one for her.

"Well, then teach me how to play one you think I'll like."

Seth's expression changed not at all. "Why?"

"Maybe because it will be fun?"

"Um, okay. I think maybe I know where Harvest Moon is. I hope you like growing stuff."

Eugenie smiled at that. She loved growing stuff. She'd just never been very good at it. But maybe if she didn't try doing it by herself, maybe if she had someone helping her, she'd have better results.

"Thanks, Seth."

"For what?"

There were so many ways to answer that question, Eugenie couldn't begin to know where to start. So she told him, "For helping out with the renovations."

He lifted one shoulder and let it drop. "It's my house, too. I should pull my own weight."

As if to punctuate the statement, he disengaged himself from Eugenie's embrace and returned to the corner of the room where only a tiny bit of flooring remained unfinished. Then he turned on the sander and went to work. She watched him long enough to know he had no intention of looking back at her, then turned around to busy herself, too. When she did, it was to find her mother still seated framed in the doorway, watching her. Lorraine's expression was as inscrutable as Seth's had been, but her gnarled hands lay palm up and open in her lap, as if she were waiting for someone to drop something into them.

Eugenie strode to the other side of the room again, and picked up the bucket of clean water she'd brought in from the kitchen to help Julien finish washing the walls. Then she walked to where Lorraine was sitting.

"Hey, Mom," she said, striving for a careless tone of voice. "Since Sophie and Chloe are going to be doing the windows, think you could take over washing the walls where they left off?"

Lorraine's perfectly penciled eyebrows arrowed downward. "Look at me," she snapped. "Does it look like I can take over washing the walls?"

Eugenie nodded. "Yeah. It does. If you can hold on to and maneuver a walker, you can probably hold on to and maneuver a sponge. Jules and I can move the chair for you as you go. But if you don't want to . . ."

"I'll just make a mess," Lorraine said.

No doubt, Eugenie thought. But they were all pretty much doing that. "It's always a mess before it gets done," she told her mother.

Lorraine huffed a dramatic sigh. "That's true. You've made plenty of messes yourself lately, haven't you?"

Maybe, Eugenie conceded. But little by little, she was getting one or two cleaned up.

"Thanks, Mom," she said. "If you'll do the bottom half, I'll do the top."

"Fine. Whatever."

Eugenie smiled again. It was fine, actually. And getting finer all the time.

Fourteen

Helen at DreamMakers was quick to remedy the Thomas situation by setting up Eugenie with a second ideal someone the following Friday night. This one's name was Michael, and Helen assured her he was both politically and socially progressive and would be way more ideal than Thomas was in that respect. She had also lightly chided Eugenie, telling her that if things like saving the planet were a concern for her, then she should have let them know so they could make her matches accordingly. Eugenie had wanted to ask where she was supposed to have told them that on their brief questionnaire, since it hadn't included any questions like, "Is there something in particular you are not looking for in a mate?" The closest they had come to that was asking about her pet peeves. And it hadn't occurred to include *obnoxious boors* since one would think that would go without saying.

At any rate, on Friday night Eugenie did arrive early enough to swill a glass—ah, she meant *order* a glass—of wine before her date arrived. She had succumbed to Helen's insistence that the meeting take place at Fourth Street Live! this time, since Helen assured Eugenie that the "downtown vibe" would inject the rendezvous with an "urban groove" that would be "wicked smexy."

Eugenie didn't know about any of that—especially the part about *smexy*—but she was willing to give it another go. She'd seen a wicked neato boudoir chandelier at Joe Ley that she wanted to buy for her bedroom, and the overtime would come in handy. She vowed that even if Michael turned out to be as obnoxious and boorish as Thomas had been, she could stomach at least a couple of hours with him in an effort to jazz up her boudoir. That seemed even more likely when he arrived looking tall, dark, and handsome in a pin-striped suit that had clearly been tailored for him, accessorized by a downright fetching smile that went all the way to his chocolate brown eyes, and begging her forgiveness for being all of five minutes late owing to his volunteer work at the homeless shelter having run overtime.

Okay, so maybe DreamMakers could conjure the occasional dream, Eugenie thought after they had exchanged greetings and introductions and Michael seated himself across from her to await the Glenlivet neat he ordered from their server. Maybe Thomas had just been a big ol' aberration.

"So you run a pastry and catering business," he said as they settled in. "How can that be possible when you're so amazingly svelte?"

Oh yeah. Definitely dreamy.

Eugenie smiled. "I maintain an active lifestyle," she said.

He nodded. "Me, too. I do the Ironman every year. I especially love the bicycling portion. I'm a major cyclist."

Eugenie was about to remark that her son was, too, but then remembered she was supposed to be child-free. Nevertheless,

Michael racked up another point for that. "I'm a runner," she told him. Even though her running activities had been a bit curtailed since moving back to Louisville. She figured all the work on the house burned just as many calories and used more muscles to boot.

"Do you run the mini-marathon for Derby?" he asked.

"I haven't yet. I just moved back to town from Indianapolis this year. But I'd love to do it next year."

He smiled. "Maybe we'll run into each other there."

Maybe they would, she thought. A lovely sort of contentment eased into her. Maybe they would at that.

The evening progressed nicely from there. Michael was convivial, articulate, and engaging, and he made Eugenie smile. A lot. They shared many beliefs and opinions in common, and they contributed equally to the conversation. By the time coffee and dessert arrived, they had covered the gamut of topics, from art to zodiac signs. It was only when Eugenie returned from a trip to the ladies' room that things turned a little . . . weird.

Not right away—in fact, the way he watched her as she walked back to the table gave her a warm, squishy feeling she hadn't felt for a long time, the kind of feeling a woman got when a man watched her with abundant appreciation that didn't cross the line into scary sexual. He simply seemed to like what he saw when he looked at her. Which was immensely okay with Eugenie, because she liked what she saw when she looked at Michael.

As she seated herself, he told her, "You know, even if you hadn't told me you're a runner, I would have been able to tell just by watching you walk. You have the legs of a runner."

There were times when such a comment would have made Eugenie uncomfortable, but somehow, there was nothing untoward about the remark the way Michael uttered it. Even coupled with his earlier statement about her being svelte, the flattery wasn't obnoxious or cloying. He simply seemed to be making an observation that arose naturally from their conversation over the course of the evening, intending it as a compliment, certainly, but not sounding as if he were working too hard to impress.

"Although," he added with a disarming little grin, "that could also be because of the heels. Those are Stuart Weitzmans, aren't they?"

Okay, now he was working too hard to impress. She knew men thought the shoe thing was a big part of womanhood—and for a lot of women, it was—but the two of them had hit it off well enough so far that he didn't need to resort to showing off how much homework he did in his wooing efforts. Even if he was right about the designer.

She brushed the feeling aside and told herself she should be pleased he was trying that hard to impress her. It meant he wanted to make, well, an impression.

"They are," she said. "I'm surprised—most men wouldn't know Weitzman from Woolite."

He shrugged lightly. "I worked my way through college in the Nordstrom shoe department."

Aha.

"Some things just stay with you," he added. "Weitzmans were always very popular. Did you know they're a favorite among pageant contestants for the very reason that they make women's legs look so good?"

Eugenie didn't know that, actually. Nor did she care, since talk of pageants naturally reminded her of her mother, and the last thing she wanted intruding into this evening was Lorraine.

She opened her mouth to change the subject, but Michael spoke again before she had the chance.

"I mean, I know Jimmy Choos and Manolos are supposed to be the be-all and end-all of women's footwear these days, but there are so many others to choose from that, well, in *my* opinion, are so much more . . . *interesting*."

Okay, now that did sound kind of untoward. Which was strange, because there was nothing in the statement that was in any way sexual, but Michael made it sound that way. In fact, coming from him, the remark had sounded scary sexual.

"You've got your Ferragamos that have been around forever, your Christian Louboutins, your Bottega Venetas, your Roger Viviers—I so admire his work," he added parenthetically with the kind of adoration she might have expected from someone talking about a da Vinci painting. "Even your better-known designers like Chanel, Gucci, Vuitton—all of them have so much to recommend them. And Escada!" he exclaimed. "Escada had this amazing pink evening sandal in its summer collection with this gorgeous metallic fringe that cascaded over the foot just so beautifully . . ."

His voice trailed off in wonder and reverence, and his gaze wandered over her shoulder, as if he were envisioning something that wasn't there. Namely, an amazing pink evening sandal with a gorgeous metallic fringe. Then he sighed. Sighed with all the dreamy idolatry of a twelve-year-old girl gazing upon Justin Bieber for the first time.

"What other designers do you have in your shoe collection, Janey?" he asked, still gazing at the imaginary object of his affections. "Tell me all about them."

Well now. This was awkward. To put it mildly. How did she tell him she'd only bought the Weitzmans because they were wildly on sale? How was he going to react when he found out they were one of only four pairs of designer shoes she owned—all purchased under the same circumstances? How disappointed would he be to discover her closet held not a single Escada but a plethora of Nike, Keen, and Birkenstock?

But the biggest question, she supposed, was, why was she so surprised to discover he had a shoe fetish? He'd been so wonderful all evening—dare she say ideal, even? She should have realized somewhere between the salad and entrée courses that, well, the other shoe was bound to drop soon.

Oh, well, she reasoned. Nobody was perfect. Michael was wonderful in so many other ways, she could overlook a little preoccupation with a particular item of women's wear. It could be worse. He could have a fetish about hunting knives.

"My shoe collection isn't really very extensive," she said. "Only a few pairs of really nice ones. I mostly buy for comfort, not style."

His gaze snapped back, utterly focused now. "What?" he said in a very soft voice.

"Um, I said my shoe collection isn't extensive," she repeated. "And that I buy more because I want something comfortable, not necessarily stylish. I love Stegmann clogs, for instance. I will pay more for those, because they're so comfy, and they last forever."

"Stegmann clogs?" he fairly spat. "Those wool monstrosities with the cork footbed that hides all the best parts of a woman's foot?"

Um, yeah, those would be the ones. "Ye-es," Eugenie said cautiously.

He gaped at her in disbelief. "You're telling me you actually prefer those over a pink evening sandal with silver fringe?"

"Ye-es . . ."

"Are you fucking *serious*?"

Okay, so maybe it wasn't a shoe fetish per se that Michael had. Maybe it was more like a shoe obsession. A shoe mania. A shoe whatever-the-word-for-get-me-the-hell-outta-here was. "Um, yes," Eugenie said. "I'm fuh . . . uh . . . serious."

He shook his head, his gaze going Arctic when it met hers. "What kind of woman would admit to something like that?"

"Maybe . . . one who's more concerned about how a shoe feels than how it looks?" Eugenie suggested.

He rolled his eyes sarcastically, snatched his napkin from his lap, and threw it onto the table like it was a gauntlet. "Oh, *fine*. Another one."

The fact that this was a conversation Michael seemed to have with some frequency did little to dispel Eugenie's concern. Go figure.

"You don't think style and comfort can go hand in hand?" he demanded. Even though a better phrase might have been *foot in foot*.

Eugenie opened her mouth to reply—actually, she did think style and comfort could go hand in hand, or even foot in foot, for that matter—but Michael lunged forward again. "Only someone who suffers from the height of ignorance could think style and comfort are mutually exclusive when it comes to fine footwear. What the hell is the matter with you?"

Again, Eugenie tried to answer his question, but he again cut her off. "I mean, you come waltzing in here wearing Stuart Weitzmans, getting my hopes up, teasing me, and then you tell me you'd rather be wearing Stegmanns?"

For a third time, Eugenie began to form a reply, but he was looking at her now as if she had just confessed to strangling kittens, and she wasn't sure what to say.

So Michael continued relentlessly, "I can't believe I've been sitting here sharing a table with someone like you. You're a monster, you know that? An absolute monster."

With that, he shoved his chair away from the table and stood. His mouth opened and closed a few times, as if he were literally at a loss for words. Finally, he said, "I'm going to do my best to forget this evening happened. But don't think DreamMakers won't be hearing about this."

Oh, Eugenie didn't think that at all. As a matter of fact, she was already considering what her own report to Helen would say.

With one final huff—literally, since he expelled an indignant sound as he did it—Michael spun on his heel and strode away from the table without a backward glance. Even before he made it a half-dozen strides, Eugenie realized he was sticking her with the check for the meal. Even so, there was no way she would call him back to sort it out. He hadn't even touched his crème brûlée, after all. No reason to risk him asking for a box for that when she could take it home and enjoy it herself.

Yeah, she couldn't wait to get home, slip into something more comfortable, and put up her feet. In fact, she could hear her Stegmanns calling out to her already.

Fifteen

By the time Saturday evening rolled around, Eugenie decided that whatever it was she and Nash were having that night, it was *not* going to be a date. Not just because she'd already had two dates with two men that week, so a third with a third made her feel like a 'ho. She had only gone out on those first dates because she was being paid to do it. Which, okay, kind of made her feel even more like a 'ho, but that was beside the point. And she wasn't calling this *not* a date with Nash because both of those earlier dates had ended badly—thereby being what threatened to become a pattern—either. The real reason this whatever it was with Nash was *not* going to be a date was because Eugenie still wasn't sure she even wanted it to be. She still wasn't sure what she expected it to be. She still wasn't sure why she'd even agreed to it. The whole thing just felt so . . . odd.

She wasn't even sure what she was supposed to wear, so she'd done what any other woman in her situation would do and bought something new. Specifically, a lovely linen top with crystal buttons and white-on-white embroidery that dressed up a pair of blue jeans quite nicely. Coupled with crystal-strewn flip-flops and matching bag (not to mention an excellent mani-pedi), by the time she was ready for Nash's arrival—a good half hour before he was due to arrive—she looked way better than she normally did when she saw him. Of course, when she normally saw Nash, she was covered with plaster dust, wallpaper remover, linoleum goo, and/or shellac, so that wasn't necessarily any kind of claim to fame.

She hadn't seen much of him since the day the two of them pondered the state of her chimney, though whether that was by his design or hers—or any design at all—Eugenie wasn't sure. Neither of them had said much about it other than upon Nash's departure the day before, when he passed her on the porch as she was arriving home from work. He had merely reiterated that he would see her tomorrow at seven. She still didn't know what his state of mind had been when he asked her out, but she had been in something of a state herself since. And it wasn't the state of Rhode Island.

Feeling restless as she awaited his arrival, she wandered out of her bedroom, past Seth's door—which was wide open, meaning he was out again doing whatever it was he did for hours and hours on end day after day—down the hallway toward the staircase at its end. Halfway to the second floor, she heard Chloe's and Sophie's voices, girlish and breathless, punctuated with giggles and the occasional chirp of laughter. Then she heard Julien's voice mingling with his daughters', deep and dramatic, the way it was when he read to them.

As quietly as she could, Eugenie made a U-turn at the landing and headed toward the room at the opposite end, the one where Nash had been working the day she won her job at HeartMenders.

The room had come a long way since then and was virtually finished. The walls were painted a pale lilac, the trim bright white. The freshly replaced window seat bore a new cushion and curtains fashioned from flower-spattered chintz, the former crowded with enough fluffy plush animals to populate the Louisville Zoo—had the Louisville Zoo been populated with fluffy plush animals, she meant. Julien had built bookcases along one wall that were teeming with all manner of girlish whimsy—pink ponies and buttery bunnies, magic wands and fairy wings, and glitter as far as the eye could see. Sophie's room was a mirror of her sister's, only with pale yellow walls, purple ponies, and rosy rabbits.

It was exactly the sort of bedroom—housing exactly the type of little girl—that Lorraine had always wanted for a daughter. *Maybe some genes really do skip a generation,* Eugenie thought. *Or maybe it's just that some social and cultural programming does.*

Still wearing his grungy work clothes, with paint flecked in his hair and on his hands, Julien should have looked out of place amid the ultrafeminine trappings. Instead, he looked perfectly at home. He sat on the hooked flowered rug, leaning against the tufted lavender bedspread with a daughter on each side of him, an oversized picture book open on his lap. At Eugenie's appearance, all three looked up, her nieces smiling and waving, but Julien continued to read to the bottom of the page before pausing long enough to greet her.

"You look pretty, Aunt Eugenie," Chloe said.

Sophie nodded her agreement. "I like your shirt."

Eugenie glanced down at the flowing, embroidered linen, suddenly feeling self-conscious. For some reason, she'd wanted to wear something sexy, and she had thought she was shopping for something along the same lines. Instead, she'd ended up with a blouse that was infinitely more delicate and embellished than what she normally wore, a garment one might even go so far as to call romantic. If one believed in such a condition, she meant.

Julien must have noticed the wardrobe aberration, too, because he asked, "Is that a new shirt?"

Eugenie picked at the hem and said, "Yep. Just bought it this week."

"For Nash?"

"No, for me," she said, ignoring the pinch of defensiveness that knifed through her.

He gave her that concerned big-brother look but remained silent.

"What?" Eugenie demanded.

"Nothing," he said.

He looked back down at the book and began to read again. But Eugenie interrupted him before he was able to finish the first sentence.

"No, you want to tell me something," she insisted. "What is it?"

He looked up again, the exact same expression etched on his features. "It's nothing," he repeated. "It's none of my business."

"Well, which is it? Nothing? Or none of your business?"

He flicked his gaze between his daughters, finally settling it on Sophie. "Do you mind finishing the book for your sister?"

Instead of looking put out, Sophie happily plucked the book from his lap and, when Julien stood, scooted over to take his place on the rug, mimicking his posture exactly. As she began to repeat the sentence her father hadn't been allowed to finish, Julien crossed to where Eugenie stood in the doorway, then tilted his head to the right in a silent indication that they should take a walk. Neither said anything until they were out of earshot of the girls, pausing near the stairwell Eugenie had just descended.

"What?" she repeated as she turned to face her brother.

"Are you sure you know what you're doing?" he asked.

She didn't pretend to misunderstand. "I'm just going to hear a friend of Nash's who has a band. It will be nice to get out for an evening. I haven't done anything fun like that for a while."

"Yeah, except that everyone who knows Nash knows he never asks a woman out just to hear a friend of his who has a band."

"Maybe he did this time."

Julien laughed lightly at that. "Look, Eugene, he's been my best friend since junior high. I love him like a brother. But the guy's a hound dog. There are probably only a dozen women in Louisville he *hasn't* tried to score with. I'd like to keep my sister in that number. She deserves better."

"There was a time when you were just like him," Eugenie reminded him.

Julien shook his head. "I was never as bad as Nash. I was at least able to have a decent relationship with a woman from time to time. Hell, I married Cassie."

And it went without saying that he would still be with her had it not been for the lymphoma. That went without saying because it was an unwritten rule in the family that no one ever talked about the lymphoma. Hell, they barely even talked about Cassie. Those subjects were things generally left to Julien to bring up, and he only did so when he absolutely had to.

"Nash has never been with a woman for more than a few weeks," he continued.

"I know that."

"And he almost never stays on good terms with one after he splits."

"I know that, too."

"You're a grown woman, and I can't tell you what to do. But

Nash is the best renovation guy I know, and he works cheap for me, and we still have a lot to do around here."

Translation: Eugenie knew what she was getting herself into, so no matter what happened between her and Nash, Julien wasn't going to compromise home renovation just because his sister was compromised. If things with Nash turned sexual and then went south—which, with Nash's history being what it was, would almost certainly happen—Eugenie would still have to see him almost daily around Fleurissant and deal with the repercussions. So she had to make up her mind about why she was going out with him before things turned sexual and went south. Was she only going out with him to get laid, something that had Marianne's seal of approval, even if it didn't have Julien's? Or was that twelve-year-old girl who still lived inside her hoping that something else might happen after the sex that would lead to the sort of happily-ever-after a twelve-year-old girl would find satisfying? Which was something that had no one's seal of approval—even Eugenie's, truth be told, because she wasn't a twelve-year-old girl anymore.

As if he hadn't already made his point, Julien added, "Whenever Nash runs into an old conquest—something that happens with some regularity, I might add—he doesn't refer to her by name. He refers to her by number. 'Oh, look, there's number forty-six,' he'll say."

Forty-six?

"Or, he'll say, 'That's number one hundred thirty-eight. She was into bondage big-time.'"

"You're exaggerating," Eugenie said. "There's no way Nash has been with a hundred and thirty-eight women."

Julien expelled an incredulous sound. "He lost his virginity when he was fourteen, Eugene. Maybe it took him a couple more years to really get going, but if you add in all the one-night stands he had with the girls who lasted more than a few dates, stretching over four decades, you're looking at a number that's pretty damned big."

Eugenie did the math, and, even with her solid C in the subject, she deduced that that could add up to an average of somewhere around ten women a year. Pretty much a new one every month from the time he was a teenager. Certainly doable—if one could pardon the extremely crass pun—especially if the person in question had a colossal sexual appetite.

"And that doesn't include the times when Nash went home with two girls at once," Julien said.

"He *never*," Eugenie said with a gasp.

Julien grinned. Eugenie's mouth dropped open. She could tell by his expression that he'd done that himself, too! Oh, there were definitely some things people should *not* know about their siblings.

In spite of that, she asked, "Did it ever occur to you, Jules, that maybe the only reason I'm going out with Nash is for the very trait you're describing?"

"Then do it with someone else," Julien told her without hesitation. "Not with Nash."

"I'll be fine, Jules," she told him. "It's just a couple of beers with a friend. Really."

"You just said it was because you wanted to get laid."

Oh, she really didn't want to be having this conversation with her brother. She lifted a hand to rub her forehead, hoping to ease a headache that flared out of nowhere. "I don't know what I want," she said wearily.

"Yeah, well, you better decide before things go too far."

She dropped her hand to her side again. "I want to have a couple of beers with a friend," she repeated. "That's all."

"So says the woman with all the fancy buttons on her shirt. Just promise me one thing before he gets here."

"What's that?"

"That when you come home—*tonight*," he added pointedly, "all those buttons will be in their proper place."

"I promise," she said.

She was confident it was a promise she could keep. After all, "tonight" was a fluid concept. "Tonight" could easily bleed into "early tomorrow morning." She would have plenty of time to get dressed before she left Nash's place to come home. And she would take her time with the buttons to make sure they were correctly aligned.

"I'll be fine, Jules," she said again. "I'm a big girl."

"Not to me," he said. "To me, you're still running around the yard with a towel tied around your neck being Strong Girl, or mooning over Tony DeFranco in *Tiger Beat,* or sitting in the mimosa tree in our backyard looking at caterpillars. You've never been a big girl to me, Eugene. You never will. So I'll say what I always did when you were a kid: Be careful."

She wasn't sure if what he'd said was sweet or something for which she should stick out her tongue at him. So she decided to just be stoic and repeat, "I'll be fine."

And she would have been, too, if not for the *chink-creak-chink-creak-chink-creak* that erupted just as her foot hit the bottom step. She spun around to head back upstairs, but Lorraine passed through the dining room just as she completed her turn and called Eugenie's name. With a resigned sigh, she pivoted again to face her mother.

"You almost made your escape," Lorraine said. "Guess I'm faster than you thought."

"I wasn't trying to escape," Eugenie lied. "I just decided to wear a different pair of earrings than these and was headed back up to my room for them."

Her mother inspected her ears critically. "Those are terrible," she agreed with a nod. "But then, the ones you wear always are. Come into my room. I have a pair that are much better for that blouse. Which I'm surprised to say looks nice on you."

Yes, that was Lorraine. Always full of the compliments. Of course she would like the blouse, even on Eugenie. It looked like Victorian underwear, which everyone—everyone except, ironically, Victoria's Secret—knew was the epitome of femininity. Any of the Brontës would have been right at home in this blouse. Provided it was under yards and yards of bombazine that it would have taken Heathcliff or Rochester all night to uncover. Those guys would have loved it—eventually—which was all that was required of a garment for Lorraine to think it was swell.

"Actually, Mom, I have a nice pair of silver hoops that I thought would—"

"Look even worse than those dinky white things you have on now," Lorraine finished for her. "When you have short hair, Eugenie, you need to add a little pizzazz to your face. And when you have short hair and a face like yours, that pizzazz needs to have pizzazz. Step down here," she commanded.

Obediently, Eugenie stepped down to the floor, level with Lorraine.

"Come into the living room, where there's better light," her mother instructed.

Eugenie did as she was told, stopping near the window, which still lacked any kind of adornment. Her mother followed—*chink-creak-chink-creak-chink-creak*—but must have been looking down to find her way when Eugenie stopped and spun around, because she barreled into her from behind with her walker, nearly knocking both of them over. Eugenie reached out a hand to steady her mother, but Lorraine recoiled with a hissed, "I can take care of myself," backing away a step—*chink-creak*—before coming to a halt. She poked her gnarled hand across the walker toward Eugenie's face, but her fingers were curled too far in on themselves for her to do more than press her knuckles against her daughter's cheek to nudge her face toward the slanting sunlight.

She shook her head in disgust. "Didn't you even put on any makeup?"

Eugenie had, but not in the way her mother applied it. Eugenie chose products designed to make a woman look like she wasn't wearing any makeup at all. Lorraine chose them to make a woman look like Boy George on estrogen overload.

"I'm going out for a couple of beers, Mom. I don't need much makeup."

Her mother expelled a rumble of disapproval. "There isn't a woman alive who doesn't need makeup, no matter where she's going. Even when I was a harried mother raising a family, I would never even think of going to the grocery store without at least foundation and loose powder. Aren't you going out with Nash tonight?"

Even though her mother already knew the answer, Eugenie replied dutifully, "Yes."

"And haven't you had a crush on Nash since you were a little girl?"

"Yes."

"And do you want him to ask you out again?"

Eugenie hesitated. "I don't know."

Lorraine hesitated not at all. "Of course you do. So you need to look your best."

Eugenie had sort of been working under the impression that

she did look her best, but then, what did she know? She'd never won the honor of being Miss anything. (Unless one included being misled or misinformed, but since those didn't come with a tiara and sash, she was pretty sure they didn't count.)

"Come on," Lorraine commanded. "After I fix your earring situation, I'll do your makeup."

Eugenie's stomach plummeted. The last time Lorraine insisted on doing her makeup, Eugenie had been forced to attend her senior prom looking like Divine. Which was only made worse by the fact that the prom theme had been "Dancing Queen."

"Really, Mom, I think I look—"

"Like a vanilla milk shake," Lorraine finished for her again. "You need some color. I said the shirt looks good on you. I didn't say you look good in the shirt."

And the difference would be . . . ? Eugenie wanted to ask. But she didn't. Mostly because she knew her mother would answer. With a reply that included bullet points.

"Come on," Lorraine repeated.

As she always did, Eugenie complied, following her mother across the living room—*chink-creak-chink-creak-chink-creak*—through the dining room—*chink-creak-chink-creak-chink-creak*—into her bedroom—*chink-creak-chink-creak-chink-creak*—continuing to the bathroom where Lorraine told her to wait while she fetched the earrings. When Lorraine joined her—*chink-creak-chink-creak-chink-creak*—she was clutching an earring in each of the hands hooked over the walker handles. Eugenie was surprised to see they weren't the Lucite, dated monstrosities she had feared they would be but instead a delicate collection of blue, yellow, and green crystals dangling in varying lengths that would compliment beautifully the colors of her blue jeans and her eyes.

"Here," Lorraine said as she thrust one hand out at Eugenie

while tightening the other on the walker. When Eugenie received that earring, her mother repeated the action, switching hands. "Put them on."

Eugenie unfastened the little white studs in her ears and replaced them with her mother's earrings, turning to look in the mirror to gauge their effect. They caught the room's light and shattered it, spraying it back out in a glitter of color that did indeed add pizzazz to her features. Damn them.

"Better already," Lorraine said. "But still not good enough."

No, of course not. *Good enough* to Lorraine meant Grace Kelly—perfect golden girl looks, married to a prince who spoke French, still thin after giving birth three times, and able to tie a scarf the way that chicly covered both the head and the neck.

"Sit," Lorraine said, pointing to the lid of the commode.

Eugenie complied again, literally twiddling her thumbs while her mother picked through the contents of the medicine cabinet over the sink, which held no medicine—those were lined up like pageant finalists on a shelf near the door—but was overflowing with bottles, compacts, tubes, pots, and wands of every color.

"You'll need rouge, lipstick, and eye shadow," her mother began, overlooking the fact that Eugenie had already used bronzer, gloss, and mascara. "And mascara," she added adamantly as she extracted a familiar pink and green tube of Maybelline and added it to the pile.

Despite the comings and goings of a dozen presidents since Lorraine had started wearing makeup, she hadn't altered her cosmetic regimen once (save the loss of the late, lamented Magenta to the Max lipstick, which even her radical letters of protest couldn't save). In addition to her Great Lash mascara and Avon accoutrements, she clung to her Max Factor foundation and powder, not to mention her Oil of Olay for beautiful skin and her

White Shoulders lotion for . . . well, white shoulders, Eugenie supposed.

"You're not even wearing eye shadow," Lorraine muttered with disgust. "How is Nash supposed to notice you tonight when you look the same way you do every day?"

This was probably a good place to insert something about how maybe the reason Nash had asked her out in the first place had had something to do with what she looked like every day, but that would just provide her mother with a springboard for giving out more tips on how to please a man, like by always talking about him and laughing at everything he said even if it wasn't funny. And since that was how Eugenie had ended up with Lawrence, it was probably best just to keep her mouth shut.

"I would think," Lorraine said, "that after all these years of mooning over Nash, when you finally have the chance to go out with him, you'd want to hook him as hard as you can and reel him in as quickly as possible."

Who had come up with the concept of men as fish? Eugenie wondered. Women were generally the gatherers in any hunting-and-gathering society, weren't they? Which meant they should be collecting men, not fishing for them. Then they should take the ones they collected and cure them with spicy preservatives and put them in a special hut to last the entire winter. That way if a woman had a man who wasn't seasoned properly or went rancid, she could just go back to the man hut and pick another one for sustenance until he stopped being tasty and nutritious. Whereupon she could return to the hut yet again for another hunk of meat.

Yeah, Eugenie liked that analogy. Even if she wasn't looking to hook *or* collect Nash. She did like the idea of him being spicy.

Lorraine withdrew the mascara from its tube and dabbed off

the excess with a tissue. "You need to set yourself apart from the other women Nash has dated."

The only way Eugenie would set herself apart from the other women in Nash's life would be if she got rid of her vagina. Of course, then she wouldn't have the very thing Marianne said he wanted. Which made for a troubling chicken-and-egg scenario that was probably best left to the macabre.

"You have to be prettier," Lorraine continued, leaving Eugenie to wonder if she meant prettier than the other women in Nash's life or prettier than she was in her everyday life. "And you have to dress better," she added as she applied mascara to Eugenie's lashes with a surprisingly steady hand. "You have to be more charming. You have to know when to talk and what to say, and when to shut up and let him talk. Nash is the sort of man who can have his pick of women. You have to ask yourself, 'What can I do to make sure I'm the one he picks?'"

Eugenie bit back a growl of discontent. Her mother was turning dating into the very competition Spalding had railed against, complete with a prize at the end that consisted less of a loving relationship than it did a trophy mate who could have gone to someone else. Then again, if her mother considered it that way, too, then dating had been a contest for a prize long before DreamMakers and reality TV turned it into such. And anyway, she'd already had this talk with Lorraine. Although every bit of advice her mother had ever given her about how to treat the opposite sex had gone completely against her grain, Eugenie had tried to follow it. By the time it became obvious that Lorraine's rules of engagement had stopped being timely at some point during the Second World War, they had been hammered so deeply into Eugenie for so long that she couldn't quite yank them out again. Even today, there was still some twisted part of her—the part that had never made it past twelve years old, no doubt—that was convinced if she was just pretty enough or charming enough, or if she behaved the right way or said the right things, then someone would love her.

Lorraine pulled away and surveyed Eugenie's eyes. "Maybe a little liner," she said as she capped the mascara.

Oh no. No, no, no, no, no. Not that. Not liner. That way lay Divine.

"No, Mom, I don't think that's—"

"Enough to make sure that the night ends the way it's supposed to. You're right. It's not. But every little bit helps."

Eugenie told herself to protest again, to stand up for the part of herself that wasn't twelve years old and behave like the grown woman she knew she was on some level. But something in her mother's expression made her hesitate. That and Eugenie's realization that her mother was hesitating, too. Instead of ignoring her daughter's wishes and unscrewing the liner top and thrusting out a hand with potentially blinding velocity to paint her daughter's eyelids, Lorraine was standing with one hand balancing herself on the walker and the other grasping the eyeliner, waiting for Eugenie to say it was okay to proceed. So, without thinking too hard about why she was doing it, she tipped her head backward and closed her eyes to let her mother sketch at will. She still had time to wash off anything Lorraine did to her, right?

"Just a little bit," Lorraine said, "and you'll look divine."

Oh, dammit.

"Now just a touch of color under the brow . . ."

"Mom, I—"

"Sit still."

"Yes, ma'am."

"Et voilà," her mother finally concluded with what Eugenie

had to admit was a damned impressive French accent. *"Tu es presque belle."*

And because Lorraine had made her choose French for her foreign language in high school, Eugenie knew that much meant "You're almost beautiful." It was the greatest compliment her mother had ever paid her. On prom night, Lorraine had only conceded that she looked *un peu mignon*. "A little cute."

When she stood to look in the mirror, Eugenie was relieved—and not a little amazed—to discover that her mother had been quite restrained in her ministrations. She was a long way from Divine and in no way seventeen. In more ways than one. She wasn't going to the prom tonight. And she wasn't a virgin. No, tonight, she was a fully ripened woman going out for beers—or something—with all the knowledge and experience of . . .

Well, okay, of a suburban mom who had only been with one man in her entire life, and he hadn't been particularly experienced himself, not to mention in any way adventurous. At least she didn't have Farrah bangs curling-ironed within an inch of their life anymore. And at least she wasn't wearing Gunne Sax. Well, not from the waist down, anyway.

While Eugenie was evaluating herself in the mirror, her mother retrieved a little makeup bag from somewhere and began to pitch each of the cosmetics she had applied into it, along with her trusted Max Factor foundation and powder, which she hadn't had out before.

"Here," she said as she extended it to Eugenie. "Put this in your purse. Make sure you wake up before Nash does, so you can shower and put your face back on before he gets a look at you first thing in the morning. And be sure to at least make him coffee, but if you have time, you should really make him breakfast. Then take it to him in bed. Even if it's just coffee, take it to him in bed.

Most women won't do that for a man these days. It will make an impression."

Nothing of what her mother said surprised Eugenie. Not that she knew Nash would expect sex tonight. Or that Eugenie should agree to it. Or that the reason she should agree wasn't because it was what Eugenie wanted, but because it was what Nash wanted. Lorraine wouldn't even counsel Eugenie to practice safe sex. Her mother had never disapproved of women who used pregnancy to ensnare a man. Lorraine had always considered that to be a resourceful thing to do. "Women only have two choices," she had told Eugenie when she was a teenager. "We may use our beauty to get what we want and need, or if we don't have beauty, we may use our wits."

Wits, not smarts. A woman using her smarts would draw on her intelligence to consider a situation or prospect and set goals accordingly. A woman using her wits relied on her ingenuity and shrewdness in any given situation and reacted accordingly. Smarts could take a long time to see an outcome materialize. Wits could move things along much more quickly. Results in nine months, tops.

"Do this right, Eugenie," Lorraine said, "and you might just snag Nash well enough to reel him right into the boat. He likes you. And he's Julien's friend. It's not outside the realm of possibility that you could convince him to marry you. Especially if you sweeten the pot."

Eugenie turned away from the mirror and met her mother's gaze levelly. "I don't want to marry Nash, Mom."

"Then why are you going out with him?"

Even in light of the frankness of their discussion, it probably wasn't a good idea to tell her mother it was because she was thinking she might want to get laid. To Lorraine, any woman looking to get laid was only doing it to pave the way for matrimony. To Lorraine, the only reason a woman did anything with a man was to pave the way for matrimony.

So she answered her mother's question with one of her own. "Why would I want to tie myself to a man who can't stay faithful to one woman for any length of time?"

"If he's married to the right woman," Lorraine said, "that wouldn't be a problem."

What a nice cryptic statement that was. Eugenie wanted to translate it to mean that if Nash were married to the right woman, he would love that woman to distraction and wouldn't have the urge to stray. But since Lorraine was Lorraine, the more accurate translation would have the right kind of woman being the kind who didn't mind a husband who strayed, provided he was discreet, came home at some point, and handed over the bulk of his paycheck.

She declined the offered cosmetic bag, telling her mother, "Thanks, but I won't need anything for overnight."

And she decided to let Lorraine work out whether that translated into a version that had Eugenie coming home before things went too far or not caring what Nash thought of her looks in the morning. Either way, her mother wouldn't approve. And at the moment, Eugenie wasn't too sure of the translation herself.

Sixteen

Stevie Ray's Blues Bar was big on bricks, beers, and bikes (the Harley kind, not the Schwinn kind), populated with lots of blue jeans, T-shirts, and tank tops, and it welcomed Nash into the bosom of its loving family the minute he walked through the door. He seemed to know everyone who worked there, right down to a busboy he greeted as "Bra," a nickname Eugenie thought unfortunate, even cruel, until she realized it was a more vernacular form of *brother* than the already vernacular *bro*. She immediately felt out of place in her Yorkshire moors blouse, so as soon as they were seated, she ordered the most American beer she could think of—Budweiser, duh—even though Nash asked for a St. Pauli Girl. Then again, after the conversation she'd had with Julien, maybe what Nash was actually asking for was another companion for the evening.

The place was surprisingly packed, so either the establishment was unusually popular or the band they'd come to hear was unusually good. For now, the music was canned, but it was in keeping with the name of the place, something dark and smoky that cried out from the singer's soul, complete with brushy drums and guttural guitar. Over all, the noise level hovered somewhere between the roaring of an angry lion herd and the humming of a contented giant, a decibel Eugenie hadn't heard since she was in college and frequented places like this when hanging out with friends or Lawrence. Her concern about her attire was ebbing by the time their server returned with their beers, and as she settled back in her chair to lift the dewy longneck to her mouth, she felt the burdens of three decades begin to wash away.

"This is nice," she said. "I like this place."

"It's practically my second home," Nash told her as he raised a hand in greeting to a group of men at the end of the bar.

"So I noticed. This must be where you escape to every night after you bolt from the house."

"I do not bolt from the house," he denied. "I just leave my place of employment to have a beer before going home the way millions of other people do every Monday through Friday." As he spoke, a woman strode past their table and addressed him by name, dragging her fingers along his shoulders as she went. He responded with a quick hello, covering her hand with his for the duration of her brief passage, and then, without missing a beat, continued, "But this is definitely an escape place for me."

She'd used the word *escape* in reference to Fleurissant for obvious reasons. That Nash would use it to refer to a place where he so clearly belonged was something Eugenie found interesting. It also made her think about Seth again, since her son was also obviously trying to escape something, if only she could figure out what.

"Nash, can I ask you a question?" she said before she could stop herself.

He had been lifting his beer to his mouth, but halted long enough to say, "Anything."

"If you were a sixteen-year-old boy"—and, really, in many ways, he had never stopped being one of those, so this should be an easy question for him to answer—"how would you spend your time over summer break?"

He studied her blankly for a moment, then his expression cleared. "Oh, right. Seth. This is about him, right?"

She nodded, picking anxiously at the label on her beer.

"I'd probably spend my summers now the same way I did when I was sixteen," he said.

"Which was how?"

He flashed a smile, but there was something about it that felt a little contrived. "You want me to tell you things that will make you feel better about Seth, or do you want me to tell you the truth?"

She stopped picking at the label and wrapped her fingers around the bottle, tight. "I was kind of hoping the truth would make me feel better about Seth."

Nash waved to someone behind her, then looked at her again. "Janey, he's sixteen. It's kind of his job to do stuff that his mother won't approve of."

Even though she wasn't all that eager to have her worst fears confirmed, she said, "Like what?"

He shrugged, his gaze flitting to his left, where a table of women half their ages—all wearing something sexy, damn them—were laughing over something one of them had said to the others. Eugenie waited for Nash to look at her again, but his reply went in their direction instead.

"The stuff sixteen-year-old boys have been doing ever since there were sixteen-year-old boys. Hanging out at the pool—or the village well or the local aqueduct—looking at girls. Driving around in the car—or the buggy or the chariot—yelling, "Hey, baby!" at girls. Prowling the mall—or the barn raising or the agora—checking out girls. You look surprised," he said when his gaze returned to her face. "You don't think boys haven't changed since ancient times?"

She bit back her smile. "No, I didn't think you knew what the agora was."

He feigned a mean face. "I'd be mad at you if I didn't go out of my way to cultivate such a dude reputation."

He cultivated that? She would have sworn he was born to it.

His gaze glanced off hers again, in the other direction this time, where another group of women—closer to Eugenie's age this time but still wearing something sexy, damn them—was sidling up to the bar. "But that's only how sixteen-year-old boys spend about eighty percent of their summer," he said. "The other twenty percent they use for wreaking havoc and/or general mayhem."

This, actually, was what Eugenie feared Seth was involved in. She didn't doubt he enjoyed his fair share of obsession with the opposite sex. But he was far more prone to acting than he was to mooning (mooning in the traditional meditative sense, not the seventies exhibitionist sense, which would indeed make it acting, and . . . and, wow, she really didn't want to go there—*Move along, Eugenie*). Her greatest concern was that he would come home one night not on his bike but in the back of a police cruiser, having committed any number of petty crimes or having indulged in any number of self-destructive behaviors. Or, worse still, that there would come a night when he didn't come home at all.

Even though she wasn't sure she wanted to hear the answer—okay, even though she *was* sure she *didn't* want to hear the answer—she asked anyway, "What kind of havoc and/or mayhem?"

Nash looked at her again, but someone else behind her must have invaded the view, because his gaze skittered to the left again. At least it wasn't a woman this time, because he did the head-bob thing guys do when they greet other guys. "In terms of my own teenage years, it was the usual," he said when he returned his attention to Eugenie. "Anything from trying to break into the school chemistry lab to swipe the materials for an M-80 to leave in Mrs. Shoemaker's mailbox to trying to find someone who'd buy us a six-pack at Fern and Moody's to shoplifting *Hustler* from Taylor Drug Store." He laughed when he saw her expression. "Nah, I'm just kidding about *Hustler*," he tried to reassure her. "Taylor didn't carry it on account of they were too moral. So we had to steal *Playboy* instead. Or else head downtown and try to jimmy the lock on the fire exit at Blue Movies."

By now, Eugenie's stomach was churning. She knew *Playboy* was a rite of passage for teenage boys, and in a lot of ways, she didn't object to Seth's looking at it, other than wishing she could sit him down and explain to him that the women posing inside were the product of cosmetics, lighting, and Photoshop and were there only because they wanted to make money or further acting careers (and that they should let Eugenie know how that was working out for them), not because they wanted to be the personal plaything of any man who might be looking at their photos. But she didn't relish the thought of a squirm-inducing (for both of them) conversation that would abolish the fantasy factor that was such a huge part of what made *Playboy Playboy*, even for adolescents who were just embarking on the good ship *Sexual Fantasy*—which, surprisingly, was less cruise ship than it was container ship. She *did* object to him looking at *Hustler*—or anything else the now thankfully defunct Blue Movies might hold within its oh-so-soiled bowels—because that way lay, if not madness, then at the very least a felony stalking charge.

"Please tell me you're joking," she said.

Nash leaned back in his chair far enough to tip it back on two legs. The hand not curled around the neck of his beer curled around his own. "About which part?"

"About all of it," she said. "Just tell me my son is normal, happy, in good mental health, and that he never does anything he shouldn't do or know about anything he shouldn't know about, and that he'll grow up to be a fine young man of sound mind and body who I never have to worry about because he's perfect in every way, and that the reason he's never at home is because he's fascinated by geology and biology and astronomy and a bunch of other natural sciences that would necessitate field study, and he wants to learn about it all firsthand because practical knowledge is the best knowledge, and that's why he stays away from home every day for hours on end, and that the reason he came home battered and bloody the other day wasn't because he was fighting but because it was like he said—he had a wreck on his bike—not that that's especially reassuring, because he could kill himself on that damned thing if he's not careful, and that neither of those things—the disappearing or the being battered and bloody—has anything to do with his dumbass father abandoning and rejecting him or his clueless mother not knowing how to talk to him, and that he's perfectly okay in every possible way and will graduate at the top of his class and be accepted to the college of his choice with a full academic scholarship, where he'll meet lots of girls who are strong and smart and would never allow themselves to be objectified or subjugated by a photo spread called 'The Girls of Egghead Land' and—"

When she got to the part about a photo spread, Nash brought his chair back down on all fours with a thump, reached across the table, and pressed two fingers gently against her mouth to keep from escaping any other fears she might unleash, just when she was getting to the part about Seth always eating organic foods and preparing at least two vegan meals a week along with two fish meals a week—though he had to be careful about mercury, so only fish farmed in the clear icy waters of British Columbia or someplace like that—to make sure he would have healthy sperm that produced healthy offspring, which, now that she thought about it, was probably a good place for Nash to stop her, so she really dodged a bullet there.

"Breathe," he said. "And let me tell you about a friend of mine, Mr. Semicolon."

Actually, Eugenie probably needed more to hear about Mr. Xanax, but she did as he instructed, breathing in deeply through her nose and releasing the breath slowly. Then she did it again. And again. And again. Only when he was confident she had regained control of her verbal motor skills did Nash remove his fingers from her mouth. And only far enough that he could quickly replace them should she succumb to another fit of hyperlogia . . . hyperlexia . . . hyperwhateverislatinfortalking.

"Seth is fine, Janey," he said softly. "Really. He's a good kid."

She managed to inhale another deep breath and expel it without incident, so she braved the question, "How do you know?"

Nash lowered his hand to the table, barely a hairsbreadth from where Eugenie's own hand lay. "Because I've talked to him."

This was news to Eugenie. She didn't think Seth talked to anyone. He was an equal opportunity ignorer, something that made her feel only marginally better about her relationship with him. She could always reassure herself that at least he didn't hate her alone. Hey, he hated everyone! So much more reassuring, that.

"When have you talked to him?" she asked.

Nash resumed his previous tipping-chair position and enjoyed another taste of his beer before answering. "He's been pitching in to help clean out the attic so Jules and I can get to it more quickly once the time comes for that."

Oh. So maybe he wasn't always gone on his bike, Eugenie thought. Maybe there had been days when he was home and she just didn't know it because he'd been working up in the attic. Not that that was especially reassuring, either, since it meant that, even when he was under her roof, she still didn't know the whereabouts—mental or physical—of her own kid.

"And he helped me repair some of the masonry on the garage," Nash continued. "The kid's actually got kind of a gift for working with his hands. Takes after his uncle Jules that way. You might not have to worry about him getting into the college of his choice. World's always gonna need laborers."

He sounded a little defensive when he said that, surprising her. For the first time ever, it occurred to Eugenie that maybe Nash wasn't quite as cocky as his dude reputation led others to believe.

"If that's what Seth decides he wants to do, I'm all for it," she said.

It was only a half lie. She did want Seth to go to the college of his choice. But if, after graduating, he decided to follow in his uncle's footsteps—and if he really was good enough to make a living at it—she certainly wouldn't object. Nash was right. The world would always need laborers. At least until the day came that humankind was overthrown by the technology they'd created and was in no way morally responsible enough to have, so said technology ended up being pure evil and taking over the world, enslaving them all.

Not that Eugenie was paranoid or anything. She just wanted her son to be prepared, that was all.

"I just wish," she said, "that Seth would exhibit some inkling of what he does want to do with his life."

"Cut him some slack, Janey. He's sixteen. Did you know what you wanted to do with your life when you were sixteen?"

She had, actually. She'd known very well what she wanted to do at sixteen. She'd wanted to live with Bryan Brown in Australia and scuba dive the Great Barrier Reef. She'd wanted to live with Sean Connery in Scotland and explore Edinburgh Castle. She'd wanted to live with Sam Elliott in Montana and raise cattle. She'd wanted to live with Omar Sharif wherever he lived and be exotic and nomadic and learn to belly dance. She'd wanted to live with Billy Dee Williams in Cloud City, extracting valuable Tibanna gas and fighting Imperial Forces. Barring any of those, she'd wanted to live anywhere by herself and do anything that had nothing to do with her life at the age of sixteen.

In short, she'd wanted to do whatever she could to get as far away from Louisville and Lorraine as possible. (Which was why she had never wanted to live with Alain Delon in Paris and smoke Gauloises cigarettes in a Monmartre cafe. There had been a chance, however small, that she might have run into her mother there at some point.) Even though she'd ended up living with Lawrence in Indianapolis and driving a four-door sedan and volunteering in the school lunchroom, she had always considered herself a success. Until, you know, she'd had to move back to Louisville and Lorraine.

Instead of saying any of that to Nash, however (because she would have also had to admit that when she was sixteen she had wanted to live with him anywhere he was, doing whatever he wanted), she asked, "Did you know what you wanted to do with your life when you were sixteen?"

He grinned again. "Yeah, but I'm pretty sure it's not what you'd want your son to aspire to."

No, it probably wasn't.

"I just wish I knew him," she said. "If you asked me right now what his favorite anything is, or how he enjoys spending his time, or what his dreams and aspirations are, I wouldn't be able to tell you. For the last few years, he's just retreated into himself and stopped doing any of the things he used to do or talking about any of the things he used to talk about. He doesn't do or talk about anything at all. He's just never there anymore. Physically or mentally or emotionally."

"I'm sure you're worrying for nothing," Nash told her. "But, look, if you want me to have a man talk with him, man-to-man about man stuff, I'll be glad to do it."

"No," she said quickly. As nice as Nash was being about all this, his was the last voice of masculine experience Seth needed to hear. She wasn't even sure Julien was the right man to be guiding her son. But at least he was a man and not a victim of extended adolescence like Nash.

When Nash looked a little crestfallen at her speedy dismissal, she hastily added, "Thank you, really. It's sweet of you to offer. But if I'm complaining about not being connected to my son, then I need to try and connect with him myself. I just have to figure out how."

Nash was about to say something else, but his attention was snatched away by a server who stopped by their table to check on their orders. Not that she was their original server, but she wanted to say hi to Nash and, hey, if they were ready for another round, she'd let their actual server know.

So began another round of Pin the Greeting on Nash, because once he was talking to someone other than the woman he'd brought to the dance, he was evidently free game for everyone else, male or female, young or old, employee or customer. Eugenie might have been offended if it weren't for the fact that he introduced her to everyone who stayed long enough for an introduction, and he included her in any conversation that lasted beyond salutation. Plus, he really wasn't the instigator in any of the exchanges. There were just a lot of people who knew and liked him. By the time the band arrived on stage, Eugenie felt as if she'd met everyone in the place, and she was working on her third beer.

That was okay, though, because they danced enough to clear any buzz that might have resulted. Any fuzziness that lingered in Eugenie's head by the end of the evening was there only because of Nash. Because of the hours she'd spent watching the comings and goings of his smile. Because of dancing much closer to him than was probably smart. Because of inhaling great gulps of his scent, all musk and muscle and man.

That, really, was her undoing, that fog of near-forgotten pheromones that enveloped her all night, thanks to Nash's nearness and the fact that he was Nash. She had forgotten how body chemistry could react to create a compound that taunted and tempted and made promises a woman wanted desperately to believe: that the sex would be phenomenal, the romance epic, and the man responsible for both nothing short of a hero. Every touch would be electric. Every thought would be frenetic. Every breath would be narcotic. And it would stay that way *forever.*

No, really. It would. Honest.

What made it worse was that the pheromones of a man like Nash were distilled to a heady, full-bodied elixir whose merest sip could intoxicate. And he served Eugenie a double shot at a time when she was parched. Even in the early stages of her relationship with Lawrence, she never felt the tug of desire—nay, the thrust of hunger—that bedeviled her when she was in close proximity to Nash for an extended length of time.

She told herself sternly that anything that happened with him would be pointless, that the only thing that could come of it would be the temporary scratching of a physical itch that would just start itching again the next time she saw him. Spending the night with him wouldn't change anything in her life or improve her situation in any way. There would be no future with him. Discounting schoolgirl fantasies, there was no past. With Nash, there was and would always be only a present that barely lasted a moment. Still, as moments went, one with him could potentially be electric, frenetic, and narcotic.

Which went a long way toward explaining how Eugenie ended up at Nash's Phoenix Hill apartment at one o'clock in the morning, instead of the house in Manitou Hills to which she had promised she would return. The night was still young, she reasoned. She would still get home before it was over. Promise kept. No harm, no foul. All quiet on the western front.

Since it was her first time in the home of her lifelong idol, Eugenie allowed herself a moment of supplication after entering the sanctuary. She had halfway expected his place to be furnished in midcentury frat house, crowded with castoff furniture—quite possibly plaid—and ugly lamps, with posters of surfers and *Sports Illustrated* swimsuit models affixed to the walls with thumbtacks. Instead, the furniture was boxy and beige, the rug a Berber remnant, maybe a shade lighter, and the lamps were fine. The walls, a different shade of beige than the furnishings, were mostly bare, save a handful of sepia-toned, parklike photographs. Although there were pale wooden bookcases along one of those walls, they housed no more than a dozen books and a sparse collection of masculine knickknacks—a couple of bowling trophies, an autographed baseball in an acrylic cube, a model of what looked like a ship in a bottle without the bottle. The rest of the space was filled with an assortment of game consoles—even more than Seth had—along with their varying and sundry accessories. All were hooked up to a big flat-screen TV beside the shelves under which was an assortment of DVDs.

Music suddenly coasted into the living room from another, and Eugenie turned to find Nash entering the living room from the kitchen with a glass of red wine in each hand. Obviously, he didn't abide the commandment that read, "Thou shalt not mix two forms of spirits in one night (even if thou do boogieth down with gyrations that are sinful in the eyes of the lord of the dance), lest thou have the unholy headache in the morning. Not to mention it could make thou do things thou wouldst regret."

Ignoring the little angel on one shoulder who whispered frantically into her ear that she was making a huge mistake being here (because the little devil on her other shoulder was shouting something about mind-blowing orgasms), Eugenie took the glass he extended with a murmur of thanks. She twirled it lightly by its stem and watched Nash over the rim, wondering what she was supposed to do next. Or what he was supposed to do next. It had been so long since she'd stood in a man's apartment after a date that she couldn't remember the steps.

"Thank you for tonight," she said. "I had a good time."

Nash was cradling his glass in the palm of his hand, his fingers curving over the bowl in the way they would cup a woman's breast. "You talk like it's about over," he said.

Did she? How odd. And interesting.

He took a step forward, bringing himself close enough to

brush the backs of his fingers over her cheek and down the column of her throat, curling them snugly over her nape. Eugenie felt the caress all the way down to her womb.

"I thought maybe you could stay awhile," he said. "I've got some of those cinnamon scones from Heine Brothers' that you like so much."

Well, if he knew she liked the cinnamon scones from Heine Brothers', then he also knew that the only time she ate them was on the weekends. For breakfast.

"Um, thanks, Nash. That was nice of you. But . . . um . . . but . . ."

But what? she asked herself. Why did she stop talking after that massively significant little word?

He must have noticed her massively significant hesitation, because the fingers on her nape curled more snugly, and he pulled her forward, covering her mouth with his. Eugenie allowed herself to get lost in the kiss for a few seconds . . . okay, maybe a few more seconds . . . just one or two more, really . . . oh, wow, now he was using his tongue, so probably a few seconds more would be okay, just for exploratory reasons . . . maybe a minute, but no more than a minute, honest . . . unless, oh . . . unless he did that with his tongue, which he did, so just a few seconds more . . .

In the next few sets of seconds, Nash retrieved her glass and set it on a shelf alongside his own, aligned his body completely against hers, and looped his other arm around her waist. Then he strode her backward to the couch and collapsed upon it, pulling her down atop himself as he went. By the time Eugenie regained her wits, her Yorkshire moors blouse was lying in a heap on the floor and her new bra—which was the utter antithesis of no-nonsense, no-frills, and was in no way white cotton—was open, and Nash was dragging openmouthed kisses from one breast to the other and back again. To her credit, she hadn't just lain there, because his shirt was hiked up under his arms and the fly of his jeans was open and she was doing a little exploring of her own and discovering how largely different Nash was from Lawrence.

Eugenie would tell herself later that it was the involuntary introduction of Lawrence into the scene that put such a screeching halt to it. But, really, when she replayed everything in her head later, she would have to admit that the brakes were slammed when the shoulder-dwelling devil was shouted down by the angel, who managed to get in one fateful word between the shouts about orgasms: *Tomorrow*.

Hearing that, being made to think about that, caused her to scramble off Nash and snatch her blouse from the floor, then put herself back together again as quickly as she could. She kept her back turned to him the whole time, hoping he might take the hint that he should put himself back together, too, but when she turned to face him, he was sitting on the couch with his pants still unfastened, his shirt still askew, his face still flushed.

He studied her hard, probably trying to figure out what the hell she was doing—well, that made two of them—but said nothing. Then again, she was the one who had interrupted them, so maybe it was up to her to be the first to speak. She just wished she knew what to say. Other than *Do you mind taking me home?*

She opened her mouth to say she was sorry but stopped herself. She had done nothing to apologize for. If she owed anyone an apology, it was herself. She was the one denying herself what she had thought she wanted tonight. She had fantasized about a moment like this with Nash for the majority of her life. When she was very young, those fantasies had always ended with the kiss. A chaste first kiss that lasted all of two seconds and didn't include any touching body parts beyond the lips. When she hit adolescence, the fantasies included quick brushes of his fingers over her breasts or between her legs. By college, she was able to picture nakedness. There had been times when Lawrence was inside her that she would close her eyes and picture Nash being there instead.

Now, finally, she had the chance to make all those fantasies reality. And she was confident that the reality would indeed supersede the fantasy, as so seldom happened. So why was she standing here fully dressed looking at him when she could be over there atop him fully naked?

Still feeling the urge to utter an apology, she made herself say instead, "Do you mind taking me home?"

Now Nash did straighten himself up, tugging up his zipper—though not comfortably, Eugenie noted—and pulling his T-shirt back into place. He stood, hooking his hands on his hips in a way that wasn't exactly unchallenging, and said, "Would you mind telling me why you want to go home?"

Well, she wouldn't if she actually knew. So she only said, "It's late."

He inhaled a breath, released it slowly. "You ask me, it's early."

"Half empty, half full."

He shook his head. "No. We were both on the same page tonight. Up until thirty seconds ago, anyway."

She didn't deny it. But she still couldn't explain it. "I'm not ready," she said. "For this. With you."

And, really, once she said that, she thought maybe that actually was all it was. Although she was ready for sex again—her brain knew it, her body knew it, even her heart knew it—she wasn't ready for sex with someone who might . . . hurt her. She knew Nash wouldn't do that on purpose. It was she who would be putting that power in his hands. Years ago, she would have been strong enough to take on Nash and bounce back afterward with fairly little bruising to her psyche. Years ago, one night with him might have been all she wanted or needed. Years ago, had she not met Lawrence, she might have even reached a point where she could be as nonchalant about sex as Nash was. Years ago, she would have let tonight follow its original course and been fine the next day. And the day after that. And the day after that. But tonight . . .

Tonight she wasn't strong enough for that, and tomorrow she wouldn't be fine. If she slept with Nash tonight, she would do so with expectations that were irrational and unrealistic. If she slept with him tonight, she'd want more tomorrow. More sex, certainly, but more beyond that, too. More of his attention. More of his time. More of his space. More of him. She may have divorced herself from Lawrence, but she hadn't divorced herself from the desire to have someone in her life the way Lawrence had been when times were good. None of the things she would want from Nash tomorrow were things he gave in any great amount. But that last, especially—himself—he had spent a lifetime making clear wasn't up for grabs. To anyone. Ever.

"You're right about it being early," she told him, crossing her arms over her midsection. Though whether that was because she was feeling vulnerable or because she feared she might be coming apart, she couldn't have said. "It is early. It's too early. For me."

She hoped he would understand she was talking about more than the hour.

"I thought you and Lawrence separated two years ago," he said.

"Twenty-six months," she corrected.

"That's a long time, Janey."

"For some things, yes."

"When I asked you out, it was because I thought this was something you might want. Maybe even need."

"When I agreed to go out with you, I thought that, too. Tonight I realized I was wrong. I'm just not ready."

He nodded, his expression changing from wariness to resignation. Then he surprised her by asking, "So when do you think you will be ready?"

She braved a small smile. "I don't know," she said honestly. "Why do you ask?"

He shrugged. Then he took a few steps forward until his body was barely a breath away from her own. "Because somewhere along the line, Janey, I realized that maybe this is what I want, too. It might even be something I need."

She narrowed her eyes at him. Was he just saying that because he still wanted to toss her onto the pile of his female acquisitions? Was he saying it now because he was trying to change her mind right this minute and get her back half undressed on the sofa? Or was it perhaps, possibly, perchance conceivable that she meant something more to him than his typical conquest did?

He lifted his hand the way he had earlier and brushed the backs of his knuckles along her cheek, as if that were Step 1, Fig. A, in the instruction manual that had come with his "How to Seduce a Woman" kit, and she began to think maybe everything he said or did was just a precursor to getting a woman into bed. Then he had to go and ruin her suspicion by dropping his hand back to his side and saying, "Lawrence was never good enough for you, you know."

Well, she knew that *now*. Now that everyone who'd ever seen the two of them together had made a point of telling her how the two of them never should have been together.

Nash tilted his head toward the front door. "C'mon, Janey. I'll take you home."

Just like that, any tension that might have lingered between them evaporated. How did he do that? How was he able to perform a virtual snap of his fingers and make everything feel right again?

She unfolded the arms she had crossed over herself and offered to help him tidy up the untouched wine still sitting in its glasses. But he declined, saying something about letting it breathe so that, by the time he got back home, both servings would be smooth and mellow and ready for consumption. Meaning he would drink both glasses himself. Along with, probably, the rest of the bottle.

And she wondered if State Liquors still stayed open till the wee hours so she could maybe go up and get a bottle for herself, too.

Seventeen

Eugenie filed her first report with Spalding about DreamMakers two weeks after making first contact. She had to give the service credit for one thing. When her first two ideal someones turned out to be less than ideal, they were quick to supply her with a third. And when that ideal someone was also not so ideal, they provided a fourth. Then a fifth. Then a sixth. And a seventh. Never appreciating, evidently, the irony of the continued use of the word *ideal* for a potential match even after it became clear that the men were all unsuitable.

Probably, Eugenie began to think around match number four, DreamMakers' slogan should be changed from "Experts in locating that ideal someone" to "Whizzes at unearthing that vaguely compatible someone who may or may not have a criminal record and/or history of mental illness since, really, we don't dig down too far."

In fact, it didn't take long before she realized that DreamMakers took on as clients only three types of people: those who had lots of money but couldn't find dates because they were unbelievably annoying; those who could overlook a lot of faults in a prospective date (including unbelievable annoyance) provided those dates had a lot of money; and those who were simply the most gullible people on the planet and could be convinced that *ideal* was just another word for *vaguely compatible*.

Because what all the men Eugenie had dated had in common—besides being unbelievably annoying—was that they all pulled in well into six figures annually. DreamMakers, she came to realize, was most suited to matching up sugar daddies—and, presumably, sugar mommies—with people who were more interested in financial security than in emotional security. All the men with whom she had been set up had evidently asked for only one quality in their ideal woman: that she produced estrogen. Okay, two things: that she produced estrogen and that she was shallow enough to overlook any undesirable qualities in a mate, provided he pulled in well into six figures annually.

Her report was as brief as their questionnaire, because she'd had no trouble summing up each of her encounters in single to-the-point phrases. She hadn't even had to have multiple-choice options of (a) through (e) to help her out. In addition to Thomas the environment hater and Michael the shoe fetishist, she had been paired with, and described accordingly, the following:

Ted—Reeked of peppermint schnapps and used the word impact *as a verb three times*

Simon—Absolutely certain Elvis is still alive and working as a consultant at a rival firm

Douglas—Much too happy about mysterious disappearance of ex-girlfriend's cat

Randy—Found the missing link!

Bob—Thinks Joseph Stalin got a bum rap

Because she had just left a midmorning coffee meeting with the Joseph Stalin fan (who could only meet at that time of day for reasons that were never made clear, but which Eugenie suspected were due to his murky marital status), and because Spalding was taking that entire day to make exploratory visits to potential dating sites, and since both of their locations had been closer to the Highlands than downtown, and since it was an absolutely gorgeous day, they agreed to meet for lunch at Seneca Park near Big Rock. Spalding arrived in his black 1964 Corvair Monza convertible—top down, natch—within moments of Eugenie pulling into the lot in her nowhere-near-as-charming four-door that didn't even boast a sunroof. They exited their cars as a unit, Eugenie carrying a bag from Queen of Sheba that contained carry-out chicken sambussa and kosta wraps, Spalding holding his *Rat Patrol* lunch box—no surprise there. What was surprising was that instead of walking over to greet her, he circled to the back of the car and opened the trunk, then withdrew a plaid blanket, which he threw over one arm.

A picnic? Eugenie thought as she watched him approach. She was going on a picnic with her boss? What exactly did that mean? She had assumed they would just scarf down their meals in the front seat of one of their cars, speculate about DreamMakers, and then head off on their merry way, Eugenie returning to Heart-Menders and Spalding dashing off to whatever old-world romantic rendezvous was left in town that he hadn't already discovered. Instead, after exchanging greetings, she followed him as he made his way leisurely to a shady patch of grass where he spread the blanket and gestured for her to have a seat before taking his own.

Which he did way more gracefully than she because he wasn't hindered by a skirt the way she was. A white skirt, at that, and a white top, so, with an eye to the sea of grass surrounding them, she scooched as close to the center of the blanket as she could without giving Spalding the impression she was actually scooching close to him. In spite of that, he glanced up at her approach and smiled. Though whether it was a smile of understanding that she didn't want to get grass stains on her attire or a smile of reassurance that he didn't mind sharing his space or a smile of encouragement that he wanted her to scooch closer still or . . .

Well, suffice it to say she just wasn't sure what to make of that smile.

Spalding lowered himself expertly onto the blanket, without having to tug at or rearrange his clothing at all—damn men, anyway—then scooched close enough to the center that, when he folded his legs pretzel fashion, his thigh pressed into hers, a sensation that spurred a funny little buzz in her belly, which immediately segued into a satisfied hum. Interesting, that.

"So, how was your coffee date?" he asked as he opened his lunch box and withdrew the thermos. She noted that the rest of his repast contained all the usual suspects.

"He was a major fan of social reform," she said as she went about the task of feng shui–ing her own lunch on the blanket. And making sure she didn't alter her position, thereby guaranteeing that their thighs brushed against each other with every motion either of them made.

"That sounds promising," he said.

"Only if your idea of social reform involves jackboots and big, bushy mustaches, my Bolshevik comrade."

He finished unscrewing his thermos top and poured something purple into the little plastic cup. "So DreamMakers' dreams include Stalinists." He looked at her again as he recapped the thermos. "I'm pretty sure HeartMenders would toss out any application on which someone's hobbies and interests included 'dressing up in uniforms with shiny brass buttons and exerting tyranny over the peasants.'"

"Permission to feel smug granted," Eugenie said. "But I'm sure it had nothing to do with the application he filled out, since the questions DreamMakers asks on both that and their world-renowned 'brief questionnaire' pretty much exclude hobbies or interests. Which is the only logical reason I can figure for why my ideal someones also included a shoe fetishist, the missing link, and a catnapper."

He glanced up at that last. "Catnapper?"

"Douglas. Instrumental in, if not solely responsible for, the disappearance of his ex-girlfriend's cat. I'm sure of it. And since there was no mention of any ransom demand being made or met, I don't even want to think about what might have been little Booboo's fate. I am mystified as to how DreamMakers can be so successful when their record is oh and six with me."

Spalding finished unwrapping his PB&J and went to work on the plastic flap of his mandarin oranges. "All these guys were loaded, I assume?"

She nodded. "Yep. Everything from a neurosurgeon to a guy who's a partner in a major accounting firm."

They ate in silence for a few moments, until each had curbed the worst of their noontime hunger. Then Eugenie withdrew the manila folder with her report from her handbag and handed it over to Spalding. He continued to eat as he scanned it, flipping over each page before looking up at Eugenie again.

"There has to be more to it—to these guys—than this," he said. "I refuse to believe HeartMenders is losing out to a service that's so careless—irresponsible, even—when it comes to their clients, and who put personal finance and physical traits above everything else. If they don't even bother to ask about the most basic things that attract people to each other, what criteria do they have?"

"Well, they did do this thing with finger measurement before giving me the questionnaire," Eugenie told him.

He nodded. "Digital ratio," he said. "That's interesting, the science and philosophy behind it, but I'm not sure it's a sound basis for matchmaking. Certainly hormones affect a lot of our traits and choices and have a big impact on us all the way back to the womb, but so does every person, scene, situation, physical stimulus, and activity we've been exposed to from day one. Biology might give us life, but life is what makes us human. Biology might generate our attraction to another person, but our humanity is what makes us fall in love with them. In love with *them*," he repeated emphatically "not with their bank account."

"Our humanity is what also makes us get hurt by them," Eugenie said. She looked down into her tea dispassionately, giving it a mindless stir with her straw. "Maybe there's something to be said for marriages of convenience instead of marrying for love. If we connect based on biology instead of emotion, we propagate the species and ensure the survival of the human race, but we don't risk ending up in despair and destroying ourselves and others."

When she looked up again, she saw Spalding poised with his sandwich halfway to his mouth. "Do you really believe that?"

"I don't know," she said. "I'm just now considering it. Before, I always figured people got married because they were in love with each other. Otherwise, what's the point? After everything with my marriage, though, I can kind of see the point now."

"The point being?" Spalding asked.

Eugenie set down her tea and picked at her lunch. "Everybody wants to spend their life with someone they love and who loves them back. But people need to survive, too, in a world that's becoming more cruel and difficult with every passing year. It makes sense for the sake of survival to align yourself with whoever has the best resources. In the twenty-first century, that means whoever has the most money."

"But survival is only part of the equation," Spalding objected. "People need other people in their lives, too, to prevent survival from becoming nothing more than simple existence. They need friends and family, co-workers, and social companions. They need someone who can provide for their emotional and sexual needs."

"But who says the same person filling the sexual role also has to fill the emotional role?" Eugenie asked. "Why can't you fall in love with one person but find physical pleasure with another? What's so strange about that?"

Spalding hesitated a moment, then asked, "You mean like your husband did?"

Eugenie dropped her head again to pick some more at her lunch.

"I don't buy it," he said. "Maybe when they're young and trying to figure out who they are, it's easy for people to get emotionally attached to one person while being sexually fulfilled by another. But when it comes to the long term, people don't separate sex and love. DreamMakers can't be successful in making lifelong matches if all they have in their stable is a bunch of well-heeled players. I don't care how materialistic our society has become, people have got to be looking for more in a mate than that they have piles of cash."

"I don't know, Spalding. Times are tough. Folks are losing their jobs, their homes, their retirements. People are looking down the road at the future, and they're not seeing much that will change any of that. Suddenly, there's a lot of stuff they can overlook in the name of financial security. Historically speaking, people have married for economic reasons since the beginning of time. Why not still do it today?"

He started shaking his head again before she even finished speaking. Then he pointed down to her report that still lay open on the blanket. "Would you marry the missing link if it meant you didn't have to worry about your financial future?"

"Me? No. I wouldn't marry the missing link under any circumstances. But some people, a lot of people, actually . . ."

She left the sentence unfinished since, really, it didn't need finishing. All one had to do was turn on the television or read the web or newspapers to see what people were willing to do in exchange for the promise of money. They would hurt, horrify, and humiliate themselves and battle, belittle, and betray others. *I Married a Catnapper* was a show that would totally make it onto cable these days. Hell, *I Married the Missing Link* would make it onto cable these days. Probably on the History Channel.

Spalding was so put out by her insinuation that he actually put down his sandwich. "I know there have always been a handful of people who think money is the most important thing in the world, and those people—those *few* people, who are in no way close to being a majority—will suffer just about anything to have it. What person in his or her right mind would base a relationship on money?"

"Lots of people," she said. "When you combine the basic human lust for money with the basic human fear of being a big, fat nobody, you wind up with a toxic compromise of principle and dignity that could suck in just about anybody. It's kind of terrifying, the world I have to bring up my son in. How am I supposed to instill in him a sense of self-worth or self-respect or individuality or any other damn thing when he's constantly pelted by pop culture references that whittle human emotion down to one quote or comic or clip that goes viral so fast, within twenty-four hours, every kid on the planet is having the same exact experience and feeling the same exact way about it, and none of them has taken it seriously and WTF, FTW, IDK, OMG, BRB, TTYL."

"Then why do you think DreamMakers is so successful?" Spalding asked.

Eugenie thought about that for a minute before replying. "I think maybe the reason they're doing well isn't so much because they're good at making matches. It's because they're good at making dreams."

"How do you mean?"

She hesitated a moment. "Can we shed our shroud of charming but archaic politeness for a minute?"

He nodded. "Of course we can. I didn't even realize we had shrouded ourselves in that."

Of course he didn't. Because he still lived in a time when that was a way of life. "Okay, look. Most people meet the person of their dreams relatively early in life. At college, say, or not long after they start working their first career-oriented job. Am I right?"

There was another pause—since he could never answer any question without first thinking about it—then he nodded. "I'll agree as long as we focus on 'most.'"

"So then anyone who's still single late in their thirties or in their forties either enjoys being single and stays that way by design, or else they're beginning to think on some level—maybe not all the time, and maybe it's not at the forefront of their brain, but on some level—that they've missed their chance to find their perfect and/or ideal someone. Will you agree with me on that?"

He inhaled a deep breath and released it slowly but finally nodded.

"Obviously, it will be a member of the latter group who hires a dating service. Still with me?"

He nodded again.

She continued, "The fact that they hire a dating service indicates that they've pretty much given up meeting someone on their own. They must have, because if they still believed in a chance encounter bringing them face-to-face with that someone someday, they wouldn't hire a matchmaker to make it happen. So by the time they do, they're already in a frame of mind that has them surrendering. Maybe not completely," she hurried to add when Spalding opened his mouth in what was sure to be an objection, "but they're not exactly in a demanding frame of mind, either. So they're already up for making concessions."

Spalding said nothing to agree or disagree with that, but his brain synapses were clearly crackling.

"I think DreamMakers has figured that out," Eugenie said, "and I think they know how to exploit it. They identify every person who hires a matchmaker as someone who has a little kernel buried deep down inside them that makes them fear they'll end up alone and unloved. HeartMenders does, too, in its own way. But where HeartMenders digs up that kernel and plants—if you'll pardon the sappy metaphor—seeds of love that will require constant nurturing and cultivation, DreamMakers leaves that kernel where it is and throws a *lot* of fertilizer on top of it."

Now Spalding grinned. Although he still didn't say anything, there was obviously something germinating in his brain.

So Eugenie continued, "DreamMakers knows that if they can make the fear in that person grow, then the person will accept as a potential suitor whatever weed grows in the garden. They'll overlook all kinds of flaws in that weed if it means sharing the same root system. 'Hey, it's green like me, it's alive,' that person says. 'Really, what more do I need in a mate? At least I won't be alone.'

"And DreamMakers uses really good fertilizer, I must say," she added. "Every time I've told them that my ideal someone turned out to be less than ideal, they immediately painted this picture of the next person on the list as being this larger-than-life individual who will be perfect for me. Only they didn't talk about *him* so much as the lifestyle he lived that he would be sharing with me. A lifestyle that, I should add, almost certainly bears no resemblance to the one DreamMakers describes. Because they made a catnapper sound like an even bigger catch than Prince Harry. They must have a really good thesaurus at their disposal."

By now Spalding had finished most of his lunch and was picking up the remnants to return them to the lunch box. "So you're saying DreamMakers does exactly what their name advertises. They make dreams."

"And HeartMenders does exactly what its name advertises," she said. "They mend hearts. I just think a lot of people these days are more into dreaming than they are mending. Certainly dreams have a better reputation than mending does. Something breaks nowadays, you just replace it with a new one. Hardly anyone owns a sewing box anymore. Mending is so much trouble. It's so time-consuming. It's so old-fashioned. Much easier and faster to just replace whatever's not working with the latest model, even if that model won't last as long, or be as reliable, as the old one could be after being repaired."

"Even if I agree with you," Spalding said, "that doesn't help me stanch the flow of fleeing clients. I'm still losing people who think their hearts will be mended if the dream made is big enough."

Eugenie began to pack up what was left of her lunch, too. She'd done more talking than eating, but Queen of Sheba made for an excellent bedtime snack. "Well, then maybe we need to stop looking at how DreamMakers sells their dreams," she said, "and start looking instead at how we can mend HeartMenders ourselves."

"You mean stop blaming the other guy for our dissatisfaction and start looking within ourselves to create our own happiness?" he asked. "Why, Eugenie. Talk about old-fashioned."

Perhaps, she thought. Or maybe doing the thing no one else was doing made them revolutionary instead. Yeah, she'd go with that. Because revolutionary was something Eugenie had never been in her life. And she was beginning to think maybe that was a big part of why her life—and herself—had evolved the way they had. Without much evolution.

"So where do you suggest we start?" he asked.

"The same place every makeover starts," she said. "We do the easy stuff first."

He grinned at that. "So says the woman who's been working on a makeover for . . . how long now?"

She knew he was referring to Fleurissant. At least, she was pretty sure he was referring to that. Nevertheless, her reply was vague. "A while now."

"How's it going for you? Have you finished the easy stuff?"

Eugenie thought about the house, about how she'd realized on her first visit to Fleurissant that there would be nothing easy about its renovation. Even things like wallpaper stripping, which she'd done for nearly every room in the house she and Lawrence had bought, and for which she should have been an expert by now, had been met with staunch resistance. As if Fleurissant hadn't even wanted the most basic changes to be completed, even if they made the house safer and more beautiful.

"Fine," she lied. "It's going just fine."

She could tell by Spalding's expression that he didn't believe her. So she only said, "Paint. We start with paint. When was the last time you painted the offices of HeartMenders?"

Now his expression indicated something that looked like guilt. "Um . . ." he said. "Well . . . It's been a while . . ."

Evidently, Fleurissant wasn't the only edifice in Louisville that had been too long neglected. "Paint," Eugenie reiterated. "A total redo of the place, starting with the reception area. You only get one chance to make a first impression, after all."

"What was your first impression of HeartMenders?" he asked.

Of HeartMenders? she echoed to herself. *Or of its owner?* For some reason, Spalding seemed to be talking about both. So she answered honestly. About both. "I thought it was old-fashioned," she told him. "Quiet. Lacking in color. Kind of tired."

His expression in response to that was inscrutable. "What's your impression now that you've had a chance to get to know the place better?" he asked.

"I'm not sure," she replied. Again, honestly. "HeartMenders isn't the easiest place in the world to figure out. It's a lot different from . . . other places I've, um, worked."

"Give it your best shot, anyway," he said.

"Okay." She thought for a moment, her gaze never leaving his, his not dropping from hers, even when her scrutiny went on for interminable seconds. "I think now," she finally said, "that it's only old-fashioned in some ways. Maybe the most important ones. Which is good," she hastened to add. "And I think maybe it's not as quiet or tired as it first seemed. But it still lacks color."

He grinned at that. "Paint, then," he said.

"Paint," she echoed.

"Since you're the expert on makeovers, I'll leave that to your trusted hands." He gave her a ballpark figure for expenses to work with, which she immediately negotiated upward. If there was one thing Eugenie had learned about renovations, it was that they always came at a greater cost than one could ever anticipate.

"So I get to totally make over HeartMenders?"

"Just the appearance," he said. "For now."

"Do I get paid extra?"

He laughed. "Not unless you're the one who rolls on the paint."

There was something about the way he said that that made her want very much to be the one who rolled on the paint. That same something made getting paid for such an act seem more than a little illicit.

"Or whoever you can find to do the job right," he said. "If that happens to be you . . ." He left the sentence unfinished, still being inscrutable. Damn him.

"Okay," she said, being deliberately vague. Spalding wasn't the only one who could be inscrutable, by God. "I'll get started on that right away."

And she would, too. Just as soon as she figured out what the hell both of them were talking about.

Eighteen

Upon returning to HeartMenders after her picnic with Spalding . . . ah, she meant after a meeting with her employer, which just happened to take place on a picnic blanket in Seneca Park, Eugenie went back to work, her mind swirling with ideas about how to revolutionize HeartMenders. She started by halting just inside the door to give the outer office a critical evaluation. She had been immediately impressed upon entering DreamMakers by the whole look of the place and thought maybe it would be a good idea if HeartMenders made a physical impression that immediate, too. Though, admittedly, her impression of DreamMakers had been that they were completely detached from reality, but that could have been a big part of why they were successful. Who wanted reality to intrude on a relationship right off the bat like that? For that matter, who wanted reality to intrude into a relationship at all?

Still, a big part of HeartMenders' philosophy was approaching the whole relationship thing with a good dose of reality (since it did have a habit of intruding on people after they started dating), so it wasn't like they could just sweep reality under the rug the way DreamMakers did. But they could get a new rug, she thought, her eye falling to one of several bare spots on the aged Persian one they had now. And maybe some new chairs—ones that had been manufactured in this century. New pictures for the walls. A new desk for Iris. Replace the fake plants with real ones. Whose idea was it to put fake plants in the waiting room, anyway? That just screamed lack of nurturing capabilities. Why would anyone trust a dating service that couldn't even match itself up with live foliage?

Iris had been sitting at her desk writing something when Eugenie entered, but she looked up when Eugenie continued to stand in the doorway just surveying the waiting room. Eugenie was reminded of the first day she walked into HeartMenders, when Iris gazed at her in the same dispassionate way she did now. So it hadn't been because she was a stranger that Iris had done that. Iris just looked that way all the time.

"Is there a problem?" she asked Eugenie.

"More like a challenge," Eugenie said.

"What kind of challenge?"

Instead of elaborating, Eugenie asked, "Iris, what's your favorite color?"

Without even having to think about it, Iris replied, "Pink."

Well, that wasn't going to help, even if Iris would be the one looking at the walls of the waiting room more than anyone else. "What's your second-favorite color?" she asked.

This time Iris did give it a bit of thought before replying, "Orange."

Okay, scratch Iris from the color wheel. "Brown," Eugenie said suddenly, not sure where the color came from. She wasn't a big fan of brown. Except maybe with regard to eye color. Especially if the brown was accented with little gold flecks that ringed the iris. But brown didn't seem like such a bad idea for wall color, provided it wasn't too dark. Brown was a warm color. The color of cocoa. And coffee. And cognac. A comforting color. No one didn't like brown, did they? That would be like not liking chocolate.

"Brown," Eugenie repeated with more confidence. "We're going to paint the office. And I'm thinking brown."

"Oh no," Iris said. "That's a terrible color. Maybe we should go with beige."

"The walls are already beige. And they're boring. We need to make an impression on prospective clients the minute they walk through the door. Beige says boring. Boring matches. Boring dates. Boring service."

"But brown is so . . . brown," Iris said. "Maybe we should do green. Green is very soothing."

"We don't want to soothe our clients, Iris. We want to make them feel confident that we know what we're doing. Brown is stable. Reliable. Wholesome. It makes people think organic."

"Because it's the color of the earth?"

"No, because organic stuff is always wrapped in brown."

"Oh. Still, it's very . . . brown," Iris repeated. "Maybe yellow would be better for the walls."

"Too stimulating."

"Red?"

"Too energetic."

"White?"

"Too sterile."

"Blue, then."

"Absolutely not. No way. Uh-uh. No."

"How about—"

"Brown," Eugenie stated adamantly. "It's reliable and steady. And we'll replace the furniture, too. Something in the bronze or amber family, I think. We can bring in brighter colors with the rug, the artwork, and accessories. Jewel tones. Ruby. Emerald. Topaz. It will give the clients the impression of richness. And it will be warm."

Warm, Eugenie repeated to herself. It wouldn't be cold, like DreamMakers was. It would be provocative and elegant instead of blatantly sexy like DreamMakers was. It would give their clients the impression of romance highlighted with a dash of reality. Good reality, though. Like moving into their first apartment and piecing it together with family cast-offs and yard sale finds. Or barbecuing ribs on the patio with sweaty longneck Coronas and lobster-claw oven mitts. Or snuggling on the sofa with a glass of wine while they watch *Casablanca,* and having him tug Kleenex from the box he brought out from the bathroom for her when the tears first started, the scene where the band played "La Marseillaise," and handing her one whenever she needed one. Or raking big piles of leaves after they bought their first house and making piles for the next-door neighbor's kids to jump into, where watching them do that first makes them think maybe it's time to start a family. Or sitting on little wooden chairs at the kindergarten, watching their son receive his first award for perfect attendance, and then going away for an anniversary trip and doing nothing but talk about what a great kid they made together, and how they never imagined life could ever be this good, and wow, were they lucky to have found each other or what?

There would be nothing in the waiting room to even suggest how, someday, Ethel Merman could walk into their lives and throw water on the barbecue, and switch off the TV right when Rick is telling Ilsa they'll always have Paris, and torch those leaf piles with the kids still in them.

Not that Eugenie could blame it all on Ethel Merman. Marriages didn't go belly-up just because another person entered them. One of the people in that marriage had to open the door and invite the newcomer in, then forget all about lobster oven mitts and Kleenex boxes and star-spangled certificates of perfect attendance. Had Ethel never shown up, someone else would have. Or else Lawrence would have gone looking. Eugenie just wished he would have clued her in to his unhappiness as soon as the marriage started to fracture. Maybe then they could have figured out a way to repair it before it reached the point where he didn't even want to try.

Before it reached the point where she didn't want to try.

Because as she looked at the reception room of HeartMenders, filled with memories about how her life with Lawrence had unfolded, Eugenie found herself wondering if she had worked as hard to fix her broken marriage as she was working now to fix a broken house, or if she had approached improving her failing marriage with as much enthusiasm as she was approaching improving a failing business. Maybe, under different circumstances, she would have been the one to open the bedroom door and invite a newcomer into the scenes from her marriage. The way Marianne had, even though she had been reasonably happy in her marriage to Dale. Even if Eugenie hadn't opened the door to another man, she might have opened it to something else that would have made her realize that she and Lawrence were simply going about the motions of their life together and not really living it.

She closed her eyes for a moment, replaying the night Lawrence came into the family room to tell her about the affair. She remembered she turned on *CSI: New York* late, coming into the program after the opening credits, while the guest-starring roles were scrolling across the bottom. She remembered being more distracted than usual—the day had been such a busy one, and the next had promised to be just as hectic. When Lawrence came into the room, she hadn't even greeted him.

She halted there, opening her eyes. Why hadn't she greeted him? Why hadn't she even looked up at her husband? She'd barely noticed his arrival, had assumed he'd come into the family room for a book or magazine or something, not to talk to her. Why had she assumed that? Had they become so distant that they had stopped even acknowledging each other's importance? Each other's presence? Had he wanted so little from her at that point that she had assumed his entry into a room was for something that had nothing to do with her? Was that normal?

Even when he'd taken his seat on the sofa next to her, she hadn't spoken to him. Hadn't looked at him. Because she had been trying to figure out what the characters on TV were saying about the fictional murder she had missed in the opening minutes. She had been more interested in that than she had been in the man with whom she was sharing her life. Sure, it was easy to say, *Hey, I saw him every day, but I only got to watch* CSI *once a week. That hour was my me time. He knew that. It's only normal that I wouldn't pay attention to his entrance. It's only normal that I would think he had come in for something other than to talk to me. It's only normal that I wouldn't have wanted to talk to him.*

Yes. It was easy to say that. Much easier than admitting that his entrance had felt like an invasion of her space—her me time. Or that she didn't want him in the family room with her. Or that she wanted to be alone. And not just for one hour, once a week, to watch TV, either.

More memories followed that one. Of Lawrence waiting in silence for her to look at him. Of him waiting for her to ask him what was wrong. Of her sensing that something was wrong but not wanting to ask him what it was. Of not wanting to know what it was. Of wanting him to go away so she could be alone for just one . . . fucking . . . hour. Of him picking up the remote and turning off the TV without asking her and saying he needed to talk to her about something important. Of the absolute rage she had felt when he turned off the TV that way. *Bastard.*

Rage. She had felt rage. Just because he turned off the TV. Even before he told her about cheating on her, even before she heard the name Dolores Hastings, Eugenie had been so, so angry at him. What was strange was that after he told her about the affair, that anger didn't explode. It ebbed. Once he finished telling her he was cheating on her, she had actually felt something akin to relief. Relief that she finally had something legitimate to be angry about. Relief that the reason the marriage was failing was his fault. Relief that the marriage would finally fail. Relief that she wouldn't have to pretend anymore that nothing was wrong.

She'd wanted out of the marriage, too, she had to admit now. Even before Lawrence's announcement. She'd wanted out maybe even more than Lawrence had. Maybe even longer than Lawrence had. By the time he told her about it, the affair had been going on for five months. But Eugenie had been unhappy for a lot longer than that. She couldn't remember the last time she'd done the things she did just because she enjoyed her life.

When had she stopped lighting the candles on the table at dinnertime because it made the table more festive? When had she stopped fixing Lawrence's favorite meals without him having to ask her to because she liked the way it made him smile when he came in from a crappy day? When had she stopped making mental notes of books and music he said he liked so she could put them under the tree at Christmas? When had she stopped running for the camera when she saw him and Seth in some kind of sweet father–son tableau? When had she taken his hand or touched his face or moved a little closer to him in bed? When was the last time she had simply been glad he was her husband?

The reason Marianne and Dale were still married, she realized now, the reason they had been able to make the necessary repairs in the face of what should have been irreparable damage, was because there had still been remnants of happiness and stability to salvage. The structure of their marriage may have taken a hit, but their foundation had been sound. The original fixtures may have been tattered and frail, but they were intact. That was why their marriage hadn't crumbled around them. By the time Eugenie and Lawrence called it quits, their marriage had collapsed under the weight of their unhappiness. There had been nothing to rebuild, nothing left to salvage. No fidelity. No trust. No love.

"Iris," she said softly, "do you think it's possible for two people to fall in love but not stay in love?"

"Sure," Iris said. "It happens all the time."

Eugenie turned her attention from the room to the receptionist. Iris's expression had changed not at all. She was her usual impenetrable self under the pile of orange hair and the pencil antennae.

"So you don't think true love exists?" Eugenie asked.

"You didn't say true love," Iris said. "You just said love."

"There's a difference?"

"Of course."

"How so?"

"Love can last a long time, but it doesn't last forever. To last forever, it has to be true love. Most people find love at some point. But not everybody finds true love."

"But that just sounds so . . ."

"What?"

"Silly," Eugenie said. "True love is so fairy tale. So Harlequin romance. So Hollywood."

"Yeah, but fairy tales and Harlequin and Hollywood had to get it from somewhere. Somebody had true love, even a long time ago, otherwise no one would have written stories and songs about it."

Maybe, Eugenie thought. But people had written about epic battles between good and evil at a school for young wizards in training, and tornado-tossed houses landing on ruby-slippered witches, and Grendel's mother taking major advantage of the all-you-can-eat Thane buffet, too. That didn't mean any of those things had really happened.

Then again, just because Eugenie was skeptical didn't mean any of those things *hadn't* happened.

"Is true love what you had with . . ." She couldn't remember the name of Iris's long-missing partner now. She couldn't even remember if the two of them had been married.

"Abner," Iris said. "His name was Abner."

"You two were married?"

She shook her head, then smiled sadly. "No. We lived in sin. His family didn't approve of me."

How could anyone not approve of Iris? Of everyone who worked at HeartMenders, Iris seemed to have the least baggage and the most even temper.

"Was it true love with Abner?"

She nodded. But she said nothing.

"Do you think you'll ever find it with someone else?"

"No," she replied without hesitation. "Not like that. Maybe I'll fall in love again someday. Maybe. But it will never be the way it was with him."

"How can you be so sure?"

"I just am."

So, according to Iris, not only did true love really exist, but it was possible to actually recognize it for what it was. Eugenie couldn't imagine how that was possible. Which, she supposed, went a long way toward explaining why her marriage had turned out the way it did. She'd never considered what she had with Lawrence to be *true* love. To refer to any relationship that way in this day and age just seemed, well . . . like she said. Silly. Certainly she hadn't gone into her marriage doubtful that it would last—had Eugenie had doubts about that, she never would have married Lawrence in the first place. But she'd never really gotten up on a soapbox and proclaimed it a love to transcend time, either.

For some reason, that made her think about Spalding and Nash. She didn't know either of them well enough to be in love with them. But she did know them both well enough to wonder about the potential.

Today, though, she had way too many other things to think about. Like buying paint for the reception room. Like figuring out what to make for dinner. Like worrying about whether or not her son was home. Like trying to make it through another evening without having to talk to her mother. And what to do about the sadness in her brother's eyes that just wouldn't go away. And how that might affect two little girls who would never have a chance to see how important a healthy, loving relationship between two grown-ups was to ensure their happiness.

"Hey, Iris," she said, "do you have a HeartMenders questionnaire I could take home with me?"

Iris grinned. “You looking to become a client?”

“No,” Eugenie stated unequivocally. “But you never know when you might come across someone who’s a potential, you know?”

Iris pulled open a drawer on the right side of her desk and withdrew not only a HeartMenders questionnaire but an application as well. The HeartMenders questionnaire, unlike DreamMakers’, was in no way brief. In fact, it looked like a college blue book. Except that it was beige. Filling out one of them could take days. Eugenie would have to get started right away.

“It will be lovely in here when we’re finished,” she said as she took all the documents from Iris and swept her arm toward the room in a wide prima ballerina arc. “It will be the kind of room where people immediately will feel welcome and want to sit down and share bits of themselves with others. Coming into this room will make them feel like they’re moving into a new chapter of their lives. One that starts with ‘Once upon a time’ and ends with ‘happily ever after.’”

Because if there was one thing Spalding Chasan knew how to do, it was match up people so they would be able to find their happy ending. She just couldn’t quite help wondering why he’d never found one for himself.

Nineteen

When Eugenie arrived home that evening, she found Nash in the middle of the kitchen. Which shouldn't have been unusual, since that was where she had found him countless other times. But this time, instead of his home improvement uniform of spattered painter's pants and T-shirt, he wore a pair of jeans—clean ones—and a navy blue polo that was hardly faded at all. He had even shaved. And gotten a haircut. In fact, the last time she'd seen him this spit-and-polished had been the night the two of them . . .

"Got a hot date?" she asked by way of a greeting. That was the only reason she could fathom for his normal state of dishabille being replaced with such a state of, um, habille.

"And hello to you, too, Janey," he replied with a smile. Before she could offer him a more proper hello, he added, "No, I do not have a hot date."

"A cold date, then," she said, still not convinced he had cleaned himself up for anyone else.

She had no idea if he had dated other women since their own aborted attempt two weeks ago, but she would assume yes. Julien was right—Nash was a hound dog who had a huge appetite for, ah, doggie treats, and who was accustomed to getting them from a variety of sources. After so many years of being regularly rewarded, he wasn't likely to heel just because Eugenie hadn't opened her Milk-Bone box for him. For lack of another canine metaphor that actually would have been even more off-putting.

"Not a date at all," he said. "What I have is a surprise."

"What kind of surprise?"

"I can't tell you. I have to show you. Outside."

"What is it?" she asked again.

"I'm not telling. And you have to close your eyes."

"Nash . . ."

"Come on, Janey. Indulge me."

Well, if she must . . .

She expelled a put-upon sigh that sounded almost convincing. "All right. You know I'll follow you anywhere."

And why had that not come out sounding as playful and flirtatious as she intended? Why had it sounded resolved and weary instead?

Nash didn't seem to notice, because he only smiled and took her hand in his as if it were the most natural gesture in the world. He said nothing until he had tugged her through the back door, but as they neared the edge of the patio, he instructed her again to close her eyes.

"I'll trip and kill myself if I do that," she said, pointing down at some of the still-buckled terra-cotta tiles.

His response to that was to return to her side and scoop her up into his arms. She was still sputtering her astonishment when he said, "There. Now close your eyes."

And there was just something in his voice when he said it that made Eugenie clam up tight. When she did, he pressed his mouth quickly and fiercely against hers. "Close. Your. Eyes," he repeated emphatically when he pulled back. Because she still hadn't done that. Even when he was kissing her.

"Oh-kay," she said, finally doing as she was told.

When he started to walk, she looped her arms around his neck and battled the urge to lay her head against his shoulder. She had to admit there was something nice about coming home from work to find a man standing in one's kitchen who immediately insisted that one take a load off—literally—and then took command of the situation himself. She didn't think she was betraying any long-fought feminist battle to admit that. She was just saying it felt good to have someone around who felt solid and essential, who smelled of the earth, and whose voice was a restorative thrum. Someone whose steady gait rocked one in his arms like the lulling back-and-forth of a porch swing.

Over the past few months, Nash had been in the house so often, and had been responsible for so much of its reclamation, it almost felt as if he had become a part of it. Eugenie had grown used to coming home from work and finding him there somewhere, sanding a ragged floorboard or patching a fragment of ceiling or rubbing oil into a banister. Often, he stayed for supper, then lingered to share a beer with Julien on the patio. There had been nights when Eugenie had been in her bedroom with the window open, three floors above the two men, and she would hear them laughing over some shared joke or bit of gossip.

Nash had begun to feel . . . comfortable. The realization of that surprised her. Nash wasn't supposed to be comfortable. He was supposed to *zing* the strings of her heart. He was supposed to splash heat in her belly. He was supposed to be the fantasy.

The ideal. The escape from reality. He was supposed to make her heart race wildly.

For some reason, that made Eugenie recall her picnic in the park with Spalding. Not that Spalding *zinged* the strings of her heart, either. Well, not the way Nash had *zinged* them for so many years. And not that Spalding's presence splashed heat in her belly, either. Not the way Nash's presence had for so many years. But Spalding was kind of a fantasy, with his classic good looks and gentle temperament. He was kind of an escape from reality with his polite manners and old-fashioned mores.

But was he an ideal? Eugenie asked herself. More ideal than Nash, who had been her ideal for a period that spanned decades? Just what was her ideal nowadays, anyway? She hadn't really given thought to what made a man ideal since she was a kid. Surely the model must have changed since she was an adolescent, hadn't it? Then again, just how many qualities did a person have to have to be ideal in the first place? In order to be ideal, an ideal someone should love you and respect you. An ideal someone should put your needs and wishes and desires on a par with his own. An ideal someone should, when the two of you were together, leave everything else behind except that which made the two of you, well, the two of you. That really would make an ideal someone ideal.

Nash halted suddenly enough to jar Eugenie from her musings, then set her back on her feet with a warning that she still better not open her eyes. She sensed him moving away from her, heard the rustle of a bush as he pushed past it, felt the scuff of the wind on her face before it swept up to tangle with the leaves stirring overhead. Then there was something that sounded like the creak of a stair, followed by the jangle of a chain. Then—

"Okay, open your eyes," he said.

Eugenie did, gasping at the sight she beheld. Where in another lifetime had stood the gazebo that had been home to pixies, but which had succumbed to neglect by the time she returned home, stood a new one—identical to the first, right down to the latticework, which would be perfect for purple clematis to twine through, and the white wicker swing that swayed on one side. Nash sat on the left side of that swing, his arm stretched across its back, smiling like . . . Well, there was no getting around it: He was smiling like a pixie.

"Oh my," she whispered reverently. Because, surely, to speak more loudly would ruin the magic.

"You like it?" he asked in his usual robust timbre.

She held her breath, waiting for the gazebo to shimmer and dissolve in light of his sacrilege, but nothing changed. Obviously, it wasn't magic that had put it there. Obviously, it was Nash who had done that.

In spite of that, she asked, "You built this?"

He nodded. "Yep."

She took a few steps forward but halted at the stairs with her hand hovering above the scrolled banister. A part of her still feared that touching it would somehow devastate it. "It's exactly like the one that was here when I was a kid," she said. She noted the gingerbread trim rimming the octagonal roof and the heart-shaped cutouts in each of the lower slats. "Exactly."

Nash beamed at the statement. "I found some old pictures of the place that had the gazebo in them. Then I tracked down a guy I used to work with who I knew could design a new one from that, with all the original specs. Once I had the blueprint, it was easy to re-create it."

"But even the swing," she said. "How did you find a swing just like the one that was here before?"

"Rummage around old houses and visit restoration suppliers

as much as I do, and you always find what you need," Nash told her. "Anything I want, Janey, I eventually find it."

She nodded. She didn't doubt that for a minute. She just wondered if Nash was talking about more than his job when he said that. Probably not, she finally decided. He was still obviously looking for something he hadn't found yet in other areas of his life. Unless maybe the search for the treasure and all its ancillary adventure was what he craved more than the treasure itself. If that were the case, then even the greatest treasure in the world would be of no value to him. Not unless that treasure stayed buried forever.

"It's beautiful, Nash," she said softly. "Thank you."

"You're welcome." He patted the cushion of the swing beside him. "Come on up."

Still a little hesitant—though maybe not because she was afraid of shattering the magic this time—Eugenie climbed the stairs. Inside, the gazebo smelled of freshly cut wood and, perhaps, a bit of pixie dust. She sat on the other side of the swing, putting a good bit of distance between her and Nash, but he either didn't notice or didn't mind. The sun was hanging low in the sky by now, slanting long shadows across the yard. Somewhere unseen, a woodpecker was tap-tap-tapping for his dinner, and the wind carried from somewhere else the bouquet of a charcoal grill. Sounds and smells of summer and suburbia. But of contentment, too.

"I think I'll be spending a lot of time out here over the next few months," she said. "I used to ride past this house on my bike when I was a kid and think how nice it would be if I could take a book and sit in the gazebo swing reading. That seemed so old-fashioned to me."

"That was old-fashioned," Nash said. "Back then. Nowadays, it's archaic."

She said nothing in response to that, only pushed the swing backward with the toe of her shoe to set it into gentle motion. *Chink-creak*, went the chain and the swing. *Chink-creak. Chink-creak*. Only now it was a comforting sound, not an anxious one.

As they sat in companionable silence, watching the evening, a cat wandered into view near the lilac bush. It was a big, buff-colored tabby, old and slow-moving, whom Eugenie had seen in the yard before. She was pretty sure it belonged to the Enrights across the street. He liked to graze on the weeds, and she was more than content to let him.

As he drew nearer the lilac bush, however, the cardinal who lived there suddenly flew out of it in a flurry of red to land on a tree branch overhead, screeching his displeasure at having such an enemy closing in on his home. Eugenie watched as he dove at the cat a few times, trying to scare it away, but the cat remained unfazed, chomping contentedly on dandelion greens, uncaring that he should be going after the bird instead. Mr. Cardinal obviously didn't understand his disinterest, though, because he continued to flutter furiously about in an effort to draw the cat away from the hatchlings in the bush. Finally, he landed on the ground only a few feet away from the cat and began to stumble, turning his wing out at an awkward angle.

Eugenie's mouth fell open when she realized what he was doing. He was pretending to be injured, hobbling closer and closer to the cat, trying to look as if he were easy dinner pickings so the tabby would come after him instead of preying on the nest that held his family. She'd never seen an animal do such a thing.

"Do you see . . . ?" she started to ask Nash.

But he softly shushed her before she could say more. Obviously, he did.

For several minutes, the allegedly wounded cardinal staggered around, adding pitiful sounds of distress to his act in an effort to be more convincing. Finally, the cat seemed to have his fill—whether it was of the weeds or the overacting, Eugenie couldn't have said—and trotted off for home. The moment he was gone, the cardinal straightened and flew back into the lilac bush to ensure that his family was unharmed.

"That was amazing," Eugenie said.

"Not to mention stupid," Nash added.

"Chivalrous," Eugenie corrected.

Nash shook his head. "Obviously no one told him it's kill or be killed in the animal kingdom."

"On the contrary, I think that's exactly why he acted the way he did. He's quite the family man, Mr. Cardinal. You don't find that very often in the wild."

Nash was silent for a moment. Then, quietly, he said, "Yeah, Mr. Cardinal is gonna fit right in with you Dashners."

There was something in his voice when he uttered the remark. As if he didn't quite understand the concept of family himself. Or that he didn't understand people who embraced it. She knew he'd lost his own parents before he turned thirty and that he had a brother somewhere to whom he wasn't particularly close. When they were kids, Nash's family had never interacted with hers, not the way the families of some of Julien's other friends, and her own friends, had. She couldn't recall Mr. and Mrs. Ridley ever being anywhere that Nash was. And she couldn't even remember if his brother was older or younger than he was. Nash had probably spent more time with the Dashners after meeting Julien than he had with his own family.

Eugenie was trying to think of something to say in response to his statement when another voice piped up from behind them.

"Hi, kids!" Marianne said jovially. "I hope I'm not interrupting anything."

But Eugenie could tell by her tone that that was precisely what Marianne hoped she was doing. She could tell that by her expression, too, as she rounded the gazebo and climbed the stairs.

"Wow, this looks just like the one that was here when we were kids," she said as she ran her hand along the railing. She was wearing her summer uniform of khaki capris and loose T-shirt, this one emblazoned with a snaky comment about the Republican party. "I always wondered why no one ever used it."

"Because whoever lived here never left the house, remember?" Eugenie replied.

Marianne leaned back against the railing, holding it with both hands. "Mrs. DePelaporte," she said.

"That's right," Eugenie said. "I'd forgotten her name."

"Yeah, she was a strange one. I don't think anyone in the neighborhood knew her. Hell, I don't know if anyone ever even saw her. Not in my lifetime, anyway. I don't think she had any family. She was pretty old when we were kids. Meals-on-wheels brought all her food for her. She never went anywhere."

Even when they were kids, Eugenie had tried to find out about the woman who lived in Fleurissant by asking Marianne's parents and their assorted neighbors. But no one had seemed to know anything about her. Mrs. DePelaporte had been living in the house when just about everyone in Manitou Hills moved into the neighborhood, and all efforts to befriend her had been met with rebuffs. By the time Eugenie and Marianne came along, the woman had reached a point where she no longer answered the front door or the telephone. Her yard was tended by a service and, as Marianne said, she'd had her meals delivered. Try as Eugenie did to recall a day when she might have seen the woman outside, she couldn't remember a single one.

It was no wonder Fleurissant had ultimately suffered such neglect. The woman living there had been hopelessly neglected, too.

"How's it hanging, Marianne?" Nash asked, barely masking his irritation at her intrusion.

"A little to the left, Nash, how about you?"

"No complaints."

"I bet."

He turned to look at Eugenie. "I'm glad you like the gazebo," he said. "It's my housewarming gift to you. And Jules and Lorraine. But mostly you. Marianne," he added as he spared her a quick glance and an even quicker salute in farewell. Then he bounded down the steps, through the bushes, and out of sight.

Marianne took his place on the swing and set it into motion once again, and Eugenie was happy to let her do the work this time. She told Marianne about the episode with the cardinal, then realized it was the perfect segue to approach the question that had been on her mind all day.

"Marianne, do you think true love exists?"

Marianne turned to stare at her through narrowed eyes. "Oh, please tell me that question has nothing to do with Nash."

"That question has nothing to do with Nash," Eugenie said easily.

Now Marianne eyed her with much consideration, as if she were trying to gauge the veracity of her response. Evidently satisfied there was no cause for alarm, she leaned back in the swing and set it into motion again.

"I never really thought about it," she said. "Except for that time Mr. Gleaves made us write an essay about *The Scarlet Letter*, and one of the prompts mentioned true love. But I didn't write about that one. I wrote about puritanical hypocrisy instead."

Yes, Marianne would have written about that over true love. Her mama didn't raise no fool.

"Think about it now," Eugenie told her. "Do you think that's what you have with Dale?"

Marianne looked at her again. "You want to ask me about my affair."

It was a statement, not a question. Eugenie was about to deny her question had had anything to do with that, then reconsidered. She really did want to know about Marianne's affair. This was as good a time as any for discovery.

"Yeah," Eugenie said. "I do want to ask you about that."

"Okay. It's a fair question. It's not like I didn't open the door for it when I told you about it."

"So what happened? Were you two having problems when it started?"

She was surprised when Marianne shook her head. "No, not really. Dale and I as a couple were fine. I as an individual was the one with the problem."

"And the problem was?"

Marianne's gaze glanced off Eugenie's up toward the purpling sky. She smiled, but there was nothing happy in the gesture. "The problem was that I wanted some me time."

Eugenie recalled her friend's derision during one of their earlier conversations. Eugenie had talked about the importance of me time, and Marianne had said it was just another thing created to turn people into more conspicuous consumers.

"So what happened?" she asked again.

"You want details?"

"Not unless you want to give them."

"I don't. But I'll hit the highlights."

She brought her legs up onto the swing and wrapped her arms around them, a posture that made her look as if she were trying to re-create her position in the womb. For the first time in all the decades she had known Marianne, it occurred to Eugenie that maybe, just maybe, she wasn't always as confident and put-together as she seemed to be. Maybe, just maybe, there were times when Marianne wanted to fall apart, too, times when she had to literally hold herself together to keep that from happening.

"I'd like to tell you," she began, "that he was this gorgeous hunka hunka burnin' love I met while I was sitting in a coffeehouse drinking espresso and wearing a beret, reading a Stieg Larsson novel. I'd like to tell you he smoldered with irresistible sex appeal, then took me back to his trendy loft apartment in NuLu. I'd like to tell you how he showed me the erotic artwork he painted for a living, then fucked me like a stallion. I'd like to tell you we met clandestinely that way for months, until Dale discovered us in bed together and shot him." She looked at Eugenie again, with another one of those sad smiles. "Yeah. I'd really like to tell you that."

Eugenie smiled back, hopefully with encouragement. "You'd like to tell me that. But . . ."

"But," Marianne said, "he was actually going bald and carrying more extra weight than I am, and he was the stay-at-home dad of one of Claire's schoolmates. Also married, but his wife was a big-shot executive who traveled a lot. We were both in the Parent Association, on the library committee, and we were in the process of phasing out a lot of the old books so we could order new ones. We were at school almost every day, sitting side by side, pulling books off the shelves to assess their condition and age, and we talked about . . . God, everything. You know, the way you do with someone you've just met, who you don't have to worry about impressing or care about whether or not they like you, because their appearance in your life will only be temporary and conditional. I love talking to people like that. I can say anything to them."

Eugenie wasn't sure she could relate. She never approached anyone that way. She always worried about the impression she was making on someone, and she always cared whether or not they liked her. Even if it was just the cashier at the grocery store or the waiter bringing her food. She wanted to be liked. She wanted to be approved of. Maybe that was another reason she had always admired Marianne so much. Because Marianne didn't get bogged down in such inconsequential stuff.

"It was just really nice talking to him," Marianne continued. "Dale and I hadn't talked that much about that many things in ages. I mean, once you know someone as well as you do after living with them for that many years, you stop talking about *everything* because you already know what they think about *everything*. Dale and I talked about the kids and his work and the stuff I did during the day, but our deep, philosophical discussions about politics and religion and the meaning of life? Nuh-uh. That had stopped a long time ago."

"Hey, you're two up on me," Eugenie said. "Lawrence and I never talked about Seth or the stuff I did during the day. All we talked about was Lawrence's work. And Lawrence's golf game. And Lawrence's latest physical discomfort. And what Lawrence needed at any given time."

Marianne uttered an exasperated sound. "Why did you ever marry that asshole?"

"It wasn't like that at the beginning," Eugenie said in an effort to defend both herself and her ex. "In the beginning, we did talk about the meaning of life and what we envisioned for our future and everything." She shrugged, then looked down into her drink. "But after Seth was born, my whole world kind of started to revolve around him, so I never really had much to contribute to conversations with Lawrence. He was at work all day, so he couldn't relate to what happened at home."

"Eugenie, you had plenty to contribute. What, Lawrence didn't want to talk about the new life that was half made of his DNA and that he was half responsible for bringing up with the right values and morals? He didn't want to talk about the needs of the woman who was raising his son in his absence? He couldn't relate to what was happening with his family in his house? I reiterate: asshole."

Well, when she put it that way . . .

"But we were talking about me," Marianne began again. "And my *me* time."

Eugenie was content to turn the conversation back to her friend. Way more content than she'd ever been to turn her conversations with Lawrence back to him. "So we were."

"He and I just really hit it off, you know? We started having lunch together in the school cafeteria, an environment that is oh so conducive to romance—not that this had anything to do with romance," she hastily interjected, "and then, eventually, we started meeting for coffee in the mornings, after we dropped off our kids at school, but before we were due to work in the library. And even when I knew something else was starting to happen that went beyond friendship, I told myself it was okay, that I wouldn't let it go too far, that I just needed a little *me* time to make me feel better about myself. It had been a long time since any guy besides Dale made me feel attractive. Hell, it had been a long time since Dale had made me feel attractive. And the next thing I knew—"

"The next thing you knew," Eugenie said, "your me time was including someone other than just you."

Marianne nodded. "But it was still all about me. It was all for me. I never thought about how what I was doing would affect my marriage. Or his, for that matter. Or how it could ultimately affect my kids. Or his."

"How long did it last?"

Marianne released the legs she had folded in front of her but didn't put them back down on the ground. "Almost a year, if you include the time before it turned sexual."

"So you had a lot of me time."

"Yep."

"How did it end? Did Dale find out what was going on?"

"No. I finally realized that what I was doing had nothing to do with me time. I mean, a big part of what makes me me is my family. I am who I've become because of what I've created with Dale and the kids. They're everything to me. If something happened to one of them, then a big piece of me would just . . . die. The time I spend with them *is* me time. The time I spend away from them . . ." She shrugged. "That's not me time. And that's when I get into trouble. When I'm not myself."

Eugenie thought about that. After Seth was born, she had completely lost sight of herself as an individual. As a woman. Even as a wife. Her entire life, from sunup till sundown, had revolved around the new infant for whom she was responsible. That had fallen to her alone, because Lawrence had to work. Her day had been nothing but feeding the baby, changing the baby, bathing the baby, trying to figure out why the baby was crying, comforting the baby, and trying to get the baby to go to sleep. Even after she'd figured out how to do all those things and recognize all those cues, she'd still needed to teach the baby. Teach him how to walk. Teach him how to talk. Teach him how to hold a spoon. And then, when he'd learned those things, she'd had to see to his education beyond the basics. She'd had to make sure he was given the proper stimuli to ensure he developed into a well-rounded human being. She'd taken him to the zoo. And the children's museum. And bookstores. She'd enrolled him in Kindermusik. And swim classes. And T-ball. Even after he started school, she still hadn't been able to rediscover herself, because by then, she had forgotten who she was. So she kept doing what she knew how to do—raise her son. She'd been a mother. And, every now and then, when she wasn't too exhausted, a wife. But she had ceased to be Eugenie. At least a Eugenie she recognized.

"I am inextricably bound to my husband and kids," Marianne continued. Ferociously, she added, "And I *like* it that way. It's not fair that there are so many messages in our society telling me that if I like being a homemaker, that if I find my purpose in being with my husband and my kids, then I'm not independent or I'm passive or I lack an identity or I don't take the initiative. Hell, *I'm* the one who created my identity as a homemaker. I rejected every fucking piece of propaganda my mother ever tried to feed me about finding my identity in myself instead of others. What could be more independent, nonconformist, and proactive than that?"

Ironic, that, Eugenie couldn't help thinking. Here Marianne had been raised by a rabid feminist, yet she had ended up embracing the most traditional role a woman could assume. Then again, maybe that wasn't ironic at all. The core of feminism was about giving women choices. Choices they'd never had when men were running things. Marianne had learned well from a strong, independent woman that she could do and be whatever she wanted.

That she had chosen to be a homemaker so devoted to her husband and kids was kind of a testament to how very much Marianne loved being exactly that. It took a strong, independent woman to choose the role of homemaker in today's world. Eugenie hoped Marianne's mother was proud of her.

"So you ended the affair and stayed with Dale for the sake of your family," Eugenie said. "That was courageous."

Marianne looked at her as if she'd just grown a third eye. "That actually would have been a really stupid reason to end the affair, Eugenie. The reason I ended it and stayed with Dale is because I love him."

Nonplussed—and a little stung by the *stupid* thing—Eugenie said, "But you cheated on him."

"Yeah, but that had nothing to do with Dale or my feelings for him. It was something in me—some absence of something or an excess of something else that I should have seen a mental health professional about instead of some dad at the kids' school."

"But—"

"That's why you shouldn't blame yourself for what Lawrence did," Marianne went on without waiting for Eugenie's objection. "Whatever happened between him and Ethel Merman, it had nothing to do with you or your marriage. It was all Lawrence's shortcomings. All his weirdness. All his shit."

"But he chose her over me. He chose her over Seth."

Marianne lifted her shoulders and let them drop. "Then he didn't truly love either one of you. And I reiterate: his shit, not yours."

Eugenie wanted to believe her. She did. Not the part about Lawrence not loving them but about it being all his fault. But there was still a part of her that couldn't. Or wouldn't. There must have been something she could have done to keep Lawrence from wanting to be with someone else. There must have been something in her that should have recognized the anger she had inside herself that had been building for so long. At the very least, she should have been able to tell there was something wrong in the marriage that they needed to fix and sit down and figure it out with him. If she had just been . . . If she had just seen . . . If she had just known . . .

Something. There should have been something. She couldn't have woken up beside him every morning for twenty years and not realized something was so wrong that he was looking elsewhere for fulfillment. How could she have known the exact consistency between soft and hard boiled he liked his eggs cooked, and which deodorants gave him a rash, and how he couldn't stand even a smudge of yellow on his neckties, and how he hated the taste of cloves and yet not known something as fundamental about him as that he couldn't be trusted to not betray her? And how could she have not recognized her own unhappiness and how much she had stopped caring about all of those things?

"So you and Dale worked it out, obviously," she said. Because that was way better than trying to answer the questions she was asking herself.

Marianne nodded again. "I had to tell him what I did. We couldn't have fixed what was wrong if I hadn't."

"How'd he take it?"

She hesitated a moment, then said, "He almost left me. He did actually spend a week at a hotel—we told the kids he was traveling for his job—but he hated the solitude and quiet and came home. We called a marriage counselor that day and got help. It took a long time. And it wasn't easy. And it changed our relationship. But you know what?" This time when she smiled, it was a happy one. "In a lot of ways, our marriage is better now, and stronger now, than it was even in the beginning. We talk now,

Eugenie," she said with even more animation. "About *everything*. We set the alarm for a half hour earlier than we used to, and Dale gets up in the morning and gets coffee for both of us, and we sit in bed for thirty minutes before the day starts, and we hold hands, and we *talk*. God, I love that. It's better than sex."

Eugenie wanted to laugh at that, but it got stuck somewhere inside her. She thought about mornings with Lawrence, back even before Ethel Merman, when she would have said her marriage was good. As soon as the alarm went off, they rolled out of bed on their respective sides, and then he headed straight for the shower while she headed straight for the kitchen. She tried to remember if they'd even muttered a groggy *Good morning* to each other and honestly couldn't remember. By the time Lawrence came down for breakfast, Seth was up, and all of her attention was for her son. Had he done his homework? Did he need a lunch? Was the track meet at home or away, and if so, where? What time should she pick him up?

She'd always figured Lawrence could take care of himself, that Seth was the one she needed to keep an eye on. But Seth had invariably had everything under control—homework done, lunch money in pocket, a ride home from the track meet, don't worry about it, Mom, I'm good. All that time, it was Lawrence she should have been quizzing, Lawrence she should have been asking about whether or not he had done everything he was obligated to do, Lawrence whose needs she should have kept track of.

Something about that did make Eugenie laugh, a couple of dry chuckles that Marianne must have thought were meant for her comment instead.

"No, really, Eugenie. It is better than sex. But then, sex with Dale at this point is pretty predictable. Nice but predictable. Our conversations in the morning, however . . ." She wiggled her eyebrows suggestively. "You'd be surprised how orgasmic a discussion about the Arab Spring can be."

"You're right. That would surprise me."

Marianne inhaled a long, slow breath and released it just as carefully, as if she hadn't breathed enough while she was talking. But it was a contented sigh, not one fraught with apprehension, as if she had made her peace with everything that had spilled out of her. "Just stop blaming yourself for Lawrence, okay?"

"I'll try," Eugenie told her. And then, because the conversation seemed to need a change of subject, she said, "I think Spalding has been flirting with me."

Marianne's mouth dropped open at that. "Ward Cleaver flirted with you? Are you serious?"

Eugenie wagged a finger at her friend. "Number one, I told you he's more like George Clooney playing Ward Cleaver than Hugh Beaumont." She brought a second finger into the wagging. "And number two, jeez, you don't have to sound so surprised."

"I'm not surprised he would flirt with you," she said. "I'm surprised he would flirt at all. I mean, c'mon. He's Ward Cleaver."

"George Clooney *playing* Ward Cleaver."

"But still Ward Cleaver."

"A twenty-first-century Ward Cleaver."

Marianne thought about that for a moment. "You know, somehow that just makes for an even bigger ick factor." She punctuated the statement with a grimace and a shudder. "You're sure he was flirting? Maybe he was just trying to—"

"Marianne, I swear to God, if you make one inappropriate Beaver reference, I'm going into the house."

"Then tell me why you think he's flirting with you. Give me a 'for instance.'"

Eugenie leaned back in the swing. "Okay. For instance, one

day, he complimented me on a necklace I was wearing by tucking his fingers beneath it to give it a closer inspection, but the backs of his fingers were touching my collarbone the whole time, and I'm not completely sure, but I think maybe he grazed it a few times on purpose before releasing the necklace again."

"I'm not sure that constitutes flirting," Marianne said. "That just sounds like he's really lame at copping a feel."

"Fine. Then there was another time when I had a question about something I was typing up in one of my reports, and he came up behind me and leaned over to read the part I was having trouble with, and he leaned in really close, close enough that I could feel his coffee-warmed breath against my bare neck."

"Again, not feeling the flirting thing here, Eugenie. Some guy breathing down your shirt is just some guy breathing down your shirt."

Eugenie frowned at her. "Then what about the time he came to work in the morning with trays of coffee from Heine Brothers' for everyone, except that, for everyone else, he just left the creamers, sugars, and stirrers on Iris's desk so everyone could doctor up their individual brews however they liked, but he handed me a medium-sized Ronda's Blend with three creamers and three sugars already stirred in, because he knows that's what I always order. Then, when he handed it to me, I could swear he deliberately botched the exchange so our fingers got tangled for a few seconds."

This time Marianne only gazed at her through slitted eyes.

Eugenie expelled a discontented sound. "So I probably shouldn't even mention the day I came in from lunch after spilling guacamole on myself, and he told me I looked ravishing, huh?"

Marianne thought about that. "Actually, that was better than flirting. That was him being nice."

Eugenie remembered another incident, too, but for some reason, she didn't want to mention it to Marianne. It was a day when Eugenie had been feeling especially exhausted and frumpy and had looked up from the computer to see Spalding leaning in the doorway of her office, smiling in a way that made her think—no, made her *feel*—as if the reason he was smiling, the reason he was happy, was simply because she was there. And when she asked him if there was something he needed, that smile crept into his eyes, too, and he replied with a cryptic, "I need a lover who won't drive me crazy. But barring that, I want to know if you've finished typing up the report on the Copeland–Madison outing."

So, did all those things constitute flirting? Or was she reading something into nothing? Or, worst of all, was it sexual harassment? Probably, it wasn't that last, because Eugenie had never felt harassed in any way at any time. In fact, she'd kind of liked one or two of the episodes.

No, actually, that wasn't true. She had *really* liked *every* episode.

She liked how Spalding seemed to have smiles that were reserved specifically for her. She liked the way his voice was a little more mellow when he talked to her than it was for her co-workers. She liked how he invited her into his office for lunch almost every day now and how they always shared at least a couple of laughs. She liked how with Spalding she *did* laugh. Most of all, she liked the funny little buzz of nervousness that sputtered to life in her belly every time she saw him or heard his voice and how that buzz melted into a satisfied little hum whenever he came within smelling or touching distance.

It was the oddest thing. Eugenie would have thought attraction to another human being would always involve gut-churning lightning strikes and psychological cartwheels and sexual pyrotechnics, no matter who the generator of that attraction was. That was the way it had been when she was a girl crushing on a boy at school. The way it had been with Lawrence during those first years. The way it had been when she was a teenager lusting after Nash.

Eugenie stretched her legs out leisurely in front of her, tipped her head back to breathe deeply of the ebbing mulberry evening, and pushed the swing into motion again. The sun was lower now, dragging fingers of gauzy pink and orange across the clouds. A few spastic fireflies had jumped the gun on the darkness, blinking halfheartedly around them. Something had been flying from tree to tree ever since the women had started talking, though Eugenie hadn't been able to tell whether it was a bird or a bat. Probably the latter, since few creatures' movements were so vigorous so late in the day. She listened again to the *thwap-thwap-thwap* of its wings and watched Marianne mull the repercussions of Eugenie's situation.

Finally, she said, "So you have Spalding wooing you at work and Nash hot for you at home."

This time Eugenie was the one to mull before replying. She had, of course, told Marianne what happened that night at Nash's apartment, and she had kept her friend apprised of ensuing developments. Marianne had listened the same way she had when they were teenagers, with much eye rolling and finger gagging and words of advice like, "If you want to fuck him, Eugenie, fine. Fuck him, and get it out of your system. But if you start talking china patterns and picket fences, I swear to God I'll hit you with a brick."

"Funnily," Eugenie said, "the Nash hotness has cooled in the past couple of weeks. I don't know if it's because what happened at his apartment that night put some reality into the fantasy or if it's that I've grown accustomed to his face or what, but the hot flashes he used to cause are more like warm fuzzies these days."

Marianne rolled her eyes and stuck her index finger in her mouth, then said, "Is that supposed to reassure me? 'Cause it doesn't."

"I don't know what it's supposed to do," Eugenie told her. "I'm just saying. What I wouldn't say is that Spalding is wooing me."

"He's Ward Cleaver. What else would it be?"

Eugenie ignored the question, if for no other reason than that Spalding was indeed the kind of man who would woo, and she just wasn't sure she wanted to go there when it came to her boss. Even if he was kind of dreamy. Even if he would doubtless woo a woman with great finesse. Even though she kind of liked the idea of being wooed by him.

"What do you think I should do?" she asked Marianne.

"About what?"

"What should I do if Spalding really is flirting with me?"

Marianne pushed the swing into motion again. "Depends on how the flirting makes you feel."

"I don't know how it makes me feel."

"Yes, you do."

"Okay, I like it."

"Then you know what to do."

It must be nice to know the answer for everything the way Marianne did, Eugenie thought. That would be a really useful superpower to have.

She hesitated, thinking Marianne didn't know the answer to everything, after all, because she'd never answered Eugenie's question about whether or not true love existed. Then she remembered everything Marianne had said about her affair and staying with Dale afterward and how hard the two of them had worked to ensure they saved their marriage. And she realized Marianne had indeed answered that question, too. In spades.

Twenty

When she went to work the next day, Eugenie was greeted with the news that Spalding would be out of the office for the remainder of that week, a serendipitous development since it offered the perfect opportunity for HeartMenders' makeover, right down to his own office. For which she selected a tawny wall color called Caramel Apple. Being sweet and old-fashioned, that just seemed like a perfect color for him. For his office, she meant. Even better, when she discovered that their part-timer Natalie had painted a fair number of her own apartments in the past with good results, Eugenie was able to hire her to complete the work before Spalding returned, since all the professionals she called wouldn't have been able to make time for the work for at least a month.

Between the new paint and the purchase of some stylish but reasonably priced reception room furnishings that would have been right at home in any HGTV remodel, by the end of the week, the new and improved HeartMenders was coming right along.

Even Iris had to backtrack on her disdain of brown once the new paint was on the walls. She said the color felt warm and welcoming. Then she took a break to make a run for a six-pack of Kit Kats.

By the time Eugenie left work Friday, she was beat. The last thing she wanted to do was cook dinner for her family, so she stopped at Stevens & Stevens for a bunch of Benedictine and bacon sandwiches. When she arrived home, however, it was to discover no one there but Lorraine. She was in her bedroom, sitting in a sturdy Queen Anne chair, which warred with the rest of the furniture, all French Provincial. Still, the combativeness of the two styles was in keeping with Lorraine's own personal style, so, really, everything in the room had come together nicely for life during wartime.

The walker was parked immediately to the right of the chair, thankfully silent when it was at rest. The television, however, was not, blaring the opening music for the *ABC World News*. When Lorraine noted Eugenie's arrival, she turned the volume down, but only enough to shout over it that Julien had taken the girls to a movie, that Seth had been gone all day, as usual, and that she hadn't seen hide nor hair of Nash, and wasn't that just like Eugenie, honestly, she was the only woman in the world who could chase off a man she was not only paying to be in her house but who would normally jump the bones of any woman who came within hailing distance.

Eugenie shrugged off that last comment—after first shouldering it long enough for it to get under her skin—and asked her mother if she'd had dinner.

"Of course not," Lorraine said. "There's barely a crumb to eat around here since *some*body hasn't been to the grocery in heaven knows how long."

Although Eugenie hadn't made a thorough grocery run in

more than a week, she knew there was plenty in the house to eat. "There's sandwich stuff," she said. "When I fixed my lunch this morning, I know there was enough turkey and roast beef in there for another couple of sandwiches."

"Julien must have used it for himself and the girls."

"There's soup," Eugenie tried again. "I got six cans of that clam chowder you like. I know you couldn't have eaten all that yet."

"It's too hot for soup."

"Tomatoes and mozzarella," she tried again, knowing she'd bought enough of both the other day to keep everyone happy for a week, since all of them—even Seth and the girls—liked that.

"I hate store-bought tomatoes. You know that."

Not that that had stopped Lorraine from eating them, anyway, Eugenie knew. At least until today, evidently. But then, what fun was scarfing down tomatoes and mozzarella when you could get so much more enjoyment out of lambasting your daughter?

Eugenie bit back a sigh. "I brought home Benedictine and bacon sandwiches," she said. They, too, were a universal favorite among the Dashner clan. "And that bow-tie pasta with sun-dried tomatoes. Would you like me to bring you some of both?"

"Well, since there's nothing else, and you're obviously not planning to cook, then I guess I don't have much choice, do I?"

Eugenie refrained from pointing out that her mother had lots of choices, that there were still tons of assisted living facilities in southern Indiana and Oldham and Bullitt counties they hadn't tried yet. But she was pretty sure her mother's question had been rhetorical, so she said nothing. Instead, she spun on her heel. After stashing the rest of the sandwiches and one container of pasta salad in the fridge, she arranged two of the former and a couple of generous servings of the latter on plates and poured two tall glasses of lemonade to go with.

She returned to her mother's room with both plates, then went back to the kitchen for a TV table, knowing her mother hated missing Diane Sawyer. She knew that, because she'd planned dinner around the newscast since shortly after the family moved into Fleurissant. It was easier than having to get up in the middle of dinner to carry her mother's meal back to her room because the program started after they sat down, or reheating her mother's plate once the show was over.

Her mother looked down at the meal Eugenie placed before her and frowned. "I don't even deserve real dishes?" she said of the paper plate that held her dinner.

Which was actually Chinet, not paper, and perfectly acceptable for a sandwich and pasta salad on a hot summer's day when the person who had prepared the meal out of the kindness of her heart—well, okay, who had stopped at Stevens & Stevens out of the kindness of her heart, and who had taken the meal out of the bag and unwrapped it out of the kindess of her heart, and who had arranged it on Chinet out of the kindness of her heart—was too damned tired to want to clean up more than she had to, but did Lorraine care about that? Noooo.

"It's Chinet," Eugenie said inanely, as if that would impress her mother. "And my dinner is on it, too."

Her mother uttered one of her put-upon sounds. "The way you neglect your household duties, it's no wonder Lawrence had a wandering eye."

Maybe it was her fatigue, maybe it was the heat of the day, maybe it was her general frustration with how life was going, but Eugenie had had enough. She was tired of hearing about being responsible for the breakup of a marriage that never should have happened in the first place. She was tired of being taken to task for not doing the things no sane woman would want to do, anyway. And she was tired of being accused of failing at things she hadn't actually failed at.

"You know, Mom," she said, "someday, I might find myself suffering from rheumatoid arthritis, too. And I might find myself alone. And I might find myself relying on Seth and his family to take care of me. I might even end up living with them. But you know what the difference between that situation and this one will be?"

Lorraine said nothing.

"The difference will be that I would never, ever, in a million years, say something to Seth just to be mean. No matter how angry or resentful I become that I have to rely on someone else to take care of me, no matter how ugly and deformed I think my condition has left me, no matter how unfair I think life has treated me, no matter what kind of leftover crap Seth and I have between us because of the way I raised him, I will never say things that are deliberately meant to hurt him. Because you don't do that to people you love. You just don't."

"Oh, and you've done so well yourself raising that boy, have you?" Lorraine snapped back. "He's as sullen as they come, and he barely speaks to anybody." She muttered a derisive sound. "And you think you're a better mother than I was."

"I know I'm a better mother than you were," Eugenie corrected her. "Because at least I notice that my son is sullen and uncommunicative. And at least I try to figure out why. And at least I let him be who he wants to be. I don't try to turn him into what I think the ideal child should be or complain that he isn't it. Maybe I'm not perfect. But I'm a damned better mother than you were."

Lorraine punched up the volume on the TV and said, "No, you're not. Sit down."

Although instinct commanded Eugenie to dump her sandwich

in her mother's lap, she instead did as her mother told her to, perching on the side of the bed as she set her plate on the mattress. It was just as well. As much as she dreaded her mother's inevitable complaints about the food's flavor, portion, texture, temperature, or caloric content, eating alone was somehow worse. Eating alone reminded her of nights when Lawrence worked late and Seth went to a friend's house after school. Or, worse, of nights when Lawrence didn't come home at all and Seth stayed overnight with a friend. There had been a time when the three of them sat down together to a homemade dinner nearly every night of the week. And not homemade from a box or bag. Homemade from fresh, organic vegetables and meats and bread from Great Harvest. Eugenie had always been proud of herself for that. It was an accomplishment to which few busy suburban moms could lay claim. But she did, once upon a time. Maybe her marriage had gone to hell and her kid was sullen and withdrawn, but, dammit, that wasn't because they never shared a table together, so take *that*, child-rearing experts.

Anyway, Eugenie didn't like eating alone. Eating alone felt like failure.

The women ate mostly in silence for the duration of the newscast, speaking only during commercials, and then only to comment on things like what someone was wearing in one of the ads or whether or not the item advertised really worked. By the time Lorraine clicked off the remote, both of them had finished their dinner, so Eugenie gathered their plates and started to head back to the kitchen.

She was halted shy of the door, however, when Lorraine asked, "You know Diane Sawyer is from Louisville, don't you? Well, actually, she was born in Glasgow—which is even smaller than my hometown—but she moved here when she was little. She got her start at one of the local news channels."

Eugenie knew both of those things, as a matter of fact, and not just because there was a million-foot image of Diane Sawyer that said, LOUISVILLE'S DIANE affixed to the very building where she worked. "I did know that, actually," she told her mother. "She started off as a meteorologist or something, didn't she?"

Lorraine shook her head. "Not a meteorologist. She was the weather maiden on channel thirty-two."

Eugenie smiled at that. "The weather maiden? They actually called her that?"

"They did. As if she were some fairy-tale little thing who just magically appeared there to give the weather, and then, poof, she was gone. As if there were no work or substance involved in what she did. Sometimes she would quote some poet or philosopher or something to show that she was more than a weather maiden—she went to Wellesley, after all. But they still called her the weather maiden."

Eugenie wasn't sure what to say in response to that, so she only replied, "Well, that was the sixties for you."

She started to leave again, but once more her mother's voice prevented her escape.

"That was how a lot of women started back then," Lorraine said. "They had to be weather maidens before they could be reporters. They had to be nurses before they could be doctors. They had to be secretaries before they could be bosses."

There was something in her mother's voice then that made Eugenie not want to leave the room. So she stacked one plate on top of the other and balanced her glass atop that, then turned fully around to lean against the doorjamb. She said nothing, though, not sure if she wanted to encourage her mother to continue but still somehow wanting to encourage her mother to continue. After another moment, her mother did.

"And before Diane was the weather maiden, she won America's Junior Miss. Did you know that?"

Eugenie smiled. Lorraine was talking about Diane Sawyer as if she knew her personally. Then again, who knew? Maybe the two of them had competed against each other once upon a time. Lorraine had been Mississippi's Junior Miss one year. But no, that couldn't be possible. Lorraine had a good decade on Diane, at least.

"No, I didn't know that," she told her mother. "She started off in pageants, too, huh?"

"She did. She and her sister both." Lorraine turned to look at Eugenie. "Her sister worked for *Vogue* magazine for a while, but now she's a big advertising muckety-muck. Did you know that?"

Eugenie shook her head. And wondered, really, how her mother knew any of it.

"They both started off in Junior Miss, and now they're both big shots in New York."

There was a wistfulness in her mother's voice now. And maybe a bit of puzzlement, too. As if she were wondering how women who had come from even smaller towns than she, who had competed in the same pageant circuit she had, had ended up wielding so much power where Lorraine wielded none. Truth be told, now that Eugenie thought about it, she wondered that, too. Lorraine had been smart and ambitious, and she'd been articulate and beautiful. Her parents could have afforded to send her to college if she'd wanted to go, but she'd been too impatient and had wanted to start living her life fresh out of high school. Still, her experiences and qualifications when she was young had been much like many other women who had gone on to achieve greatness. So why had greatness passed by Lorie Higgenbotham?

Funnily, her mother answered that question without Eugenie having to ask it.

"But that's how it was," Lorraine said a little wearily. "Some of us became . . ." She gestured toward the darkened television. "Network news anchors." She dropped her hand back to her lap. "And some of us stayed weather maidens." She sighed heavily, then looked at Eugenie. "And then there were those of us who never made it into the studio."

"But you made it," Eugenie said. "Maybe not to the network news in New York, but you were Miss Mississippi. And fourth runner-up for Miss America. You were Mrs. Kentucky."

Lorraine nodded but said nothing for a moment. Thinking the conversation had come to an abrupt end—it was Lorraine's turn to talk, after all—Eugenie pushed off of the doorjamb and started to turn around again. But again, her mother's voice stopped her.

"Did you know," she began, signaling that she was about to say something she didn't think Eugenie knew at all, "that during my tenure as Mrs. Kentucky, I was invited to take part in what was supposed to be an inaugural conference on women's issues at Transylvania University?"

Wow. That actually was pretty impressive. Yet for some reason, this was the first time Eugenie was hearing about it. "No, Mom. I had no idea. That must have been pretty exciting. Especially for that time."

"I was very excited," she said, "and so flattered to be included. They even put me on a panel with some other notable ladies from the state. One who was the sole female member of the Kentucky House of Representatives at that time. And another who owned a chain of used-car lots in western Kentucky. And a writer, a lady professor from Midway College, who had just published a book about feminism, which I bought and read beforehand so I would be able to ask her questions and comment on things she said. It was quite a good book," she added parenthetically, sounding surprised to have enjoyed it. "I thought she had some interesting ideas about women's place in society."

Now it was Eugenie's turn to be surprised. Her mother had enjoyed a book about feminism written by a feminist? Lorraine had thought, all the way back in the sixties, that women even had a place in society, let alone a place touted by an early feminist? This was a side of her mother Eugenie had never seen. And it was a conversation she should have had with her mother decades ago.

She started to ask her mother who the woman was—maybe she needed to read this book, too—but Lorraine started talking again, so Eugenie waited.

"There must have been a thousand people in that room listening to us talk. I was so nervous. They asked me to speak about how the roles of wife and mother were evolving with this new feminist movement, and even though I was terrified, I thought I did a very good job defending my traditional choice to stay home and raise a family. I talked about how important mothers were to society as a whole, and how the home would always be the heart of the family, no matter how many strides women made outside it, and how essential it was to keep our husbands happy because that contributed to better productivity in the workplace, which increased the GNP."

Eugenie couldn't quite stop her mouth from falling open at that. She'd been in complete agreement with her mother until she got to that last bit. It was surprising enough that her mother knew what the gross national product was. But even more astonishing was the idea that she'd actually believed she was helping to keep the GNP healthy by meeting Douglas Dashner at the door with his nightly martini and slippers. And not figuratively, either—she'd actually met Douglas at the door with a martini and his slippers every evening she was able to manage it. Thanks to that simple act, Lorraine had concluded, all of America had benefited, lining its commercial coffers because Douglas sold more appliances at his shop the following day.

That kind of went beyond June Cleaver, Eugenie thought. That was getting straight into Stepford wife territory. Clearly those Van Heusen "show her it's a man's world" advertisements had worked. At least on Lorraine.

"I was glad I spoke before the lady professor, though," Lorraine continued. "She was *very* impressive. Very smart. Very confident. Very charismatic. I found myself so admiring her while she spoke, because she was so passionate in her beliefs. But I felt bad for her after she finished, when people were supposed to ask questions. A lot of women raised their hands after I spoke. And some had had questions for the business lady and the legislature lady. But no one raised a hand when the lady professor finished. It just felt so awkward. So I asked her a question myself."

Such a considerate gesture, Eugenie thought. *And so unlike her.* Then again, her mother admiring a feminist was so unlike Lorraine, too. For that matter, so was speaking on a panel in front of a thousand people. Why had she never heard about any of this before? Why had she heard only her mother's complaints and bitterness?

Lorraine went on, "I asked her what she thought would be the biggest long-term obstacle to feminism. The one thing that had the greatest possibility to prevent the women's movement from realizing its goals. And do you know what she said?"

Eugenie shook her head. "No. What?"

"She said the greatest obstacle to feminism was women like me."

It wasn't the professor's response that surprised Eugenie. Women like her mother *had* been an obstacle to feminism. Not because they chose traditional roles, but because they thought women should reject any role besides the traditional ones based solely on the fact that they had a uterus. And it didn't surprise her that the professor would have told her mother that. What surprised Eugenie was that the woman would tell her mother that in front of a roomful of people. It was just incredibly rude to belittle someone in front of an audience. Where had the woman been raised, a barn?

So Eugenie was only sharing her mother's indignation when she replied, "She said what?"

"She said women like me were the greatest obstacle to feminism," Lorraine repeated. "To a room filled with what must have been a thousand people. She said that women who kept assuming traditional roles and who relied on their beauty and sex appeal to land a successful husband so they could get by in the world should be ashamed of themselves for pandering—yes, she said we were pandering—to the patriarchy. Let me see if I can remember exactly how she put it."

Lorraine paused, pretending to ruminate on the matter. Eugenie knew it was pretend rumination because no human being worth their salt would forget the details of such a public attack. Sure enough, after a few seconds, Lorraine said, "I remember now. She said some more about how women like me made it impossible for women like her—who relied on their brains and hard work to get by in the world—to be taken seriously. She said when women like her—who didn't have big breasts and blond hair and long legs—tried to make the point that there was more to women than breasts and hair and legs, they were accused of being motivated by jealousy and sour grapes. And then she finished with, 'Mrs. Dashner, you'd better appreciate your beauty pageant looks and sex appeal while you can, because it won't last forever. And when your husband leaves you for a new-and-improved Barbie doll, you'll realize what a mistake you made in finding your identity in your big breasts and blond hair and long legs.' I was a blonde then, if you'll recall," she said as an aside, in case Eugenie didn't remember that. "And then she repeated, in front of what must have been a thousand people, that I should be ashamed of myself, and why didn't I just stop pretending I was a fine, upstanding wife and mother and go to work at the Playboy Club, where the women at least had the decency to be obvious about what they had up for sale and didn't try to hide it behind wholesome suburban values." She nodded once. "Yes. That was exactly what she said to me in front of what must have been a thousand people."

Neither woman spoke a word after that. Until Eugenie remarked, "Wow. She must have been a total hag."

Silence hung between them for a moment more, then Lorraine smiled. It wasn't a huge smile, but neither was it one of the brittle, derisive ones she normally stocked in her repertoire. "She wasn't even wearing mascara."

Eugenie gaped dramatically at that. "In front of all of those people? She should be ashamed of herself."

Lorraine looked down at the gnarled hands that had lain motionless in her lap since she finished her dinner. "You know, don't you, Eugenie, that I only wanted you to get further in this world than I did? And that that was the reason I was so exacting about your appearance while you were growing up?"

Actually, Eugenie hadn't known that. And her mother must have realized that on some level, because she phrased the question so similarly to how she phrased the ones about Diane Sawyer, which she hadn't expected Eugenie to know the answers to. Because Eugenie wasn't sure what to say in reply—since this was coming out of nowhere and she'd barely had time to register the question, let alone think about it, let alone form a response—she remained silent.

"You were a plain girl," Lorraine said, "and you were growing up in a world that was very unkind to plain girls. When you were born, women didn't have many options. The pretty ones married well and had good lives. The plain ones went to work and lived the rest of their lives alone. I didn't want you to go to work and live alone. I wanted you to marry well and have a good life."

Eugenie inhaled a breath in preparation of speaking, then realized she still didn't quite know what to say.

"I only wanted what was best for you, Eugenie. And I knew you would never have the best, looking the way you did."

It didn't hurt anymore, hearing her mother tell her how she had been an unattractive child. Eugenie knew she wasn't beautiful. She'd always known that. But she knew she wasn't hideous, either. Even if she had been, that wouldn't have meant she was doomed to a life of misery. Yes, society had always favored the beautiful people in the world, and it continued to do so today. But it had also always favored the rich. And the powerful. And the ingenious. And the gifted. And the tenacious.

There were a lot of ways to get ahead in a superficial, unfair world, regardless of the time period. Getting ahead didn't have to mean clawing one's way to the top of the food chain. There were lots of ways to be happy. Lots of ways to be successful. Lots of ways to fit in. That was something her mother had never figured out. To Lorraine, her beauty was the only valuable thing she had to barter, and the only consumers of beautiful women when she was growing up were men. Whether her conviction of that was the result of the society into which she'd been born or the education she'd received or the traits encoded on her DNA, Eugenie didn't know. Really, it didn't matter. The point was that her mother had only known one way to get by. She'd only tried one way to get by. Even when the world changed in ways that opened more avenues for her to explore, Lorraine Dashner clung to the only thoroughfare that was familiar. She hadn't changed with the world. She hadn't adapted. So she hadn't survived. Not the way many of her contemporaries did.

"You know, Mom," Eugenie finally said, "instead of trying to change me to fit the world, you could have tried to change the world to fit me. That's what Marianne's mother did. And you disliked Mrs. Weatherly enormously because of it."

"I didn't dislike Andrea Weatherly because she was trying to change the world," Lorraine said. But she didn't give any reason for why she had disliked her.

So Eugenie asked, "Then why did you dislike her?"

"Because—" She halted, glanced up at Eugenie, then back down at her hands. "I disliked her because she was pretty and had married well, and because she had two daughters who were pretty and would have married well, but she couldn't be happy with that. Even having everything the way she did, she still wanted to change the world. That was just greedy. Why couldn't she be happy with what she had?"

"Because it wasn't enough, Mom," Eugenie replied immediately, wearily. "Because it's better to be treated like a human being than like a beauty queen."

Her mother's head snapped up at that, her eyes fierce.

"Or like a brainy professor," Eugenie added. "Or a savvy businesswoman. Or an exceptional politician. Or any other single identifying role a person might play. Mrs. Weatherly knew her daughters could be a million different things—all at the same time, even—and she wanted to give them the opportunity to be all of them. When she saw a hole opening in society that would allow for massive cultural change, she jumped through it and started ripping it wider so her daughters—and other women—could climb through it, too."

Her eyes narrowing in anger, Lorraine said, "And I grabbed my sewing basket and tried to stitch it shut, is that what you're saying?"

Eugenie shook her head. "No. I'm saying you grabbed my hand and held it tight to keep me from climbing through, too, even though I wanted very badly to see what was on the other side. But you didn't do it to be mean. You did it because you were afraid of what those women might find on the other side. You were afraid of the great unknown."

Lorraine relaxed at that, but she dropped her gaze to the hands in her lap again. The beautifully manicured, lovingly tended, horribly disfigured hands.

Eugenie wanted to tell her mother that she shouldn't have tried to hold her back. That she should have let her find her own way to the other side, trusting that if she encountered something terrible there, she would come running back to her mother's side. And Lorraine should have realized that if Eugenie found something wonderful, she would have come back and taken her mother's hand and led her to the place where anything was possible.

But Eugenie knew a mother's love wasn't always farsighted or reasonable. And she knew a mother's fear was sometimes so overwhelming, it could blind and cripple. Her mother had been wrong, and Eugenie wanted to think she would have done a better job of it in the same situation. But the truth was, she hadn't made the best choices herself. She'd fallen out of love with the man she married, and her son barely spoke to her. So who was she to judge her mother's choices? She just wished her mother had chosen differently. But then, she wished she had chosen differently, too.

Still standing framed by the doorway, half in her mother's bedroom and half out, she told Lorraine, "You still have a chance to change the world, you know. If you really want to."

Lorraine's response was to pick up the remote control and turn the TV on again, then flip idly through the channels. Eugenie tried to convince herself that her mother's action was a metaphor for someone wanting to see what was out there in the world that might be worth exploring. If she stopped her channel surfing on the Discovery Channel, say, that could have been hugely significant. Or if she paused at the Travel Channel. Or Lifetime. Or even the Family Channel. Hell, especially the Family Channel.

Eventually, her mother did stop surfing—on the History Channel. But when she saw that it was an episode of *Biography* about Eleanor Roosevelt, she switched the TV off.

Eugenie lingered in the doorway a moment longer, to see if her mother would say something that might jump-start their conversation. As contentious as it had been, they had spoken more to each other tonight than they had in years. Even more important, they'd said things to each other, things both had needed to hear.

But had they listened? Eugenie asked herself as she pushed away from the doorway and started back to the kitchen. That was the question. Had they listened?

Twenty-one

When Spalding returned to work on Monday, there was something different about him. Namely, his necktie. Instead of a sedate and very Ward Cleaverish diagonal stripe, or even a slightly more daring but still very Ward Cleaverish vertical row of tiny diamond shapes, this one was a bold red number with vintage, Picasso-esque swirls and trapezoids in sky blue, pea green and canary yellow. In other words, in no way lacking in color. Which of course made Eugenie remember their last conversation, when she'd told him her place of employment—and, by extension, her employer—lacked color. He was also armed with a new iPod touch, paper-thin and ultramodern. Granted, it was still filled with Frank Sinatra, Sam Cooke, and Petula Clark, but all in all it wasn't nearly as old-fashioned as the last one. Too, he looked more than a little refreshed, not nearly as weary-seeming as he had on so many occasions since she'd joined the HeartMenders team.

Now if he started doing something to make a little noise, something to negate that "quiet" designation she'd also applied to her place of employment—and, by extension, her employer—that day in the park, he'd be four for four.

In a word, *Hmm.*

His impression of the new-and-improved HeartMenders offices could be summed up in one word: *Wow.* Because that was the one word he kept using, every time he entered a new area. *Wow,* Eugenie, the reception area looks amazing. *Wow,* Eugenie, your office looks amazing. *Wow,* Eugenie, Marco and Natalie's office looks amazing. *Wow,* Eugenie, my office looks amazing.

Okay, so maybe his impression could be summed up in two words. She was just glad he liked the almost-final product. She had been most worried he wouldn't approve of her renovation of his own office. He was more than a little proprietary of how he kept his personal work space, but he *had* used the word *offices,* plural, when he told her she could paint. And she'd figured that old adage about it being easier to be granted forgiveness than permission was probably true. So in addition to the new paint—and still staying in budget—she'd bought him a new rug, desk, chairs, and filing cabinet, too.

That last was something whose reaction from Spalding she braced herself for, because it had the potential to blow up in her face. His filing system consisted of lots of piles of crap placed in arcane but strategic places throughout his office, a system Eugenie still hadn't figured out, even having worked there for months. But she'd finally decided that if he was so adamant about not giving up paper files, then he could at least learn to keep them organized someplace where other people who worked for him could find them.

Unless, you know, he really hated the system and wanted to go back to the arcane piles of crap. In spite of all the work she'd completed over the past several months, there were some things, Eugenie knew, that simply defied renovation.

Although he claimed his office looked amazing, when he saw the filing cabinet—along with the piles of crap lined up neatly beside it, a silent indication he should put them in their proper place as soon as he had the time—he did hesitate. Then he looked at Eugenie, as if he wanted to challenge her over it. Instead, he smiled at her and said something about change being good, then promised he would get to storing the files at his earliest opportunity. Eugenie then risked showing him where she stashed the packages of brightly colored folders and organizational tabs and braced herself again.

But he only echoed his promise to get right on it and told her, "Really, Eugenie. Change is good."

Interestingly, Eugenie was starting to think that, too.

What she liked best about the remodeled HeartMenders was how quickly it had come together. Unlike some houses, which would remain nameless but whose initials were Fleurissant. Still, even Fleurissant was immensely more livable now than it had been even a few weeks ago. By the time summer ended and Seth and the girls started back to school, the house would be . . .

Well. It would be a place they wouldn't be ashamed of when they brought their friends home to visit. Even better, she could actually envision a time now where Seth might actually do that at some point.

At least, she was able to envision that until one day toward the end of July when Lorraine called Eugenie at work to tell her Seth was in trouble. For one thing, Lorraine had never called Eugenie at work. For another, Lorraine never took much of an interest in her grandson—possibly because her princessy granddaughters were more her style but probably more likely because her grandson didn't take much of an interest in her. Put both developments together, and any alarm Eugenie might have felt about the situation was multiplied tenfold.

"What do you mean he's in trouble?" she asked her mother, heat splashing into her belly, her heart rate doubling.

"I mean he came home a few minutes ago hurt and bleeding," Lorraine told her.

"Bleeding? How bad?"

"He has a big gash on his chin, and his lip is split," Lorraine said. "And he's holding his side like maybe he has a broken rib, and he's walking a little hunched over, like maybe he hurt his"—she lowered her voice—"privates."

"Oh, Jesus," Eugenie said. Classic injuries from fighting. Or, more accurately, from being beaten up.

Why the hell hadn't she talked to Seth about his absences before now? Yes, the two of them had made some headway where communication was concerned—and she was really starting to kick ass at Call of Duty—but they were still dancing around each other when it came to meaty subject matter. She was familiar again with her son's favorite bands, books, and movies, and she'd learned how to pwn n00bs, and she knew Dave Wiens had six consecutive wins in the Leadville Trail 100 under his belt. But she still didn't know if Seth was happy.

Even if communication with him was still in a tentative state, she should have insisted he tell the truth about his disappearances and increasingly ragged state. She should have denied him privileges until she got to the bottom of it. No gaming. No biking. No anything until he told her what was going on. What had obviously been going on for some time now. Maybe since the day they moved to Louisville.

Her mother gasped loudly at the other end of the line, and Eugenie pictured Seth collapsing to the floor in a pool of blood. "What?" she demanded. "What happened?"

"Don't you *dare* take our Lord's name in vain in front of me, young lady," her mother told her.

Eugenie relaxed some. Clearly Seth wasn't lying in a pool of blood if her mother was taking her to task for her profanity. Even Lorraine would put pageant queen righteousness second to grandmother concern. Probably.

"Where is he now?" Eugenie asked.

"In the bathroom," Lorraine said. "I heard the shower switch on."

Eugenie looked at her watch. It was a quarter past four. Less than an hour until quitting time. Spalding wouldn't mind if she left early. Especially for something like this.

She found him sitting in his new faux IKEA chair (since they didn't have any real IKEAs in Louisville) behind his equally faux IKEA desk, reading the contents of a bright red file folder. On the desk before him were two others, one green and one yellow. He'd adapted beautifully to the coded system Eugenie had organized and had been meticulous about keeping the files in order. He'd also continued to wear his brightly patterned neckties and had added a dark blue suit to his wardrobe. And he'd begun subscribing to a music service for HeartMenders—all jazz and big band—so the office was never quiet anymore.

Check, check, check, and check.

Today's musical collection consisted mostly of show tunes. Currently, "Wonderful Guy" from *South Pacific* was playing. And Eugenie couldn't quite ignore the serendipity of the selection.

When he looked up to see her standing framed by the doorway, he smiled. That warm, fuzzy smile that made her feel warm and fuzzy inside. He'd been smiling that way a lot lately. "Nice job on the Nielson–Rothstein report," he said. "I think they're going to work out well."

"Thanks," she said. "I agree. Listen, do you mind if I leave a little early today?"

As if he sensed her concern, his expression shifted to a more sober one, and he closed the folder. "No problem. What's up?"

She was torn between giving him some throwaway response about something coming up at home or telling him about Seth. So she said, "Something's come up at home. It appears Seth has been in a fight. And that he lost. Badly."

Spalding's worry was obvious then. "Is he okay?"

"I think so. But I may need to take him up to Immediate Care. My mother described injuries that might include a broken rib and stitches."

"Go," Spalding told her. "You need to be with your son. Call me later, though, and let me know how he is."

She nodded and closed the door until it was nearly latched, then hesitated and pushed it open again. She had thought Spalding would have returned his attention to his work, but he was still looking at the door—and, now, at her. But he said nothing, obviously waiting for her to tell him why she hadn't left yet.

"Spalding?"

"Yes?"

"Can I ask you a favor?"

"Anything."

"Could you . . . Would you mind coming home with me? Maybe having a little talk with Seth?"

He looked surprised by the request. And, really, Eugenie was surprised to have made it. When Nash had offered to talk to Seth, she'd been quick to tell him she would do it herself. And she had done it herself so far. But that had been almost a month ago, and she still didn't know what was wrong in her son's life. Maybe there were just things Seth couldn't or didn't want to share with her, whether it was because she was his parent or not a guy or for some other reason she didn't understand. Maybe because she just didn't know the right things to say herself.

"You want me to talk to Seth?" Spalding asked, his voice laced with bafflement.

She nodded.

"But I've never even met him."

"I know. But I'm kind of thinking that might actually be helpful."

"How?"

"Because his built-in snub feature won't have any data on you yet to process. It will take him at least a few minutes to find something to dislike in you, and that might provide a window of opportunity to deactivate it."

"How do you figure?"

"Because you're immensely likable, that's why."

His lips parted fractionally at that for a moment, then curled into a smile. "And here I was beginning to think you hadn't noticed."

She smiled back. "It's impossible not to notice," she told him. Then, thinking *What the hell*, she admitted, "I noticed a long time ago, Spalding. That first day I walked into HeartMenders, in fact. You're a good guy."

For the tiniest, scantest—but most unbelievably charged—

moment, neither said a word. Then Spalding rose, cornered his desk, and crossed the room to Eugenie. He grabbed the door and pushed it wider, then extended his hand for her to precede him. They could talk more later about other things. In fact, later was probably a good time for lots of things. Not all of which—necessarily—included talking . . .

Twenty-two

The garage door was open when Eugenie and Spalding arrived, offering a view of Julien's Mustang convertible on one side and Seth on the other, working on his bike. If he wasn't riding his bike, he was tinkering with it, often turning it upside down, as it was now, to remove the wheels or chain or some part she couldn't identify for esoteric adjustments completed in almost ritualistic fashion. Julien had promised Seth a small outbuilding specifically for his bike stuff once the rest of the house was finished, but for now her son had to share space like the rest of them.

He was so intent on his efforts that he hadn't heard their arrival. Or perhaps he had heard but was pretending he hadn't, which was more likely. The thread of anxiety winding through Eugenie loosened some at the realization that he wasn't hurt so badly that he couldn't partake of his usual activities like bike tinkering and grown-up ignoring.

Spalding joined her on the driveway after parking his car behind hers.

"I hate it that he's hurt," she said softly when he came to a stop beside her, "but maybe this will at least keep him home for a few days. I hardly see him since we moved. He's usually up and out of the house before I am."

"That bothers you," Spalding said, his voice lowered, too. He obviously detected more in her concern than the fact that her son had been injured.

"Yeah," she said. "It does."

He gazed at Seth for a moment, who had yet to look up from his work. "Why does it bother you? I thought kids his age were supposed to be pulling away from their relationship with parents to find their own way in the world."

"Not like this, they aren't. As much as I've worked on changing the way things are between him and me, neither of us is ever in the same place long enough to really do what we need to do to get back on track with our relationship. A lot of times he's out of the house before I'm even up, and he doesn't come home until after supper. There have been nights when it's been after dark by the time he comes in. I have no idea where he goes during those hours in between. And he's always alone," she added, piling higher her concerns. "He never does anything with anyone else. I've tried to get him to hang out with Marianne's son D.J.—and D.J. seems to like him—but Seth would rather be alone."

"Have you asked him where he goes or if he's with anyone?"

"Of course."

"And what does he tell you?"

"Nothing," she said. "He either acts like he doesn't hear me and just keeps walking up to his room, or else he says he hasn't been anywhere. Sometimes he says things that can't possibly be true."

"Like what?"

"Once when I demanded to know where he'd been, he told me he rode his bike to Lexington and back."

She looked at Spalding, expecting to see the eyebrow that always shot up when something he heard didn't jibe with what he suspected was true. But his expression changed not at all. "And you don't believe him."

Eugenie crossed her arms over her midsection. "Of course I don't believe him," she said. "How could he ride to Lexington and back in one day? It's seventy miles one way. And that's on the interstate. He'd have to take U.S. 60, and that would make it even longer." When Spalding still said nothing, she added, "He's doing something he shouldn't be doing. I know it. I can feel it. And the fact that he came home today all beaten up just proves that."

There was another moment of hesitation on Spalding's part before he asked, "Why do you automatically assume he's doing something he shouldn't be?"

How did one explain that sixth sense parents developed over time to someone who had never been a parent? How could she say, *I just know, that's how,* without sounding the way mothers did when they didn't know what else to say?

Finally, she told him, "I just know, that's how."

She was almost afraid to look at him after that, fearing she would see that indulgent *Sure, Eugenie, whatever you say* expression Lawrence had always tossed her way when she said something similar to him. Instead, Spalding looked as if he were giving what she'd said great consideration.

When he finally replied, he turned the tables on her. "When you were Seth's age, how did you spend your summers off from school?"

"Mostly reading," she told him. "Sometimes Marianne and I

would go to the pool or hang out at the mall, but her folks kept her pretty busy over the summer with camp and trips to visit family out of town. I used to walk to the library once a week to return books I'd read and check out new ones."

"Reading," he echoed with something that sounded almost like distaste, even though she knew for a fact that he loved books. "That's all you did all summer long?"

"Yes," she said, the word coming out more defensive than she'd wanted it to.

"An activity I assume you participated in alone."

"Yes, but reading is a solitary activity, anyway."

"So is cycling if you want it to be."

"Yeah, but I—"

"What was it you liked so much about reading?" he interrupted.

"Books offered me a nice escape."

"Bikes do that, too. Only it's as much physical as it is mental. What was it you wanted to escape?" he asked before she could object again.

Reluctantly, she told him, "Before my folks split, it was my mother's constant efforts to turn me into something I wasn't and never would be. After they split, it was . . ."

When she didn't finish the statement, Spalding finished it for her. "After they split, you wanted to escape the very same thing Seth is trying to escape now."

"But it's different for him after his parents' divorce than it was for me after mine," Eugenie was quick to object.

"Why?"

"Because *I'm* different," she said emphatically. "I'm not my mother. I would never try to turn him into something he doesn't want to be."

"No?"

This time Eugenie made no effort to hide her defensiveness. "No. Never."

"Even though you don't want him leaving every morning and staying out all day before coming home at night? I mean, he does come home, Eugenie. And it hasn't been in the back of a police car or anything."

"Yet," she qualified. Before he could argue further, she hurried on, "How do I make sure he never does if he won't even talk to me about the really important things in his life? I try to engage him with those things, I really do. I'm not like my mother there, either. I couldn't talk to her about anything without her turning it into some kind of litany about all the ways I didn't measure up. But I don't do that to Seth. He should be able to talk to me about everything."

Spalding laughed outright at that. "Eugenie, he's a sixteen-year-old boy. The last person he wants to confide in is his mother."

Eugenie's chin actually came up a notch at that. "That's not what Marianne says. She talks to her sixteen-year-old son all the time. They're buds, she and D.J."

Now Spalding gave her the indulgent look she used to hate getting from Lawrence. "Well, with all due respect to your friend Marianne, there's a lot that D.J. doesn't talk to her about."

"Marianne says he talks to her about everything."

"Then either Marianne is lying or D.J. is. My money is on the latter."

"How do you know?"

"Because, Eugenie, I was a sixteen-year-old boy once upon a time. And I had a mother. With whom I had a very good relationship. To whom I talked. And with whom there was *a lot* I didn't share."

It was the first time Spalding had ever mentioned any family besides his aunt Maisy, and Eugenie suddenly found herself wanting to know more. Were his parents still around? Did he have siblings? What had the dynamics in his family been like? He knew so much about her situation and family life, and she knew almost nothing about his. Why was that? It wasn't like he was nosy and kept asking her personal questions. She was the one who offered up daily snippets of herself and her home life, without him having to ask. He was just the kind of person who was easy to talk to, and who always seemed to be interested in whatever she had to say. Which was something that just made her reveal even more.

Yet she knew almost nothing about his life outside of work, even though she knew so much about everyone else's there. She knew Natalie sewed her own clothes and Marco was taking sailing lessons and Iris's go-to karaoke song was "Many Rivers to Cross." But she didn't know anything like that about Spalding.

"Come on," he said as began to walk forward. "Introduce me to your son."

The clink of metal against metal grew louder as they approached the garage, then changed to the sound of metal against concrete, then metal against metal again as her son laid down one tool and picked up another. Still oblivious to their approach—or, again, just ignoring it—he jerked hard on the bike's front tire, an action that resulted in an irregular whir followed by the grinding of something that had obviously not been repaired the way he intended. So he halted the spinning wheel with his palm and scraped up another tool to *clink-clink-clink* on something again.

He remained absorbed in his work until Eugenie and Spalding stopped only inches away from him. Only then did he . . . Well, actually, he continued to work without acknowledging them. He just seemed to work a lot harder. His injuries weren't as bad as

Eugenie had imagined—though, admittedly, her motherly mind's eye had formed visions more suited to an episode of *CSI*, most likely one that involved a body being thrown into a meat grinder—but they were ugly. The gash on his chin was already forming a scab, as was the one on his lip, so he probably didn't need stitches. Her mother hadn't mentioned a black eye, but there was the shadow of a bruise forming beneath his left one. He winced as he reached for a wrench that lay some distance away from him, then held his side as he straightened again.

Eugenie started to reach forward, to help her son in some way or offer him an affectionate touch. But Spalding curled his fingers lightly over her wrist and pulled her arm back to her side, a silent warning not to. She would have been offended by his meddling if she hadn't realized he was right. The last thing her son would want when meeting another Y chromosome for the first time would be to have his mother cooing over him.

"Are you okay?" she asked.

Seth nodded silently in reply.

"Gran called me to tell me you came home hurt. You want to talk about it?"

"Bike accident," he said.

"You think maybe we should take you up to Immediate Care? That chin looks pretty bad. You might have a broken rib. They could do an x-ray."

"I'm fine."

Clearly, he wasn't fine. And clearly, he wasn't going to say any more about it. She wanted to press. She didn't want to see Seth's face marred by a scar for the rest of his life if that cut did need a stitch or two, and if he did have a broken rib, they might need to tape it. But when Spalding gave her wrist another gentle squeeze before releasing it, Eugenie let the subject lapse. For now.

"Seth," she said instead, "I want you to meet my boss. This is Mr. Chasan."

Without looking up, Seth muttered, "Hey."

Eugenie opened her mouth to tell her son to at least look at the person he was speaking to, but Spalding did the cautionary wrist touch again. So she didn't.

"Great Surly," he said by way of a greeting.

Eugenie snapped her head around to glare at him. What, she couldn't touch her son affectionately or tell him to look at the person he was speaking to, but it was okay for Spalding, a total stranger, to complain about his surliness to his face? She was about to open her mouth to defend her son—even if she did agree with Spalding that her son's surliness was indeed great—but before she had a chance, Seth glanced up, looking in no way offended.

With something akin to pride in his voice, he said, "Thanks. I try to take good care of it."

Well, that was certainly true, Eugenie had to agree. Seth cultivated his surliness with all the care and nurturing one might show a money tree. If, you know, money trees actually existed. Still, what kind of mother would she be if she allowed the two of them to sit here and praise the very trait she wanted most to abolish in her son?

Once again, she opened her mouth to object. But this time, Spalding smiled and told her, "Surly is the brand name of your son's bike."

So Eugenie closed her mouth again. Oh. Okay. In that case (the capital *S* case, she meant), it was all right for Spalding to compliment Seth's Surly. Just as long as he kept his comments about Seth's lowercase surly to himself. Then she realized how readily—and how with absolutely no surly—Seth had replied.

He'd just spoken more words to Spalding in that one response than he had to Eugenie all week.

"Is that the Pacer?" Spalding asked.

"Cross-Check," Seth corrected. At least, Eugenie thought he was correcting Spalding's identification of the bike. Unless *cross-check* was a new slang word teenagers used to confirm something as true. But Spalding nodded as if he knew what Seth was talking about, so Eugenie was going to go with the former.

As if he knew what she was thinking—and didn't he always?—he grinned at her and said, "Just be glad he isn't riding Surly's Big Dummy. If he'd said that, you would have been sending him to bed without his supper for calling your boss an idiot." He turned back to Seth. "This is one of the first completes they offered in that model, isn't it?"

Seth nodded. "Yeah, but I've made some modifications."

"I can see." Spalding completed a couple of steps forward and gave the bike a closer inspection. "You added some eyelets. Carrying a heavier load than usual?"

Seth's gaze darted to Eugenie, then back to Spalding. She might have thought she detected a little panic in his expression, but she couldn't imagine why he would feel panicked. It wasn't like she had a clue what they were talking about. Had eyelets been something more commonly used by people like the Unabomber, Spalding probably wouldn't have been so matter-of-fact about it.

"Yeah, sometimes," Seth replied, sending another furtive look Eugenie's way before returning it to Spalding.

"And you've put slicks on it," he continued. "How are those working out?"

Seth eyed him warily for a moment, but then, to Eugenie's surprise, he stood. Not without difficulty—he held his side again and moved more slowly than usual. When he was up, he looked

Spalding in the eye, giving him his full attention. Unbelievable. Eugenie hadn't seen her son give anyone even a quarter of his attention since they'd left Indianapolis. Whatever language Spalding was speaking, Seth was clearly glad to have met someone equally fluent. Without his usual slouch, he stood nearly as tall as Spalding, who hovered at six feet. A few months ago, he'd only had about three inches on Eugenie's five six. He would be as tall as Lawrence by the time he graduated. He might even pass his father up.

"They're working really well," he told Spalding. "I took off the knobbies after we moved. The slicks don't have as much wear in the long term, but they're better for the terrain."

Spalding nodded. "You changed the forks and hubs, too, I see."

"Needed to make it my own, dude."

"No fixed gear?"

Seth nearly snarled his disgust. "Fixters are posers."

"True enough," Spalding agreed.

At that point, Eugenie stopped trying to follow the exchange, since the language they were speaking was one she'd never be able to conjugate. One or two words jumped out here and there that sounded familiar, and she knew the gist of it was cycling in nature because of the way they kept pointing to the bike. Beyond that, she was clueless.

But then, she was always clueless when it came to Seth, so why should today be any different? Maybe Spalding was right. Maybe she was like her mother when it came to a lack of communicating with her child. But she wasn't like Lorraine in any other way, she hurried to reassure herself. Eugenie did *not* want to change Seth and turn him into something he didn't want to be. She loved him exactly as he was. She just wished he was the kind of kid who talked more. And that his grades were better. And that he kept his room tidier. And that he was more social, someone who had lots of friends. And that he liked the same books and movies she did. And that he didn't game so much. Really, she just wished he was more like other boys, boys like D.J., for instance. Or even—

Oh, crap. Crap, crap, crap. Eugenie *was* like her mother. She did want Seth to be different. At least in some ways. Ways that would make him easier to understand. Ways that would make him more manageable. Ways that would make it easier for her to be a mother.

"So, what's the farthest distance you've covered?" Spalding asked Seth, bringing her back to the matter at hand.

Except that Seth's bike travels weren't the matter at hand. Seth's fighting was. She started to point that out, then stopped herself. Seth had started to relax around Spalding—a benefit of being countrymen from the Land of Tandem, she supposed. He had stopped throwing her those wary looks whenever Spalding asked him about his bike. So Eugenie dipped her head to study a chipped nail, pretending she had stopped paying attention.

After a moment, she heard Seth say, "Cincinnati and back."

Cincinnati? she wanted to scream. That was a hundred highway miles away on the interstate! God knew how many it was taking the back roads! Either Seth was lying through his teeth, or he had put himself at enough risk to bring himself grievous bodily harm. Either way, she was going to kill him.

Spalding seemed in no way surprised or bothered by the revelation. "Where were you headed today?"

After a very telling pause, Seth said, "Indianapolis."

Eugenie's stomach clenched tight. Not because it was as far away as Cincinnati, but because her son had just said he wanted to return to the place where he was from. The place where he had lived his entire life up until their move here. The place where his closest friends still lived. The place that held his history. The place where his father dwelled. The place from which she had removed him.

He hadn't been fighting. He really had had an accident on his bike. All those other times he'd come home looking like he'd been fighting but telling her he was riding—to places as far off as Lexingon and Cincinnati—he'd been telling her the truth. He'd spent full days and hurt himself no telling how many times, all because he was working himself up to go back to the place they had left behind. Because he wanted to go home.

"Indianapolis—that's a long trip," Spalding said.

"No longer than Cincinnati," Seth replied.

"Guess it depends on the route you take."

"Guesso."

Spalding turned to Eugenie then. "Eugenie, I need to get going soon, but I'm absolutely parched. Can I beg you for a drink of water or something?"

In other words, she thought, *beat it while I talk to your kid the way you asked me to.*

"I made some fresh lemonade this morning," she said. "How does that sound?"

"Great."

"Seth?" she asked. "You want some, too?"

"Sure," he tossed over his shoulder.

Funnily, he wasn't being his usual surly self when he did that. The reason he tossed the single-word reply over his shoulder was because he was facing Spalding completely and directing his attention to something else on the bike. It was the first time in a long time that Seth hadn't ended a conversation where an opening presented itself for an ending. In fact, it was the first time in a long time Seth hadn't ended a conversation where an opening hadn't presented itself for an ending.

Which could only mean one thing. It must be a beginning.

There was enough fresh lemonade in the house for all three of them, but Eugenie made another pitcher, anyway, to give Spalding and Seth time to get a good conversation going. Then she washed up some leftover dishes and inventoried the fridge for a future grocery run, to give them time to keep the conversation going.

When she finally delivered their drinks to them in the garage, she found Seth on his back under the bike and Spalding handing him a wrench while he held on to the front tire. The latter had also shed his jacket and tie and rolled up his sleeves, and his hands were streaked with the black and brown remnants of bike offal. So she manufactured an imaginary problem in the kitchen that required her attention and told them she'd be back in a few minutes. Then she exited the garage through the big front bay and circled to the side window that was missing two panes so she could eavesdrop.

They were still speaking cyclese, their comments punctuated by the clanging of metal and the whirring of tires. Spalding was obviously as big a biking nut as Seth was, because both their voices were infused with the sort of enthusiasm that only the truly passionate displayed.

Marianne's words came back to haunt Eugenie again, about the secret to talking to one's kids being to adopt one's kids' interests, whether one liked them or not. Even if Eugenie would never be a passionista when it came to the things Seth liked, she knew she was going to have to make an effort if she wanted to generate even half the reaction in him that Spalding had.

The two of them lapsed into silence for a moment, save the mechanical touches, until the whir of the tire turned into silence, too. That was when each exclaimed in triumph, a sound that was followed by the unmistakable slap of two hands high-fiving.

"Now you'll be able to make it up to Indianapolis," she heard Spalding say. Without an ounce of concern, too, she marveled. Obviously he didn't find anything wrong with a sixteen-year-old boy traveling a hundred-plus miles of back roads on a piece of metal that weighed as much as a stick of butter. "I haven't made a trip like that for a long time," he added. "Should be a nice ride."

"It is," Seth told him. "At least as far as Seymour. Brown County is awesome."

"You've already made a bit of a trial run, then."

"Yeah. About a month ago."

"I'm sure it will be good to go back for a visit," Spalding said. "You must miss your dad a lot."

"I don't miss my dad. He's a dick."

The remark surprised Eugenie. Not just that Seth had such an opinion of his father but because of his tone when he said it. There was no venom, no anger, no resentment. There was just a flat sort of matter-of-factness he might have used when uttering any number of remarks. *I got a B on my essay. It's supposed to rain. My dad's a dick. What's for supper?*

Spalding seemed stumped by the response, too, because he said nothing for a moment. Then, in a voice that was at once cautious and penetrating, he said, "Look, Seth, you do realize that anything that happened between your parents has nothing to—"

"Do with me," Seth chorused with Spalding's *do with you* as he finished the statement. "I know. It has to do with the fact that my dad is a dick."

Again Spalding hesitated, still obviously not sure how to proceed. Probably, he hadn't planned on the conversation becoming quite this personal or quite this specific. Frankly, Eugenie hadn't planned on that, either. She hoped Spalding wouldn't be mad at her later for putting him in such a spot.

Finally, he said, "There was probably a lot of different stuff involved in your parents' split."

"Yeah, probably," Seth said. "But my dad cheated on my mom. That was the main thing."

"Well, maybe it was and maybe it wasn't. What happened was between them and probably goes back a long time, even before your dad started cheating."

Eugenie was grateful to Spalding for not sidestepping that issue. Seth knew about Ethel Merman. He'd met her on a couple of occasions both before and after the split was final. Neither Eugenie nor Lawrence had said a word about the affair or how long Ethel had been in the picture. But Seth wasn't an idiot. For all Eugenie knew, he'd figured it out before she had—the part about Lawrence cheating, anyway, if not whom he was cheating with.

That said, Eugenie wasn't going to try to dissuade her son of his notion that his father had cheated. Lawrence *had* cheated. Let him be the one to dissuade Seth. As far as that went, Eugenie wasn't going to try to dissuade her son of his notion that his father was a dick, either. Lawrence *was* a dick. Let him be the one to dissuade Seth of that, too.

"Both of them love you," Spalding continued. "And both of them are going to be a big part of your life even if they're not married to each other anymore. Your dad—"

"Mr. Chasan?" Seth interrupted him.

"Yes?"

"It's okay. I've had this conversation with my school counselor and a shrink my parents made me see while they were going through the divorce."

"Oh. So. How'd that work out?"

"Fine. I know what happened had nothing to do with me. I know it was all between my parents. And I know my dad is a dick. He's not the reason I want to go back to Indianapolis. I want to go back up there to see my friends and hang out in Broad Ripple. My dad can go fuck himself."

Eugenie winced inwardly. She'd never heard Seth utter the *f*-word, and although it didn't surprise her to hear it rolling off his tongue, she was a bit bothered by how easily it had. Still, it did give her a sort of good-news/bad-news reaction. The bad news was that her son's profanity had escalated. The good news was that he still knew better than to use it in his mother's presence. Maybe there was hope for him yet.

Spalding was silent for another moment, then, with a jollity that was obviously tempered by having been blindsided—he was essentially Ward Cleaver, after all, and Wally and the Beave had sure never dropped the *f*-bomb—he said, "Well, all right, then. You want to get to work on that fork crown now?"

There was more bike talk followed by more bike sounds, and Eugenie tried to curb her disappointment that that was going to be the end of it. Really, all she'd learned about Seth was that he thought his father was a dick, that he used more profanity than she'd realized, and that she'd been remiss in not taking him back to Indianapolis to visit the friends she should have realized he missed. She'd just been so caught up in her own crap since returning home that she hadn't been as focused on her son as she should have been. But it was hard trying to rebuild a life after a divorce and move forward. It was like learning how to walk and how to talk and how to hold a spoon all over again. Eugenie was barely able to keep her own life on track, let alone keep Seth's where it needed to be. Trying to be a breadwinner and a homemaker and a mother all at one time. It wasn't easy for Eugenie.

Nor, she supposed, had it been for her mother.

Once again she was struck by the similarity. Lorraine had had to be breadwinner, homemaker, and mother all rolled into one, too. And she'd had to do it at a time when it was even harder for a woman to make a living than it was now. And Lorraine had had double the number of children Eugenie did.

"So what's your dad like?" she heard Seth ask Spalding.

That question, too, surprised her. It wasn't like Seth to take an interest in anyone other than himself. Especially a newcomer like Spalding. Having just voiced such a low opinion of his own father, it seemed odd that he would care about anyone else's. Unless maybe he didn't want to stop talking about fathers just yet. In case maybe his opinion about his own wasn't set in cement, and he was still sending out feelers about other people's relationships with their own paternal units.

"My dad isn't around anymore," Spalding told him. "He died when I was fourteen."

The clanking and whirring sounds halted abruptly. Eugenie held her breath as she awaited Seth's reply, but he said nothing. Probably, he had no idea what he was supposed to say when he encountered a tragedy like that. She didn't think her son had ever been confronted by death at such a close range.

Spalding didn't seem to take offense, because he continued easily, "He had an aneurysm. A blood clot in his brain," he clarified, in case Seth wasn't familiar with the term. "We were at a

Colonels game. That was the minor league baseball team Louisville had before the Bats. Way before you were born. Anyway, we were up in the stands in the cheap seats—that was all we could afford—and he'd just bought us both hot dogs, and a Coke for me, a Schlitz for him. I remember the Colonels were playing the Blue Jays. It was the fifth inning, tied up. One guy was on second base, and the batter hit a ball that looked like it was going to go way the hell out into right field. My dad and I both stood up, yelling our heads off, and when the ball arced over the right fielder and those two guys started to run the bases, we grabbed each other and started hugging and laughing like idiots."

It wasn't just the bike sounds that had stopped, Eugenie suddenly noticed. It seemed like all sounds had stopped. The birds chirping nearby had fled at her appearance, the breeze ruffling the leaves overhead had stilled, and the blood pumping between her ears had slowed when she heard Spalding speak of his loss. For some reason, she envisioned him sitting now, on the riding mower that had been parked by Seth's bike. She pictured Seth having crawled out from beneath the bike to sit next to it on the grimy garage floor. One knee was probably bent with his forearm braced atop it, as was his way when he sat like that, and his hair was probably damp with sweat and hanging over one eye. She really should encourage him to get a haircut.

She heard Spalding sigh softly, and in her mind's eye, he had slumped forward a little on the mower, hooking his fingers loosely together as he continued to talk. "The last guy had just crossed home plate, and my dad and I were laughing and squeezing each other in this massive bear hug when the aneurysm hit him. He went down like a sack of potatoes, and there I was, my arms empty, my euphoria shattered, and my dad . . ." There was another sigh, this one more ragged. "My dad gone. Forever."

Out of nowhere, a bright red cardinal landed on the gutter above Eugenie, cocked his head, and stared down at her. She held her breath as she gazed back at him, not wanting to startle him or make him think she posed any threat to his family. Finally, he cheeped, but only twice, a couple of quick whistles to his mate to let her know he was nearby. Then he flew away again, a flutter of crimson arcing over the trees.

Seth's voice ambled through the broken window in its wake. "So . . . then . . . I guess your dad wasn't a dick."

Spalding expelled a single, unhappy chuckle. "No. He wasn't a dick. My dad was the greatest dad in the history of dad-dom. Losing him, especially like that, was . . ."

Heartbreaking, Eugenie finished silently when Spalding didn't.

"Not long after that, the Colonels moved to Rhode Island," he hurried on, clearly not wanting to dwell on the memory. "They became the Pawtucket Red Sox. Everybody in Louisville was outraged. Except me. I was kind of glad to see them go, you know?"

This time it was Seth who said nothing for a moment. Then, "Yeah, I do," he replied quietly. "There's a part of me that wasn't all that sad to leave Indianapolis. Don't tell Mom, though," he hastened to add.

Too late, Eugenie thought. But she was smiling when she thought it.

The soft scrape of metal against cement kicked up again, then more clinking of metal against metal. Several moments passed as the two men submerged themselves in their work again.

Then Spalding said, "I keep thinking I'll go to a Bats game sometime, but in all the years they've been here, I never have. You like baseball, Seth?"

"Not really," Seth replied. "I'm more into basketball."

"Who's your favorite team?"

"Dude. I'm from Indianapolis. Butler."

"Right. Forgot. Heartbreaker on those back-to-back NCAA losses."

"Yeah."

"Maybe they'll make it to the final game again this year."

"Uh, hel-lo. *Of course* they'll make it to the final game this year. And they'll win this time. Stevens rocks."

There was more than a touch of good humor in Spalding's voice as he told Seth, "Unless Louisville knocks their asses out of the tournament before they even get to the Elite Eight."

"Hey!" Seth cried. But he was laughing when he said it.

Tears sprang to Eugenie's eyes at the sound. She couldn't remember the last time she'd heard Seth laugh. But as she continued to eavesdrop on him and Spalding, she heard it come again. Then a third time. And with each new outburst, a coil of something cold and unwieldy loosened inside her.

She turned to lean her back against the garage wall, the great, weighty tension that had bunched her shoulders and tightened her gut for so long gradually beginning to ease. When her gaze fell on Fleurissant, she waited for the stress to advance again, knowing there was still so much left to do there. But the house was awash in late afternoon sunshine, looking buoyant and blooming in anticipation of all that was to come. At its topmost angle, a bright red cardinal perched. He whistled twice, to let his mate know he was still close by.

And this time, he didn't fly away.

Epilogue

Summer drew to an end the way it always did in Louisville, panting and sweaty and cross. But that didn't stop Eugenie from organizing a Labor Day get-together for friends old and new. Marianne and her family, of course, were there, but also the Burdens from up the street, who had twins Sophie's age, and the Sicilianos from two blocks over whose son was a friend of D.J.'s . . . and now a friend of Seth's, too.

Nash had arrived fashionably late, of course, with a woman named Sarah, and— Oh no, wait. Sarah had been the woman he was with when she and Spalding ran into him at Stevie Ray's a couple of weeks ago. He had introduced this woman as Suzanne. Anyway, he was there, too, striving for at least an eight on the Nash Ridley Charm-o-Meter in light of all the people, especially the female people, he was meeting for the first time.

Spalding was manning the grill at the moment, Ward Cleaver on vacation wearing big ol' Bermuda shorts and the circa 1957 tiki shirt Eugenie had found at Elizabeth's Timeless Attire for his birthday just last week. He was assisted by a woman named Caroline whom he and Eugenie knew from HeartMenders. Not because she worked there, but because she was a new client whose replies on her beige book questionnaire, Spalding had decided after much deliberation, made her a perfect someone for Julien. Whose own beige book had, admittedly, not been filled out by him, but who knew him better than his own sister, right? Caroline was a single mother who had lost her husband to ALS a few years ago. She and Jules had been exchanging wary glances since her arrival, and it was Eugenie's hope that they would be exchanging phone numbers by the time she left.

Lorraine was spending the afternoon stretched out as well as she could be on a chaise longue near the pool, still far enough away not to get her bright pink silk separates wet. She was wearing her best pair of rhinestone sunglasses, flipping through a coffee-table book about Paris and sipping the champagne cocktail Marianne had made for her with instructions to "Keep them coming, Marianne. I'm going to get to Paris today, one G.D. way or another."

Eugenie smiled. Her mother was actually going to get to Paris the right way soon. Lorraine's seventy-fifth birthday was coming in the spring, and Eugenie was planning a trip to Paris for the two of them. She'd already made a reservation at a small pension on the Boulevard Saint-Germain. Second floor. With a balcony. The proprietor, Anatole, had promised he would arrange for a chaise longue, too.

It was a beautiful day in spite of the oppressive heat, the grass browned by drought, and the sky gritty and taupe thanks to the ozone warning the meteorologists had issued that morning. It was beautiful because everyone was finally settling into this new-

and-improved family situation, which really was new and improved. And Fleurissant . . .

Well. Fleurissant was obviously happier, too. Thanks to the house's age and temperament and how set it was in its ways, it was never quite going to be the place it was in its prime. But it had come a long way since its abandonment. Its white wedding-cake exterior was crisp and clean, its red front door a marzipan hibiscus at its base. Baskets of purple petunias lined its front porch now, and gauzy curtains framed its windows. The fountain was the only part of the house they hadn't tried to re-create, possibly because the pool fit so nicely in its spot near the gazebo, whose latticework was half woven now with ivy.

Change really was good, Eugenie had decided at some point over the summer. But so, in a lot of ways, was status quo.

She threaded her way through the crowd that filled her backyard, greeting her new friends with waves and her old friends with kisses, until she reached Spalding. He was kind of a new friend, too, but she kissed him, anyway. On the mouth, since he was special that way. And because June never would have kissed Ward in public like that.

In fact, June wouldn't have done a lot of the things Eugenie did. But that was okay, because Eugenie wouldn't do a lot of the things June did, either. She wouldn't wear crinolines under her skirts. She wouldn't turn her too-young kid loose without supervision so that he could strand himself in a giant coffee cup high atop a billboard downtown. And she sure as hell wouldn't vacuum in pearls. But if June wanted to do all those things—or if Lorraine did—it wasn't Eugenie's place to judge. It was only her place to live her life and be herself the best way she knew how.

"The house looks great," Spalding said as he flipped a bratwurst with one hand and slipped the other around her waist. "All that hard work is definitely paying off."

"You're right," Eugenie agreed. "But I don't think she'll ever quite be finished. She's going to be a work-in-progress for the rest of my life. And she's going to need constant care to keep her from falling apart again."

"Yeah, but that's okay," Spalding said. "There are lots of people around here who love her and will take care of her now." He grinned. "The house, I mean."

Eugenie grinned back. "Of course."

He was right, naturally. Fleurissant—and its owner—were doing way better than they'd been when they first met. Where before had been destruction and loss was now rejuvenation and hope. Where before had been emptiness and expiration was now wholeness and breath. Where before had been silence and solitude was now animation and joy. Because where before had been only the heartbreak of loneliness in the house on Butterfly Way now was the fullness of family. Maybe there were still a few flaws that required tending and a handful of fractures that needed to be filled. But the foundation was sound, and the bones were good. Better now, even, than they had been before.

Eugenie really did love the house on Butterfly Way. Now more than ever before.